THE MAGIC OF BETRAYAL

EMERALD LAKES BOOK TWO

BRITT ANDREWS

Copyright © 2020 Britt Andrews

All rights reserved. No part of this publication may be reproduced, distributed, or transmitted in any form or by any means, including photocopying, recording, or other electronic or mechanical methods, without the prior written permission of the publisher, except in the case of brief quotations in book reviews.

The unauthorized reproduction or distribution of a copyrighted work is illegal. Criminal copyright infringement, including infringement without monetary gain, is investigated by the FBI and is punishable by fines and federal imprisonment.

Please purchase only authorized electronic editions and do not participate in, or encourage, the electronic piracy of copyrighted materials. Your support of the author's rights is appreciated.

This book is a work of fiction. Names, characters, places, brands, and incidents are the products of the author's imagination or used fictitiously. Any resemblance to actual events, locales or persons, living or dead, is entirely coincidental.

Cover by: Jodielocks Designs
Formatting by: Inked Imagination Author Services
Developmental Editing: Cassie Hurst with Inked Imagination Services
Editing By: PollyAné Nichols from Proofs By Polly
Proofreading by: Black Lotus Editing
Photography by: TalkNerdy2me
Samantha La Mar www.thetalknerdy.com

Thank you for securing your seat in Britt's weenie wagon.

Please read the rules below and we do hope you'll ride with us again.

We ask that you please keep all body parts inside the vehicle for the duration of the ride.
This includes tits. Nobody needs to be losing a titty.

Please, secure your seatbelts and get comfortable. There will be ample opportunity to explore the sex scenes at an appropriate time, but safety first.

You may wish to bring a towel. Or two. One for your face tears and one for your... other tears.

Handheld fans are permitted.

Drinks are also permitted as past riders have been known to get thirsty AF.

HOLD ON TIGHT AND ENJOY THE RIDE!
(Name of your sex tape)

TRIGGER WARNING

This is a full-length RH romance, intended for adults 18 and over, which includes MMFMMM content. It ends on a cliffhanger and contains domestic violence including physical, mental, and sexual abuse and other themes that readers may find triggering.
This is the second book in a paranormal RH series.

Kai

Chapter One

The lingering echoes of Saige's gut clenching screams had dissipated, but they would haunt me forever. They tore right into my soul, shredding my heart, delivering jolts of panic to my system that I'd never experienced before. Bagheera was roaring inside my brain, claws out, tearing around, hackles raised. I was in a frozen state, unable to soothe him, and was stuck standing at the foot of her bed, staring at her.

Blood was still running freely from her nose, her normally lively body slack and disturbingly still. Bagheera refused to back off, so he was right there at the forefront of our connection, but he wasn't choking like I was, he was cursing me for not moving, gods dammit.

Someone rushed past me, knocking me out of my trance.

"Tell us everything, Cam. Quickly," Fischer demanded, climbing right into the bed with our woman, taking her hand in his and checking her pulse. Cam must've called them.

"She woke up, started telling us she'd been in the demon realm, she was about to say something and started complaining of a headache. Within minutes, she was screaming in agony, and then the bleeding started. Then she was just... like this," Cam explained, the fear in his tone was evident.

Boss is scared. Shit.

Sloane moved to sit beside Fischer, running his hand over Saige's forehead. "I don't sense anything malevolent or demonic right now. No curses or hexes, so that's something. I'm assuming that she was pulled there again because there's something there that keeps calling to her. It's like her body knows she needs to go there for something, and whatever the fucking reason, she keeps getting yanked across the realms. Remember the case we had in Sydney two summers ago?"

"Yeah, you're right," Fischer agreed. "That poor man kept getting pulled to the other side of the world... until his soul splintered from his body."

My heart was racing, but I still couldn't fucking move.

"Kaito," Cam growled, which had us growling in return. "Get your ass over here, now."

Opening my mouth to reply, my voice was a low rumble, "I'm going to get Gran. She'll know what to do."

Before anyone could say otherwise, Bagheera burst out of my skin, the shift smooth and very fucking welcomed at the moment. Sprinting out of the room and jumping down the entire flight of stairs, the mudroom screen door hit the side of the house as we charged outside. Roaring our fury and fear to the sky, we raced to Gran's cottage where she was already at the door, obviously having heard the chaos.

Bagheera handed the reins back to me and I shifted with ease, telling her everything as quickly as I could. Her face paled briefly but in true Bette fashion, she squared her shoulders and lifted her chin in determination. I could see the wheels turning in her mind and I threw up every prayer, wish, and hope I could to the stars that Sprout would be okay. I wouldn't even entertain another scenario.

"She will appear to be sleeping for now, Kaito. Don't worry, I know something that will help. I'm going to need your assistance, though. We need to go fetch some supplies. Are you okay with leaving your mate?" she asked, placing her small hand on my arm in comfort. My eyes widened at her use of the 'm-word' and she smiled, answering my unasked question, "Of course I know she's your mate. A blind mage could see that, child."

After last night, there was no doubt in my mind that she was my true mate. Ggods, the scent of her, the feel of her body gripping me, there was no other explanation.

Taking her hands in mine, I breathed out a long exhale. "I can't just sit up there. As much as I need to be near her, right now, I just need to do something that will ensure that this never fucking happens again. Tell me the plan, please," I begged, squeezing her fingers gently, but with an undertone of urgency.

"First things first, we need to gather some crystals from the cave, and then head to The Pig. All of the supplies we need are there, and we can create what I have in mind. A magical tether, something that will keep her locked in this realm, no more of this spirit snatching once we get her back. We won't let them take her, Kai. Do you understand? These evil creatures have no business with my granddaughter and I will have their blood if they don't fuck off. Let me grab my stuff, go tell the others where we're going and what we're doing. Prepare them that this might take some time, so they need to relax." Gran turned her back to me, rushing inside, and I blinked a couple of times before shifting back and tearing it up to get back to the guys.

The scene before us nearly broke our heart. All of our brothers were surrounding our sweet witch, Cam wiping the blood from her face with a damp cloth while Fischer was stroking her hair and Sloane was sitting at the end of the bed with his hands clasped together. Our throat tightened with emotion, but we shook that shit off, because there was a plan, and it was going to work. It had to. Shifting to myself, I walked over to where Cam was perched on the bed.

"Listen, Gran has a plan. I'm going with her to create what she called a tether, when it's finished, it will keep Saige from being pulled across the realm. No more of this shit. She said to tell you all that Saige will be fine for now, and that we should all relax because it might take some time to get this tether complete," I explained, sitting my bare ass on the bed.

"But how does she know that Saige will be fine? We have no fucking clue what's going on wherever she's at. What if she's in danger? That's not a stretch considering these things keep happening and coming after her," Cam snarled, his emotions running really fucking high. All of ours were, but I had to keep them locked down because otherwise, I might shift and stay that way until this passed. The thought of that made me feel like a fucking coward, and Bagheera swiped a huge paw at the insinuation that being in his form was cowardly. My brow creased slightly from the mental discomfort his pissy cattitude was causing. *It's not like that, Baggie, and you know it. I have to be able to help her, we can't lose her.* His answer was a pitiful whine that just solidified my resolve to get this shit done.

"There's nothing we can do for her right now, Cam," Sloane snapped, but when Fish shot him a glare, he added a little gentler, "but we can work on this tether with Bette and get her back to us as soon as possible. I'm going to go with them, another set of hands on deck can only expedite things."

Fischer continued lovingly stroking Saige's hair, not shifting his focus from her face for a moment. Sloane noticed and stood, moving to stand by the headboard, his hand reaching out to Fish's face. That seemed to get his attention and Sloane tilted Fischer's head back slightly, staring into his eyes that I'm sure looked as sad as a kicked puppy's.

"Fischer, we'll get her back, everything will be as it should. I'm going to help Kaito and Bette, the sooner we get this figured out, the sooner we'll get her back," Sloane reasoned, always the realist, he gripped his chin as he lowered his face to press their foreheads together.

"I'm... scared," Fish whispered, his awe over the fact that he was feeling such a thing was clear as day.

"I know. It will be okay. We'll fix it. Breathe." Sloane's alpha tone rippled through the tense air and I found myself nodding, like he was addressing me as well.

"Do whatever you need to do. Just hurry. Who knows what hell she's going through right now," Fischer noted, and a growl came from Cam. Obviously, he did not appreciate the idea that our girl might very well be in a bad situation without us there, and no way to get to her.

Sloane leaned in then, sealing his lips over Fischer's in a hard kiss, and Cam and I shot each other a 'what the fuck' look, because Sloane *never* did shit like that. Always insisting that his 'arrangement' with Fish was strictly sexual, but this was like watching two people in love with each other, making an unspoken agreement of trust, sealing the contract with a kiss. *I'm going to have to investigate this later.*

"We'll be back soon. Call us with any changes." Sloane determinedly walked from the bedroom and I called out a hasty goodbye as I darted out to keep up with him. *Let's do this shit.*

Outside, we found Bette sitting on a moped, sporting a helmet that had a unicorn horn and fake rainbow tail hanging off the back. When she saw us, she lowered riding goggles over her eyes. "Hurry up. I already ran and grabbed the crystals we will need, let's get to the shop. There's no time to waste."

With that, she fired up her rainbow colored bike, revved the little engine, and then tore down the driveway, popping a small wheelie before sending up a dust cloud in her wake.

"That woman is unreal," Sloane mumbled, hopping onto his bike as I did the same.

"She's amazing," I breathed and held my hand against my heart for a moment before we were following a tiny cackling witch on a moped. What a time to be alive.

WE'D BEEN at it for six hours.

Six fucking hours with no change from Saige. She clearly wasn't going to be waking up on her own, so I was getting more and more impatient with each passing minute and Bagheera was downright pissed.

The three of us were sitting on stools at the counter in The Pig. Bette had hung a sign saying 'Sorry, we're closed' and Sloane threw a shadow spell against the windows so nobody could be nosy about what was going on in here.

Bette had done most of the prep work since we had no idea about the magical properties and ingredients of what she was trying to create. A mixture of five different crystals, twenty different ingredients that varied from herbs to shriveled up mushrooms, and a couple drops of something she said was 'the best thing since banana hammocks'. After two hours of continuous chanting from the three of us, boom, we had a pentagram shaped pendant the size of a half dollar. It would be worn as a necklace, the green specks of the herbs mixed in nicely with the shimmer of the different crystals. Sparks of purple, green, pink, blue, and white glimmered spectacularly and I couldn't help but imagine how nice it would look on Sprout's chest.

None of us had ever created something like this before, so we were combining our knowledge and hoping for the best.

"How did you hear about something like this, anyway?" Sloane asked Bette, who was doodling dick cartoons on a notepad.

"Well, my daughter... she had a bit of a demon obsession. When she went down that rabbit hole, I started some of my own research. They're pretty isolated, so there's not a ton to read about demons since the ones that are actually in our realm don't flaunt it. They exist between the shadows, hiding their true forms, and the powerful ones can use their powers without the victim ever knowing. Nasty creatures, honestly." She scrunched up her face in disgust. "I was trying to prepare for the worst, so this should tether Saige. I already gave her a bracelet that will let her sense if a demon is near, and protect her from possession."

"It's a decent idea." He nodded in thought. "Let's hope it

works. Cam just texted and said there's been no change, so I'm counting that as a win," Sloane informed us as he strummed his fingertips on the glossy wooden finish.

"How will we know when it's done?" I questioned, getting really impatient.

"See how it still has a soft pink glow to it? When it's done, it won't be glowing at all, the magic will have been absorbed completely into the pentagram, and then it will be safe to try," Bette explained to us as she added arms, legs, and top hats to her collection of dick doodles.

My mind couldn't stop wandering to what Saige was doing right now. I'd already cleaned every surface in this damn shop, the bar top was practically sparkling, and there wasn't a speck of dust on anything. Ugh, it was driving me fucking insane. Bagheera hadn't stopped his relentless pacing since this morning and as much as he was starting to annoy me, I couldn't bring myself to scold him. I understood completely. I hated not being productive, wasting time drove me nuts.

Hopping up to look for something else to do, Sloane's arm snapped out and pulled me back down onto my stool.

"Would you sit the fuck down for two gods damned seconds, K? I swear by the light of the fucking moon, if you don't settle down, I am going to slap the shit out of you," Sloane barked and anger began to rise in my chest. But... he was right. Ugh. A whimper from Bagheera slipped out of my mouth and Sloane's expression softened. Before I knew it, he'd wrapped his arms around me in a tight hug.

"Don't start purring, you freaky feline. This is a show of solidarity and support. But you really need to try and chill out, brother. We're doing everything we can," he reassured me, stepping back and gently slapping my cheek.

"How long will you boys be in town? Saige told me about who you work for and what you're doing here. I'm just curious how long it will take to close on that property, or what the situation looks like. She's my number one everything, and this is a discussion that needs to happen." She leveled each of us with a stare and Bagheera growled through the bond at the thought of ever leaving our mate.

Sloane took it upon himself to respond first, standing up and stretching while he spewed our lies, "The timeline depends on our boss, really. We forwarded all of our videos and pictures from the warehouse, so it's in his hands for now. We'll be here in case he wants hands on deck to handle any paperwork or needs us to check out anything else on site. At a minimum, I'd say three more weeks, but real estate is a fickle bitch, so could be a couple of months."

Bette nodded, thinking over what he had said. I watched her face, trying to determine if she knew we were full of shit. In ten years, I'd never once felt bad about sticking to the cover, completing mission after mission, hitting our marks, stealing items we were sent after. I'd never felt this... guilt. And that was because now, it was personal.

Was I in love with Saige? I wasn't sure, I'd never been in love with someone in a romantic way. I loved my brothers and I'd do anything for them, and I felt the same way for Sprout. When the mate bond flared from Bagheera the first time we'd laid eyes on her, I couldn't believe it. Just like that? Instantaneous? Love at first sight? How could something like that ever happen in real life?

What I did know was that I'd kill for her. I'd killed for lesser men, and there'd be no hesitation when it came to her protection. She was a delicate and precious treasure, one that I planned to cherish for as long as she'd let me, which hopefully, would be forever. I was already falling into a serious downward spiral headed straight towards obsession and total admiration.

"If any of you hurt her, I will chop off your cocks and give them to Randy Roger to hang in his wind chime garden in his backyard. You get one warning. She's been through enough and is still the most resilient witch I've ever known. Affairs of the heart are the ones that break people, and I won't stand for it."

"All due respect, Bette, it'd be more likely that she'd be the one to break their hearts if we're being honest here," Sloane murmured, running a hand through his dark hair. His ice blue eyes were frosty as ice chips, and a hint of sadness flashed before it was lost forever. *What was that all about?*

"Then let's just plan on nobody getting their hearts broken, yeah?" I said, suddenly feeling done with this conversation. My woman was laying in bed, lost to us, and I couldn't process the thought of ever being separated from her.

"Let's pick up some food and head back. We can bring the pendant with us so the moment the glow stops, we can put it on our girl. We need to eat, even if we don't feel like it," I suggested, tired of sitting here doing fuck all. "I'll probably need to go for a run after lunch. Bagheera is in a downright shitty mood and if I don't let him have a proper feline freak out, who knows what we'll be in store for later."

"Sounds like a plan. Order from the Chinese place. I could eat there every day!" Bette exclaimed, clapping her hands before putting the pendent into her bag. "Let's get the fuck out of here. See you suckers at home!"

And with that, she flounced out of the shop without so much as looking back. Sloane and I just looked at each other before shaking our heads and chuckling over her antics.

"I'll call Wok n' Roll, go make sure the backdoor is locked and warded. That douche-mage was lurking around here last week and I don't want him trying to pull any kind of fuckery," I told Sloane, pulling out my phone and looking up the number to call in the food.

"On it."

I placed an order with enough food to feed a fucking army, and after Sloane and I made sure everything was good to go, we headed over to the restaurant to pick up our deliciousness. My stomach rumbled so loud, I nearly mistook it for Bagheera getting bitchy again.

"Last one to the house has a micropenis!" I hollered at Sloane, attempting to lighten the mood and laughing as he cursed me, both of us running to our bikes with backpacks stuffed with Chinese food. It was fun when we did these races since I *always* beat him. My bike was faster, and he would be such a pouty bitch over it.

The laughter felt forced from my lips as the shadows from massive clouds drifted over the sun, matching my emotions. The excitement I would've normally felt over beating him in any competition no longer felt as good as it usually did.

THE SUN WAS SINKING in the sky, casting hues of pinks, oranges, and purples in its farewell.

Bette had given Cam and Fischer the rundown on the tether once we returned. With nothing left to do but wait and worry, we'd all stuffed ourselves at lunch and afterward, everyone decided to take a nap, exhaustion setting in after the huge surge of adrenaline we'd all felt. But I had to run. We stood on a large rock, staring at the sky, just lost in thought. This whole situation was beyond fucked up, and after Bette's questioning earlier about our timeline, there was so much weighing on my mind and conscience, I was having a hard time dealing with it.

What kind of a mage lies to their mate? A scum bag. An unworthy one. And on the other hand, one that is keeping his woman safe, one who has a secretive job, one that could put her in further danger. For every positive, a negative was right there waiting, and I'd ruminated on this line of thinking all gods damned day.

My usual cheery attitude was nowhere in sight, and a flare of concern came through the bond multiple times today, my panther checking in to make sure that I was okay, that the depression I struggled with off and on was still in check.

And it was, for now.

It had been years since I'd had a really scary low time, but it happens. There was no trigger, no event that set it off, it was just how my brain was wired. A chemical imbalance, that's what the healers told my parents when I was first diagnosed at age seventeen with MDD — *major depressive disorder.* It was so much easier to just say MDD, especially when I would be so fucking depressed. The less words needed to use to give a history, the better.

Learning coping skills and utilizing therapy services had been monumental in taking my life back from the darkness, the suffocating sadness that seemed to hit like a ton of bricks without any justification or warning. I refused to let it happen right now, though. Saige would be fine, this tether would work, we would all figure out what the next step would be in our relationship, and perhaps a transfer was possible if we convinced Larson to buy this fucking building after all. We'd spearhead the project and oversee the development of Radical Inc. Kingstown Branch.

Maybe he'd be more interested if we played it up as a recruitment and training center. Sloane and Fischer had said the space was there for it, that could be a great change of pace for us. Train the next generation and all that shit. Like Karate Kid. My stomach twisted uncomfortably though at the conversation we'd have to have sooner rather than later about our real careers and why we were here.

The dead sprint back to the cottage passed in a blur, and our muscles were screaming, but the anxiety was ebbing away, so it was fucking worth it. Shifting fluidly back into my body, I entered through the back patio and snagged the pair of shorts I'd left, quickly slipping them on. There was no sound coming from upstairs, so the others must have still been snoozing. *Good, they needed their rest.*

Grabbing a cup and filling it with water from the tap, I slammed three of them before taking some deep breaths. *There, that's much better.* Stretching out a bit, I felt like myself again. *I can do this. This is my gods damn mate and I'll be a son of a bitch if some demon fucks think they're going to take her from me. I'd die before I ever allowed that to happen.*

Taking the stairs two at a time, I turned the corner and my heart melted at the scene before me. Our beautiful woman was lying in the middle of her bed, Cam's arm underneath her head, his face buried in her hair. Fischer took up the other side of her, his arm thrown across her waist, his body pressed as closely as possible. Sloane was sprawled across the bottom of the bed on his stomach, but his grip was firm around her ankle. My pack. My family.

Figuring I should shower before staking a claim in the puppy pile that was happening, I intended to do just that, but as I walked past the dresser, I saw the pentagram tether, and it wasn't glowing.

It. Wasn't. Glowing.

"WAKE THE FUCK UP, ASSHOLES!" I shouted, and the guys all leapt from the bed, jostling poor Sprout as they landed in pure attack mode. Should I have felt guilty? Maybe? But I felt fucking proud as hell, my team was still as quick as ever and ready for any trouble that should come our way.

Their wild eyes scanned the room and when they landed on me, all three of them wore matching scowls and began to stalk my way.

"Now, now, boys," I held my hands up in surrender, "let's not do anything hasty. It's time to get our girl back!" I scooted backwards when they didn't stop advancing on me. "What? Would you rather I left you sleeping and took the role of the sole hero when she comes to?"

They froze. Ha.

"As I thought. I believe the words you're searching for are

'Thank you, Kai. You're the best friend a mage could ever ask for, I'll never stride towards you in anger ever again, and you have the nicest looking cock—'" I'm not even going to lie, a girly ass scream left my throat as Sloane barreled into me, tackling me to the ground.

"Stop. Talking. Feline," he growled, pushing his weight down on top of me.

I smirked up at him. "Is that the world's largest magic wand or are you just happy to see me, Sloaney?"

"You wish, K." He chuckled, hopping up and giving me a hand.

"What do you mean it's time?" Fischer asked, as his curiosity got the best of him and he joined Cam in eyeballing the necklace.

"Well, you heard Gran. When it stops glowing, that means it's party time, right? Someone go get her, I'm going to take a lightning fast shower, and then we're gonna get our woman back where she belongs."

"I'll do it, hurry in the shower, K. I want her back as soon as possible." Cam's no nonsense bark to his voice had me spinning on my heel and speed walking to the shower.

We were going to get her back. My Sprout, my mate.

Saige

Chapter Two

Something cold and smooth pressed against my cheek as my eyes fluttered open. Voices drifted into my ears, but they sounded distorted and I couldn't figure out what the words meant. My head was pounding, like the lingering effects of a bad hangover, and I felt groggy, like my brain had been reduced to nothing but a pile of rubble. *Where am I?*

Willing myself to open my eyes was a task in itself, my eyelids felt like lead weights. Once my eyes focused, I realized that I was laying on a stone floor, wearing the purple velvet robe from before. *At least I'm not naked this time. I'm back in Besmet, and I came here this time while I was fully awake. Good, that's not terrifying at all.* And the voices... definitely angry voices now, angry demonic voices. *Get up, get up, get up!* Attempting to push myself up on wobbly arms, I crashed back down to the floor almost immediately, my body was just too weak to respond the way I needed right now.

"Who are you and what are you doing in His Royal Highness, King Thane Carlisle's throne room?" an incredibly deep voice questioned. I glanced over, seeing it was one of the royal guards, judging by the uniform. Trying to think of something to say, I rolled over onto my back to buy myself some precious time, and my eyes widened when I took in the sight before me.

At least thirty demons stood around me, some men, some women, all with an assortment of different looking horns on their heads. They looked human aside from the horns, but more

THE MAGIC OF BETRAYAL

importantly, they all looked like soldiers. Like the kinds of demons you don't want to fuck with. I might have to bullshit my way out of this and fast.

Looking over to the man I recognized, I scrambled to come up with something to say. "I–" my voice cracked, throat dry and scratchy, "I'm here to visit your son."

Well, that certainly drew some less than desirable looks from the audience, and the king's eyes narrowed as he studied me, his eyes traveling over my entire body— not in a lewd way, but like I was undergoing some kind of assessment I knew nothing about.

Rubbing his knuckles under his chin, he sneered, "Bram's taken a whore? Well, it's about bloody time! Let's get the boy here to collect her, shall we?" He was staring at me, but his eyes had a sort of glazed look to them, like he wasn't really seeing what was before him. Just as my mouth opened to inform the bastard that I was not a whore, my skin started to tingle and the air before me rippled in the outline of a man. What the hell?

Fascinated and terrified, I stared up as Bram —I guess that was his real name— materialized before my very eyes. *Holy shit. Demons can teleport?* He stared down at me, his eyes widening when he realized the situation he just walked in on.

"I found your whore laying here like street trash, son. She claims she's here to see you. Next time, make sure you keep your toys from wandering the halls," the king grumbled, but I couldn't tear my gaze from Bram. His honey eyes were practically glowing, his jaw ticking in response to his father's words. I silently plead with him with my eyes to not ask questions, needing him just to play along. I didn't want this demon king to know anything about me.

Bending down towards me, he extended his hand in invitation, one I gladly accepted because without his assistance I'd probably be 'whorish street trash' for the remainder of the day with how exhausted I felt. When our hands connected, that same jolt of electricity zapped through my body and the magnetic pull

I'd felt before was almost buzzing as I fought the urge to plaster myself against his body and breathe in his scent.

Leaning down, his mouth hidden by my hair, he whispered, "Don't speak."

"Bram, I'm glad to see you finally breaking your celibacy. You know damn well we're having a crisis here. Now, get that commoner out of my fucking throne room and into your bed. With a little luck, you'll impregnate the whore," his father barked, and my eyebrows lifted to my hairline. Impregnate? Celibacy? What the actual fuck is going on here? Bram squeezed my hand in warning, reminding me to keep my mouth shut.

"Sire, I apologize. The woman is a wild one and after we'd mated earlier, she must've slipped out of my room while I was coming down from the knot. Won't happen again, will it?" His grip tightened as he pulled me against him, his other hand cupping my ass, earning cheers and laughter from the crowd. The loudest laughter was, of course, coming from the king of this castle. Creepy ass demon fucker.

"No. I'm sorry," I mumbled.

"You're sorry, what?" Bram bit out, playing the part well.

What the hell does he mean... Okay, right. He's royalty.

"I'm sorry, my prince," I amended, squeezing his hand to express my disgust. A smirk pulled at the corner of his mouth.

"Well, my boy! Don't let us deter you. I'll see you tomorrow morning for breakfast," he reminded Bram, then turned on his heel and began to stride across the room. Just as our shoulders sagged in relief, he spun back around, his gaze flicking between the two of us. "And just to be clear, if I find you sneaking around my castle again, I will slit your throat, whore to the prince or not." With that, he left the room, and without having to say a thing to his guards, they followed him like lemmings.

"Holy. Shit," I breathed. "That was fucking crazy! What the hell was he talking about, impreg—" my words were cut off as I was pulled into Bram's hard chest, his mouth dipping to my ear.

"There are spies everywhere, tiny warrior. Hold onto me, we're getting out of here before anything else fucking happens," he whispered, his breath igniting a shiver that ran down my spine. My hands lifted of their own free will, wrapping around his waist. *Wonder where we're going...*

"Oh! Oh, Bram, no, don't you dare—"

I screamed like a total asshole, at the top of my lungs, nothing held back as my soul left my body. It felt like someone had a giant vacuum and sucked us through it with no resistance. It was pitch black... oh wait, my eyes were closed. Derp. Whatever, I was too fucking scared to peek at what was going on out there.

We landed with a bounce on something soft, and my eyes flew open. The room was spinning so I squeezed them shut again. "Ugh, why the fuck did you do that?" I groaned.

He looked down at me like I was a few cards short of a tarot deck before shaking his head. "We just jumped back to my living quarters, it's still within the castle, but this is *mine*. You handled that well, most non-demons get sick," he informed me, and I felt the surface I was laying on shift. Inhaling and exhaling slowly, my bearings returned, and I felt brave enough to crack a lid.

"You thought landing us on your bed with a chance I was going to barf was a good idea?" I questioned, both eyes now open wide and taking in the expanse of the huge bedroom I was in. A black silky comforter was spread across the huge mattress, the stone walls towering high above us. Gargoyles were carved into different places along the perimeter of the ceiling, silently watching every move. They looked scary as hell. Fitting, I guess, for a demon prince's bedroom.

Bram had walked over to the sitting area where a fully stocked mini-bar stood in against the wall. "The blanket is replaceable. I was mostly concerned with you being so weak from whatever had you laying on the floor in a psychopath's castle, and that your legs would give out when we landed and you'd crack your head on the floor. Now, tell me, what the hell were you doing there? I explicitly warned you last time not to get caught snooping around."

"For the last time, I wasn't snooping. I don't know how I ended up there! After our last meeting, or whatever you want to call it, I woke up in my room and it wasn't five minutes later, my head felt like it was going to explode. By the stars, I'd never felt anything so painful in my entire life. It was awful! Have you ever thought you were dying? Because that's what I thought was happening. Next thing I know, I'm here. Again," I fired back at him, sitting up and crossing my arms over my chest.

Turning to face me, two glasses in hand, he walked over and handed me one as I studied his face for a moment. He really was unique. Easily over six feet tall, in fact, he was probably close to Cam's height, but narrower in his build. His hair was a dark auburn, shaved close on the sides and longer on the top to where it was constantly falling into his eyes. I'd never seen someone with the amount of freckles he had, and I was positive there were more hiding under his short beard. The most noticeable trait though, were his eyes. Amber yellow with specks of brown and his black rimmed glasses just amplified their beauty.

Taking the glass from him, the dark liquid swirled, and I didn't hesitate as I lifted it to my mouth and threw back half of it in seconds. A burn ignited in my mouth and throat unlike any liquor I'd ever encountered before I gasped and choked out, "What the fuck is that? Poison?"

Bram threw his head back and laughed as my throat died a fiery death. Flipping him double birds just made him laugh louder. "Hahahahaha," I mockingly laughed. Dick.

"You are captivating. It's called Dragon Fireball. It's whiskey made with actual fire from the beasts. Obviously, it's most enjoyed when sipped, not slammed. But street trash always take things too far, don't they?" He lifted an eyebrow, a grin causing his features to light up, somehow him repeating his father's words caused me to see the ridiculousness of them, and I grinned in response as his joke pulled me from my grumpy mood.

"Warn a girl next time, yeah?" I chuckled, choosing to ignore the whole dragon fire bullshit, and the burn was now nothing more than a nice warm tingle that was moving from my throat down my chest and arms, overtaking my whole body. *Oh, this is nice. Like a blanket, a snuggly and soft blanket.*

"Come, let's talk in the sitting room. Do you think you have the strength to walk?" he questioned, studying me.

"I'm feeling much better now. I should be fine, thanks," I replied as I scooted to the edge of his monstrous bed and let my feet drop to the floor. Straightening my spine, I stretched out with my arms overhead. My muscles were definitely tired, but they didn't feel like dried up raisins at this point, so I'll take it.

Bram led the way to the seating area where a large black rug held a massive couch that looked like it was going to be the comfiest one in the entire world. Sitting down in the far corner, I turned to face him, putting my back against the armrest, and kicked my feet out in front of me on the cushion. He dropped down about a foot from my bare toes, reaching forward to put his glass down on the coffee table. I wasn't ready to give mine up yet, so I took another small sip.

"So, I have a question," I began, laughing when he startled.

"I'll answer it if I can, tiny warrior. Not all questions are meant to have answers," he replied ominously.

"Okay, well, first of all, what the hell did your dad mean by impregnating me? What was that about? He wants you walking around knocking up presumed whores? Of all the things I could've anticipated, that was not even on the radar," I ranted, talking a mile a minute.

"He wants me to have heirs. At this point, I think he'd be happy no matter who birthed them. Just so long as the family line stays intact. I'm his only surviving child, so it's really up to me to continue the family name, or that's what he believes, anyway," he confessed, rolling his eyes. " I told you, my father has no respect for the lives of others, and I want no part of his plans."

He had told me that before, and judging by the general disgust that his tone was drenched with every time he spoke of the man, I think I had to believe him at this point.

"And you're celibate?"

Bram turned and gave me his full attention, and it was intense to say the least. He had this... air about him, he seemed so professional and put together, and then it's like his inner psycho would catch a glimpse of something that intrigued the beast inside. The beast was awake right now, I could see it with how his amber eyes practically glowed.

"I am," he grumbled, an emotion passed across his face, but I couldn't place it.

"Why?"

"You're forward, asking about my sex life when you don't even know me."

But, I did feel like I knew him. He was easy to talk to, and his mannerisms were so unexpected that he reminded me a little of myself. Or maybe that was just the Dragon's Fireball talking.

"Well, I've never met anyone who was celibate, so I'm curious, and your dad is the one who brought it up originally," I reminded him, taking another sip of the poison.

"I've not found anyone of... interest in a long time," his gaze penetrated mine, burning through me. "What's the point of fucking if it doesn't make you feel anything? Excitement, heat, passion, wickedness? Why bother if, when you're balls deep, buried to the fuckin' hilt, and you've got no desire to completely and utterly fucking own that person?" He leaned in closer to me, his voice becoming husky, and his eyes narrowing. The dark centers began to expand and I sucked in a breath. "The desire to fuck harder and harder, wanting to slam your soul into theirs so violently, they're so gods damned intertwined they'll never be untangled. That's what I want. The obsession. The whole 'I can't think of anything else except her sweet cunt and tight ass. Her hot tongue, how sweet she tastes, and how I'd fucking kill for her.' Oh, how I'd fucking kill for her."

"You're, uh, a little intense, yeah?" I asked, trying to shake the redness from my flaming cheeks. What a filthy talker.

"You'd be intense too if you hadn't had sex in forever," he chided and I nodded my agreement because, yeah, it wasn't so long ago that I was in that predicament. Look at me now, catching dicks left and right like a gods damn snake charmer. A small smile tugged at the corner of my mouth and Bram's nostrils flared. Leaning in, he inhaled deeper. *What is with all the men lately and all the sniffing?*

"I can smell sex on you. Of course, you'd be spoken for, fucking hell." He rose off the couch and began pacing so hard, I was concerned the rug beneath his feet would be worn down from his speed. Actual words were no longer coming from his mouth, just a series of growls and mumbles. Shit... his face was a mixture of pain and anger.

Standing slowly, so he didn't startle, "Bram?" I questioned softly.

No response, just more pacing. I could barely pick up on anything distinguishable coming from his mouth, but I swear I heard the words mate thrown in there and that had my stomach flipping. *Poor guy really needs to get laid. His psycho dad was totally right. Eek. Not my job, though. I already have four cocks to entertain.*

Steeling my spine, I spoke up louder this time, "Bram!"

The massive demon came to a dead stop inches away from me, snapping out of whatever the hell episode he was having.

"That's okay. I'll win you, take me to your man, let us settle this like gentlemen," Bram proposed, puffing out his chest. "If you were in your true form, I'd be able to scent him better and track the unworthy scum down myself," he growled.

"What the hell goes on in this place? You physically fight other men for ownership of a woman? Have you lost your gods damned mind? I make decisions for myself, a man will not take that from me. Never again." I bumped right up against his chest, poking a finger against his rock hard pec as I gazed up into his amber eyes that were looking a little like they were glowing.

Bram stood stoically, and I feared for a moment that I might have fucked up. I didn't know this dude, at all. He'd already displayed some interesting behavior that called into question the stability of his mind, but maybe that was just a demon thing? Regardless, I might've peed myself just a teeny little bit while we engaged in this epic staredown. Just when I was about to break, he threw his head back and laughed. And laughed. He laughed so hard, tears began streaming down his thin face, causing his freckles to glisten in the lighting of his sitting room.

My eyes darted back and forth across the room, growing more and more uncomfortable by the moment, so I figured what the hell and threw out a few laughs of my own.

Suddenly, Bram gripped my upper arms and leaned down until we were nose to nose. "You, tiny warrior, will be mine one day. Mark my words. Something about you speaks to the beast inside of me." His hand lifted and he twirled a strand of my hair around his fingers. "Every time you've visited me here, all I can think about is when I'll stumble into you the next time. You smell like leaves crackling on a raging fire, like fresh steel and wet soil after the rain, my favorite scents. Plus, you have this faint vanilla smell to you that is purely delicious. Tell me, my sweet, if you weren't meant to be mine, why does your scent slam into me and completely overtake my senses? And why is it when I touch your skin, it feels like an electric current is sparking through my body?"

He feels that, too? Inhaling through my nose, his aroma invaded my brain, and I nearly stumbled against him, feeling pulled by an invisible tether. I fought it.

Stepping back from Bram, he dropped his hands, his brow creasing as he stared me down, waiting for some kind of response. "Regardless of how I may or may not speak to your inner beast, I still make my own choices. Remember the shriveled up snail?" I reminded him, hoping that it might get him to back off.

"Do I remember it? Woman, that was the moment that I knew all I needed. Just envisioning you fired up and ripping that scum's cock from his body?" He groaned loudly, running his ring adorned fingers through his red hair, fucking it up a bit, just adding to the unhinged look he had going on at the moment.

Well, that didn't work like I'd hoped.

"First of all, I'm not actually here. However this keeps happening, it needs to stop…"

"You are here, though. It's a physical projection of yourself. You can eat, drink, fuck… all the essentials." He winked. "Oh! Why didn't I think of this before? I split my time between here and the human realm, tell me your name and I'll find you there. I have unlimited resources at hand." Bram chuckled, pulling his phone from his pocket and handing it to me. "Put your number in there."

I couldn't give this guy my personal information. With being stalked by demon shadows as it is, this would just escalate matters. The thought crossed my mind to ask him about the shadow demons, but I quickly dismissed that idea, wanting to find out more about him first before deciding to trust him. His phone lit up and I lifted my eyes with a 'what the fuck' look. His background image was a drawing. A full color, *extremely detailed* drawing of me. On his back, piggy-back style, while he was in full demon form, my fists wrapped around the horns on his head like he was some kind of rodeo bull. His wings spanned out wide, not even fitting within the dimensions of the screen, his tail wrapped around one of my legs and coming up between his own, covering his demon dick. Thank the stars, because of course, we were obviously naked. I wasn't prepared to see whatever he was packing. *Oh shit, it was probably scary looking. Eek!*

"What. Is. This?"

"Your future, my warrior queen. I drew that a couple days ago, isn't it amazing?"

I lost it. Laughter bubbled out of me like a force of nature, while tears began streaming down my cheeks. *How is this my life? Oh moon maidens, is this some kind of cosmic joke?* Bram was now howling with laughter right along with me and neither one of us had a clue exactly what the fuck was going on.

"Okay, okay, Picasso," I gasped out between trying to catch my breath. "Here." My fingers flew across his keyboard, and I entered some bogus phone number and put my name as Marigold. Giggling internally at that, I handed the phone back.

"Marigold," he breathed, rolling the alias over his tongue and I couldn't help but wonder what my real name would sound like in that tone. The dude was crazy as bat shit, but he really was uniquely beautiful. I'd never seen another man with such distinct features.

"Yep. That's me." I shot him double finger guns and he pretended in full theatrics that I'd actually shot him, I found myself giggling yet again.

"Come, I want to show you something," Bram offered, holding out his hand. Eyeing it momentarily, I figured I may as well take it. Despite his… instability at times, I did feel surprisingly safe with him. He seemed like the kind of guy that would kill first and ask questions later.

"Where are we going?" I put my hand in his, and those tingles from before zapped up my arm as a small groan left my lips at the same time a louder one left his. "What is that? Why does that keep happening?"

"Don't worry about it, Goldie," he replied, not giving it a second thought, pulling me with him through the giant room until we reached a door. *Goldie, hmm, that's kind of cute, actually.*

"Hey, wait. If we're leaving this room, to go out, you know…

in public… can I borrow some clothes? I don't want to walk around looking like I'm searching for Hyrule all day."

Abruptly stopping, he turned back with the biggest smile on his face. "I'd love for you to wear my clothes, what better way to scent mark you than to have you draped in my clothing?" He dropped my hand and disappeared before reappearing across the room, flinging open a door and striding inside, I didn't even have time to shriek over his vanishing act.

Moments later, he popped back before me and this time, I did shriek. Loudly.

"By the moon, Bram! I'm not used to your Houdini shit, warn a witch. You're going to give me a heart attack!" I shouted, and he had this dreamy look on his face. "Why are you looking at me like that?"

"My name sounds scrumptious coming out of your mouth, Goldie girl." He winked and my face flamed as he handed me his clothes, "I'm sorry I startled you. Here. Put these on, they should fit."

Grabbing the first article of clothing, I held it up. It was a black t-shirt with a deep V down the chest, well worn, soft as a kitten. *Damn, I bet he looks like sin with this on.* He held out the second item, a pair of tight yoga pants, also black. They'd be way too long, but at least they'd be easy to roll.

"Turn around, demon boy. No peep shows today."

Bram spun around without a single protest and that won him some brownie points. Dropping the purple velvet robe, it pooled around my bare feet and I quickly slipped the clothes on. The shirt was bordering on obscene. The gals were large and in charge, but I felt strangely sexy in his clothes. And they smelled like Heaven. *Maybe I can keep them.*

"Alright. I'm all set, but I don't have any shoes," I noted as he turned back to face me.

"Damn, Goldie. The stars really broke the mold when they traced the curves of this body. By Saturn's brightest rings, you are the sexiest female I have ever laid eyes on," Bram's voice dropped an octave with each word spoken, and fire raced up my spine as his eyes burned a path over my body.

My blush deepened and I felt it crawling down my neck, heading straight for my chest. "Thank you," I replied shyly.

"Here, take these socks and boots. They'll be way too big, though."

"Oh, ye of little faith," I chided, slipping my feet into the socks and boots, and with a flick of my wrist, the boots shrunk to the perfect size. "See? I can do cool shit too, demon boy."

Bram studied me for a moment longer before shouting, "Here we gooooo!!!" Wrapping me in his arms, and poof, we were swirling, and then we weren't.

"Ugh, what part of warn a witch do you not understand, you demonic dickhead?" I groaned, rubbing my temples, but Bram was already walking off, not listening to shit I had to say. *Well okay then, guess I'll just go fuck myself.*

"Hey! Come back here, mister! I'm scolding you," I called out, stomping over to follow him, my vision tunneling on his back.

"Who, me?" he called back over his shoulder, still not stopping.

Huffing with indignation, I mumbled, my feet tromping through grass, "No, not you, I was talking to the other freckle-faced nut —oof—" I slammed into a Bram brick wall. "What the heck are you doing, you are really starting to p—" I shut up. My eyes scanned the landscape and my mouth dropped open.

We were standing on a cliff that overlooked a massive forest with rolling hills, and tinkling streams weaving in and out of the trees. Houses of all sizes were sprinkled throughout the vast land, smoke from chimneys rising towards the sky, lights from their homes lighting up the night like beacons.

"Wow, this is beautiful," I sighed. A green witch's dream, really. All of this growth? Ahh, I lowkey wanted to get down there and roll around, touch all the trees, and trail my hands through the tall grass.

"Would you like to go on a walk with me? I can tell you a little more about this realm?" Bram offered, and the slight insecurity in his tone had my heart softening, and the anger I'd felt earlier dissipating.

"I'd love that!" I jumped up on the balls of my feet a few times in excitement.

He grinned, reaching for my hand. "I'm going to jump us down, and then we can walk like normal people, okay?"

As much as I didn't appreciate the sensation of jumping, maybe this time wouldn't be so bad since he'd given me a warning.

"Alright, let's do this." I grabbed his hand and a moment later, we were standing in a dense evergreen forest, the trees towering high above us, the cool air nipping at my nose. The jump had not jolted me as badly since I knew what was going to happen, so I immediately began wandering around, slipping between the trees, and letting myself enjoy the rich pine and cedar scent the forest was offering.

"This was one of my favorite places to play when I was a boy. The trees are excellent for climbing, makes it easy to hide from your friends and pounce on them when they least suspect it," Bram told me, keeping pace behind me.

"Oh, if this was where I'd grown up, I would've been out here every day! These trees are monstrous. The ones on my land don't get this big. I love them!" A flash of white in my periphery had me slamming to a halt. *Maven?*

"Did you see that?" I questioned, pointing to where the white flash disappeared.

"See what?" Bram asked, his body already stiffening in preparation for... *what? Are we in danger out here?*

"There was something white, it reminded me of my pet back

home," I confessed, walking over to see if I could catch another glimpse.

Bram relaxed. "Oh, yeah, these woods are overrun with white foxes. Little shits are troublemakers."

I froze in my tracks. Prickles of awareness tickling the back of my neck, *oh my gods*. What were the odds? No, there's no way this was a coincidence. Demons hunting me? Check. Their forests are running rampant with white foxes like Mave? Check. *What the fuck sticks? Is Maven a... demon fox?*

"What is it, Goldie? Are you cold? You're shivering," Bram observed, wrapping his frame around me, holding me tight. Without conscious thought, I nuzzled my cheek against his chest and one of his hands came up and began to run through my hair.

"I'm okay, just tired," I lied, not wanting to talk about this Maven conspiracy that my brain was trying to run away with. I wondered if there were some way to see if he was a demon fox, like a spell we could try that would reveal the truth. Thinking back, I couldn't remember when Maven actually showed up. Well, I remember when I first started seeing him, he'd stuck to the forest for a while before getting brave and approaching me. It was a brutal winter and I felt bad for him, so I let him in the house. Gran about lost her shit over that, but he loved it. Snuggled right up against me in bed, and I never kicked him out again. That was about five years ago now.

"Let's get you back to my place then. I can make you something warm to drink, run you a bath? Whatever you wish, I'll make it happen, Goldie."

Warmth did sound good, and maybe a nap. Definitely a nap since I had no idea why I was here or how I'd get back home again.

WAKING up in Bram's giant bed, the sun was shining outside and I had lost absolutely all sense of time. The satin sheets felt delicious against my skin and I stretched out like a cat, only to remind myself of Kai. Sigh. How long was I going to be stuck here? I missed my guys. Tears pricked my eyes and I rolled my face into the pillow.

They must have been so worried. I could barely recall the events that happened before darkness took me and I woke up here, the pain was the focus of my attention, but I did remember their panic, the fear in their shouting. *Is my body just laying there in my bed still? Are they all sitting around me like I'm Snow White? I need to figure out how to get back, and soon.*

A snore that was most assuredly not my own startled me, and I sat upright, eyes wide as I frantically searched the room before lowering my gaze to the bed. That sneaky little demon. Bram was snoring like a freight train, an arm slung over his eyes, the sheets low on his waist. Outrage tried to stir, but was pushed down by curiosity. My greedy eyes trailed over every exposed inch of his skin.

Black tattoos covered much of his body, all of them some type of rune or symbols that I didn't understand. They must be important to his culture, and that would explain why I was clueless. On his chest, right above his heart, there was a bare spot. Like he was holding that place for something important.

The freckles that smattered his face covered his whole body, I realized. Dark russet hair sprang from his chest, trailing down, down, down to fun town. A peek of thick curls peeked just over the sheet and I froze when I realized he was naked under there. Shaking my head, I rolled over, and swung my feet off the mattress. *I need coffee. Stat.*

Padding silently through the room, I searched for the kitchen that ended up being just off of the sitting area, so it wasn't too difficult to locate. My stomach rumbled, *when was the last time I ate anything?* Food and coffee, in that order. I wonder if I can eat here... but my stomach was growling so that was a good sign.

"GOLDIE!?" A panicked shout from the bedroom made me stop and run back to Bram. *Oh shit, is he in trouble?*

Bursting into the room, I glanced around, finding the demon sitting on the bed, hair askew, eyes wild.

"What is it? Are we in danger? What's wrong? Is your dad on the way to kill me?" I whisper shouted as I looked around.

"Oh, by the stars, you scared the shit out of me. I thought you'd left again. Whew!" Bram flopped back on the pillow and I stared at him, mouth open. *What does one say to someone who is like this?*

My hands were pressed to my chest, my heart racing as I tried to take some deep breaths. "I thought you were in trouble, holy moon maidens, you need to learn some social skills. You scared me half to death."

"Nobody will harm a hair on your head ever again, Goldie. I guarantee you that," Bram growled, his eyes flashing with darkness. *And now we're back to scary demon prince.*

Bram

Chapter Three

Propping myself up on my elbows, my brain whirled with murderous intent. No man or beast would ever hurt my Goldie, not unless they wanted to experience the most pain they'd ever felt in their miserable existence moments before I flicked my wrist and incinerated their bodies from the inside out. I wonder if that would soften her toward me at all. She could pretend she didn't feel the mate bond, but she was full of shit, and I was an extremely patient man.

After getting sick and tired of my dad's bullshit, pimping me out, trying to get me to make babies right and left, I swore a life of celibacy. This dick had not felt the caress of a lover in nearly fifty years, so I could wait for my little warrior to come to terms. It had been written by the stars, fate itself brought us together and I wouldn't lose her now.

"Alrighty then," my ray of sunshine chirped before clapping her hands in front of her chest, "but now that you're up, can you please make me some coffee? Oh, and I need food. Like, real bad. A breakfast buffet would be fantastic!"

This, I could do. Swinging my legs off the side of the bed, I stood tall, stretching out my long body with a groan. Cracking an eye when I heard a soft gasp, I watched as Goldie slapped her hands over her eyes. *Okay. Definitely not the response I was going for. Fuck, maybe there's something on it?* Peeking down at my retired dick, I breathed a sigh of relief that it was still as magnificent as ever.

"Bram! Can you like, throw some shorts on? I don't need to see your peen first thing in the morning, okay?"

"So you would like to see it at other times of the day? That can be arranged."

"I'm going to the kitchen. Get dressed, you... flasher!" She "insulted" me. *Wow.* What a stinger that one was.

"Whatever you say, tiny warrior. This demon dick belongs to you now, so it shall obey your orders."

She threw her hands up in the air as if I was the one being impossible. How does she not feel what I feel? How does she not feel the magnetic force between us? How the fuck else does she think her ass keeps getting pulled into Besmet while she's dreaming away in her bed? I wonder if her lover is there right now, cuddled up against her, not realizing she's actually here, peepin' my demon dick at six in the morning.

Grumbling, I waltzed over to my closet and snagged some gray sweatpants, the kryptonite to women from her realm. With my confidence restored, I strutted into the kitchen like a god about to gift his goddess with the best coffee in all the world.

"By the moon, what are you doing?" I choked out.

Goldie swung her head back to look at me, her shapely body on all fours on the floor digging through a cupboard. "I'm looking for coffee! What's it look like?"

Gritting my teeth, I inhaled deeply through my nose.

"Well, it looks like you're presenting yourself, if I'm being honest." I leaned against the fridge and stared down at her juicy ass.

Her pouty lips fell open and she scrambled up onto her feet, wiping her long red hair out of her face.

"What the hell do you mean, presenting myself?" She stepped up against me, her tits grazing my chest. Clearly, the woman doesn't know their reach. Lucky me.

"It's what a female demon does during mating. It's an offering to her mate, getting into position and preparing to be mounted," I whispered and smirked as her eyes widened. Maybe I could kiss her? Well, I could try... I leaned down and looked at her mouth, just before I made contact, she spun away.

"No. Not happening, demon boy. Where is your coffee machine? If I don't get some within the next five minutes, I'm going to have a total WF," she threatened, like that meant anything to me, but regardless, it didn't sound like something pleasant.

Smirking, I snapped my fingers and a carafe of freshly pressed coffee materialized on the kitchen island, and I watched her face go from confused to absolutely gleeful.

"Oh, my stars, how the fu– no, doesn't matter. Coffee!" she squealed, rushing over to me and giving me a quick hug before hustling over to the delicious smelling liquid. Right as she was about to ask for a mug, I snapped my fingers again and two mugs appeared.

Snapping once more, I conjured up some cream and sugar, and she went about making her perfect creation before scooting over to hop on a bar stool. Following her lead, I poured myself a cup and slid onto the seat beside her.

"Gods, this coffee smells amazing. Thank you," she breathed, lifting the mug to her lips for a long sip. She paused, closed her eyes, and gave a satisfied smile before taking another long drink. "Sooo goooood."

Damn, I could watch her drink coffee all day long. "You're welcome. Oh! You wanted breakfast, too. Pancakes? Bacon? Sausage?" I asked with a wink and she shoved my shoulder playfully.

"Uhm, yes? All of the above?"

Snapping my fingers had the countertop filled to the brim with stacks of pancakes, and an assortment of breakfast meats. Goldie's stomach growled and mine answered, I was pretty damn hungry too. Grabbing some forks from a drawer, I slid one to her before stabbing a sausage link and shoving it in my mouth.

"This smells fucking delicious. Gah, I'm so hungry." She snagged a plate that was stacked with a load of pancakes and smothered in butter and syrup. Not wasting any time, we both descended on the spread of food like a pack of goblins. Who knows how long we sat there stuffing our faces and drinking coffee, but holy fuck, I felt like I was going to blow up.

"Ahhhh, I totally overdid it. That was the coolest shit I've ever seen though, I wish I could do that. Snap my fingers and make things appear in the blink of an eye." Goldie leaned back against the barstool, rubbing her full belly, and satisfaction spread through my body at knowing I did that. Provided for her. Something I would always do.

"I'll teach you sometime. It's not that hard, just takes some practice and a little bit of focus. For example, you wouldn't want to try to conjure a plate of breakfast sausages and instead have a plate of dildos land in front of you. Well, unless you're into that kind of thing? I can get some dildos here in a real fuckin' jiffy. Just say the word..."

She was laughing, then groaning, "Oh my gods, don't make me laugh right now. I can't take it. Too full. And no, no plate of dildos, thank you very much. I think I just need to lay down for like half an hour and digest some, then I'll be good to go. Well, after a shower..."

"Come on, let us digest together in bed," I announced, spreading my arms wide as I hopped off the stool, snagging her hand in mine and tugging her behind me as we slowly made our way back to my bedroom. Once we stepped inside, I dropped her hand and sprinted across the floor, catapulting myself onto the bed, bouncing on my stomach, and flipping over onto my back.

"You're ridiculous," she laughed, "but that did look kind of fun..." She ran to the bed and launched herself, twisting in the air to land on her back, yelling out a warrior cry that had my cock twitching.

After a moment of laughter from both of us, we laid there in silence for a few minutes, my mind thinking about all the things I knew for certain. First, she was my fated mate. Not all demons were lucky enough to find theirs, and with our numbers dwindling, the chances of such a blessing happening were getting slimmer and slimmer. For the past one hundred years, our race had been stricken with fertility issues, we were lucky to have a hundred purebred demons born each year and for a world of our size, that simply wasn't sustainable for our future.

My father had sent a team of his highest ranked and most trusted advisors to the earth realm to tackle the problem head on. Khol, Asrael, Eronne, and Thijs had all been earth side for the past century. One goal: make babies. One problem, no babies had been made.

They started with humans, and while some were able to conceive, none of the pregnancies lasted past twelve weeks gestation. The human women were not strong enough to carry a demon spawn, and it appeared to have a negative effect on their minds. After a few years, they switched to witches. And not a single pregnancy happened. Nothing. It seemed there was nothing to be done. The team had confided in a few talented mages and witches—well, more like tortured and killed—to access certain spells that might increase chances of conception.

Still, nothing worked. So The Four continued, their frustrations growing with each day that passed and they were forced to stay earth side. That was the stipulation set by my father, you can't return until you have a live birth. A demon hybrid, one that could further the race and end our struggles. In the beginning, I'd been completely on board with this plan, survival of the fittest and all that. Now? Shit, I was kind of happy that there had never been a successful spawn, who knows what the fuck my father would put them through... and if it was a woman? Ugh, I couldn't even think about what she would be put through at his hands.

And now, not only was our fertility practically nonexistent, but parts of our world were starting to die. Forests that were once green and lush were dying, the trees blackening to the point that when the wind whipped through the forest, they would crumble into ash. It didn't make any sense. My father was convinced that there was dark magic at work, possibly the witches earth side that knew what we'd been up to the past century were sick of our shit and decided to curse us.

Good thing they couldn't just enter Besmet, you needed to be a demon to open the portal. And that's why I was confused by the witch laying beside me in the bed right now. A fated mate was always the same species, at least for demons, and how was she able to project herself here? It didn't make sense and I had a suspicion there was much more at work here than met the eye. The only person I would confide in would be Khol; if my nutty ass dad got wind of this, he'd probably kill her on principle, and then I'd have to kill him because fuck if he was ever going to get his hands on my woman.

"It's peaceful here, for a demon realm," Goldie murmured, breaking the quiet.

"Mmm, yeah. It can be. It can also be bloody and darker than your worst nightmare. But here? In this room? Nobody would dream of disturbing us."

"Are demons violent? I admit, I don't know much at all about your race. Until recently, I hadn't even realized that you existed. How is that possible? To be so elusive that the masses don't know that you're not myths?"

Rolling onto my side to face her, I studied her round face, slightly pink cheeks, full lips, and hair fanning out across the dark blanket we were sprawled out on. So beautiful.

"Demons are quick to anger and violence. We like to deliver swift and precise responses. Dicking around is not in our blood,

THE MAGIC OF BETRAYAL

we don't do things by halves. Once a demon's mind is made up, that's pretty much it. Getting us fired up is not a wise decision as once the rage kicks in, there's really nothing that can stop it."

"So do any of you live in my realm? What does your real form look like? Do you really have a tail? Oh shit, I'm sorry, that was probably too personal." She slapped her hands over her face, embarrassed.

Chuckling, I reached over and pulled her hands away, looking her in the eyes. "Some do live there. Have you ever heard of the notorious gang that runs Port Black?"

"You mean The Exiled? Yeah, who hasn't heard of them?"

"Well, all five of them are demons. Really powerful fucking demons. They were booted from here years ago and they made a life for themselves in Port Black. My father wrote them off, so we don't communicate with their crew at all anymore. As for my true form?" I laughed. "It mostly only comes out if I get really worked up, pissed off, usually. Or during sex, but like I said, that's been a while. And yeah, of course I have a tail, you saw it in the drawing, remember?" I winked and her eyes widened. "Maybe I'll show you sometime in person, we'll see. You've already seen my horns, those actually weren't fully elongated. They're quite impressive."

She seemed to process my words for a moment, which made sense. I was giving her a shit ton of new information. Her eyes met mine again and she shrugged. "I'd be lying if I said I didn't want to see your tail, but we can save that for another time. So, the snapping thing you do, is that your only power? What all kinds of powers do demons possess?"

"Procuring items is a fairly basic demon power. The higher ranking the demon, the more powers they can master. It's similar to witches and mages. Not every demon gets every power. For example, I am able to do telekinesis, voice mimicry, dream walking, and shapeshifting. Once I ascend to the throne, all of my father's powers should transfer down the bloodline to me. So I

37

will be able to do everything he can, which includes deal making and biokinesis. That's why I keep telling you to be careful around him, he can make your body go boom with the flick of his wrist. He's a kill first, ask questions later kind of king," I told her sternly, the tone of my voice hopefully bringing across the severity of the situation.

"I will do my best to never piss him off. I hope I don't run into him again, ever... and that will make it very easy to stay true to my word."

"Good. I just want to keep you safe, Goldie."

"I'm not your responsibility. And hopefully, I can figure out a way to stop myself from being sucked into this realm! I don't want to be here or anywhere near the king, for that matter."

Her words pinched my gut in an uncomfortable way. She would be here, though. She would be the next Queen of our realm, she just didn't know it yet. Oh well, plenty of time for her to warm up to the idea before it would ever have to happen.

"You mentioned a shower, how about you go do that and I'll make us some more coffee, and then we can go out and explore some more?" I offered, trying to sweeten her up with caffeine and adventure.

"Yes, that sounds perfect." She sat up and scooted to the edge of the bed. "Can I borrow some more clothes? Do you think you could procure me something a little more... feminine? A basic tank top, underwear, a bra? Leggings? Oh, sweet, sweet leggings, the appropriate at all time of the days pants," she sighed dreamily at the thought.

"Sure thing, tiny warrior. Everything you need is in the bathroom."

She padded off to the bathroom and I starfished out like the princely stud I was. She'd be wrapped around my finger in no time.

While she showered, I got her clothes in order. Black leggings with a black tank top that I personalized with a hand drawn creation. Getting dressed myself, I paused when my phone began ringing.

"Yeah?"

"Is that any way to greet your oldest friend and mentor?" Khol chuckled.

"Sorry, man. I'm trying to get dressed. What's up?" I asked, putting him on speaker as I slid my pants down before slipping into a pair of jeans.

"The report I've been waiting for will be done tonight. Get over here around eleven. We'll read it together. I'm confident this is what we've been waiting for. We'll discuss how to proceed after it's official."

"I'll be there. Any news on the bitch's whereabouts?"

"Nothing yet. It's a matter of time now, the team is closing in on her. Vengeance shall soon be mine." He noted with a darkness to his tone that would have lesser men pissing themselves. Khol was an extremely powerful demon, and he was getting sick and tired of the never ending assignment he was on. He was due for a break.

"See you soon." I ended the call, slipping a shirt over my head.

"Bram?" Goldie's voice carried through the entrance of the closet and I gave my dick a squeeze at the sound of my name on her lips. By the fuckin' moon, I needed to have her soon. But not until I won her fair and square from whoever the fuck her body was with now. My forehead started tingling, a tell that my horns were itching to break free and I took some deep breaths to force myself to chill out. *It's all good. She's here with me. Not him.*

"In here. I laid your clothes out, they're on the bed. Let me know when you're dressed," I called out.

Three, two, one... "BRAM! WHAT THE HELL IS THIS!?"

Poking my head out from the closet, a giant grin across my face, I laughed my ass off as she held the tank top up, examining the artwork on the front that immortalized how she'd gotten the nickname tiny warrior. A snail, well, a dick snail would be more accurate. A snail shell with a shriveled up penis as the body, two sad as fuck looking balls dragging behind the thing, it's droopy antennae hanging off the head of the dick. Fucking glorious.

"I can't wear this! Did you draw this too? By the fucking stars, Bram. I can't even with you." She tried to be serious, but she started smiling at me anyway, and that lit my heart on fire.

"Fine. I'll take it off, but it is completely appropriate. You're a warrior and every male here should know about it," I conceded, but in reality, all I did was put a glamor on the image so that she wouldn't be able to see it, though everyone else would. Laughing maniacally and congratulating myself on how much of a kick ass evil genius I was, she snatched the pile of clothes and disappeared with them. *Hope she likes the cheeky booty panties I stuck in there.* A more scrumptious ass didn't exist in all the realms combined. *Fact.*

She walked back into the room, looking like a goddess. Her curves were on full display, and she tugged at the tank top around her middle.

"What are you doing?" I questioned.

"It's a little tight, don't you think?" she asked, continuing her stretching at the material.

"No. It's perfect. You're perfect."

"I don't normally wear such form fitting shirts," she confessed, her cheeks reddening. Was she... self-conscious? The fuck?

"Well, maybe you should start, Goldie. You have a sexy as hell body and it'd be criminal to hide those curves under baggy ass clothes."

Her gaze lifted and met mine, the tension building between us. I knew she could feel it. The bond, pulling tighter with each minute we spent together. I couldn't wait to complete it.

"Thanks. So, what's on the agenda? More exploring?"

"Hmm, maybe. Let's just go see what kind of trouble we can get into, how about that?" I offered, and she smiled, nodding her agreement.

We both headed towards the door when a pained sound from behind me had me running back to her. She was doubled over, arms wrapped around her torso.

"What is it? What's wrong?" I ran my hands over her body, checking for any visible injuries, but nothing appeared to be amiss.

"Hurts. Oh fuck, it hurts, Bram. Something is pulling my insides!" she shrieked, dropping to her knees.

"Breathe, Goldie. Just breathe. It'll be okay..."

Panic rose in me like a tidal wave. *What was happening?* Her wailing turned into screams and each one tore my heart apart, her pain a living thing inside my body.

"I... can't... breathe..." she gasped, writhing on the floor, and then her form began flickering, like a busted neon sign.

"Oh fuck no. They're trying to steal you back. Don't let them, stay with me, Goldie, please," I called out to her, desperation lacing my tone, but I couldn't give a fuck about that right now. My horns sprouted from my head and I felt my tail elongating, tearing my jeans, my muscles bulking out as my body grew to its full size.

"Bram... thank you..." she gasped just before another soul piercing wail filled the room.

"I'm going to track you down, tiny warrior. I will find you. I pity the bastard who would dare to steal you from me like this," I told her, a threat and a promise in those words.

I blinked once and she was gone, the scream the only thing left of her in the room, and even that dissipated into silence moments later and I was left demoned out in my full form, alone, again.

Fischer

Chapter Four

With clasped hands we all sat around Saige, creating a supercharged magical circle that would hopefully be forceful enough to return her to her physical body. Gran was in charge, taking to the role easily as she ordered us about and gave directions. None of us gave a shit though, the severity of the situation having each of us admitting that we were not the most qualified person in the room for this task.

Gran was sitting on Saige's left side, having already placed the necklace around her chest. Cam was on her right, Sloane beside him, Kai was sitting cross legged at the bottom of the bed, and my hand was firmly holding his and Bette's. We'd gone over the spell, we all knew what we needed to say.

"On my start." Bette looked to each of us, her face the picture of focus.

She began, and all four of our voices joined in, our chanting creating a melodic cadence that caused each of our magics to manifest. Soon wisps of color, yellow for Kai, blue for Cam, red for Sloane, black and silver for me, and dark green for Bette, all intertwined and began wrapping around our arms, moving through each of us, and into Saige.

Return to us, for all our sakes, we call you back to Emerald Lakes.

Sweat broke out on my brow, the hair around my neck growing increasingly damp with each pass of the words that left my mouth. I'm sure the others were feeling it too, but I couldn't take my eyes off my sweetheart. The pentagram began glowing, a sign we took to mean whatever the hell we were doing was working. Bette and Kai both squeezed my hand in encouragement.

"Louder, boys, come on! It's working, the color is coming back to her face, drop your mental shields and let's do this shit!" Bette shouted before diving right back into the chant with renewed vigor.

Maven had been pacing on the floor when we'd started, but he dove through the circle and nestled right on top of Saige's chest, laying his snout right on the illuminated necklace. Her body began seizing and horrible, awful sounds came from her throat. Noises that would haunt me for the rest of time.

"Come on, baby girl. Don't fight us. Come home, little witch," Cam pleaded, his voice cracking as our hair began to stand on end like we'd been electrocuted.

We call you back to Emerald Lakes. We call you back to Emerald Lakes. We call you back to Emerald Lakes.

The second the last word left our mouths, a blinding flash lit the entire room and Saige's scream filled the space.

"It's okay, it's okay, we've got you," Kai called out, placing a hand on her thigh. The purple robe she had been wearing was gone, seemingly traded in for some normal comfortable clothes. *So freaking weird how the clothes come with her when she goes back and forth.*

Saige's eyes scanned the faces surrounding her and she visibly relaxed as her hands found Maven's fur. Her hair was stuck to her face, the exertion it took to bring her back apparently not only having affected us.

"Are you hurt, baby girl?" Cam stroked her cheek in such a gentle gesture that should not have been possible from a man of his size.

"N-not anymore. The pull that brought me back was excruciating though. Does someone have water?" she rasped, clearing her throat.

"Right here, Red." Sloane stood and snagged a water bottle from the nightstand, unscrewing the lid before handing it to her.

Maven hopped off of her chest, and Cam and Bette helped her sit up. She drank generously before giving the bottle to Bette and collapsing back down to her pillow.

"We can't tell you how worried we were, sweetheart. Were you safe? Did anyone harm you?" I questioned, needing to know if she'd been hurt, and how I could fix it.

"Safe enough. I did meet the demon king, though. Serious bastard, but the guy who I'd seen before, he's actually his son, and he showed me around and kept me away from his shitty dad." She paused, rubbing her face with her hands and Maven slithered up to her once again, pressing himself against her side. "So, how did you call me back?"

"Well, that was all Gran, Sprout. She took charge and is the reason you're here. Thank the stars." Kai all but pounced on Bette, wrapping her in a heartfelt embrace, his low words were for her alone, but I could hear the thanks and the sincerity in his voice.

Saige laughed softly, taking Bette's hands and the two Wildes witches stared into each other's eyes in an intimate moment that made me feel a bit like an intruder. Wanting to give them some space, I moved to stand and Bette's hand snapped out, latching onto my arm.

"I don't think so, Fish-boy. No running off. I'm exhausted, that spell took a lot out of me. I'm going to head to my house in a few minutes and you guys can fill her in. Deal?"

We all nodded our agreement, and I realized in that moment that Bette was a total alpha boss witch. She would've been one hell of a team lead in her heyday.

"Thank you, Gran. For everything. I love you so much." Saige's voice wavered as her emotions hit home.

"I love you too, child. No thanks needed, I know you'd do the same for me. The necklace you're wearing, it's a tether. It

THE MAGIC OF BETRAYAL

will keep you firmly in this realm, no more astral projecting. I'd hoped the wards we placed after the shadow demons appeared in your room would've stopped it, but the pull must've been too great. This will for sure put a stop to it. So don't fear, you won't ever go back there," Gran informed her, and I raised an eyebrow when instead of relief, a flash of another emotion danced across Saige's face. Was it sadness? Longing? Uncertainty? Whatever it was, it made me wonder if she was okay with never returning. *What the fuck went on in the time she's been gone?*

Bette rose from the bed, making her way to the door, before turning back. "I'll stop by in the morning for breakfast. French toast and bacon. Or maybe sausage? By the stars, I love sausage..." she trailed off, her eyes tracking across our bodies wistfully for a few moments before exiting the room with her usual flair.

"What can we do, baby?" Cam questioned, lying beside her, holding her hand, Kai on the other side.

"I feel like a shower is in order, I'm all sweaty. Maybe some food then? Pizza? What the hell time is it anyway? Was I gone long?" She asked, each question coming out faster than the last.

"Slow it down, Red. Last thing we need is you getting stressed right now. You were out for close to eighteen hours. It's almost midnight, so no take-out places will be open in this tiny ass town. Any other requests for food?" Sloane told her the facts, and I thought his straight from the hip no bullshit attitude was exactly what she needed right now.

"I think I have some frozen pizzas. That'll work. Thank you, Sloane." She smiled at him and he returned it before muttering about preheating the oven and leaving the room.

KAI WAS BURYING his face into her neck, his purrs erupting from his chest at a volume I'd never heard from him before. Saige's giggles had my mouth lifting at the corner, watching Kai sniff her, and lay kisses up and down her throat. Suddenly he jerked back, eyes wide.

"What is it, Kai?" Cam demanded.

Kai shook his head, bringing Saige's hand up to his nose, running it up and down her wrist and arm, taking deep inhales.

"I just... thought I smelled something familiar, but that doesn't make any sense."

"Something or *someone?*" Cam pushed, wanting more information, and I listened eagerly.

"Thought I smelled Johnny for a second, that damn Acqua Di Gio cologne he's always got on, and don't get me wrong, that scent is there, faintly... but there's something else that's stronger, and I've never scented that from him." Kai processed his thoughts aloud and then Saige piped up.

"Does it smell like old books and coffee?"

"That's it." Kai snapped his fingers with a dramatic flourish that only he could pull off, "But Johnny doesn't have that smell. It just startled me for a moment."

Kai leaned back down and continued the sniff and kiss fest, and when her hand came up to playfully push him back, he caught hold of her wrist and brought it to his cheek, the two of them staring into one another's eyes with a longing that I could feel from where I was standing.

Silently shuffling over to scoot onto the mattress myself, Cam shot me a look that relayed his relief. We'd all been beside ourselves when our girl went unconscious, but losing someone important had always been Cam's biggest fear. Well, at least for the past fifteen years.

"You scared me, Sprout," Kai confessed, running his fingers down her cheek.

"I was scared, too. I'm so glad you all figured out how to ensure that doesn't happen anymore, this is where I belong." Saige leaned in and pressed a kiss to Kai's mouth.

Cam folded his huge frame around our girl, dropping an arm over her waist and snuggling his face into her hair and neck.

"Baby girl..." he rumbled, a deep sigh leaving his lips before continuing, "I would've burned down all of the realms combined to get you back. We all would have. Did you learn anything of interest while you were there? Anything that would help explain the prophecy or why this seems to keep happening?"

Sloane returned just then with two pizzas and a basket loaded up with water, diet Dr. Pepper, and beer. Saige started laughing at the sight.

"You look like a pissy little red riding hood with that basket, Sloane," she giggled, bringing a smile to all of our faces.

"First of all, Red, let's get one thing straight. I'm not little anything, and if we're going with that story, you should know I'm the big bad wolf and I'm here to eat up little Red," he glowered, my dick throbbed at the sexual current that ran through his words. Jesus.

Saige's cheeks blushed, nearly matching her fiery hair.

"Get over here with that food, man. Sprout was just about to tell us more about her time in Besmet." Kai explained, helping her sit up.

"Red. What in the name of Jupiter's cock are you wearing right now?" Sloane's eyes nearly bugged out, and we all turned our attention to her.

"It's just a tank to—" She looked down at the same time Kai's howling laughter filled the space. "That dirty fucking demon dickheaded dingleberry..." she shrieked, outraged.

"Is that a... penis snail?" Cam questioned, his eyebrows nearly hitting his hairline.

"It looks like the saddest fucking creature in all the galaxies, where did you get it? Is that a thing that lives in the demon realm? Fuck, that's the shit nightmares are made of." Sloane visibly shuddered and I laughed like hell.

"So, there's this man—"

"Better not be, Sprout." Kai's eyes narrowed and a growl built in his chest. By the moon, he was turning into a jealous fuck.

Cam's eyes also narrowed and I took it upon myself to get these alpha dickheads to stop making fools of themselves.

"Enough. Let our girl tell us her story. There are other men in the world, you know this, right? It's not like she mentions another dude and that means she's dating him. You guys are going to growl yourselves into an early grave if you keep this shit up. Knock it off."

Cam and Kai both looked sheepishly at me and then Saige, muttering apologies.

"Thanks, Guppy," my sweetheart smiled at me and I longed to press my lips against hers.

Sloane had prepared her a plate of food and handed it to her, loaded with pizza, extra parmesan cheese sprinkled on top, and a fresh can of diet Dr. Pepper. After thanking him, she immediately tore into the food, sighing when she took a deep drink of her soda. The other guys slid off the bed, moving to grab their own food.

"So, like I was saying, there's this man. He's the demon prince, and the two times I projected there in my sleep, I ran into him."

She went on to explain how she'd woken on the stone floor of the castle, coming face to face with the demon king and his guards, telling us how this prince had protected her from his lunatic father.

"There's something about him that just made me feel safe so when his father was all," she deepened her voice, "'what are you doing here, you trashy whore?' I told him I was there to see his son, knowing he'd get me away from the king," she explained.

"I'm sorry, he called you what?" Cam gritted out, his jaw ticking.

Saige put her hand on his cheek and pulled his face down for a soft kiss. "It's fine, I'm home. Don't worry about it, big Daddy," she winked and Kai groaned. *Fuckin' Kai.* I laughed to myself.

I know I'd just scolded the others for being jealous pricks, but I'd be lying if I said I didn't feel a twinge at the thought of another man doing what I should have been. Protecting my family was my number one priority in life. But I was thankful on the other hand, who knows what would've happened had this prince not been there for her.

"But, oh my GODS, I almost forgot." Saige's abrupt change to anger had all of us steeling our spines, ready to defend against some unknown enemy.

"MAVEN!" she shouted and the grumpy fox barely twitched an ear in response, he'd nestled in between her thighs on top of the blanket.

"What is it, little witch?" Cam questioned, staring at the fluffy animal.

"MAVE!" She tapped him on the head with her index finger and his eyes cracked open the tiniest fraction, but they were filled with death. Saige began running her hands over his fur, lifting his head to inspect his face.

"What the hell are you doing to that fox, Red?"

"Is there a way to tell if an animal is really an animal? Or if they're a shifter... or a demon? When I was in Besmet, Bram took me to the forest and he told me that the woods are infested with white, trouble-making foxes. Now, you tell me, what the odds are of that, and the fact that I have an arctic fox sitting on my bed right now?"

Kai grunted, eyes flashing yellow. *Oh shit, here we go.* The shift came so fast that Bagheera's paws hit the floor before Kai's shredded clothes did.

Saige screamed. Legit screamed, a high pitch sound that had Cam wrapping his arms around her and pulling her onto his lap. Right... she hadn't met Bagheera yet. At two hundred and fifty pounds, and an impressive eight feet long from tip of the nose to tip of the tail, yeah, that might be kind of terrifying.

The stubborn as fuck fox didn't even move. The balls on this little animal were astounding.

Bagheera towered over top of Maven, teeth on full display as he leaned down to thoroughly sniff the hell out of him. Maven did have the decency to roll over onto his back, which, in the animal world was always seen as a sign of submission. *Good. The fluff ball doesn't have a death wish.*

And, I take it back. He's a wild animal. Just as Bagheera started to get closer to his face, the little grump gave a half second warning with his own snarl before launching himself up and biting the big black cat right on his nose. A wail came from Bagheera and he shook his head violently, a few drops of blood hitting the bedspread. Sloane intervened and grabbed Maven's snarly ass before Bagheera could retaliate.

"Just go put him in the bathroom for now, Sloane," Saige offered, and Sloane quickly deposited him in the room and shut the door. That was probably the best choice if they were going to continue this bullshit alpha fight.

Saige slowly crept off Cam's lap. "Umm, hi, Baggie..." she addressed the bleeding feline softly, and his huge head turned in her direction, his tail slowly changing from the flicking of an annoyed cat, to one that had just laid eyes on something that he'd decided was his.

The mattress creaked beneath his weight as he moved to her, dropping down into a crawling position that mirrored hers and looked ridiculous, but perhaps it was meant to put her at ease. Looked more like a predator stalking prey to me, but whatever. I took a big bite of my pizza, eager to see how this was going to play out. A hand on my back had my attention turning elsewhere, though. Sloane had materialized beside me, the heat of his hand warm enough to give me dirty thoughts.

As if he knew the effect he was having, his hand trailed lower and he palmed my ass, taking his own savage bite of his pizza, his tongue licking his bottom lip after he swallowed and I gulped. A sexy smirk tugged at his mouth, and my own mouth gaped when his hand ran up the crack of my ass through my jeans. He turned his attention back to the introduction that was happening on the bed, leaving me wondering what the fuck had gotten into him to start giving me public displays of affection. Even if it was hidden, this was a first. *And earlier, when he'd been so gentle and caring before going to The Pig with Kai and Gran?*

This was a new side of Sloane, and it was one I wanted to explore further. Was he finally ready to have a real talk about whatever was between us? The thought made my stomach clench, but before I could think on it further, commotion from the bed had my head snapping towards that direction.

"Baggie! Quit!" Saige squealed, her body squirming underneath the big cat as he nuzzled, purred, and licked her face. That's another first. *Are all men and beasts destined to act completely out of character around this woman?*

"Alright, let her up, Bagheera. She needs to finish eating, let us talk to Kai and see what he thinks about the fox," Cam ordered, and after one last lick, this one up the side of Saige's throat, he was gone in the blink of an eye and I was left staring at Kai's bare ass.

"Hello, Sprout." Kai's sultry voice had me rolling my eyes, but I moved over to them, nonetheless. His lust was evident, as his mental shields dropped and the room was being invaded by it.

"That was crazy! He... you... you're so big!" Saige exclaimed, grasping onto Kai's biceps as he hovered above her.

"Oh, Cub... if we had a dollar for every time we heard that..." he trailed off suggestively and Cam's eyebrow raised at the use of a new, more sexual nickname for her. Cam's lust was breaking through now and permeating so strongly I could hardly breathe.

"K, put some damn clothes on, you animal. Nobody wants to see that pale ass," Sloane scoffed, standing near the bottom corner of the bed.

"I bet yours is paler, Sloaney Baloney, but fine. If you can't handle this heat, I can cover up as not to offend your little sensitive eyes."

Kai went to move off of our girl, but Sloane moved lightning fast and cracked his palm right across his ass and Kai yelped, "Yes, like that! You know how I like it!"

Sloane scowled and we all laughed, but I saw the handprint that was left on his ass, and I definitely didn't miss the way Sloane's icy eyes were burning through my body when I glanced at him after taking in the mark he'd left.

Cam stood, letting Sloane slide in his spot and I moved to where Kai had vacated, the two seamlessly sharing our girl, knowing we needed a turn to be next to her as well. Saige leaned against me and I lowered my face to hers, needing to be closer.

"Guppy, I missed you," she breathed, running a hand through my dark curls that had fallen into my eyes. By the stars, this beautiful witch... and she was mine. At least for now.

"Oh, sweetheart. I'm just so glad you're back here safely and we've found a solution to prevent that from happening again," I whispered, getting closer. "I will fucking destroy any man, mage, or demon who harms so much as a hair on your head, I swear to the moon, Saige. They will not know what beast is coming for them until it's too late, and it won't be death that I deliver," I promised, my voice changing slightly, my power rising inside of me, seeking something to twist and splice.

"What... what will you do, Fischer? Tell me," she begged, and I was the tiniest bit surprised to see that she was clearly getting aroused by my darkness, if her increased breathing, dilating pupils, and wriggling thighs were any indication. I noticed Sloane's hand trailing up and over the curve of her hip, drawing little patterns over the material of her leggings.

I loosened the restraints that I kept locked around the monster inside of me and he peered out at the goddess before us. *Well fuck, if she liked the couple of glimpses she'd gotten up to now, she was going to love this shit.* Letting my mind drop into the swirling black abyss that I lived in while I worked, I allowed the words to flow, my voice dripping with the blood I'd let run if anyone ever harmed this woman.

"I'd convince their minds that they're in a coma, hook them up to fluids, and the bare minimum nutrients to ensure that they'd continue to survive. Then I'd search their minds to find their greatest fears, and I'd take those and devise the worst kind of nightmares they could ever imagine. Burning in hell would be a mercy in comparison. After a few weeks of that, I'd bring them out of the coma, let them see my face again before pushing them back into that hellscape. *Nobody. Hurts. You. Ever.* It will be the last thing they do, I fucking swear it."

My nostrils flared as I exhaled sharply, and then her lips were crashing against mine. Groaning, I slipped my hand between her and Sloane, tugging her closer to my body, half of my weight resting atop her. Her tongue slipped between my lips and I was in real danger of coming in my pants. Then Sloane's lust hit me like a sledgehammer and I grunted when his hand landed on my hip, squeezing Saige between us even tighter.

"Boss, why is this the fifth hottest thing I've ever seen?" Kai whisper shouted from the foot of the bed.

Saige laughed against my lips, moaning when I chased her mouth, biting her bottom lip and then licking the sting away.

"You're killing us, kitten," Sloane rumbled, rolling onto his back, adjusting himself.

"Blame Fischer, he just disintegrated my brain and panties when he went all evil like that. Holy moon maidens, I need a breather." Saige sat up and started fanning herself with her hand, "Ugh, I'm too hot. I'm going for that shower now. A cold one."

"Need help in there, baby?" Cam offered, his huge arms crossed over his chest.

"No!" she shouted, pointing a finger at each of us as she got out of bed. "And nobody follow me either. I'll never cool off if you do. Oh, Kai, before I let Maven out, what's the verdict?"

"If he's anything other than a fox, it's from some kind of magic I'm not familiar with. He smells like a fox, and usually, when we encounter other shifters, there's some kind of double consciousness that we can sense," Kai explained, and Saige nodded, opening the bathroom door.

Maven stalked out and his eyes zeroed in on Kai. *Oh hell.* His pace never slowed or faltered as he made his way across the room and lifted his leg as soon as he was in range of Kai's foot.

"You little shit!" Kai jumped, but not before a few drops of fox piss had landed on his leg.

Maven chirped and then flew out of the room at an impressive speed.

Sloane was full bellied laughing at this point and I had to admit, if Maven really was just a fox... he had the balls of a fucking lion. Saige disappeared into the bathroom so we took it upon ourselves to clean up the plates and empty drinks, and Cam went downstairs to grab some fresh sheets and bedding.

When our girl emerged from the shower, it was clear exhaustion had taken hold now that the adrenaline had worn off and she'd eaten, the inevitable crash was coming. We all laid out on the bed with her, and while she explained more about her time in Besmet, we asked our questions, which generated more questions. But in the end, our girl fell asleep with her head nestled against my chest, at the center of our team, like she'd always belonged there. I was beginning to believe in fate, for the first time in my life.

Saige

Chapter Five

I'd woken up surrounded by men. Boxed in the middle of my bed in the most delicious way. *How is this my life?* Not wanting to disturb anyone, I eased myself into a sitting position, I simply couldn't lie down another second. Honestly, I felt... normal. No lingering tiredness, no unsettled feeling of doom, this felt like any other morning. Well, plus the added bonus of four sex gods in my bed.

Cam's grip on my thigh tightened briefly as I shifted to put my back against the headboard, his golden hair fanned out across the pillow, his light eyelashes lying peacefully against his skin. My beautiful protector, he'd been such a safe haven for me the past week, someone I could count on, someone who I knew without a doubt wanted what was best for me. Cam was just genuinely a good, decent man. And stars knew those are hard to come by, but he didn't just crave control. *He needed it.*

Fischer was sprawled out as much as the tight squeeze could allow, one arm thrown over his head, the other resting across his stomach. My eyes took in the dragon wings tattoo chest piece that adorned his body, the rainbow of colors popping in even more as they contrasted with his beautiful skin. He looked so peaceful in his sleep and I smiled softly, happy that he could at least escape to his dreams for a break that he wasn't able to find during the day. I wanted to take his pain away and make him smile, he was so gorgeous when he smiled.

Sloane was laying in a ball with his cheek resting on Fischer's thigh. Even in his sleep, his broodiness was evident. *Does the man never relax?* Then I remembered the one time I did see him truly at ease, and that was with his dick crammed down Fischer's throat. Fuck. The memory of that was enough to get my blood heated. Sloane had opened up to me a little bit, giving me hope that perhaps there might be something between us that could grow, given some time and some mutual respect.

Movement at my feet drew my attention, my eyes landing on Kai's, a saucy smirk on his face.

"Hi," I whispered.

"Let's go get some food and coffee... don't wake them yet, they need the sleep," he whispered back and I nodded eagerly, my stomach giving a growl at the prospect of breakfast. Kai slipped out of his spot and held his arms out to help me stand in the middle of the bed, encouraging me to hop over Cam with the assistance of his tight grip on my hips.

Curvy women around the world, get yourselves some men who can toss you around like a ragdoll. Hottest shit ever.

I brushed my teeth quickly, ran a brush through my hair, and snagged my robe to pull on over my nightgown. Kai took his turn after I finished, and then we crept out of my room silently, my hand tight in his hold.

Moving to the kitchen, I saw that the damage caused from my magical explosion the other day had been taken care of, I'm assuming by Gran. The vine that had broken the window was nowhere in sight and the window replaced. Sighing, I reached for the coffee and I was suddenly spun around, Kai's dark eyes boring into mine and I swallowed roughly.

"Gods damn, Sprout. I've never been more scared in my life." His hand pushed my hair back from my face, like he needed to see every inch of me, and I knew that if he could pull my soul open and get a look at that too, he would, just so that he could lay claim to every single part of me.

"Kai." His name nothing more than a breathy whisper in the

silence of the kitchen.

In a flash of movement, my ass hit the countertop, my legs coming alive with a mind of their own as they wrapped around my shifter, pulling him as close as possible, his hard cock pressing against my core.

"You. Are. A. Goddess." Each word was delivered with a purposeful thrust of his hips, my own hips moving to meet his. "Look at how needy you are for me, Cub." He ground against me once more, a moan escaping my lips.

"I want you, Kai."

A deep growl echoed against the kitchen walls and Kai tugged my head to the side, exposing the length of my neck to his mouth. His hot tongue ran a line of fire from my shoulder up to my ear just before I felt a nip of teeth against my earlobe.

"Tell me what you want, Cub." His voice rumbled in my ear and my belly clenched low. "I need to hear you say it."

"Please, I feel empty. I need you to fill me up and make sure I never, ever forget where I belong."

"Fuck." He grunted, lifting me, and walking us over to the table. "I'm hungry, Cub. Slip those panties off and lay back." His tall, lean frame towered over me, and when he bit down on his fist as he watched me wiggle out of the lace that was separating us, I felt my heart speed up it's already furious tempo.

"I'm going to sit right here," Kai said as he lowered into the chair at my feet, his hands pushing my knees apart, his gaze laser focused on my cunt, "and feast on my girl, but don't worry, Cub, I'll fill you up just as soon as I've had my fill of this pretty pussy."

Holy shit.

Kai's mouth landed on my center, his tongue moving like it was making love to my clit. Long, determined licks and the tightness of his hands on my thighs had my hips thrusting upward, seeking every bit of his mouth that I could possibly get. When he slipped his fingers inside of me, I called out his name like a prayer.

"That's right, little Cub. You're mine. Mine." His fingers twisted upwards, hitting that sweet spot that promised detonation, but just as I felt that crescendo, he pulled back and I whimpered at the loss.

"When you come, it'll be around my cock," he rasped, pushing his shorts down and resuming his seat on the chair. "Come sit on this dick, Cub." He stroked himself, fisting the wide base in his hand, and I moved with the purpose of a woman with an addiction. Straddling his legs, his hands squeezed my ass as he guided me to slide down all the way, our bodies joined as closely as possible.

"Oh, Kai, please..." I begged, not knowing how to complete the request, but he knew what I needed.

His mouth found mine and our tongues dueled for domination. Kai's big hands encouraged my hips to grind, "That's it, take me deep. Tell me, Cub, tell me you're mine."

Looking into his eyes, the yellow flashing against the black, "I'm yours, Kai, fuck. Gods, I love how you feel inside of me."

My head was pulled back, Kai having wrapped my hair around his hand, my back arched when his mouth found my nipple. By the stars...

A flicker of movement had my focus transferring to the entryway of the kitchen. Sloane was frozen in his tracks, the bulge in his gray sweatpants evident. Our stares locked onto each other just as Kai started pumping into me from below.

"Ah, ahh, Kai. Oh, fuck." My fingernails sank into the curve of his shoulders, and his hand snaked between my legs, seeking out my throbbing clit. Noticing my attention had shifted, Kai turned his head, a smug ass look on his face.

"Get over here, man. Look at this beauty wiggling around on my cock. Have you ever seen anything so hot?"

Sloane quickly crossed over to us, his fingertips moving slowly over the half moon indentations that my nails had left on Kai's skin. Sloane leaned in, his tongue running over one of the

THE MAGIC OF BETRAYAL

marks. Oh holy rings of Saturn, they're going to kill me. Kai groaned, and his cock somehow got even harder.

"The sounds you make, kitten..." Sloane rasped, running a hand through his dark hair, his icy blue eyes staring a hole through me. Kai never stopped bouncing me up and down, encouraging my hips to slam against his, his big hands sinking into my ass cheeks. Sloane caught my chin in his hand, his thumb running over my bottom lip, my breath rushing over it with every movement Kai controlled.

"Open, kitten."

My mouth opened on its own when Kai's palm cracked across my ass, and Sloane seized the opportunity to slip his thumb into my mouth.

"Suck."

"Oh fuck, Sloane," Kai grunted, and I followed Sloane's order. My tongue caressed and licked his finger, just like I'd do to his dick.

Kai was gritting his teeth, but I was chasing the release now, my movements speeding up with each passing second. I needed this.

Sloane leaned down and let out at a slew of the filthiest dirty talk I'd ever heard in my life.

"Fuck her, brother. How's her cunt feel? Warm and wet like you want to just move in there and never leave?" Kai and I both groaned. "I can't wait to feel this mouth wrapped around my cock. She heats up like a furnace, don't you, kitten?"

He removed his thumb from my mouth and reached down, tugging on one of my nipples, giving it a pinch that pulled a squeak from my throat.

"I'm gonna..."

"Yes, you are, kitten. Squeeze him, take his cum. All of it."

"Fuck. Fuck. Fuck," Kai chanted when I began to convulse around him.

"Come with me, Kaito," I begged, his eyes fluttered closed at my wish and when they reopened they were yellow.

"Not like this," he growled, standing up, pushing me back onto the table, never having pulled out, he leaned over me, and started... rutting? Is that the right word? The speed with which he was fucking me was animalistic. My screams were bouncing around the walls of the kitchen, and I couldn't even be bothered to care.

"By the moon..." Sloane's voice sounded far away, a mixture of awe, lust, and was that panic?

Kai's back was going to be bloodied when this was over, shit, I might be, too.

His growls continued, and all I could do was hang on for dear life as another orgasm built rapidly. Turning my head to the side, Sloane was inching closer, and I held my hand out to him, but just as he went to take it, Kai snarled and bit him. *Fucking bit him.*

And I felt a smile tug at my lips as I got even wetter for Kai, widening my thighs to let him hit deeper, despite the pain. That familiar pull I'd had the first time he walked into my shop was in full force as his hips slapped against mine, his chest flush against me, I felt like I wanted to get inside his damn body.

What the fuck is happening?

"It's okay, kitten," Sloane told me firmly.

Kai grabbed my face then and made sure I was focused on him and only him while growling, "Don't look at him, Cub. Stay with me."

Stay with him? I never want to be detached from him again.

"Kai, I'm going to come, oh my gods."

A moan came out of my mouth at the same time that my orgasm crashed over my body, and that quickly turned into a scream as a sharp pain exploded where my neck met my shoulder, and then the purest ecstasy I'd ever known claimed my body.

"WHAT THE FUCK IS GOING ON?" Cam's voice boomed, Kai's hips slowing, my own legs falling open, completely useless. His tongue lapped at the mark he'd no doubt branded me with, sending a shiver down my spine.

THE MAGIC OF BETRAYAL

I faintly registered talking coming from the other three guys, but I couldn't make sense of a single thing. All I knew was that Kai's grumbles and growls had given way to purrs and the sweetest words.

"You're everything, Sprout. I'd never, ever harm you. You are so beautiful, you're mine," Kai murmured against my throat.

"What just happened, Kai?" I questioned softly, wanting this moment between us.

"You threw me into a rut. I'm sorry, Sprout. I've never had it happen before and I didn't anticipate that. Did I hurt you? Fuck," Kai cursed, leaning up over me, fear on his face.

"You probably broke her damn vagina, you shithead," Sloane announced. "I know you almost took a chunk out of my arm."

"You should know better than to approach a shifter in rut. I know you know that, Sloane." Fischer chastised him, but looking at his arm nonetheless.

"She wanted me, too," he grumbled quietly. He was right. I had wanted him, right up until the point of Kai sinking his teeth into his arm and then all I could think about was how Kai would protect me against anything, even his best friends and that was something a man had never given me before. That devotion, putting me first. My hand trailed over the bite on my neck and my clit thumped thinking about how thoroughly owned I'd just been. *I fucking loved it.*

"Right. Kaito, a word," Cam ordered, an edge to his voice that had me cringing.

"It's alright, Sprout. I'll be back." His lips pressed gently to mine and I sighed as he pulled back, the warmth of his body leaving me. Kai stalked after Cam butt ass naked, no shame whatsoever. Boy had nothing to be ashamed of and he knew it.

"Are you okay, sweetheart?" Fischer asked, offering me his palm and helping me sit up on the table.

"Arms up, Red," Sloane said, holding my nightgown up so that he could slip it over my head. Once I was covered back up, the ache between my legs became more prominent as I scooted down to the chair.

"I'll be one hundred percent once I get some coffee," I hinted, a cheesy smile on my face.

"I got you, sweetheart," Fischer told me, moving towards the kitchen with purpose.

"What's rut?" I asked Sloane without removing my eyes from Fischer as he prepared the coffee.

"Ah... I think maybe Kaito should explain, he'll be able to do it better than I could since pyros don't experience that," Sloane informed me and I tried hard not to push, but that was... it had been like he was trying to burrow his dick into my womb, and surprisingly that thought made me feel smug as hell, like I had some ownership over this shifter, that my body could do things to his that no other person had done before. A whisper sounded in my head, a single word, *mine*.

My body suddenly felt warm and needy. Not a sexual way, but I *needed* to see my shifter. Rising from my chair, I moved to leave the kitchen, vaguely hearing Fischer asking if everything was alright. Voices were carrying down the stairs and I drifted up them like Sleeping Beauty being called to the damn needle.

"How long have you known? You could've hurt her, Kaito!" Cam's voice boomed as my fingertips trailed along the handrail.

"I'd never hurt her!" Kai snarled.

Pushing open my bedroom door, I found the two mages chest to chest, big dick energy making me suck in a breath.

"Alpha," I breathed, my limbs beginning to tremble. *Where the hell had that come from?*

Both men turned their heads toward me at the same time.

"Oh fuck, Cub." Kai left Cam standing where he was and pulled me against him. My heart fluttered at the name.

"I need, I need—" I whimpered, not knowing what I needed, just that I needed something from *him*.

"Hush, Cub. I know what you need. You need your Alpha to

praise you, Cub. Need to feel me close, isn't that right?" Kai's hand ran down my hair, petting me in soothing strokes before scooping me up with his arm locked under my knees and walking us over to the bed. He laid me down gently and slipped in right beside me, his arms engulfing me, my cheek pressed against his chest.

Cam disappeared into the bathroom before returning and handing a rag to Kai. I couldn't really focus on what he was doing though, the shaking was overtaking my body. The door clicked shut and I guess Cam decided to take off and give us some privacy.

"What is this, Kai? What's happening?"

"You did so good earlier, Cub. You took your Alpha like a queen," he told me, his hand running up and down my back, the trembling beginning to subside with each word of praise he showered me with. He pushed my hair over my shoulder, eyes flashing when he saw the bite mark on my neck. "Look at you with my mark. Fuck," he purred, leaning in and running his tongue over the wound, and I shivered as he kept licking me.

"Gonna clean you up so good, little Cub," he swore, his lips and tongue making my belly clench with need. "A more captivating woman has never existed, the way I feel when I'm buried deep inside you, it's like I've always belonged there, Cub. It's like your body was made just for my cock, I've never felt anything as exquisite as your wet pussy clenching me, urging me to mark you with my cum and my teeth."

A little moan left my mouth and my thighs clenched, his cum slowly leaking from me and making a hell of a mess on my thighs, but I reached down and slid my fingers through it, pushing it back inside of me. "Fucking hell, that is the number one hottest thing I've ever seen," he breathed in awe. His words had elation pumping through my body, I felt cherished, special, and needed.

Kai began purring contentedly, his hands caressing, his

tongue never ceasing, and the panic and urgency I'd felt when he'd left me in the kitchen dissipated completely.

"Alpha," I whispered, pulling back to look into his eyes. "Are you mine?"

"Oh, little Cub, I was born to be yours," he declared fiercely, his hand pulling my face to his so that he could kiss me and seal his promise.

"Saige, listen… we need to talk," Kai's voice was soft and comforting, but those were not words a girl wanted to hear from her man, so of course, I startled upright and he followed.

"What's wrong?" I questioned, trying to keep the anxious tone to a minimum. I mean, he'd just told me he was mine, so what could he possibly want to talk about?

"Nothing's wrong, come here." He pulled me onto his lap so that my legs wrapped around his hips, our chests flush against one another. Kai gently lifted my chin so he could stare into my eyes before leaning in and dropping sweet kisses on my mouth and moving to my jaw. "I should've talked to you sooner, but I had to be sure." He purred in my ear and a shiver raced down my spine.

"Sure, about what?" I smiled softly, trailing my hands down his chest.

He leaned forward, pressing his forehead against mine, inhaling deeply. "You're my mate, Saige Wildes."

My eyes flicked up to his, *his mate?*

"But how can that be, Kai? I'm not a shifter." I shook my head, trying to process this information, but from everything I knew of shifters, their mates pretty much always shared that affinity.

"It can happen. Fated mates on their own are a rarity, but there have been instances of shifter's being mated to different magically gifted individuals." His hands never stopped moving their circular motions over my back.

"Well yes, but, how do you know? Like, you have no doubt that we're mates?" I asked, and I needed to hear his reasoning on this, because I know what I had felt in the aftermath of whatever had just happened downstairs, but I wasn't exactly up to date on shifter mating habits.

"Hmm, well, from the moment I met you, I've felt this protectiveness over you, a need to provide. I even made the food for you and Fischer's date. Yeah, I like to cook, but I felt almost... compelled to do that. To take care of you, even while you were on a date with another man." Leaning forward, Kai pressed his lips to mine softly before continuing. "So when I knew you were in trouble, and Cam and I hunted you down in that magically doused forest you created, I started to wonder if maybe this was something more. But what are the odds of such a thing? So I pushed it down, we had more urgent things to deal with. While we were having sex with Cam, something in my brain flipped," he confessed, sighing.

It wasn't hard for me to remember that event and when the supposed switch flipped.

"Was it when you were sniffing my soul out of my vagina?"

Kai sputtered, his eyes wide before tossing his head back and laughing like hell. *These dudes better quit fucking laughing at me all the time.*

"You're so perfect for me, Sprout. I swear." He wiped his eyes with his hands, a big smile lighting up his beautiful face. "But yeah, probably happened around that time. What can I say? I loved the scent of you, knowing how turned on you were? Fuck."

My cheeks flamed, there's just something deliciously dirty about having a sexy man's face between your legs and sniffing like he's gonna do lines of coke off your pussy. *Very fucking weird experience, but also, need that to happen again...*

"What does being mates entail? I mean, obviously I feel a strong connection between us, and that feeling I had after we had sex downstairs, that was new."

Kai sighed, bringing his hand up to my cheek. "So, it means we're bonded. I want you, always, forever. Bagheera and I are in complete agreement about you, and so our intimacy downstairs most likely snapped the bond in place."

I furrowed my brow at that.

"You should have told me before we did that, I feel kind of like I didn't get a choice in the matter, Kai," I muttered, feeling kind of pissed off about it.

"Sprout, the bond never would have happened if you didn't want it. It's not the act of sex that caused it to happen. The other night we were together and nothing happened, and that's because it wasn't on the radar, but earlier? Some part of you had to have wanted this with me, you can't force a mate bond on someone who isn't willing," Kai explained, looking pained. "I'd never force you to do something you didn't want. If you need time, or..."

I wrapped my arms around his neck and buried my face into the crook of his neck. "No, that's not it. This has just been a really fucking weird week."

Kai began purring as I ran my fingertips through his thick hair. *I have a mate. A forever mate... didn't see that one coming.*

Of course Kai wouldn't force me into something, none of the guys would. Oh fuck. They know what happened. Ohhh, Daddy was not a happy Daddy. Shit. What does this mean for the rest of them?

"I can practically hear you thinking, Sprout. Talk to me," he urged.

"The others... I can't, I mean—"

"Our relationship with each other is just that, ours. I love that you're with all of us, and earlier, with Sloane... I'm sorry. I'm not a jealous fuck, at least, not with the other guys. I'm going to have to guess that it was due to being in rut for the first time, my instincts were screaming at me that you were mine and I had to have you to myself. Sloane knew what was happening, he should have known better."

My whole body relaxed, thank the stars.

. . .

"What does Bagheera think about sharing?" I questioned.

Kai smiled. "We both just want you to be happy, and we know that what makes you happiest is all of us. Coincidentally, everyone being together makes us very happy."

I thought that over for a moment. The love these guys had for each other was unconditional. Their bond was so strong and I found myself wishing that I'd grown up with a tight knit group like theirs. But maybe I'd get the next best thing and get to keep them as mine.

"I still don't want to share you, though. Not with another woman, ever," I confessed, and pulled back when a growl began building deep in his chest, the rumbling causing my nipples to pebble.

"There will never be another woman for me. Look in my eyes, I'm deadly serious right now, Saige." Kai gripped my chin, not roughly, but firm enough to get my full attention on his face. "I am yours. Yeah, we haven't known each other long, but fate wrote it in the stars that we're destined. You never have to worry about other women, they no longer exist."

He was being one hundred percent truthful, the conviction in his eyes was enough to make me squirm under the intensity of it all.

"It's so bizarre. I feel like I barely know you, and yet, I feel like you're this extension of myself that I never realized I was missing until right now."

"I know. But don't worry about that, Cub. I'm going to wine you, dine you, and sixty-nine you until you know everything there is to know about me, and when you do fall in love with me, you won't have a single doubt in your pretty head that I'm the fucking mage for you."

Laughter escaped my mouth, just moments before Kai's lips crashed against mine in a searing kiss. Gods, this man kissed like he had something to prove, and he spent the next couple of hours doing just that.

Sloane

Chapter Six

Speeding towards the apartment on my vintage Indian, the bite on my arm throbbed, reminding me that I was suddenly dealing with a big, big fucking problem. *Fuck!*

Mates. They're fucking mates.

Of course they are. Nothing about this gods damn mission had been straightforward, so why start now? The sight of her soft body wrapped around Kai, the snapping of her hips as she rode him, my cock had been so hard in that moment, I probably could've stabbed someone with it. My bike roared as I gave it more gas, a perfect representation of how I was feeling on the inside.

I'd bolted after the first hour of listening to them fucking upstairs. Cam had joined us in the kitchen, looking stoic as ever. The air had been heavy with the discussions that we'd need to have sooner rather than later, but nobody was brave enough to start throwing them out there. As far as I knew, Kai had never experienced a rut, and I knew I'd never fuckin' seen it before. The way he'd fucked her into that table, it shouldn't have been possible for any man, supe or human, and I couldn't look away even if I had wanted to.

There would be no separating Kai and Red now. I could only hope that this shit with her mom wasn't going to be as bad as I was anticipating. Red was a good person, but damn, she was fucking up my world. For my entire life, the three of them were all the family I'd really needed. My father was a disgusting piece of existence, and thanks to him, I'd been an only child. My twin sister had been stillborn thanks to an 'accident' that ended with my mom 'falling down the stairs'.

Yeah, by the time I was seven years old, I knew that story had been a crock of shit. For years, I'd begged Mom to leave him, we could've gone to literally any of the guys' houses and they would've taken us both in, but she wouldn't do it. It's not like what happened in our home was a fucking secret. A broken arm here, a bloody lip there, Mom wearing her big sunglasses in the dead of winter, the sky as grey as my outlook on life. By the time I'd turned sixteen, all I'd had was resentment for her and hatred for the piece of shit who'd fathered me.

So, I worked my ass off, and made my own fucking luck. The thought of not being in control of my life, my career, my finances... *fuck, did that burn me up*. The fire inside of me was swirling, seeking an outlet, and I was only slightly concerned that the tiniest bit of oxygen to the flame right now would cause a fucking inferno that I didn't want to deal with.

My mind raced with all the possible outcomes of this situation... *what would happen to the team? Would Kai stay here? Would they all? Would* Fischer?

Snarling, I ripped the helmet from my head and hung it off the handlebar. Movement drew my eye and I caught the back of a man darting around the corner of Vlad's bookstore. Intrigued, I quickly hopped off my bike and leaned around the building just in time to see him disappear around the back corner of the store. There was just something about his movements, this dude was sneaking.

A flame ignited in my palm, just in case, and I peered around the corner. A blonde guy was at the backdoor of the shop, his hands pressed against the frame. This must be the abusive ex... *perfect*.

"I can't tell if you have a death wish or if you're just plain stupid," I called out, my hands behind my back, fire whirling, ready and waiting for action.

Douche-mage, as Kai lovingly calls him, turned around, a ball of water swirling like a cyclone in his hand. A dark smile slashed across my face.

"Ah, you must be the bad boy asshole," Bryce observed, sizing me up.

A deep chuckle left my throat. "Nah, douche, that's you."

Bryce tossed his head back and laughed, but not before I saw the flash of fear on his face and a sort of manic look to his gaze. "I should've known that whore would be fucking all of you. Not surprising that you'd all want a piece of that ass."

Leaning my head to the side, my neck cracked, the urge to fight quickly rising.

"Hmm," I hummed, walking towards him. His back was pressed against the door, the water ball in his hand pulsing with power. "You think you're a top dog, Bryce? You aren't shit. Nothing but a throwaway, I can guarantee you that you don't cross Red's mind, *ever*. Seems that's not the case on your end though, is it? You just don't understand that you need to fuck off."

What was this guy doing here again? Kai had mentioned he'd seen him slinking around in the dead of night last week. If he was hoping to catch Red off guard, he'd be in for a fucking surprise.

"See, I think that's where you're wrong. Saige needs a firm hand, she craves it. Aren't you concerned at all that she's going to destroy your little crew?" Darkness flashed in his eyes, but I kept my own face impassive, I wasn't giving this guy a scrap ammunition to use against any of us. He was up to something, and I was going to find out what.

"Actually, quite the opposite," I lied, because I was concerned, but fuck if I was going to let him know that. "She's really talented at bringing us all together," I hinted, the innuendo clear.

Bryce's face deepened to a dark red that had him strangely resembling a tomato with hair. A slight shift in his shoulder was all the warning I got before he launched the ball of water in my direction, having turned it to ice before it left his hands.

Bringing my hands around, I held them before me and willed a wall of flame into existence, the ice melting before it even had the chance to reach me. My feet carried me forward, right through the fire, and just in time for another round of ice daggers shooting straight for me. A wave of my hand had a wall of heat taking care of those as well.

"You wanna fight me, douche? Get over here and let's do this shit. My fists are itching to fuck up your face," I taunted, and then Bryce was sprinting at me, two ice knives gripped in either hand.

My heartbeat increased in anticipation. Just as he reached me, I dropped into a crouch and spun low on the ball of my left foot, sweeping my leg out, throwing him off balance and causing him to crash into the pavement. A wave of water propelled him upright and we circled one another. He must have a decent amount of power to be capable of the things I'd just seen, but he wasn't as strong as I was. *No fucking way.*

"Why are you here, Brian?" His eyes flashed when I called him by the wrong name on purpose. "Didn't you get the memo enough times? You're not wanted. You're nothing but a piece of shit woman beater."

He snarled. "Like I said, she loves it. She'll be back, begging for my cock, and the other things I love doing to her. She bruises so prettily."

All I saw was red. Launching myself at him, I hadn't given him time to react and his eyes widened just before I tackled him to the ground. My fist swung through the air, connecting with his cheek, his head snapping to the side. He rallied quickly, though, blasting me with a shot of water that pushed me backwards. His foot came up and he kicked me squarely in the chest, sending my back flat against the warm asphalt.

Rocking back on my shoulders, I jumped up fluidly, not seeing the ice shards he'd fired my way. The kiss of pain tore through my upper arm, leaving a few rips in the black t-shirt I'd been wearing. A small trickle of blood ran down my forearm and I smiled maniacally.

"You should probably run, motherfucker," I said, calm and deadly.

"Bring it, fire bitch."

Well, that's a new one.

Dropping the barriers on my magic, the fire rushed to freedom, erupting from my body like a volcano. I was a walking flame, fire circled every inch of my body, nothing more than an extension of who I was on the inside. I'd worked my ass off to be able to master this skill, and it was fucking rare that a mage could completely push his power from the inside out. I was going to grab this son of a bitch and turn him into char.

Bryce's eyebrows lifted to his hairline, finally realizing he stood no chance in this fight. The fire that surrounded me began to turn black, white, blue, and purple. Temperatures climbing, the air just giving more fuel, I was reaching cremation level. Vaguely registering the sound of a bike, I advanced on Bryce, one goal in mind. *Burn. Burn. Burn.*

"Sloane!"

Blinking, my hands were suddenly stretched out in front of my chest, the magic building, ready to launch out and protect me.

"Gods dammit! SLOANE!"

Fischer?

My concentration wavered for just a second and Bryce turned his back and ran away like the fucking rat he was. Glancing behind me, Fischer was standing about fifteen feet back, a panicked look on his face.

"Take a breath, man. He's gone. You know you can't burn people alive in broad daylight, and we're supposed to be blending in. Kill it." His deep, soothing voice had my hackles lowering, the flames shrinking in on themselves.

"He needs to die," I gritted between clenched teeth. Adrenaline still coursing through my bloodstream, the urge to chase him was simmering in my blood.

"Yes. He does. But not like this. Not today. Not where our cover could be blown," Fischer reminded me, and I inhaled a deep breath, letting the flames burn out completely.

"Fuck!" I stalked over to Fish. "He wants to hurt her. I can't allow that. I can't allow him to be in a position to ever hurt any woman again."

Fish nodded, grabbing my wrist and tugging me toward the building. "We should have this discussion in private. You never know who is watching."

Frustrated with myself for losing my head like that in public, I agreed with him with a short nod of my head, letting my feet carry me up to the apartment. Thank fuck my clothes didn't burn up. I'd learned long ago that I could control the flames, nothing got incinerated without me intending it to, but the moment was so close from getting out of control, it wouldn't have surprised me if they had burned off. Tugging my shirt off, I tossed it onto the island, pulling a bottle of water from the fridge and chugging over half of it before leaning forward, my forehead pressed against the cool metal of the appliance.

A barstool slid across the laminate, scuffing softly as Fischer thought aloud. "We need to do some more digging into the backstory with the ex. Is he a local? From everything I've seen of the people that live here, his behavior doesn't mesh with the feel of the community."

He was right. It didn't fit. How was it that Red was with this asshole for so long and nobody knew or stepped in? But then, I lived that life, I knew all too well how easy it was for people to look the other way versus sticking their nose where they felt it didn't really belong. How did she get mixed up with a guy like that? She's stronger than I'd given her credit for because somehow she'd gotten away from him. Something my mother was never capable of doing. *Fuck, this is the kind of shit I don't need to be thinking about.*

"We need to figure out what he's up to." I pushed away from the fridge and sat down beside him, finishing the rest of my water. "This is the second time now that one of us has caught him snooping around here and he's very out in the open with how aggressive and abusive he is. Whatever he's up to, it isn't good. He's pretty powerful, too," I gritted out, because it pained me to make it seem like I was giving this idiot a compliment in any way.

"I'll find out where he lives, works, all of that. Once I know his routine, I can see who he talks with, see where he goes, and read his emotions," Fischer offered and I nodded, agreeing with his line of thinking.

"You could always just—"

"No."

"Fischer. He's filth. Scum of the earth. We'd know right away then. I'll be with you."

"I said no." His tone was firm with an edge to it, one that I knew meant he wasn't willing to budge an inch.

"Fine. We'll do it your way." I backed off, if he wasn't willing to use his affinity to its fullest extent, then that was on him. Fish was able to insert himself into another person's memories and thoughts. As far as we knew, he was the only mage capable of such a thing, and he used that power as little as possible. The last time he'd done so, we'd been on a mission that ended badly, a lot of people were killed, which wasn't his fault— but he'd gone off the deep end. Scary shit.

Glancing at him from the corner of my eye, I could see his fingers tapping rapidly on the countertop, a glazed look to his eyes, a tic in his jaw. He was reliving it.

"Tell me where they are, Chan. We've been at this for days now, we don't need to turn it into weeks," Fischer's rough voice skated across my skin as Cam, Kai, and I looked in on the interrogation through a hole in the wall of the dilapidated warehouse. Chan was cuffed to a chair, his

sweat drenched hair hung in his swollen eyes, a waterfall of blood running from his nose and ears, then there was the little matter that he'd nearly bitten his own tongue in half trying to fight Fischer from getting inside his head.

"Fuck. You," Chan grunted. I was surprised the man could still speak.

Chan's organization had been kidnapping witches and mages, studying their powers, experimenting on them. Fucking bastard. One of Radical's spies had gone missing while undercover and we suspected she'd either been made, or was seen as being too tempting of a lab rat to ignore.

Fischer laughed a deep, dark laugh. A laugh that had the hair on my arms raising and Kai's eyebrows lifting. The darkness was coming and if Chan thought things had been bad before, he was about to get a fucking wake up call. We're the only ones who have ever seen that monster and lived to remember it.

"Just remember, this was your choice, Chan."

Fish sat down in front of our captive in a metal chair.

"Look at me," he ordered. Chan didn't move.

"Look at me!" Fischer's voice was no longer his own, the monster that lived inside of him that he kept on a tight leash was in the room now.

Chan's head snapped upright, his eyes nothing but an endless pit of the darkest black. If I'd been able to see Fischer's, his would've been matching.

Not the appropriate time to have your cock wake up, but he was so deliciously devilish when he gave in to the beast.

Chan released a high pitched squeal, his face wincing in pain as Fischer pushed his way into his mind. The shit fucking hurt, I knew first hand because we'd all practiced our powers on each other at one time or another, and it helped to have first hand training so we were all familiar with all the different possibilities. If you'd just allow him in, drop your barriers, it was more of an uncomfortable pressure, a presence that didn't belong.

If you resisted, well, it would feel as though your skull was splitting down the middle. Chan was probably really fuckin' regretting his decision to be difficult, but it was too late now. He wasn't the first person Fischer had done this to, and he wouldn't be the last. We'd seen this show before, but each time it was equally disturbing.

"Where are they, Chan? Hmm, let's see what I can find out. What secrets are locked away in here?" Fischer practically sang the last part of his questioning.

I heard Kai mutter, "fucking hell," beside me. Fish tried holding back his darkness until it was truly needed, and when he let it out, it was almost like he became a different person. It was unsettling the way his honey oak eyes changed to pitch black, even the smile on his face changed. The hairs on my arms lifted as I watched him.

Fish hopped up and began pacing around the table. "Really, Chan? Everyone knows toilet paper goes over, not under. I'm disappointed. And for fuck's sake, you don't put ketchup on steak. I should kill you on principle alone."

Chan's screaming bounced around the cavernous warehouse, the sounds of rats scurrying along the concrete floor reached my ears. When the rats know it's time to fucking bail, you should take the hint and get the hell out yourself. But this was Fischer, my family, our monster. We'd never leave him. Watching him in his element was everything.

Fischer's fist swung out and connected with Chan's nose, blood spurted from his face as though a tap had been turned on.

"You're a sick fuck, Chan. You've not only been taking adult supes, but kids?" *Fischer growled. Pulling out a sharp knife from his pocket, he flicked it open and in a flash, had it buried to the hilt in Chan's thigh.*

Looking to Cam for his reaction, Kai began growling low and dangerous.

"News to me... Fish will get the information. Then he dies," *Cam snarled.*

"Had... no... choice," *Chan told Fischer, his voice full of panic.*

"Fuck that. Drop your shields, you piece of shit."

A beat of silence and then more screaming. Fuck.

Fischer turned to look where we were hidden, his face a deadly calm mask and his eyes black as night that had a shiver running down my spine. His thick curls were sticking out in all directions, he looked absolutely deranged, and I reveled in it.

"They're being held in some shit neighborhood in Cleveland." *His tone was dripping with darkness and the promise of blood.*

We moved out from behind the wall. "Get the details, see if you can find out who ordered him to do all of this, then we gotta hustle. Who knows what they'll do to them when they realize Chan's been made, and that won't be too much longer considering his phone has been buzzing non stop the past two hours," *Cam instructed, leaning back against the crumbling brick wall, the scent of his leather jacket becoming stronger as his arms crossed over his barrel chest.*

Fischer stepped up behind Chan, the man clearly sensed the predator at his back, his begging and pleading becoming pathetic. Nothing was going to save his ass now. Fish place his hands on Chan's head, his hands trembling with exertion. The desire to get out of this shithole and go rescue some people was riding me hard, seeing Fischer in all of his glory had my own demon wanting to party.

"They're in a basement, there's cages..."

Another growl erupted from Kai, and fire flared in my own palms. They're dead. All of them.

"Crying. Some of the younger ones are crying."

Cam slammed his hands down on the table, finally losing his calm demeanor.

"8734 Sycamore Lane. That's where they are." *Fischer sagged, Chan's head hung limply, blood and drool dripping from his chin.*

"Let's go, we'll call it in and get someone in the area on it. I'm going back to the hotel to pack. Leave him here for the rats," *Cam snarled, turning and heading for the exit.*

Kai followed, leaving me with Fischer. The exertion of his work evident by the shiny sheen of sweat on his pretty face.

I'd stepped up behind him, running a hand down his muscular back, a gasp leaving his lips. Spinning around, his hands gripped my shoulders and I looked into his black eyes.

"Still not back yet, pet? Do you need a session with your Master?" I murmured.

"I feel dirty, like I can't shake the feel of that fucker's mind. He needs to die."

"Allow me."

Calling on my fire, I tossed the large flame and it hit Chan on the back of his head, the rest of his body catching within seconds. Blood curdling screams that only a man being burned alive could make reverberated through my bones, cutting off sharply about three seconds later. My fire burned with the heat to rival a cremation furnace, so he was reduced to nothing in no time at all. The smell wasn't overwhelming, thanks to the high temperatures, but still, I didn't want some burned asshole so close. I let my fire build in my palm and aimed it at the skeleton before letting it loose and watched with satisfaction as it slid clear across the floor to the other side of the huge room.

Fischer leaned forward, his hands now sinking into his dark hair. "Fuck!"

Grabbing his hair myself, I pulled him up. "Listen, pet. You're a fucking beast, and my monster wants to play with yours. My darkness will pull you back to the light."

He groaned, grabbing my neck, and pulling my mouth to his. Sweet fucking stars.

Pushing him back, I reached for what was left of the rope lying on the table. "Turn around. Hands behind your back."

Fischer obeyed and I quickly secured his hands.

"This is going to be rough, pet. I hope you're ready for this," I whispered in his ear.

"Fuck this out of me, Master. Bring me back."

My dick surged to a painful thickness. I loved his begging, but it wasn't necessary. Not with how turned the fuck on I was after watching him work. Pulling the packet of lube from my back pocket, I ripped it open and sat it on the table next to his hip. Reaching down to his waist-

band, I hastily undid the button on his jeans and unzipped them, pushing them with his boxers down to his ankles. That'd just have to work for now, I needed to be inside of him. Shimmying my own jeans down, I pressed myself against his ass, groaning at the feel of our skin together. My hands found his cock, and I squeezed his balls, earning a moan that had my own tightening.

"Please..."

Pushing him down so his chest was flat against the table, his legs spread as wide as the restriction of his jeans would allow, I dropped down behind him, sucking on two of my fingers.

"You want this, pet?" My voice husky and deep.

"Yes, Master. I need you."

My fingers ran down his crack, swirling his hole. Fucking hell, he's so tight. A whimper filled the air when I pushed in, and I quickly pulled out, spreading him with both hands before leaning in and running my tongue from his sack to his ass. His body jerked at the contact, a chorus of 'oh yes' and 'more' driving me further.

"Tell me how much you love this, pet. Now." My palm cracked his ass, his tan skin reddening with the blow. I loved marking him.

"Taste me, this ass belongs to you, Master."

Fuuuuuck.

"Gods damned right it does," I snapped, leaning back in to work him up so good he'd forget all about Chan. The only fucking mage who belonged inside of him, his mind, his body, was me. My tongue licked and speared, and Fischer began moving his hips, grinding his cock against the table, searching for friction of any kind.

My fingers pushed easily inside of him and he squeezed tight at the intrusion, but he was begging for more. Chan's body was nothing more than a pile of ash at this point, and I fisted my cock with my free hand, groaning at the contact.

Standing up, I slapped Fischer's ass a few more times, his hole squeezing my fingers gloriously with each smack.

"What do you need, pet?" I questioned, reaching for the lube.

"Your cock, Master." He panted.

"Quit fucking the table, pet. I'm the one who is going to give you what you need." I squeezed the lube out onto my fingers and coated my dick with it. Bracing myself by gripping his hip tightly, I pressed the head of my cock to his asshole, pushing just enough to have him squirming, trying to fuck himself onto my dick.

Smirking, I leaned forward, breaching his tight ring of muscle that had my balls jumping, and my head tipping back on a groan.

Inch by inch, I slid inside of him, his pleas building the tension higher and higher.

"Stop teasing me, fuck me like you fucking mean it," he snapped and I cracked his ass so hard, the sting on my palm had me wincing.

"You don't tell me what to do, pet. You're not in charge here. If I want to fuck you long and take hours to do so, I fucking will. If I want to fill your ass with my boiling hot cum and let you stay in this position with it leaking from your body, then I will. If I want to make you gag on my cock afterwards, never letting you get the release you're looking for, I will. Do. Not. Test. Me."

Slamming forward, my balls touched his as I was buried to the hilt. He cried out, and I fucked him viciously, his grunts were music to my fucked up soul.

"Sloane!" he cried, chanting my name like I was some kind of deity that could save him from the brink of insanity.

Feeling the familiar shiver of impending orgasmic bliss, I slipped two fingers into his ass with my cock, stretching him even further. Fischer cried out in surprise.

"That's it, pet. Take it. I could fuck you through this fucking table. My balls are bursting and I'm going to give you all of this hot load right up your cock loving ass. Grind against me, work my cock."

Despite his hands being tied behind his back, he rocked his hips like a good boy, and wiggled around on my dick like it was his personal throne. Pulling on the rope, I freed his hands.

"Get up there." My dick slipped from his ass, and he climbed up on the table, legs spread, and a hand pumping his cock wildly. His eyes met *mine as he looked over his shoulder, and I was looking into the gaze of Fischer, not his monster. Good.*

"Make me come, please," he begged.

Grunting, I stepped up, and slammed into him once more, thrusting in and out, hitting a new angle with the leverage I was now able to get.

"Shit, shit, shit."

"Squeeze my cock, Fischer," I groaned, fire licking down my spine, I was going to burn the fuck up if I didn't come soon.

He clenched hard and I lasted another few thrusts before I was shooting ropes of cum into his ass. Fish cried out beneath me as he came, my name on his lips, and my handprints branded on his ass.

"Fucking. Fill. Me. Up." Each demand was met with a push of his hips.

"Fuuuuuck!" I shouted, breathing heavily, collapsing on his back, little movements from my hips ensuring that all of me was inside of him.

We were frozen like that for a few moments before I stood and slipped out of him, a string of cum still connecting us.

"You fuck like a monster," he chuckled.

"Because I am one. But so are you."

We cleaned up and got dressed quickly. Just as we were about to walk out, Kai came running in, a wild look in his eyes as he searched the room, when his gaze landed on the ashy remains of Chan, he cursed.

"What is it, K?" Fischer asked.

"The address was wrong. There was a note left there that said 'Fuck you, brain mage. Better luck next time.'"

Fish's eyes widened. "But, I saw it. That's not possible!"

"They knew we'd find Chan. Someone planted those memories to protect the real location. It's likely he didn't even know it in order to make sure you didn't get a hold of the truth," I mused, my fists clenching at my sides.

"That's all that was there? A note?" Fischer inquired, his fingers tapping against his thigh.

Kai looked away, and my stomach clenched. Fuck.

"Tell me, damn it!" Fischer roared.

"Ten bodies. Fresh. Our agent was amongst them. All of them gutted," Kai said softly and glanced at me, something passing in his eyes that made me swallow hard. Fischer noticed.

"What aren't you saying?" Fischer breathed, teeth clenched.

Kai looked down at his feet, running his hand over his face before he quietly told us, "A few of them were teens."

"Motherfuckers!" Fischer yelled, running over to the table and throwing it across the room, the clanging of the metal nothing more than a loud reminder of our failure. The chair was next, Chan's ashes flew through the air, sunlight coming through the window catching them as they filtered down to the ground.

"It's not your fault, Fish," Kai said, approaching slowly.

"The fuck it isn't! And now he's dead so I can't even do a more thorough search. Fuck, I must've missed something. I missed something, didn't I? DIDN'T I!?"

"Fischer!" I barked, my dominant tone in full force. His head swung in my direction, tears were welling in his eyes. Fucking hell. His knees hit the ground, and that was the mission that had sent Fish into a swirling hole of darkness and murder that still plagued him.

"I can't do it, Sloane. Leave it." He stood up and walked away, leaving me sitting here to stew over what the fuck we were going to do when it seemed every day brought forth new bullshit, the stars were intent on fucking up my life. They should know by now though, I don't go down without a fight. And I won't lose my brothers. I fucking refuse.

My phone vibrated in my pocket, and I absentmindedly slipped it out and tapped the screen to see a text from Larson requesting a call. *Fuck. The hits just keep on coming.* I replied asking for a few moments as I beelined for the bathroom, locking the door and flicking the air vent on before turning the shower on full blast. At least Kai wasn't here with his damn cat ears.

Hitting call, Larson picked up after a couple of rings, his deep voice coming through the line.

THE MAGIC OF BETRAYAL

"Sullivan. I trust things are going well? Has the girl woken up?"

"Yes, things are going well. She woke up late last night, there's some bizarre shit going on in this town, Sir," I replied, unsure really where to even begin and why I had this weird as fuck tight feeling in my chest thinking about spilling these details, the whole thing was starting to fuck with my head.

Larson hummed to himself, and I could just picture him sitting behind his huge ass mahogany desk, a glass tumbler clutched in his large hand, dark amber liquid swirling as he pondered what I had said.

"Tell me everything," he finally responded and the tightening in my chest increased.

It took me several minutes to tell him all about the shit that had happened, and I left nothing out, well, except for Kai's mate bond. That was a highly personal bit of information and not something I was willing to go behind his back on. He'd tell Larson when he was ready.

I'm an operative, one of the fucking best in the whole damn field, and it was time I remembered that. We're going to find this woman, hand her over to Larson, get awarded with personal time off and have unlimited company resources at our disposal to get some gods damned answers for Cam. I could only hope that Red was innocent in all of this. My brothers would be crushed if she weren't, especially Kai. He would be destroyed beyond belief if she wasn't. Thank fuck he was the only one mated to her.

The other two were just obsessed. And I got the appeal, she was sexy as sin, but at the end of the day, this was an assignment. A job. How would Red feel when she realized the three men she was fucking had been lying to her from the start? Fuck, she might be the one kicking their asses to the curb. Either way, I didn't see this ending well.

"Very bizarre indeed."

What was maybe even stranger was that I could swear to the moon I could hear him smiling.

"Her mother will show up eventually, and we must be prepared to act when that time comes. With the girl being unwell, it wouldn't surprise me if Laura showed up sooner rather than later. She might be a shit mother, but I think her curiosity might be stronger than her maternal instincts. I'm sending in reinforcements, can't be too careful."

Reinforcements? What the fuck? We didn't need any fucking back up.

"Sir, all due respect, we have this situation well in hand. It will look suspicious if more guys show up in this little town, we caused quite a stir just by moving in."

"Hmm, I see your point. Good call. I'll just send one then, I'll make sure he's briefed on everything and ready to jump in as soon as he arrives." He paused, "And Sullivan?"

"Yes, Sir?" I asked reluctantly. *What are people going to think when they get wind of Larson sending in a fifth man? Is this person going to be expected to "get close to Saige" like we had? We don't need anyone else seeing how deep we are into this mess.*

"I don't think I need to remind you of the importance of this mission?" he questioned, his voice hard.

"I'm a professional, Sir. You assigned us to this for a reason. We know what we're doing and I'm the best you've got."

Shit, was that too forward?

A laugh came through the line. "You're ballsy, I'll give you that. Keep up the good work. The new player will arrive tomorrow morning."

The line went dead.

Well, fuck me.

Saige

Chapter Seven

Normal. That's what my life had been up until very recently, and now, well... shit was anything but normal. I'd fallen into the pattern of daily life, basically on autopilot at all times, not even realizing that I'd been missing key parts of myself.

Kai had been sleeping over every night, and I'd never slept better than I did when he wrapped his strong arms around me and purred deeply against my neck. We'd whispered and laughed late into the nights between kisses and some of the hottest sex I'd ever had, I was one lucky witch. We'd talked about our favorite things, our dislikes, Kai had confided in me about his struggle with depression, and I told him about what it was like growing up with the type of mother I had. Kai was so attentive to me, his fingers always finding a point of contact on some area of my bare flesh and my desire for him never stopped. In fact, the more we had sex, the more I craved him.

The other guys had backed off a little, though Cam and Fischer had popped into the shop several times while I was working, often just sitting at the bar and keeping me company. But I was beginning to miss them. However, I knew this intimate one on one time was what Kai and I needed, and I'm sure Baggie was pleased with all of the attention. Last night, Kai allowed Baggie to take over for a while, letting him run through the forests and who knows what other kinds of shit that panthers liked to do. In the end, I wound up sleeping with a huge panther playing big spoon, Maven was the little spoon, and I was squeezed right between them. Bagheera was a gorgeous animal, his fur was sleek and shiny, faint spots barely showing on his coat. In certain lighting, his coloring glimmered like an oil slick, making him look like he belonged in another realm.

It had been a few days now since I'd woken up from my sleep coma... *what the hell am I supposed to call it anyway?* It was time to face reality. Today, the guys had some work to do, something about meeting up with another co-worker, and after I'd assured them five hundred times that I'd be fine, they relented and left me to my own devices for the day. Maven and I were headed to the park to meet up with Miranda for some girl talk and wine, she'd been texting me constantly asking me about the guys and I needed my friend so I could just get everything out there.

The sun was shining, the weather eagerly catching onto the fact that it was June now and summer was in full swing. The warmth on my skin reminded me of Sloane's hands, and my thoughts turned to that sexy asshole... he'd been quiet lately. I'd thought we'd turned a corner, especially after what had happened between us in the garden, but I was getting all kinds of mixed signals from the guy, and I wasn't going to chase him. Either he was interested, or he wasn't, but I was starting to get the feeling that he might be feeling intimidated by my relationships with the others. He just seemed like someone who thrived on structure and routine, and here I was knocking it all to shit. I felt for him, really, but I wasn't vindictive or nasty. My feelings toward Cam, Kai, and Fish were legitimate, and I'd told Sloane where I stood regarding him. The ball was in his court.

Heading down to Peridot Park, Miranda and Annie were already waiting for us at the pavilion, and I smiled when I saw the chalk artwork that Annie had been busy creating. There were a ton of little Maven drawings, many of them depicting ice cream cones and a stick girl who obviously was Annie.

"I love these drawings, you'll have to make me some new ones

THE MAGIC OF BETRAYAL

to hang at the shop," I told Annie as her little pink faced cheeks lifted from the ground to take us in. Squealing, she tossed the chalk and gave me a fast hug before setting her sights on Mave.

"Hey girl, long time no see." Miranda smiled at me from the picnic table she was sitting at, her chocolate brown hair fell in thick waves and was so shiny, I wanted to touch it. But I wouldn't, because I did that to someone the last time I was in this pavilion and it was awkward as hell. Not that Miranda would bat an eye over it, she was used to my quirkiness... but I was trying this whole new thing called thinking before I act. So no, do not touch the shiny.

Sighing, I sat down across from her, dropping my backpack on the bench beside me. "No kidding. It's been kind of crazy lately."

Annie and Maven were running around the park, her laughter was the sweetest sound. Not even grumpy Mave could resist her cuteness.

Miranda wiggled her eyebrows, making me laugh as she leaned forward. "Tell me everything. How does it work dating three men? Are they cool with it, like, for real? No jealousy? Do you keep them on a schedule?"

"Okay, settle down," I giggled. "No. There's no schedule, and, so far, no jealousy. Kind of crazy right? It's actually been... amazing. They're different from one another, so I feel like each relationship is defined and its own 'thing'. I get distinct things from each of them."

"And?" she prompted, smiling at me like a kid who was about to be handed a lollipop.

"And what?" I played dumb and she kicked me under the table, "Ow! Okay, fine, you violent witch. The sex is fucking mind blowing. Unbelievable."

Miranda squealed and clapped her hands in front of her chest; she really was my personal cheerleader. Every witch needed one of those. Someone in your corner that you knew you could always depend on. That kind of friendship was rare and hard to come by, so once you had it, you didn't let go for anything.

Whispering, she asked, "Do you... you know... do it with more than one of them at once?" Her cheeks bloomed into a nice pink and I had no doubt mine matched.

"Well, I have. A couple of times, and that was just next level shit."

My smile grew as I thought about those couple of times, and damn, I needed to figure out how to get that to go down again.

Miranda sighed. "Girl, you're glowing. I'm so happy for you, you deserve it."

Studying my friend, she looked better than she had when I'd given her the moonstone a few weeks back, but she still wasn't one hundred percent.

"How are you, babe? Sleeping better?" I asked, scanning her face for the truth she may not give me with words.

"Yeah, the stone seems to have done the trick. Annie's been good too, as usual. It's just a lot, working, full-time mom life, keeping up with the house..." Her finger traced the wood pattern in the table and I frowned slightly at the change in her demeanor. She was so strong, but she was clearly tired. Then, in true Miranda fashion, she rallied. "I think I need to get laid. We should go out sometime soon."

Barking out a laugh, I shook my head. "Gods, I haven't been dancing in forever, maybe for my birthday? It's coming up, ya know?"

"Hell yes, that sounds like exactly what I need. I'll let my mom know I'll need her to keep Annie at their house that night. I'll need a kid free zone to bring back my catch of the night." She winked and crossed her fingers.

"You need a man who has his shit together, who can take care of you for a while." She was prepared to snap at me over that, but I held up a placating palm. "Listen, babe, I know you can take care of yourself, and you do, but you deserve someone who adores you, protects you, who helps carry the load equally. And a big dick probably wouldn't hurt, either." I rushed the words out and we both laughed like hell. Taking a deep breath, I took her hands in mine, and looked into her chocolate brown eyes. "Whoever snags you is the luckiest guy in this realm," I told her, and that was the truth. She was a genuinely good person with a huge heart, and Annie would just be a bonus dose of goodness.

THERE WAS a young couple walking our way, hand in hand, and when I realized who it was I made sure to look closer. Sam Campbell, the depressed teen that Fischer had pointed out to me a month ago at the cookout, was strolling along with a love struck expression as he gazed down at his girlfriend.

"Who's that with Campbell?" Miranda asked, tracking them just like I was.

"Oh, that's Robin. Mayor Edgerton's daughter. Must be a new relationship because news like this would've already been spread through town like wildfire otherwise," I noted and my bestie nodded.

"They're so cute together! Look how happy they look. Ah, young love," Miranda sighed dreamily and I chuckled. But she was right.

My phone vibrated snapping me out of my staring and I laughed when Kai's 'name' popped up, one of his own choosing. I hadn't told anyone yet about the mate bond, I just wanted to keep that information close to my chest for now, at least until all of this weird shit settled down and we had more time to explore what our relationship was going to look like.

Alpha Beast: Hey, Sprout, just wanted to say I miss you, and I can't wait to bite you and then lick it all better.

By the stars, heat bloomed between my legs just thinking about it. He'd been biting me constantly during sex and it was the hottest thing ever, but then when he licked the marks afterward?

It made me want to wrap myself around him like a monkey and insist that tongue never leave my body.

Another text came in before I could even consider what to say in response to his message.

Alpha Beast: Daddy wants to know if you're being safe. I told him to back off but he got that dad look on his face where he just looked so *disappointed* in me that I let it go. So, are you?

Sighing, I ran a hand down my face.

"What's up?" Miranda questioned, looking up from her own phone screen to see what had me being dramatic.

"Well, the guys have been really attentive, and I love that. It makes me feel special, but Cam in particular, can be over the top. I've been taking care of myself for a long time, and I don't need a guy to protect me. Don't get me wrong, it's nice to have someone care like that, but I'm capable, aren't I? I just don't want them to think I'm some helpless witch who can't handle my own shit, you know?" Damn, that was a lot of word vomit, but the feelings of anger were stirring now that I had everything out there and a small part of me felt irrational.

Miranda laughed, shaking her head. "Tell me how you really feel, huh? I get it. You were with a guy who essentially stalked you and had to know every move you made during the day, so I understand that any kind of attention like that might be upsetting to you. And hell yes, you're capable; you're awesome. Some men are just like that with those they care about, there's a line between being controlling and caring, between being possessive and being protective. Just make sure you know which it is before you blow up on him. Maybe just talk about it," she suggested, and I knew she was right.

"I'll do that later when I see him," I decided aloud. Shooting a quick text back to Kai to let them know I was at the park and completely okay, I sat my phone down and fanned my face with my hands. "Good grief, it's hot all of a sudden."

"You have been running hotter lately, probably the exposure to such hot dudes all the time."

Maven's bark drew our attention to where Annie was chasing him near the big oak that grew out over the lake.

"Not too close to the water, Annie!" Miranda called out, but my gaze was firmly locked on the side of the tree, the spot that I had healed when I'd been here with the guys last. Seeing the darkness along the side of the trunk had me hoping to the stars it was just a shadow, that I'd get over there and there'd be nothing wrong with the beautiful tree.

But deep down, I knew that wasn't going to be the case. I hadn't even thought about how I'd used my magic out here that day, but it made sense that the big tree would've been affected the same way everything else was that I dared to taint with my affinity.

My legs were carrying me to the lake, Miranda's voice behind me, asking what was wrong... but I couldn't speak yet. Not until I confirmed what I was seeing.

We stopped right against the tree, my hand running down the blackness that was spreading outward almost like veins in the body.

"Shit, shit, shit!" I cursed under my breath.

"Trees get sick sometimes, Saige. It'll be okay. You can heal it, can't you?" Miranda asked, placing a hand on my shoulder. She understood that the death of living things hit me much harder than the usual witch, my powers being so connected to life.

"Yeah, yeah, of course. But I need to do some digging first to see what the problem might be before I start pushing magic into it," I replied. However, the fact of the matter was I wouldn't be touching the tree or anything else with my powers, not until this mystery got sorted out. What a mess.

We walked for a bit, Maven and Annie darting back and forth across the paved walkway. It felt great to spend time with them, yet my mind was having a hard time not thinking about all of the shit going on that my bestie didn't know about. I didn't tell her about everything because she had enough on her plate, I didn't want to add to her stress.

We'd been sitting on the bank of the lake, our toes dipping in the water, laughing about things that had happened when we were in school, catching up on what we'd each heard about old classmates, but the sun was starting to sink lower in the sky, and I still needed to swing by the grocery store on the way home.

"Well, girls, I think it's time for Mave and I to head back home," I said, stretching out my back once I was standing.

"Aww, man, can't he spend the night with me?" Annie asked, her eyes wide like a little puppy.

Glancing a look at Maven, I swear to the stars, he shook his head no.

"Not tonight, hon. We need to get home so you can eat dinner and take a bath. What do you have there?" Miranda asked, leaning down to take the paper from Annie's hand.

"It's a picture I made for Saige," Annie smiled, waiting for me to look at it.

Miranda laughed and handed it over to me without peeking.

It was a beautiful forest, so green and alive. But the forest wasn't the focal point of this painting. No, it was the large pentagram drawn into the center of the forest floor. The drawing itself was beautiful, she was incredibly talented for her age, but there was something ominous about it and I suppressed a chill that ran down my body.

After thanking her for the artwork, we went our separate ways. I had a stop to make before I could go home.

PULLING my bike up to Dinner Thyme, I rested it against the wall and ran inside quickly to grab a couple bottles of wine, and an assortment of meat and cheeses. Hell yes. Pushing my cart down the aisle, I passed by Randy Roger, who was dressed immaculately in a terry cloth romper with snakeskin cowboy boots. *By the moon, the confidence on this mage.*

"Seasons greetings, Saige, it's been a while. You look lovely, darling."

"Love the outfit, Roger. Where'd you find that?" I smiled, but for real, I really did like it and kind of wanted one for myself.

"Oh, this old thing?" He brushed his hand through the air, like I was the one being dramatic and I giggled. "Stole this right from your gran's vintage trunk. Don't tell her, she turns into a real hag when I borrow clothes without permission. But I figure it's easier to just do whatever I want and then beg for forgiveness." He winked and I shook my head at his ridiculousness.

"Your secret is safe with me, Roger, but you know she's going to find out... and there will be hell to pay when that happens."

"Pfft, I'll win her affections back with the tequila jello shots I have in my fridge at home." He snapped his fingers dramatically, "Oh, that reminds me, I need to grab some limes. When you see Captain Cuke-zuke, let him know I'm ready for a rematch, and this time, eggplants and leek are acceptable weapon options."

Before I could even process what had just come out his mouth, he sauntered down the aisle, shaking his ass like he was born to. Strange duck, that one, but I adored his live and let live mentality.

My phone dinged and I smiled when I saw a text from 'Big Daddy'. Laughter slipped out from my lips at the name change, Kai must've done it when I was sleeping. Accurate though.

Big Daddy: Everything okay, little witch?

Me: Yes, Dad. **eye roll emoji** Everything is just fine. At the grocery store, the meat hasn't attacked me, don't worry.

Big Daddy: I have some meat that wants to attack you.

Bloody hell.
Me: Omg, Cam.
Big Daddy: Be safe, baby girl.
Me: Always. Gotta go, I wanna get home. I'm hungry.

I sent it off with four kiss face emojis and shoved my phone back into my pocket. Keeping in mind the advice my bestie had given me, I took a deep breath. I knew I needed to just talk with him about the coddling, and I should probably do it soon seeing as how my moods were zero to sixty these days.

The bottle of wine I wanted was a little out of reach, so I was stretching to grab it when a hand landed on my ass. Sucking in a breath, I froze. A large body pressed up behind me, and I was trying to figure out which of the guys had snuck up on me. Sighing, I closed my eyes and leaned back as a hand swiped my hair to one side of my neck, their lips hovering over my skin.

My nose wrinkled when a familiar magical signature skated along my body. That's when the scent hit me. His cologne. His smell. A hard ridge pressed against my butt and I stiffened, his hand clamping over my mouth before I could scream, his other arm snaking around my waist and securing me tightly to his body.

"I knew you still felt it, Saige. Look at how you respond so beautifully to my touch," Bryce growled in my ear and bile rose in my throat.

Shaking my head no, I called on my magic, vines immediately burst from my palms, wrapping around his wrists to pull him away from me, just as his hand was pulled from my lips, I opened my mouth to let out the loudest call for help, but instead, all that came out was water.

My eyes widened when Bryce spun me around toward him, his face furiously red and scary. The vines fell away, my panic caused me to lose focus on anything except for the fact that I was drowning. Bryce was fucking drowning me in the middle of the grocery store. Clawing at my throat, all I could do was watch as he chuckled deeply.

"Here's the deal, pretty. You. Are. Mine. You are always going to be mine. Your boyfriends won't be in town forever. You're nothing but a warm hole for them to fuck while they're here on business. They're not built for Emerald Lakes, they're always going to want more. Can you give them that?"

My heart was racing, tears stinging my eyes as I slowly suffocated. *When had he gotten this powerful?* This was next level magic.

His hand trailed down my waist, and he tugged on my t-shirt before leaning in to whisper in my ear, the heat of his breath and the feel of his hands on my body making me gag stronger on the water.

"You know I always enjoyed your body, but most mages aren't into fat witches, so maybe back off a bit on the snacking, hmm?"

Despite the fact that I was drowning, my face flamed in humiliation. I'd been trying so hard since I left his abusive ass to work on body positivity. He had always made comments about my weight, and I was ashamed that just one comment had me sinking back into a haze of embarrassment. My vision began darkening, bright circles floating across his hateful face.

My phone was going off in my pocket, the vibrations relentless, but I was helpless here. Scraping my hands down his arms, I prepared for the worst. Was he really going to kill me here, like this? No, he wanted my submission, and that was something I swore he'd never get again. *What's one more psychological blow?*

Nodding my head, and dropping my eyes and arms, I let myself go limp in his hold.

"That's what I thought."

The water evaporated instantly, as if it'd never been there to begin with and I started hacking, sucking in gulps of air.

"She's fine, she just choked on a sip of water," I heard Bryce telling someone who must've come to check on the alarming noises coming from this aisle. Peeking up at him, he was smiling, raising a friendly hand in a wave as his other hand gripped my wrist so hard I stifled a cry of pain. His grip twisted and I felt my bracelet break in his palm, pretty perfect symbolism for how all of my confidence just snapped and fell to pieces within three minutes of being in his presence.

Sometimes the most evil monsters wear the prettiest masks.

Bryce cupped my face with his hand, swiping his thumb across my cheek, clearing away the tears. "You know I love you, I just... I need you to stop pissing me off, Saige. The last thing I'd ever want to do is hurt you, but you're hell bent on pushing me to that point. You make me crazy." Releasing my wrist, the bracelet fell to the floor, destroyed. The little crystals rolled all over the ground.

My breathing was rapid, I couldn't think coherently, all I could do was stand there with hands on me that had no business being there, and the next thing I knew, his lips were on mine. Gentle, soothing, like he really did love me. And all I did was stand there. *Pathetic. Weak.*

"Do you feel what you do to me?" He pressed his hard cock against my stomach and I whimpered, a sound he mistook for want instead of what it really was, fear. Bryce had no concerns about anyone seeing us, the store was dead, and he lived to push his luck. My phone was vibrating again and I was positive it was the guys. A strangled sob came out of my throat when Bryce cupped my crotch through my leggings, pressing against my clit with his middle finger. *No, no, not again. I can't go through this again.*

"I will have this. Soon." He stepped away from me and my knees hit the floor, "Oh, and Saige? This stays between us or I will drown every last one of those motherfuckers in their beds and leave them for you to find." And with that, he turned and left me a shaking, crying mess.

Abandoning my cart, I practically sprinted to the single person restroom and locked the door behind me. All I could hear was whooshing in my ears, like I was under water, and my hands were trembling as I gripped the sink. *Fuck. What the fuck am I going to do? He fucking touched me, kissed me, tried to drown me!*

My green eyes gazed back at me through the mirror, looking even more vibrant than usual due to the redness surrounding them. Black streaks from my makeup had me looking like a crazy person, like a weak person. Heat prickled at the base of my neck, spreading throughout my body in mere seconds. *I'm not weak.*

The vibrating in my back pocket snapped me out of the stare down I was having with myself and I saw Fischer's name flashing up on the screen. *Fuck, how am I going to talk to anyone right now and not have them pick up immediately on the fact that something is very, very wrong with me?*

Feeling guilty as hell, I let it go to voicemail, there was no way I trusted my voice right now.

Me: Hey, sorry. Forget my phone in the bathroom at the store. Checking out now, gotta run.

Fischer would tell the others and at least I had a little bit of time to compose myself. I hated liars, I mean, it was really one thing that made my blood boil and here I was lying to the guys, and trying to figure out how I was going to be able to keep what had happened with Bryce to myself. He was a lunatic, and he'd somehow powered up in the time we'd been broken up.

My mind was racing and I felt like I couldn't take a deep breath. All I could do was hope that the guys would understand my reasoning for keeping this from them. I knew they were powerful in their own right, but they were just businessmen dealing with real estate issues, Bryce obviously can drown them just as he promised. He was dangerous and unstable as a three legged stool. I couldn't give him that opportunity.

Leaving the restroom, I grabbed my cart and threw in a bunch of wine, it was definitely going to be a wine night. Needing to get home quickly, I made as little small talk as possible with Joanne while she rang up my things, and I quickly loaded my backpack up with the groceries. Maven was curled up in the basket on my bike and he slowly lifted his head when I made a clicking sound with my tongue.

I need a shower, I'd have one of the guys get my bike tomorrow. A shiver of disgust rolled through my body when I thought of Bryce touching me like that. The look in his eye so familiar, and I knew had we been somewhere private he would've taken what he'd wanted. My hands were shaking and I could feel the tears rising up now that the reality of what had happened was settling in like a dark cloud that I couldn't outrun. Shots. That's what would help.

Changing my path and heading to The Pig, I had one goal in mind. Drink all the drinks and hopefully numb myself to the feelings of violation and fear, then I'd head home and wash away the disgust and unwanted touches. Everything would be okay. It had to be. But Bryce was in my head now, and I wasn't sure that I'd be able to forget the comments he'd made. His words always had a way of cutting me so deeply and effectively destroying any self confidence I might've mustered up.

Placing my hand on the door of The Pig, the lock recognized my magic and opened, admitting myself and Mave. The hairs on the back of my neck stood up before I walked through the threshold and I turned my head to see who was watching me. A gust of wind blew my hair over my face, the breeze felt really good on my heated skin, but I didn't see a single soul. Shaking my head, I walked through the door and made my way to the bar.

Bram

Chapter Eight

Gods damn, I was one grumpy son of a demon king.

Fuckin' Khol sent me on this mission, and while in the past, I might've lived for the thrill of it, the possibility of maiming and killing... I just wasn't feeling it. Khol had pulled off the impossible, he had a daughter, a daughter who was not only a demon, but more demon than witch. That means that somewhere in her line, a demon would've done this before, maybe it had something to do with the fact that Laura had been a green witch? They were givers of life, so I suppose that made sense.

Apparently, his daughter was shacking up with the entire team he'd sent here, those guys were brutal. I'd know, I helped train their asses. Sullivan and I had a healthy competitive streak between us, but he was that way with pretty much every person who so much as raised an eyebrow at him. Khol and I were fairly certain Laura would be showing up eventually, and we'd be here to snatch her when she did. The witch had some explaining to do.

Speaking of disappearing women... Goldie. I hadn't seen her since she'd been taken from me, and I'd texted and called the number she'd programmed in my phone so many times, but there was never any answer. The thought of her being in trouble had me teetering on the edge of homicide for the past few days, my next plan was to stalk her to the fullest extent over social media, but she had absolutely zero accounts. Then, before I could come up with my next plan of attack, Khol ordered me here, telling me there'd be plenty of time for pussy chasing when this mission was complete.

She was so much more than that, but I wasn't going to admit all of that to any other demon just yet. My father's reach was wide and all encompassing, and while I trusted Khol, the less he knew for now, the better.

The guys were all headed over to their girl's house this evening and by the stars, they were obsessed with this witch. Immediately upon my arrival, I had my ass parked in a chair and been given the sternest talking to I'd ever gotten from anyone aside from Khol and daddy dearest. Thinking about it now had a smirk pulling at my mouth, they were so easy to rile up.

"Johnny, have a seat," Cam directed me to the seating area in their living room and I plopped down on a chair, knees spread wide. Hopefully, they cut to the chase fast so I can get the fuck out of here and focus on more pressing matters. Like Goldie, pressing herself against my—

"Should've known he'd send you," Sloane mused, sitting his grouchy ass down. He looked kind of tired, which was interesting since this was an easy as shit assignment. Why aren't you sleeping well, Sullivan?

"Sup, Scorch? Burn anyone up lately? I'm itching for a fight." *I pinned him with a stare and he grinned. He was just as sick of a fucker as I was; he wasn't fooling me.*

"Been too long, man. Don't talk about it, makes my fingertips burn," he bantered back, leaning forward in his seat, resting his elbows on his knees, and flicking his fists open to release a flame on each tip of his finger.

"Don't burn anything, Saige will kill us. Or Gran will," Fischer piped up, sitting down with a bottle of water.

A growl rumbled from the kitchen and I directed my attention to Kaito, who was getting snacks or some shit. The guy was always eating, or preparing shit to eat.

"Who pissed in his kitty litter?" *I asked the room as a whole and*

THE MAGIC OF BETRAYAL

Sloane chuckled, "Okay, you guys are wound tighter than a virgin's butthole, what the hell is going on?"

Cam spoke first, unsurprisingly, seeing as how he was their leader and everything.

"Saige is ours," he said simply, crossing his arms over his chest.

"Let's clear the air right now, shall we?" I held my hands out in front of me, "I have no interest in Saige. First of all, I'm here to do a job, and you guys know damn well I'm celibate. Not to mention, I have my eye on a little witch named Goldie. She's the most beautiful woman in all the realms and that's where my focus is, aside from this assignment. Second of all, we've been working together for how long now? You know I'd never do any of you dirty, I've always had your backs. Now, let's just focus on completing this mission so we can move on with our lives. I don't want to be here long, I have more... pressing matters."

Kai sauntered into the living room, moving with a grace that only a cat boy could pull off. "Well, the problem is you haven't met her yet. She's..." He sighed, dropping onto the rug, his legs crossed as he stared off into the distance.

"Okay, lover boy. I see you've got it bad this time, but for real, I'm not interested. Even if she had fourteen karat gold nipples and a diamond studded vagina, not gonna happen."

Fischer choked on his drink and Sloane slapped him on the back a few times, everyone seeming to be much more at ease now that they'd hypothetically pissed all over this poor woman in a show of alpha dominance that I could appreciate. I'd do the fucking same to anyone who ever got near Goldie, and I still had her lover to fight. Oh, I couldn't wait for that day. She'd see my physical prowess and fall in love with me so hard.

"We're actually headed over to her house in about an hour or so, if you wanna come hang out?" Fischer offered, but I shook my head.

"Thanks, man, but I think I'm going to go get the lay of the land, stretch my legs a bit." I'd jumped the main distance of the trip here, but since the guys didn't know I was a demon, I'd rented a car in Kingstown *and drove over from there, but the leg stretching suited my excuse for not wanting to go watch them drool over Khol's daughter.*

And I wanted to go out into town and explore a little, not only was that ingrained in my head from all the training I'd gone through, there was too much energy buzzing through my bones for me to be able to sit still for any length of time. Plus, the sooner this shit was over, the sooner I could find my saucy redheaded warrior woman.

From what I'd seen so far, this was an odd town. The people who lived here were strange, and that's saying something coming from someone like me. When I'd arrived at the apartment, I felt the stares from across the street, two women dressed like it was tea time with the Mad Hatter were eyeballing me so fucking hard I gave them a wink and pushed my glasses up my nose as they returned the wave, giggling and whispering to each other.

I was effectively disguised as my earth side alter ego, Johnny Carson. There weren't a ton of demons residing earth side, but it was just safer to have this glamour on the off chance a rogue demon did recognize me. Being the heir to the demon throne was reason enough for a lot of these demons who had a bitter taste in their mouths from my father's rule to try to kill me. Not that they'd succeed, but whatever. I was still sexy as shit in this form.

Heading to the right out of the apartment, I passed by the magic shop that was named The Mystical Piglet. *Interesting name choice, I like it. I'm going to have to check that place out tomorrow, maybe there's some goodies in there I can pick up for my love.*

Up next was a crystal shop that looked quaint and appeared to be more jewelry like than the crystals I'd spotted in the window of the magic shop next door. I'm going to have to check these places out tomorrow, and I had seen a bookstore that was on the opposite side of The Mystical Piglet. I did love some good books. Mainly ones that talked about war and murder, shit like that, although, I had been meaning to pick up The Lion, The Witch, and The Wardrobe ever since I'd googled Aslan when Goldie said she was trying to meet up with him in the wardrobe in the throne room. I admit, I'd felt like an idiot when I realized he wasn't her boyfriend, but a fictional lion. Regardless, I wanted to see why she was trying to meet him.

Hitting the corner, I took a right and strolled down the mostly vacant sidewalk. This town was cute. A word I rarely used, but it was the best one to describe it. Emerald Lakes had a total European feel that reminded me of a small city center in The Netherlands. Brick businesses pressed up against one another, making use of every square inch of space available. *I wonder if Goldie's ever been to Europe, I'd like to fuck her at the top of the Eiffel Tower.*

My body jolted to the side as someone bumped into me. It was my own fault, not having been paying attention with visions of my woman spread eagle for me with Paris as the backdrop.

"Whoa there, big boy," the guy who ran into me cautioned.

My eyes widened as I took in his appearance. He had a curly ass mullet that I hadn't seen the likes of since nineteen eighty five and was absolutely rocking a strapless terry cloth romper. By the light of Jupiter's cock, I seriously hoped he tucked his shit into his waistband because otherwise, someone was going to be playing one eye peek-a-boo as soon as he sat down.

"Apologies, I wasn't paying attention to where I was walking," I replied, holding out my hand to greet him.

"Ah yes, I can see the stars in your eyes. Lucky lady... or guy?" He shook his head and smiled, sliding his hand into mine with a firm grip. "I'm Roger. Welcome to Emerald Lakes."

"Nice to meet you, Roger, but how do you know I'm new here?" I questioned, my eyebrow lifting in question.

He barked a laugh like I was a dipshit. "Everyone knows everyone here, and I would have remembered seeing such a striking specimen."

Well, shit.

"Right, well, thanks for the welcome party. I'm off to explore.

See ya around, Roger." I backed away from him before shit got even weirder. I'm a crazy bastard, but something told me that guy could give me a run for my money. The crazy lived in his eyes.

The wind was picking up and I pushed my hair back off my forehead, but I caught a scent on the air that had me stiffening. All of me. My demon dick included. Gods, I must have really been having withdrawal because I could smell her. My heart ached in my chest as I thought of how badly I wanted to see her again. Following her pretend scent, I stood in front of a grocery store called Dinner Thyme. I chuckled, able to admit to myself it was a good pun.

There was a bench in front of the store and I figured I might as well take a few moments to survey the townspeople some more, there was much more to them than met the eye. Step one on a new assignment was always to stake out the location and get a feel for the people in the area. Passing by a pastel blue bicycle, I glanced down and saw a white fox snoozing in the wicker basket attached to the handlebars. *Hmm, I didn't think that type of animal was common in this realm, or at least in this particular area.*

Sitting down on the wooden bench, I was going to try to bribe the stars to give me what I desired most. It had been a while and I wasn't exactly what one would call a good boy, but I was desperate.

Oh mighty stars above, you sent me a beautiful witch to love.

Now I'm alone, *no witch to bone.*

I'm not *sure why I'm trying to rhyme, on this bench outside of Dinner Thyme.*

I've been a bad boy, *but it's not my fault I love to destroy.*

THE MAGIC OF BETRAYAL

. . .

PLEASE FATE, you sparkly bitch, give me back my Goldie witch.

AMEN.

Do you say amen after something like that? Seems appropriate. Respectful. Nodding to myself, I felt certain that the universe would hear my plea.

A clicking sound ended my thoughts and prayers session and I cracked an eyelid just as the white fox hopped out of his basket, following a woman who had hair the exact same shade and style as—

What the fuck? My eyes dropped down to her ass, and that was literally all the confirmation I needed. *Bleeding hearts and stars unite!* Standing abruptly, I almost called out to her, but then I remembered that she wouldn't recognize me in this form, and what was she doing in this town of all the stars damned places? Her scent was hitting me like a freight train but there was sadness radiating off of her from the way her shoulders were hunched and her head down.

Who hurt her? I'd crack their chest like a crab leg and peel their ribs off of their spine one by one, I swear to Saturn... My brow furrowed as she hung a left and walked back toward the way I came. *Where are you going, Goldie girl?*

Maintaining my distance, I walked along the opposite side of the street and watched as she stopped in front of The Mystical Piglet, tilting her head back to look up at the dark apartment windows above, the guys would be long gone by now. Stepping behind a large tree, I watched as she held her hand up to the door where it recognized her magical signature and opened.

Just as I thought she was going to go inside, she whipped her head around and I wondered if she'd felt my presence as keenly as I was aware of hers. *Is Goldie hiding something from me? That's not going to fly.* Thankfully, I was already in my other form and I didn't want her knowing my true identity, oh no. I needed to see what she was up to here. Sending my powers out in a wave through my body, I made sure that my demon characteristics would be well concealed, even to another demon. My scent would be nothing more than Giorgio Armani.

A BELL CHIMED when I pushed through the door of the shop, her scent hitting me like a freight train. My nostrils flared, the desire to breathe in as much of that smell as I possibly could was riding me hard. Display shelves were set up to the right and a long wooden bar ran nearly the whole length of the store, with shelves rising to the ceiling and down to rows of drawers.

Perhaps the most interesting thing was that Lizzo was blasting through surround sound speakers. Not seeing anyone, I made my way around the place, checking out what all was sold here. This was a typical magic shop, but it had more of a homely feel to it. Cozy, welcoming, like the owner had really poured their heart and soul into it.

Nearing the back, there were strands of beads hanging in the doorway that probably led to the restroom. Since I was standing off to the side, she didn't see me when she walked through them and made her way to the front of the store, clutching a bottle of tequila in her hand.

Clearing my throat at a pause in the music, she shrieked and swung the bottle in a wide arc, and I thanked the stars I hadn't been standing any closer or she'd have smashed me right in the head.

"By the moon, you scared the shit out of me!" She held her palm over her heart, her face pale as a sheet of paper. Tilting my head to the side, I took a moment to really look at her face. She was upset, her eyes were a little red, and the parts of her face that

THE MAGIC OF BETRAYAL

weren't white as a ghost looked red, from tears or from washing her face. Why was my little warrior so sad? Was I going to have blood on my hands before the night was through? *How is Goldie here before me? Fuck.*

"I'm sorry, I figured you didn't hear me over the music..." I trailed off, gesturing to the bumping bass and the lyrics filled with body positivity and women empowerment.

Holding up a finger, she turned and walked back to the bar, killing the music with the flick of a button on a receiver that was on display between stacks of books. She put the tequila on the bar top, and gave me her full attention.

"Sorry, but we're actually not open right now, I was just stopping in before heading home for the night. Needed to, uh, get a drink." She gestured to the tequila, looking slightly embarrassed.

Unable to look away from her, I held her gaze as I approached the bar and pulled a stool back before sliding onto it, resting my arms on the smooth but worn bar top. "No worries, I'm new in town and I saw the lights on so I figured I'd just pop in and see what the place was like. Do you work here then?" I questioned. I was going to find out the answers to my questions and take advantage of her not knowing who I am.

"Oh, well, welcome to Emerald Lakes, then. And yeah, you could say I work here. I own this store," she replied with a huff. She was definitely off from something that had happened, her usual sunshine demeanor was nowhere in sight. But how could she own this place? Khol's daughter owned the...

Oh. Fuck it to hell. Fucking fuck all the fucks.

"You okay, buddy? Need some water or something?" she asked hesitantly, and I swallowed down my demon that was awake and pissed. Like, big time pissed. He wanted nothing more than for me to flip her over this bar, hogtie her, and give her a lesson on what happened when you lied.

Not responding, I reached for the liquor and popped the top. Her eyes widened as I lifted the bottle and took a swig. *Shit, I'm going to need a lot more than a bottle of tequila to counter the level of fucked my mind had just gotten.*

"I'm good, you just remind me of someone," I rasped, wiping my mouth with the back of my hand.

Taking the bottle back from me, she grabbed a couple shot glasses and poured us each one.

"An ex?" she asked, tapping her fingers on the bar.

"No. We haven't really labeled what we have yet. She's mysterious, and I just found out recently that she lies, too. Not sure where that leaves us," I replied, trying hard to swallow down the snark in my tone.

"Well, fuck liars, and fuck exes. I know she's not your ex, but I'm saying fuck you to mine." She raised her glass and waited for me to do the same. We clinked glasses and threw our shots back with ease.

"Is he the reason you were crying?" I bit out and she wiped at her cheeks, as if she could disguise the fact that she'd been crying. It was obvious.

"Yeah. He's a dick. That's why I had Lizzo blaring, I needed some girl power to lift me up and remind me that I'm worth it. I've tried so hard to get over all of the psychological abuse that I went through for years with him, and I thought I'd been doing so well, but then all it takes is one encounter with him and I'm spiraling." She bit her lip, her eyes welling with tears and I couldn't handle that. Despite the fact that I was still livid with her, it was taking literally every ounce of willpower not to walk out of here right now and find that motherfucker.

"Feel free to have another drink, sounds like he's a real gem." I pushed the bottle closer to let her know I was serious before I continued. "So are you seeing anyone else?" I asked, because obviously I was a sick fuck who wanted to hear the words from her mouth.

After pouring two more shots, she downed one and offered the other to me, but I held my hand up and shook my head no. I needed to keep my head right now, I couldn't get intoxicated around her, I didn't trust myself. No fuckin' way.

She chuckled, "Yeah, actually. Three guys. Can you believe that?" She tossed her head back and laughed deeply, on the verge of hysteria.

I didn't know what to say, so I just sat there like an asshole. This really complicated my plans for killing her boyfriend. Damn it all to hell.

"It's still new, but damn, it's been great. They're all so wonderful, I'm not sure what will happen in the future though, because they're not from here either. They're in town on a long term business assignment. Well, it could be long term, but I guess technically it could end anytime. So who knows where that will leave me at the end?" She sobered at that thought and clearly didn't like the taste of that reality so she quickly took the third shot.

"How are you getting home?" I asked quietly.

"Home? Oh shit! What time is it– oh moon maidens, I'm so rude, I forgot to ask your name. I'm Saige, by the way." She held her hand out for me to shake and I slid mine into hers with zero hesitation, watching the way her eyebrows lifted as our bond sizzled to life between our touch.

Dropping my hand, I held my watch out for her to see. "Oh hell sticks, I've gotta get home."

"I'm Johnny. Nice to meet you, Saige." I answered her question as she bustled around the space, distracted.

"You'll have to come by again when we're open and I can show you more of what I sell here? Damn, I'm going to be in a lot of trouble, my phone is dead." Holding it up, she showed me the black screen before shoving it into her backpack.

"Let me give you a lift home. It's dark out now and with your ex being in the area, I'd feel better about giving you a ride. I'm parked out front, do you live close?"

She looked up at me, her big green eyes studying me, trying to determine if I was trustworthy or not.

"It's just a two minute drive, would you mind? I'd really, really appreciate it! I left my bike at the grocery store, but I'm buzzing enough right now that I wouldn't want to drive it home anyway."

This woman, I'd never wanted to punish someone as badly as I did her in this moment. She doesn't even know me and she's going to hop in my car? There's a team of fucking assassins living above her magic shop and she's banging seventy five percent of them, hell, probably one hundred percent for all I knew, her ex is out there causing a scene, and she's just going to accept my good guy vibes? I'm not a good guy. I'm a fucking demonic asshole and my hands were itching to slap the hell out of her ass.

"I'll go start the car. Just come out when you're ready." I had to get some air before I did something unsavory.

She'd slid into the front seat of my car with her fox gripped to her chest a few minutes after I'd started the engine. Actually got into my car, a fucking *stranger*, but wouldn't tell me, *her mate*, her real name or phone number. My forehead was tingling and I knew I was seconds away from 'demoning out'.

"Thank you, Johnny. I appreciate this, can I give you some money for the trouble?" She looked at me from across the console and I swallowed a growl. She looked so innocent and beautiful, those wide green eyes staring into my soul and I felt myself soften toward her. A little tiny bit. That's all she was getting.

"It's not a problem. Where are we going?" I squeezed the steering wheel so tightly my knuckles popped.

"Just pull out and follow the road for a few miles, my drive is on the right, I'll give you a heads up before we get there."

Glancing over at her, she was staring out of the window. I looked down and was met with the face of a fox, it's lip curled up in a silent snarl. *Ex-fucking-scuse me*. Lifting my own lip in return, the fox snapped at me and put his paw on the console, like he was telling me to fuck right off. Ballsy little shit.

We headed down the road and I didn't speak because I didn't trust what might come out of my mouth. She lied to me. Gave me a fake name, a fake phone number... how could she do that to me? How could she deny the pull between us like that? My throat clenched at the thought of her betraying me like that. Did she not realize I would have found her regardless? She was mine and the sooner she accepted that, the sooner I could give her everything she'd ever dreamed of.

I WAS GOING to need to drop her off and make a quick exit because if I had to watch the guys pawing at her I really might go nuclear and nobody needed to see that. They didn't know I was a demon either, and it needed to stay that way.

"This is it, on the right," she murmured and I slowed down to take the sharp turn into her driveway.

Immediately, I could see four silhouettes standing near the house and I took a deep breath as they all turned toward us. Here goes nothing.

Cam

Chapter Nine

Why? Why does she pull this shit?

"Yo, boss. You okay?" Kai asked, pulling my focus out of my own head and to where he and Fischer had sat their asses in a couple of chairs on the patio out back. Saige was supposed to have been here twenty minutes ago, and her phone was going straight to voicemail. The house was locked so we were all just anxiously piddling around waiting for her to show up.

"Fine," I grunted, my jaw ticking in anger. But it wasn't anger, not really, it was the fear that something had happened to her. Her phone was always on her, and she knew how worried we'd been lately, so why wouldn't she let us know she was running late?

"Her phone probably just died, you guys need to chill out," Sloane snapped, clearly sick of the abundance of emotions he was having to deal with on the daily. Well, he was just going to have to get over it because I was all in, and Kaito was mated to her, for fuck's sake.

"Hey, we have every right to be worried, asshole," Kai growled, Bagheera clearly in agreement and making his feelings known.

"Ugh, whatever. I'm going on a walk, I can't stand to be around you all when you're like this. Get your heads out of your asses. We're still on a mission here, or have you forgotten we have a job to do?" Sloane's tone was dripping with venom and before I could make a move to grab him by the throat, headlights illuminated the side of the house and we all hopped up, making our way over to the garage.

"Who is she with?" Fischer wondered, squinting his eyes to try and make out the vehicle, but the lights were too damn bright.

The large SUV pulled into the spot in front of the garage and I had to take some deep breaths, she'd gotten a ride home from Johnny. Fucking Johnny, who she had never met before in her life. The man in question rolled down his window as Saige scooted out of the passenger side door, putting Maven down on the grass.

"Found this one in her shop, figured she needed a lift home since it was dark out."

Kai stood there for a moment before stepping up to the car and shaking Johnny's hand, thanking him for looking out for her. Fischer also expressed his thanks, but all I could do was give him a short bro nod before turning to wait by the door. I just... couldn't process this right now.

Sloane was leaning against the house with his arms crossed over his chest, an unreadable expression on his face as he observed the situation. *Dear gods, he better keep his smart mouth shut tonight. I am not in the mood.*

Johnny backed out and his taillights faded down the driveway, leaving us all standing there. Fischer had Saige in an embrace, but I could feel her eyes on me. Nope, I couldn't bring myself to look at her right now. Sloane made a noise under his breath and I think he'd finally realized how on edge I was.

"Sorry guys, I got held up at the store longer than I thought. Then I headed to the shop to grab some stuff and lost track of time when my phone died," Saige told us, her voice quiet as she walked over to unlock the door, keeping a hand on the house to steady herself. *Was she drunk?*

"So, I see you met Johnny," Sloane piped up, filling the silence.

The door swung open and all of us filed inside behind her. "Oh, you already met him? He's a nice guy, he stopped at the shop when he saw the lights were on and offered to give me a ride home when I realized how late I was."

Glancing back at Fischer and Kai, we had a silent conversation. Our training had made us experts in that. And it was agreed—she was hiding something.

Everyone made it to the kitchen and Saige began pulling meats and cheeses from her bag along with a couple bottles of wine and a suspiciously half full bottle of tequila.

"Were you drinking alone?" Fischer questioned, holding up the bottle of liquor.

She spun and put her back to us as she pulled a large tray out of a cupboard. "Huh? Oh, well I had a few shots, and Johnny had one with me. I've just been a little stressed out with everything that's happened."

Yeah, I suppose that made sense, it had been a lot to take in for everyone. We were used to strange things happening and learning to roll with the curve balls that the stars threw our way, but for Saige, this was quite the upheaval from her routine life.

She began plating the food and grabbed some dill pickles from the fridge along with a variety pack of crackers.

"Want to watch a movie in the living room?" she asked us, wringing her hands together in front of her chest.

"A movie sounds great. I'll just take this stuff to the living room, someone bring beer." Sloane picked up the plate and high tailed it out of the kitchen.

Kai and Fischer moved in on Saige, speaking in soft tones, but I was still too angry to even be in the same room with her. Instead, I grabbed a few bottles of beer and the wine, and trudged to the living room, leaving them to have their discussion.

Sloane was sprawled out in a corner of the large sectional couch and I tossed him a beer before putting the other shit down on the coffee table. There was a large recliner opposite the couch and I secured my own drink before beelining for that chair. That way I wouldn't have to sit beside her.

The three of them came into the room, Saige's giggle made my chest clench. Man, I needed to get my shit together, but I could feel her eyes on me, so I stared down at my cell phone, still unable to make eye contact. I was disappointed, the woman acted recklessly during a time where she should be taking every fucking precaution to be safe.

Thunder rumbled and I cursed softly, having lost control of my power for a moment. Everyone looked in my direction and I lifted my beer and downed the whole thing.

"I'm going to head back to the apartment. I'll see you guys later."

I needed to just get some space, I couldn't do this shit tonight.

"You okay, man?" Fish asked, concern lacing his tone.

Grunting in reply, I left the room and headed for the mudroom, slipping into my big black combat boots. I'd just pushed through the screen door to head for my Harley when the door opened and slammed shut, letting me know someone had followed me.

"Cam," she whispered.

Freezing in place, I waited for her to say something else, because I knew I needed to keep a tight lid on my mouth right now.

"I'm sorry, okay? My phone died, and I lost track of the time. Are you really so pissed at me that you're going to leave right now?"

"Am I that pissed? Really, Saige?" I spun around and advanced toward her, stopping when she backed up against the screen door.

"It wasn't my fault, Cam. It was an accident. Why are you so upset?" Her voice was now steady and firm, and I already knew where this was headed, but I couldn't stop it. Nope. This was happening right the fuck now.

"Let's see, you've been projecting yourself into another realm, you were in a coma like state for hours with blood pouring from your nose and ears, you've seen horned shadow figures, we've concluded that demons are indeed after you for some unknown reason, and you acted carelessly," I growled out, my voice low and rumbling.

She opened her mouth to respond to that, but I cut her off with a wave of my hand.

"No, I don't want to hear it. You didn't even make sure that your phone was adequately charged. What if you'd been in trouble?" I questioned, stepping into her space now, electricity zinging up and down my spine as another burst of thunder came from above.

"I'm not a child. I'm not weak. And I can take care of myself. I've been doing it for twenty-seven years, you overbearing caveman." Her face was getting redder with each passing moment, her anger rising to match mine.

"Then stop acting like a child!" I boomed, a flash of lightning lighting up the sky.

Her mouth opened in shock, but I continued, "This isn't about the phone, I'm not happy about that, because it wasn't okay to leave us here wondering if you were fine or lying somewhere bloodied and unconscious. That, I could've gotten over easily," I chuckled without humor, "but the part that has me so upset, is that you let a random dude into your shop, drank with him, and then willingly got into his fucking vehicle, Saige. A stranger! Do you understand how stupid that was? He could have been anybody. Did he tell you he's our business associate, or did you just think 'Oh, he's nice, so I'll just get into his car—'"

My rant was interrupted when her palm slapped my cheek.

"I said I was sorry, Cam! You don't get to stand here and berate me, I'm not your fucking employee."

Lifting a hand to my face, the sting of her slap still fresh, she'd gotten me good. Tears were welling in her eyes, but I didn't think it was because she was sad. She was probably an angry crier. *Well good, I'm fucking angry too.*

THE MAGIC OF BETRAYAL

"I'm going home. We both need to cool down." I turned and walked away, straddling my bike, my breaths still coming in heavy pants. Firing up the engine, I didn't look over at her when I drove by, for all I knew she had already gone back inside.

Raindrops began falling from the sky and I unleashed a torrential downpour, not caring that I was absolutely soaked, I was hopeful the rain would wash away some of this anger. This fucking fear of losing somebody I cared about. Fuck, I couldn't go through that again. The only way I was able to tolerate the jobs the guys and I did was because they were all trained and they didn't make careless decisions that put themselves in danger. Honestly, I would be feeling the exact same way if any of them ever pulled a stunt like this.

I drove around for about an hour before heading back to the apartment and trudging upstairs, soaked to the bone and still in a piss poor mood.

"Hey Jacobs, you good?" Johnny was sitting in the living room watching something on TV.

"Fine." I stepped out of my boots and ripped my shirt over my head making my way to the washer and dropping it inside, then quickly ridding myself of the rest of my clothing and putting that in with the shirt. Johnny had seen me butt naked many times over the years and I really couldn't give a shit less right now. I needed a shower.

He didn't look my way when I walked through the kitchen and headed for the bathroom, and when I came out after my shower, he had pulled out the sofa bed and was snoring like a lumberjack. Well good, I wouldn't have to interact with anyone.

Just as I was about to go into my bedroom, a hand grabbed my arm and pulled me into another one, backing me up against the wall with a growl, letting me know Kai was back and he was furious.

"What the fuck, Kaito?" I barked and he pressed himself up against my chest, getting in my face, eyes flashing yellow.

"I understand that you have some real issues from what you went through when you were younger, but if you ever disrespect my mate like that again, I will kick your big ass. Do not fuck with my woman, Cam. Sort your shit out and tell her about your past, because your relationship with her will suffer until you do. I'm going back to the cottage. Get yourself straight."

He brushed past me on the way out, and I just stood there breathing heavily and letting the weight of his words sink into my brain. Shit. My hands ran through my wet hair, and I wanted to pull it out.

Slipping into bed naked, I laid awake staring at the ceiling, the reminder of my childhood bringing the ghosts that I tried to keep buried to the forefront of my mind.

"Cam! Hunter! Get your shoes on, we need to leave in five minutes!" Mom called out to us and we dropped our Nintendo controllers. I flicked the TV off and we raced to the front door. Mama B was already closing the trunk of the van, everything all packed and ready for our annual week long vacation in the mountains. The cabin was the highlight of our year, and we were bursting with anticipation. Swimming, fishing, bonfires, cooking out. I loved everything about it.

Swinging my arm around my brother's shoulder, we made our way to the car and hopped inside, all smiles.

"Mama B, did you bring the gummy worms? We can't have a road trip without them!" Hunter questioned and Mama B held up a package of neon sour worms, a Jacobs road trip staple.

"You should know I'd never forget the worms, sweetie. Now buckle up, let's get a move on so we can get there before it gets dark out." We did as she asked and Mom slid into the passenger seat, reaching over to take Mama's hand as we backed out of the driveway.

I tried so hard to remember every detail I could about that moment, the last time we were at the house together as a family. It had been fifteen years now, but just the thought of them made tears prick my eyes. I could almost hear their laughter and happiness in the dark and empty room with me. Sleep likely

THE MAGIC OF BETRAYAL

wouldn't come easy tonight, but I closed my eyes and focused on my breathing in an attempt to push the memories back down.

SUN WAS SHINING through the curtains, so I must have overslept. Not surprising given the fact that I'd tossed and turned for what felt like hours the night before. But I felt good now that I had some semblance of what I wanted to do with Saige. I was feeling like a real asshole, but I still believed I had a right to be upset and I needed her to understand where I was coming from, and that I wasn't just being a dick who wanted to boss her around or track her every move.

Pulling out my phone, I typed out a message and sent it off before I could think too hard on it.

Me: Can I take you out tonight? I want to talk to you about some things and apologize for last night.

Not waiting for a response, I rolled out of bed, and slipped on some sweats. The scent of fresh coffee pulled me to the kitchen, I was such an addict. Music met my ears and I lifted my brow in surprise as Johnny danced around the kitchen, grinding his hips to the beat of the song.

"Never would've guessed you were a Lizzo fan," I chuckled, grabbing a mug and filling it up with piping hot coffee.

"Just distracting myself, not much else to do in this town. There's a lot of things you don't know about me," Johnny replied, taking a drink of his own coffee.

"Why do I have a feeling that I want it to stay that way?" Shaking my head, I took a sip of my drink, and stretched backwards to loosen my back up a little.

My phone vibrated and I pulled it out, unlocking the screen and finding a message from Saige.

Little witch: Sure. What time are you thinking?

She must still be pissed. No emojis, and that was a really short reply for her standards. Not that I blamed her.

Me: I'll get you at five. I'm taking you to dinner first, but we'll be on the bike, so dress accordingly.

Little witch: *thumbs up emoji*

Laughing, I tucked my phone away and found Johnny studying me from across the island.

"What?" I grunted, drinking some more of my coffee.

"Oh, I was just wondering how the mission was going. We haven't seen anything to indicate that Laura is going to show up any time soon, right?" he asked me, tapping his fingers on the countertop.

"Nothing concrete, but we figure it's only a matter of time now," I guessed. Who knew when this woman would show up again?

"And Saige doesn't know anything about the assignment?" he questioned, a hint of suspicion in his voice that I didn't appreciate.

"No, of course not. We wouldn't compromise a mission, you should know that. Though, when Saige was unconscious we did find out from her grandmother that her mother has an obsession with demons. We think that they're probably after her for something her mom is responsible for," I speculated, sitting down on one of the empty stools.

"And I heard there's a prophecy? Tell me more about that."

Taking a deep breath, I recited the damn thing from memory.

> "A witch, a mix of green and red,
> Save a race before they're dead.
> Hurry, witch, find your five,
> If there is hope to survive.

> Change, rise, manifest,
> A soul so pure soon possessed.
> Before the year of two and eight
> The chosen one must find her mates.
>
> If she should fail to meet her task,
> To another the role will pass.
> Evil will consume her heart,
> Her soul captured by the dark."

"Interesting." Johnny ran his thumb over his mouth, his navy blue eyes lost in thought as he worked through that puzzle. Good luck, buddy. Nobody knew what the fuck it meant.

"So, how's Larson? You've seen him in person more recently than I have. He was pretty amped up about this assignment."

"He's actually doing really well," Johnny responded, a flicker of emotion passing over his face, too quickly for me to fully analyze. "Things are looking up for Khol, and being this close to getting some closure from the Laura debacle has him in great spirits."

"Makes sense. She did a number on him." Johnny lifted his head and widened his eyes a little bit, like maybe I had insider information, but I didn't, so I waved him down. "I'm just judging off of how he acted when we met with him to get the orders. The man rarely shows any emotion at all and it was pretty fuckin' telling that he was so pissed."

He chuckled. "Yeah, no, you're right. She has no idea who she fucked with, but do you get the vibe that there's more going on here than meets the eye?"

Nodding, I had to agree with that, something just felt off in my gut, and I always trusted that feeling. It'd never led me astray before.

"Who knows, man. There's a lot of interesting people here, that's for sure."

"How do you think Saige is going to react when you guys come clean about why you're here? Or will you not tell her? Seems like a big fucking mess," he pondered out loud, taking a drink of his coffee.

I ran my hands through my hair and groaned. "Ugh, I don't know. We need to discuss it as a team first, and then discuss it as the guys who are dating her. I didn't see this happening, me finding a woman like this, or a woman who would be interested in all of us like that, but here we are. I'm not giving her up, and I think the others are in agreement with that, but I'm just focusing on one day at a time and trying to live in the moment."

"Must be some woman to bring the alpha team to their knees..." he mumbled and I chuckled.

"She's so that, and so much more, man. So much more."

Damn, I was nervous. Nervous to see her after our fight, nervous to tell her what I needed to, nervous to see if she'd forgive me for my behavior yesterday. It wasn't a feeling I was used to, and I didn't appreciate it.

I'd slipped on a grey and black henley, and paired it with some black Levi's that had rips in the knees. My long hair was pulled up in a knot on the top of my head, and I wore my signature black boots. Sloane and Fischer were sitting in the living room watching some Marvel movie and I smiled to myself as they laughed over something on the screen. We usually didn't have much downtime, so I was glad to see my guys getting to cut loose and relax a little bit.

"Where you taking her, Cam?" Fischer asked when I entered the room, patting my pockets to make sure I had the essentials. Keys, wallet, phone.

"We're going to grab dinner somewhere first, then heading to the lake. I want somewhere quiet where we can talk," I told them and they watched me warily.

"You'll feel better once you get it out there, and you know our girl, she'll want to support you and be more understanding about your... need for control." Fischer smiled encouragingly and Sloane grunted.

"More like his brutish caveman behavior, but sure, we can go with need for control," Sloane shrugged. Fischer threw a pillow at his head, hitting him square in the face.

"Be supportive, Sloane," Fischer scolded, crossing his arms over his chest.

"It's fine, he's just jealous. Don't wait up for me, boys." I winked at them, then took the stairs two at a time. I just needed to fix this fuck up of mine and get my little witch where she belonged. With me.

THE ENGINE of my bike idled at a soft rumble as I put the kickstand down. Just as I was about to flip the key and head for the door, movement caught my eye and I looked up just in time to see Saige come through the screen door and make her way to where I was.

Stars have mercy.

Leopard print skinny jeans, a black corset style top that accentuated her natural hourglass figure had her hips popping in all the right ways, heeled black boots came just over her knees and I swallowed roughly. She was my vision of a wet dream. Smokey eyes, dark purple lipstick, and two thick braids, I swear on Jupiter, my heart felt like it was going to beat out of my chest.

"Hi," she said, stepping right next to me where I sat frozen on my bike.

"H-" I cleared my throat, "Hi." *Fuck, I can barely speak.* "You look amazing, little witch."

A blush popped immediately and I smiled slightly as she looked up at me from under her dark eyelashes.

"Thank you. I figured this would work for being on the bike." She shrugged. We both just kind of stared at each other for a moment, neither sure of exactly what to do next. We needed to talk, but not yet, and not like this.

"There's a helmet in there for you." I pointed to the saddlebag. "Hop on, baby. Let's go get dinner."

Holding onto my arm, she swung her leg over the seat, pressing her soft body against my back. Oh gods. Giving myself a quick adjustment, we headed back into town. There weren't a lot of options in terms of restaurants, but there was a small Italian restaurant that I'd gotten take out from last week and it had been pretty good.

We pulled up in front of *Come and Spaghet It* and I killed the engine. Helping her slide off the bike, we hung our helmets on the handlebars. Just as I was turning to head toward the door, she slid her hand into mine and intertwined our fingers, looking up at me with vulnerability. *Well, I can't have that.* Lifting our hands, I pressed a kiss to hers and pulled her tightly against my front, my free hand finding her cheek.

"I'm so sorry, baby. I know we have to talk about last night, and we will, but I can't have you looking at me like you're questioning if I still want you or not. Because I always want you." My voice sounded rough to my own ears, and I felt my dick waking up again, pressing into her stomach.

"I'm sorry I slapped you. I don't know what came over me, I'm not a violent person and I feel so terrible about it." She took a deep breath and tears were shining in her green eyes.

"Hey, hey, it's okay. I deserved it, I was an asshole."

"So you forgive me?" she asked quietly, her cheeks pink with her emotions.

"Oh, baby girl." I didn't know what else to say so I leaned down and pressed a gentle kiss to her full lips, intending to keep it short and sweet since we were standing in the middle of the sidewalk. She had other ideas and suddenly her arms were wrapped around my neck, her tongue licking at my mouth, seeking entry. Groaning, I opened my lips and met her tongue with mine, caressing and loving the way we just fused together.

Clapping from somewhere had her smiling against my mouth and pulling back slightly. We both looked across the street where those two seer women were clapping, and jumping up and down at the sight of our PDA.

"Don't stop on our account, love birds!" the shorter of the two called out.

Saige laughed. "You two are so bad! We're going in for dinner now, hope you enjoyed the show!"

"Spoilsport!" the taller woman shouted, but they were both still smiling at us like we'd made their whole damn week.

Saige tugged my hand and led me into the restaurant, and I let hope fill my chest at the great start of the night. Hopefully, we could get everything out on the table and our relationship wouldn't detonate before it really even began.

Saige

Chapter Ten

Dinner was great. I'd eaten my weight in salad, breadsticks, and baked spaghetti, and Cam had devoured his chicken parmesan. We were both slightly groaning as we walked out of the restaurant, my body tucked close to his. We still hadn't had a deep discussion about what had happened last night, but I knew it was coming and my face heated with shame when I thought of how I'd lost my temper and slapped him, how I was lying to them all about Bryce and his threats.

The look on his face, or rather, the lack of expression damn near killed me. I'd ran back inside and gone straight upstairs, stripping out of my clothing and putting on my nightgown, slipping into bed with tears running down my cheeks. When Fischer and Kai slid into bed and held me, I really lost my shit. Ugly crying. Like, the absolute ugliest, big sobs, nose blowing, rapid breathing... the whole nine yards. And they'd just held me close, soothed me, while Fischer ran his fingers through my hair and Kai purred against my neck.

I must've passed out because next thing I knew, it was morning, and my face felt sore and raw from the tears and wiping them away. Fish and Kai were still in bed and I just snuggled in closer to Fischer, having missed him a lot lately. I needed some one on one time with him, soon. Sloane had either slept in the guest room, or the couch in the living room. He usually stayed when everyone else did, and I appreciated that Sloane had actually made an effort not to be upset with me. They'd come over to see me and I was late, and then turned into a soggy noodle. What a night of fun. Cam interrupted my thoughts and brought my focus back to him.

"Where are we going now?" I asked Cam as he led me away from the bike and down the street.

"Thought we'd just walk off some of those carbs and maybe head down to the lake for a bit? It's so nice out, we might as well take advantage." He leaned down and pressed a kiss to my head, our feet still moving in the direction of Peridot Park.

"Sounds great," I agreed, and it really did. The lake was so relaxing to be around, the water calling to me almost as much as plants did.

We walked in companionable silence until we found the perfect spot to sit. Underneath a beautiful cluster of giant weeping willows, not too close to the water, but the view was still incredible. Plus the long branches gave the illusion of privacy, and this was going to be an intimate discussion, I could already tell by how nervous Cam was getting.

"This work, baby?" Cam motioned to a lush spot that was flat and cushioned with springy green grass.

"Perfect. Do you have a blanket in your backpack?" He nodded, slipping the bag from his shoulders and pulling one out. We spread it out together and collapsed on top of it, lying on our backs and staring up at the trees.

The urge to use my magic was strong, being out in nature like this always brought it to the forefront of my psyche, but I wasn't using any of my magic these days, not until we figured out what the hell was going on.

"What are you thinking about?" Cam asked, taking my hand and pulling me closer to him so I was resting my cheek on his chest.

"Just that I wished I could use my magic. It's getting antsy at being locked down."

"I bet. I'm sorry you're going through all of this shit. You don't deserve it." His hand trailed up and down my back, his fingertips tracing the line of my hip and then back up.

"Nobody deserves this shit. I mean, I went from a normal girl next door kind of life to... whatever all this is. Doesn't happen every day, thank the stars," I laughed.

"I love that you find the good side of everything, you're always so positive. Does that ever get exhausting?" he asked me, and I pondered his question for a moment before answering.

"No, I mean, not really," I tried to explain. "It's just part of my personality. Why get bent out of shape over things you can't control? Things could always be worse, so I try to see the good things in every situation. It's definitely not always easy to do, and it doesn't always happen either. But it helps me stay in the moment and be thankful for what I do have." I wasn't sure I was explaining it correctly, but I felt him nodding in understanding.

"That's a good outlook to have, I should start taking notes," Cam responded as his fingers played with one of my braids.

We laid there together and I reveled in all of his gentle touches and the steady pounding of his heartbeat beneath my ear.

"Saige, listen. I am so sorry for my behavior last night. I was worried and I acted irrationally. I'm still upset, but I need to explain to you why. It's not easy for me to share, and I hope that you'll hear me out." His heartbeat sped up as he talked, and I was thankful he wanted to open up to me enough to tell me more about himself.

We sat up, facing the water. I pressed myself against his side and firmly grasped his hand; I wanted him to know that I was supportive. If it was easier for him to not have to look at me while he explained, then I would just hold his hand and hope that he could feel that I was someone he could trust with his secrets.

He sighed, "First, I want to talk about what happened yesterday. I'm sure you now know that Johnny is a co-worker of ours and he's safe to be around, but you didn't know that when you were alone with him in The Pig, and you didn't know that when you accepted a ride from him. What if he had been working with the demons or if he was just a bad dude?"

"I know, I've just had a rough couple of weeks and I wasn't thinking like that. Emerald Lakes has always been such a safe place for me, and it's hard to just throw everything I've ever known out the window like that." I snapped my fingers for emphasis.

"But you have to start doing that, Saige. We don't know enough about all the strange occurrences going on to not be at the top of our game here. Careless decisions are dangerous decisions, and I'm not willing to let you get hurt anymore. Do you have anything you want to say?" he asked softly, his thumb rubbing over my hand.

"I don't like being talked down to, Cam. You made me feel like I couldn't be trusted to make my own choices, and I think it triggered me a little bit due to what I went through in my last relationship." His face snapped over to look at me and I cut him off before he could speak, "No, I know you're nothing like him, trust me. But he was very controlling and condescending. Yesterday, I felt like you didn't want to hear what I had to say, the only thing that was important in the moment was making sure you let me know how badly I'd fucked up. And then I did the unforgivable and slapped you. I'm so ashamed of myself, and I hope that you'll forgive me for it because I know I won't be able to forgi—" My words were cut off when Cam cupped my cheek and turned my face toward his, leaning down, he gently pressed his lips to mine.

"I was a fool, baby girl. You're already forgiven, I don't want you beating yourself up over it anymore." He pressed his forehead against mine and I closed my eyes, after a few moments he pulled back and focused on the lake again.

"You mentioned being triggered by my reaction yesterday and I think that's a good way to explain why I reacted the way that I did. But in order to fully understand why, I have to tell you a story. And it's not a good one..." He trailed off, swallowing roughly like he was trying to loosen his throat up to speak the words he needed to.

"You can tell me anything, Cam. I'm here for you, okay?" I encouraged him and after a moment, he started talking. I didn't interrupt because it was like he was reliving the story. The way emotion skated over his face and his eyes kind of glassed over... whatever he was about to tell me, it was going to be difficult for him to do so.

"It's not really a secret that I'm not the greatest with words and relationships, but for you, I am going to try hard to change that. I really want this to work, little witch. When I was sixteen years old, my moms, yeah, I had two moms," he chuckled, "and they were everything to me. Loving, understanding, I loved them with all my heart. My ten year old brother, Hunter, and I had been conceived by the same sperm donor, but our mothers took turns carrying us. Mama B was my biological mom, and she was the strong silent type, it's not hard to see now where I might get that from. Mom was more of an extrovert, life of the party kind of woman, and that's exactly how Hunter was, too."

Cam took a shaky breath and I leaned my head against his shoulder in silent support. My heart was already clenching at the way he'd used past tense words in his descriptions of his family. I already knew where this was headed, and while I was excited to hear more about the man beside me, I felt really bad for him.

"Every year since my brother and I had been born, we'd go on a vacation to The Meridian Deep mountains and we always rented the same cabin every year. We'd stay for a week or two, and it was the highlight of our year. It took us about five hours to drive there, and we'd eat gummy worms, play Game Boy, and read comic books on the way. My brother was a few years younger than me, he'd be twenty five this year... anyway, we'd been at the cabin for about a week.

"Hunter and I were down at the lake swimming, it was so warm out that evening, and the water was the perfect tempera-

THE MAGIC OF BETRAYAL

ture for a swim. Mom and Mama B were up on the top deck grilling some food for dinner and we could hear their music and laughter all the way down in the water.

"It was late, but we always stuck to our own schedule when we were there. Fireflies had started lighting up the darkening sky and the twinkle string lights from the cabin reflected off the water. These are all things I remembered after the fact." He cleared his throat and wiped his hands down his face.

My stomach twisted unpleasantly because this happy family vacation was about to take a dark turn, and I wish I could stop it.

"Mama B yelled down for us to head on up for dinner, and Hunter swam over to the ladder, climbing up onto the dock to walk back. I stayed behind though, I just wanted a few more minutes to float around on my back and look up at the stars, it was relaxing and it felt like one of those moments in your life where everything is just good. But that ended in an instant. An orange glow lit up the sky and I righted myself in the water and saw the exact moment a large fireball blasted the side of the cabin.

"Just as I was about to scream, I saw a group of people standing off to the side, their attention on the burning house. Whoever the pyro mage was launched three more fireballs while the others stood back and talked amongst themselves. Instead of helping, I choked. I slipped underneath the dock and waited. And waited. I think I'd convinced myself it was a nightmare. There was no way that I could believe my family had just been burned alive inside of our vacation home. But I'd heard my moms' screams, and I knew it was real.

"Over an hour passed before the first responder lights lit up the scene and I swam out from under the dock and pulled myself up. My whole body was shaking and I remember running my thumbs over my fingers, over and over and over again. They were so wrinkled, and I couldn't comprehend how my skin would ever go back to the way it was before. Just like I would never get to go back. Somebody must've seen me because within seconds, I was swarmed by paramedics and was hauled into an ambulance. The cabin was nothing but a pile of smoldering ash when the backdoors of the vehicle slammed shut.

"That day I lost my moms and my only brother. Since I was only fifteen years old, I moved in with Fischer and his family. Our parents had been very close and he lived across the street. Sometimes, it still feels like a bad dream, like I could just close my eyes and reset everything."

Tears were trailing down my cheeks and I couldn't stop them. This was a heartbreaking story, no wonder he didn't like to talk about it. The way he told it, I could tell he was trying very hard to detach himself from the emotion, but his voice had cracked several times and each one felt like a fissure to my heart. This was a life event that shaped him into the mage before me.

"I'm so, so sorry..." I breathed and ran my hand up and down his broad back. *This* was why he was so protective of the other guys and me, *this* was why he has to be in control of every situation, so he knew the probability of the outcome. *This* was why he exuded daddy vibes and made me feel safer than I ever had in my life. I knew it wasn't his intention, but damn it if I didn't feel like shit for how sick with worry he must've been yesterday when my phone was dead.

"So, you see, I have some control issues and it doesn't take a shrink to figure out where those stem from. I've been like this with the guys ever since, but for some reason, when it comes to you, it's just an over the fucking top reaction. There's this pull, in here," he took my hand and pounded it against his chest, "and I can't fight it. A stronger man would tell you to stay away from me, from us, but strength left me the moment you sassed me, disobeyed me, cussed at me, fucked me, called me daddy... you're my own personal storm that I didn't fuckin' see coming."

"Cam." His name was nothing but a breathy sigh from my lips.

"I can't lose you, baby girl. I can't lose anyone else."

I watched this beautiful, broken man, tear down his walls and show me his heart with his bare hands. Cam reached out to me and cupped my cheek in his massive palm. We didn't speak, we just connected; our eyes saying everything that needed said. This moment was transcending all words. Our souls were twisting around each other, he was giving me this part of himself. I felt his thumb brush a tear off of my cheek, his pupils suddenly dilating into black endless pools. He looked sharply away from me and gazed out across Emerald Lake, pain etched across the planes of his face. Suddenly, everything I knew about Cam clicked into place and it was like I was seeing him for the first time. He was so, so much more than just an alpha asshole; he needed vengeance, and I was going to help get it for him.

My ears popped suddenly as Cam pushed himself up off of the spot we were sitting on. I couldn't tear my eyes from him. He was radiating energy, and the air was becoming more and more pressurized. I could hear the sounds of the teenagers across the lake laughing and enjoying the late evening sun.

A boom so loud erupted from the heavens, I was positive the gods themselves couldn't have recreated it. Laughter turned into screams as the thunder kept coming, louder and louder. Cam tipped his head back and looked to the dark skies above us, he opened his mouth in a roar, the thunder an extension of his pain and his inner turmoil.

Fat raindrops began falling to the earth, the sky splitting open as purple and blue electricity began coursing up and down his hands and forearms. He had been dancing between heaven and hell for so long and now the devil was calling for him, reaching out for his heart. The devil could fuck off. *Cam is mine.*

The rain began falling in waves, unrelenting and savage in its escape from the clouds. I stood up and wiped my now drenched hair out of my eyes. Cam was moving towards the lake, every purposeful stride sending out aftershocks of thunder. Everything felt slow, I was moving toward my big guy before my brain processed the movement, I felt like his magic was pulling me directly to where I needed to be. His hand reached behind his neck as he roughly grabbed a hold of the collar of his henley and ripped it up and over his head, revealing his naked back to me.

I inhaled sharply. How I hadn't seen his back yet was a mystery to me, but I knew without a doubt this was the first time. I think that was on purpose on his part.

The cabin.

In full technicolor, was forever enshrined across his entire back and shoulders. The blues of a beautiful lake with a dock started at his lower back, a stepping stone pathway leading up a sloped bank through a sparse pine forest. The simple a-frame cabin's slanted roof was illuminated with twinkling white string lights. Above the beautiful vacation scenery was a sky that was an exact mirror of what I was living in real life right this moment. Harsh, unforgiving lightning was streaking across his expansive shoulders, purples, blues, whites, and golds. The detail was so realistic, I was concerned I may actually get shocked if I ran my fingers over the beautiful artwork.

Cam heard me behind him, and he spun around. His breathing was ragged, water pouring off his face, his arms lifting as he grabbed his top knot and his soaked hair fell to his shoulders. My eyes tracked the water that was pouring from the ends before snapping my eyes back to his. Water was dripping down my face and he brought his hand to my mouth, his thumb tracing my bottom lip, pushing the tip of it inside my mouth when I opened for him.

This was happening. My stomach flipped as his arm snapped out, his hand closing firmly around my throat, tipping my face up toward his and then everything just exploded. The lightning crashed down around us, lighting up Cam's face, the look in his eye should have scared me. It should have had me trembling with fear, but instead, a loud moan came from my mouth and he stared down at me with a burning intensity that I'd never seen.

My hands went to his belt, trying to get his fucking pants off as quickly as possible, but he smacked my hands away, grabbing the hem of my shirt and dragging it over my head and I launched myself at him. I needed this. He needed this.

He caught me, his large hands finding my ass and lifting me easily so I was able to wrap my arms around his neck and my legs around his waist. Cam carried me quickly back to the little hideaway we'd been in before underneath the willows and I released him from my hold as his hands unclasped my bra, I worked on my boots and my pants. All I knew was that I had to have him, and the storm he'd created was so powerful, even if there were still people out here, they couldn't see anything more than five inches from their face.

When I stood after getting my jeans and panties off, he was standing before me like some kind of fucking viking god who bent the rules of the atmosphere to his will. Electricity was coursing over his skin, his hair curling from the water. The sky lit up with a bolt of lightning behind him and I whimpered as his eyes trailed down my generous figure with the hunger of a predator who'd just spotted their prey.

"Baby," he growled and my cunt clenched.

My chest was rising and falling rapidly, my breasts shaking with the effort.

"Lay down on the blanket. Spread those delicious thighs and show me what's mine."

By the stars...

My brain short circuited, but I found myself dropping onto the blanket, my eyes locked with his as I laid back and kept my feet flat, spreading my legs open.

"Wider. I wanna see how wet you are."

Well, if he keeps talking like that, my pussy is going to put out a downpour that will rival this storm. I spread my legs as far as they would go and thunder cracked loud enough that I jumped.

"Touch yourself, show me. Show me how badly you need me, baby."

My hand slid down my stomach and I felt immediately how turned on I was, my fingers slicked easily up my slit and I circled my clit, never breaking eye contact with him. My hips began grinding and my other hand found a hard nipple that I tugged on and Cam cursed under his breath.

"Please," I begged.

"You need me, baby girl? You need Daddy to fuck you, is that it? You want this inked, pierced cock inside you? Tell me and you'll get it." I watched as his hand gripped the cock in question and he pumped it a few times.

"I need you, Daddy." I bucked my hips up into my hand. "I need you right the fuck now. Give me your pain."

His eyes flashed and then he was on me, pressing me down into the wet blanket beneath me, our mouths tangling together, nipping, sucking, licking. My head was spinning and just feeling his dick grinding against me was nearly enough to set me off.

"Gonna taste you, need your sweetness all over my face. I've been thinking of almost nothing but your pussy for the past week," he grunted against my neck and all I could do was moan in encouragement as he slid down and threw my legs up over his shoulders, he put his hands under my knees, spreading me wide and completely at his mercy.

He ate me like a starved animal. My head rocked back and forth and I sank my hands into his hair, shamelessly fucking his face and guaranteeing that mouth of his wasn't going anywhere until I came in it. Thunder rolled when he slammed three fingers inside of me, and I cried out at the fullness, but if I could take his cock, I could handle his fingers.

Pulling his face back, I opened my eyes and looked down at him between my thighs, like he was at the altar, worshipping me, or maybe he was damning me with him. Whichever it was, when the sky flashed with light and I saw my cum glistening on his mouth and chin. A part of me wanted to feel embarrassed, but then Cam flashed a savage smile before his tongue licked his lips clean and I found that I really didn't give a fuck. *Fucking. Hot.*

"You taste like heaven. Be a good girl and give Daddy all of it, little witch. Come for me." He lowered his mouth and twisted his fingers, I saw stars explode behind my eyelids as I jerked and thrusted my cunt against his mouth, screaming out his name as his tongue swirling and lapping at my clit, ensuring I rode out every soul shattering moment.

"I'm going to claim you completely tonight, baby. Right here with the stars and moon as witness, I will make you fucking mine," he promised and my body shivered with desire.

"I need you, Daddy. I'm yours, but I need to taste what's mine. It's only fair." I raised an eyebrow and crooked a finger at him as I sat up and he moved toward my face, his cock jutting out and ready for my tongue.

"Kiss it."

Smiling, I grasped his hip and rose up onto my knees, pulling his tip right to my mouth. I pressed a feather light kiss to the crown, his piercings flashing in the storm.

"Lick me, baby."

Leaning down, I ran my tongue from his balls, over the barbells I could feel under the smooth skin, and up to the tip, swirling around his crown, tasting his unique flavor that I needed more of. Looking at him from under my lashes, I opened my mouth and slipped my tongue out, waiting for his next instructions.

His hand landed on the top of my head and he moved swiftly, sliding his dick deep inside of my mouth and I loosened my jaw, giving him free range to fuck it however he wanted. His head was thrown back and water ran down his abs, and when he hit the back of my throat I gagged slightly but when he went to pull back, I held his hips there, letting myself adjust to the feel of him in my throat. Relaxing, I swallowed.

"Fuck!"

His thrusts became short, but deep, and I swallowed every single time his cock hit the back of my throat. My hands squeezed and toyed with his balls, and I wasn't sure how he would react to this, but I really wanted to try. Slipping my hand further back, I brushed his taint and he grunted, but didn't stop me from advancing further. Everything was wet, and I just wanted to see how he would respond. I'd never done anything like this with a guy before, but the idea of it excited me. A lot.

My other hand cupped his sack and I pushed my finger between his ass cheeks, hitting his hole and he shuddered. Still didn't stop me, and my intentions were clear. *Fuck, I was so turned on.* Applying a little pressure and swirling the tip of my finger against him, I pushed in and he groaned. He was so tight, and hot. *Fucking hell.*

"No, not coming in your mouth." He stepped back and my hands fell away from him as he dropped down to the blanket and flipped me around so I was on my hands and knees. "You're a filthy girl, and now I'm gonna fuck the hell out of you."

A scream tore from my throat when Cam pulled back on my braids and slammed home all the way to the hilt, not giving me a moment before he was fucking me so hard, my back arched as he pulled my hair harder, my hips angling so he hit me so deeply, all I could do was make incoherent noises. His chest pressed against my back, and I opened my mouth when his fingers sought entry. Cam pressed his fingers against my tongue and then retreated. A crack on the ass had me squeezing his cock and squealing at the sting, but his palm came down again and again and I knew I wasn't going to last long.

"I'm going to fuck you here, little witch." His wet fingers pressed into my tight ass and I squirmed, looking back at him with wide eyes. "But not tonight. I'm going to stretch this hole out nice and good so my cock will feel so fucking good for you, baby girl. And then maybe Kai can fuck your cunt while I'm buried back here." He slipped a second finger in my ass and the image he'd created of both of them fucking me at the same time set my orgasm off like a rocket.

"Daddy!" I shouted, dropping down to my forearms, ass straight up in the air as he continued to fuck me relentlessly.

"Say it. Fucking say you're mine, baby girl."

"I'm yours, I'm yours, I'm yours," I chanted, eyes rolling back in my head when he spanked my ass so hard one last time, it set off another orgasm, and he bellowed out his release as his seed flooded my greedy cunt, squeezing him as if I needed all of it painting my walls, marking me as his.

Cam pulled me up, still inside of me, and wrapped his arms around my body, kissing my neck as our bodies quivered with the aftershocks of our passion.

"I'll never get enough of you, little witch," he breathed against my throat before he ran his tongue from my shoulder to my ear.

"Good, because I love the way you fuck me with your fancy peen," I replied and he barked a laugh, falling over beside me, bringing me down with him. The rain continued on for another half an hour while we just laid there, tangled up with each other, naked, and all the things we felt for each other were raw and out in the open. Nothing could touch us here, and I think we both needed the time to connect and solidify our relationship. I was falling hard for Cam and I just hoped that when he learned the truth about what had happened to me the night before with Bryce, that he'd understand I was only trying to keep him and the others safe. Because as much as he couldn't bear to lose me, I couldn't lose them either. Especially not to Bryce.

Kai
Chapter Eleven

My muscles burned deliciously as I held my one handed tree pose, breathing deeply through my nose, focusing on the center of my body, feeling my strength, and letting the air in my lungs flood life into me. I loved yoga. I'd started doing it as a teen after my affinity manifested and it had helped me immensely with my angsty teen moods and anger issues that stemmed from the constant battle Bagheera and I had been locked in for dominance.

Lowering myself down to my mat, I switched hands and moved fluidly into the wounded peacock pose. Whenever I decided I was done with Radical life, I had dreams of teaching yoga, and maybe offering cooking classes. My two loves. And that thought had my mind turning to my beautiful mate and how I'd like to fold her up like a fucking pretzel. Smiling, I pushed into an upward dog, stretching my hamstrings and arms before sliding down into downward dog, the stretch in my spine and chest making me groan.

Cam hadn't returned last night, so I hoped that meant he and Saige had worked through whatever the fuck happened between them the other night. I didn't like when my girlfriend and... well shit, what exactly were the others now? My boyfriends? A laugh slipped from my mouth as I sprayed my mat down with disinfectant and wiped it down. Regardless, I didn't like them fighting, and I didn't like having to get in Cam's face, either. But, by the moon, the man was stubborn as a bullfrog on the best of days and I didn't need him standing in the way of his own happiness.

This worked. This thing we all had going on, it was everything I could have ever hoped for and if I needed to be the glue that held everything together when one of us wanted to try to self sabotage, then you might as well call me fucking Elmer. I was going to make sure we were all stuck together forever. There was no other option for me, not after the mate bond snapped into place and Bagheera and I still loved the fact that the others were loving on our girl.

As I stood, Johnny cleared his throat and I glanced over to where he was sitting on a stool in the kitchen.

"Hey man, sorry, didn't even realize you were there. I zoned out," I explained, rolling my mat up and walking over to where he was.

"You're pretty flexible for a guy," he commented, swirling his coffee in a mug that said 'Good chives only!'

"See something you liked, Johnny boy?" I winked and his eyes snapped up to mine narrowing slightly.

"I'll let you know when I do," he grumbled.

He'd been a moody fuck since he got here and I wasn't sure why, but now was as good a time as any to ask him some questions.

"What's up with you? You seem off. Are you not sleeping? I know the couch bed isn't exactly the greatest..." I grabbed a cup of coffee for myself and slid beside him at the island.

"No, I haven't been sleeping that great, but I don't think it's because of the bed. I'm just trying to work out this puzzle so that I can get the fuck out of here."

"Hmm, well, so far nobody has any information on a Laura Walker, but we have to be discreet about who we ask because the last thing we need is for word to spread that we're here looking for someone. That would blow our whole fucking cover."

"True, but couldn't Fischer just erase the memory of the

conversation afterward?" He wondered and I paused for a minute to think about that, but then the door downstairs opened and closed, and the stairs creaked and groaned with the weight that could only be from one of us.

"Daddy's home!" I shrieked, and Johnny spit his coffee out over the counter, choking and coughing.

"Gods dammit, Kaito," Cam chastised me, but a grin was on his face and he looked good. Happy. Really fucking happy.

"'Daddy'? Did you just call him 'daddy'? I knew you guys were into some freaky shit, but this takes the cake," Johnny sputtered as he snagged a paper towel and began mopping up his coffee mess.

We both busted up laughing, Cam looked to Johnny and just said, "Long story," then went straight to the coffee machine to get himself all fixed up.

"So many questions..." Johnny trailed off, shaking his head at our antics.

"So tell me, boss, how did it go last night with our girl?" I was practically bouncing up and down on my seat, unable to keep hold of the pure happiness that was bursting out of me knowing that my... fuck, what am I going to call them? My lovers? Yeah, let's go with that. Knowing that my lovers had sorted everything out and everyone was safe and content.

"It went great. We went to Come and Spaghet It for dinner, then walked to the park. I told her everything."

I raised my eyebrows at that and he quickly added, "Not about the assignment, I mean everything about my past."

I nodded and Johnny looked between the two of us.

"So I take it she was understanding and you spent the night? You have this... freshly fucked aura about you right now, but it might just be the sex hair you're rocking." I laughed and Cam punched me teasingly in the arm.

"She's an amazing woman, she was more than understanding.

THE MAGIC OF BETRAYAL

Gods, I could live inside her," Cam groaned, running his hands through his wild hair.

A shatter had both of our heads whipping to Johnny where he'd abruptly stood, holding his destroyed coffee mug in his hands, blood mixing with the coffee and pooling on the floor.

"Holy shit, dude! Are you alright? Here, let me help," I offered, reaching for his hands to pull him to the sink, but he moved suddenly and stepped out of my reach, dropping the mug into the trash.

"It's alright, I'm going to take a shower." He spun on his heel and quickly made his way to the bathroom, likely trying to avoid dripping more blood all over the damn floor.

"What's up with him? He's been acting weird," Cam commented, tossing me a roll of paper towels as he wiped the counter and I cleaned up the floor.

"Not sure, but you're right. I was just asking him about it before you came home. I don't think he's sleeping well, but something's definitely up. He probably needs to get laid. I mean, he definitely needed to. Celibacy is hard on the mind when you're hearing about how great sex is all the time. Whoever his mystery woman is, obviously isn't here, and who knows how long it's been since he's gotten some action." I shook my head. A man had needs.

"Kai, I almost confessed everything to her last night. The lying is eating me alive. It started out as a mission, but this has turned into so much more and I feel like our future is with her, don't you? Something tells me she is not going to react well to the fact that we kept this from her, especially when she realizes exactly the kind of work we are involved with. We've killed a lot of fucking people, K. She's so sweet and wouldn't harm a fly, what if she doesn't want us anymore when she realizes what monsters we actually are?"

Cam was panicking, I could tell because he was usually a man of few words, yet, here he was talking almost as much as Sprout.

"I know, boss. I know. How do you think I feel? Bagheera put his paw down and claimed his mate, we both did... if she hates us for this, I don't know how we'll handle it." I inhaled a shuddering breath, because it was a possibility she would be really pissed. "But we don't have a choice in the matter right now. Do you really want to cross Larson on a mission that is so important to him? He'd fucking kill us if we fucked this up," I firmly reminded him while running my hand through my hair. "Hopefully, the woman makes an appearance soon and we can be done with it. Speaking of, have you given any thought as to what comes next?" I questioned, holding my breath and waiting for his response.

"I love the job, Kai. The traveling, the excitement, saving people, killing bad guys. I'm not sure who I am without that, what would I even do with myself without my career?"

"Well, I was thinking..." I trailed off when he groaned teasingly. "No, no, hear me out, big man. I think this is a good idea."

When he crossed his arms and looked at me expectantly, I swallowed and then pitched my idea to him.

"We already have a location. The warehouse in Kingstown. It's massive and the old processing plant that's underground would be perfect for affinity training. What if we can convince Larson that it'd be a great investment for expansion and we could turn it into a training facility? We're the best of the best, we could run it for him," I explained, my stomach twisting as I waited to hear his response to my idea.

His brow furrowed and I could see the wheels turning in his head as he did his leader bullshit, working out all the logistics in his mind at a rapid fire pace.

"Actually, I think that's kind of genius. He'd be a fool not to go for it, more and more people are signing up for the training program and there's even been a waitlist the past year. Seems everyone is realizing that it's one of the best bets to get you to the top of your game and setting yourself up for a career. I like this. A lot. We'll need to talk about it with Fischer and Sloane, but I think Fish will be all for it. Sloane is going to push back though, he loves the spy life."

Nodding, I opened a granola bar and munched on it while we sat in companionable silence and thought about our future.

"Let's wait to talk to Larson about anything until we have everything figured out, because you know he's going to ask, and I'd rather have some numbers and statistics for him before pitching the idea. It'll make this look more like a planned change versus a spur of the moment thing. He's more likely to take us seriously that way," Cam decided, and I agreed with a thoughtful nod. We needed to plan this accordingly.

I'D THROWN myself headfirst into planning mode. I decided that I'd wait to tell Fischer and Sloane about my idea until I had it completely prepared, knowing that it would be better that way because then I could actually answer their questions without sounding like a fuckin' amateur.

One thing I figured out quickly, I didn't like financial shit. Talk about boring. By the stars, if I had to look at any more bullshit reports, I was liable to set the whole folder I'd collected on fire. Cam offered to take over that part when he'd found me holding a lighter underneath the pile of papers over the kitchen sink. Not my proudest moment, but for real, fuck math.

I'd spent several days typing up proposals and ideas, trying to put all of my thoughts together, and the more I researched and thought about this project, the more excited I became for the possibility of a future here. Closing my laptop, I debated what to do next. *Damn, I'm bored.* I took a deep breath and my nostrils flared. *Mate.* Jumping off the bed, I sprinted down the hallway, and slid into the living room in my socks. I smiled savagely at Saige, who had just noticed me, her eyes wide as I stalked toward her.

"What's a pretty cub like you doing up here alone?"

"Kai... I just came up to say hi. I'm on my lunch break, but I only have ten minutes before I need to get back downstairs..." she backed up and put the island between us. *Silly witch, that's not going to stop me.*

We circled around, my eyes flashing with the thrill of the hunt. *I wonder if she'd run from me.* That thought had my cock turning to steel, thinking of her trying to escape me in the woods, tackling her, and fucking her into the dirt.

"Kaito... I can't be late. Don't look at me like that, bad kitty!"

I was positive my eyes were yellow now, all animal.

"Run," I growled, and her mouth opened when I gracefully pounced onto the top of the island. She didn't hesitate, squealing and turning to run toward the bedroom. Snarling, I dove off the counter and chased her. She was just about to slam my bedroom door shut in my face, but I got my foot in the door at the last moment and she screamed, diving over my bed and pressing herself against the wall.

"I can hear your heartbeat, Cub," I spoke quietly, my voice rough in my throat.

"I'm sure you can."

"I can smell how turned on you are, too." A smirk tugged at my lips and she shook her head, like she could try to lie.

Crossing her arms, she sassed back, "You're losing your mind, pussy cat."

Not giving her a single clue as to my intentions, I launched myself across the bed and tossed her down onto the mattress, crawling on top of her and pinning her wrists above her head.

"You're lying, Cub."

She was wearing one of those sexy as hell vintage pin-up dresses that had her amazing tits practically falling out as she laid, panting beneath me. Single mindedly, I ran a hand up her leg. She was wearing pantyhose, but when I hit her thigh, a purr erupted from my throat when I realized she was actually wearing fucking stockings.

Flipping her dress up, I groaned as I took in the black lace garter belt, thigh high stockings, and matching black lace thong.

"Cub," I purred, "look at you. Aren't you a fucking treat for your Alpha?"

She whimpered and tried to hide her face. "Ah, ah, don't you try and hide from me. Who did you wear this for? You didn't put this on without plans of this exact scenario happening." I palmed her throat, making her look at me as my eyes trailed back down her body. Fucking hell, she looked like sin.

"Kai," she moaned, squirming under my hold and my predatory instincts flared again, the urge to mark her and claim her were the only thoughts driving me.

Slipping down, I lifted her dress to her hips, and growled my approval at how delicious she looked.

"You're a vision in stockings, Cub. I'm almost sad the others aren't here to see you like this, but we can plan something that involves all of them..." I trailed off my thought, and she sucked in a breath, her eyes dilating with lust.

"You like that, don't you, dirty Cub? The thought of all of us fucking you together? Hmm, we need to start prepping you to be able to take as many of us at a time as possible," her breathing hitched, "because I can't wait to feel you squeezing my cock at the same time as you milk one of theirs."

Pushing my sweats down, my cock sprang free. I pulled her thong to the side and slid inside of her, her wetness making it easy.

"Yes, Alpha. Fuck me. I need you."

"You're gods damn right you need me, Cub, and I'm going to give you all of me. But tell me, how do you want us to fuck you? Tell me what you think about in that head."

My hips swiveled and she clenched the bedding as her hips lifted and grinded against me.

"I've never done anything like that before," she sighed and I pumped myself in and out of her, not in a rush to get off just yet.

"Mmm," I purred, the thought of us being her first made me extremely fucking happy. "Maybe you want to let me fuck your ass with Cam buried deep inside your cunt? Or should we let Fischer be the first to take your ass? Sloane can fuck your mouth while we fill you up so good."

Her pussy started fluttering against me, the mere thought of what I was describing too much for her to handle. Smiling, I increased my movements.

"That's right, Cub. We'd take such good care of you, taking you to places you've never seen. Sloane and Fischer would love to have you between them, or maybe I could be in your pussy, Fischer in your ass, and Sloane in his?"

Fuck that's hot. My balls twitched.

"Yes, yes, gods, I want that, Alpha!" She cried out and rolled us so that I was on my back and she was straddling me.

"Show me how much you want it, and maybe I'll tell your other boyfriends just how naughty you are. We'd fuck you so good, Cub." She sank down on my dick and I grunted.

She rode me hard and I pushed her dress up her thighs so I could see those fucking stockings before my control snapped, and I pulled her down and pressed my mouth against hers, jacking my hips up and slamming in and out of her.

A strangled cry came from her mouth and she clenched around me so hard, it bordered on painful, but the best fucking kind. Turning her head to the side, I latched onto her shoulder and bit down, her blood pouring into my mouth as she screamed and I exploded inside of her. She rode out her orgasm as I twitched inside of her tight pussy, my tongue lapping at the bite I'd left on her skin.

"Why does it feel so good when you lick me after you bite me?" she asked in a daze as her walls still lightly pulsing against me.

"You just love my tongue, Cub," I replied against her neck, flattening my tongue and letting it slide over the wound.

I moved us so we were laying side by side and she moved her panties back over herself and tugged her dress down.

"Gods, that was amazing." She smiled at me and my heart felt like it was going to burst from my chest. Satisfaction flared through the bond with Bagheera and we both felt like a couple of smug assholes for making sure our mate was nice and fucked.

After we cleaned up, we walked back into the living area to find Sloane was reading a book sprawled out on the couch, not even lifting his eyes to acknowledge us. Saige squeezed my hand and when I glanced down at her, her cheeks were pink. She was probably wondering if he'd gotten home while we were getting busy in my room, but it didn't bother me at all.

"Hi, Sloane," she greeted him when it became obvious he wasn't going to.

The asshole just grumbled and turned the page and I scowled at him. Fucker was in major denial.

"I'll let you get back to work, Sprout. Text me when you're done? Dinner tonight at your place?"

"Sounds good, I'll be done around five." She wrapped her arms around my neck and tugged my lips down to hers, she kissed me passionately and slowly, making my dick wake up again in a real hurry. She pulled back and kissed the side of my mouth, biting her bottom lip as she moved away from me and turned to disappear down the steps. Her goodbye left me standing there with a hard on and an open mouth.

"You gonna stand there all day with your mouth open like that? I have something I could put in it, if that's the case..." Sloane sniped, turning another page of his book without looking up at me.

Sighing, I dropped into a chair next to the couch and ran my hand through my hair.

"Fucking hell, that woman... I have no words." I smiled like a damn nerd, but I was blaming the sex filled state my brain was still stuck in.

Sloane's phone started buzzing across the coffee table, and I saw the screen before he snatched it and ignored the call. 7th Circle Penitentiary. His fucking dad.

"Has he been calling often?" I asked gently, it was a sore subject and one that needed to be handled delicately.

"Every other day or so." He shrugged and continued reading, pretending it didn't fuck him up on the inside any time he had to think of that piece of shit, but I knew better.

"What do you think he wants?" I asked, not really expecting a response.

A few moments passed and Sloane laid the book down on his chest, finally looking at me. "Fuck if I know. I haven't spoken to him in probably ten years."

I nodded, because I remembered the last time he'd spoken to his dad. After we'd graduated our training program, his dad had reached out to him for the first time since he'd been locked up. Sloane didn't recognize the phone number when he answered the phone and that's all the in that fucker needed to get inside his head. Sloane told his dad about how he was in the top ten percent of his training class and all his dad had to say was 'I knew you didn't have what it took to be at the top'.

The guy was absolutely toxic and anything he'd want to say to Sloane would just be with the intentions of ripping him to shreds. There had been far too many nights when we were kids that Sloane would show up knocking on my bedroom window and I'd pull him inside and clean up his wounds.

Faint tapping had me turning my head away from the cooking show I'd been watching in my room. Sloane's face flashed in the window and I scrambled over to let him in; he could climb the tree easily enough to get up here, but if he fell, that would have hurt like hell.

"Hey, what's up, are you alright?" I asked as I gave him a hand so he could step inside my room. His black hood was up over his head but I

saw his shoulders shake and my gut twisted because I knew what his face would look like when he took his hood down.

"Sloane, hey, it's okay. You're safe here, let me see, man." I reached out and put my hand on his shoulder and he hissed in pain. I pulled my hand back so quickly, you would've thought I'd burned it.

Snagging his hand, I pulled him into my bathroom, putting the toilet seat down and directing him to sit. Pushing back the hood, I schooled my features and kept my face blank. My poor friend. His bottom lip was busted, as was his left eyebrow, and dried blood streaked down his face. His eyes were focused on the floor and I knew he was embarrassed, but he shouldn't have been. His dad was an asshole, and he was a big dude. We were still just kids, our affinities not even awoken yet. Well, besides Cam, but he was the oldest of us. Lucky bastard.

Pulling out the first aid kit, I started patching him up. I'd done this so many times now, it was just second nature, but there was something different this time. There was something swirling inside of me that felt like a scratching against whatever it was inside of my head that made me, me. Dismissing that, because that sounded absolutely insane, I cracked an instant ice pack and handed it to him to put on his face.

"How bad is the rest, Sloane?" I asked softly, the need to protect my best friend was almost suffocating. I'd always looked out for my friends, but this felt different, stronger, hungrier.

"Why can't I just fight back, K? I freeze like a little bitch every fucking time and the beatings are getting worse. He will kill me one day." His voice trailed off and his ice blue eyes glistened as he looked at me with fresh tears in his eyes and anger flared through my veins. I'd never wanted to kill anyone as much as I'd wanted to kill Sloane's father.

"It's not your fault. He's your dad, he's not supposed to do this. I'm so sorry, Sloane. When we get our powers, we can fight back. You won't be defenseless anymore," I promised as he unzipped his hoodie and dropped it onto the floor.

"By the stars, Sloane." My eyes pricked with tears because I couldn't process the state my best friend was in. There were cuts, but mostly just

huge patches of bruising. Purples, blacks, greens, yellows. Not all of these were new, he was getting beaten daily.

"It really hurts here," he pointed to a spot on his side where his ribs were. They were probably broken.

Swallowing a growl I hadn't known I was capable of, I bit out, "Let me grab an ace bandage and wrap your ribs, okay? It'll help."

Ugh, my headache was escalating, and I never got headaches. My skin felt itchy and tight. I'm probably just disgusted by what Sloane lives with across the street. *It was absolutely unacceptable, but my parents had already called CPS, and so had the school, and so had Fish and Cam's parents. Nothing ever changed. He was stuck in that house with that monster, and since Mr. Sullivan was also Sheriff Sullivan, it wasn't likely to change any time soon.*

He stood when I approached with the wrap, holding his arms above his head with a wince.

"I'm going to kill him one day, Kaito. With the stars as my witness, I swear it. He will pay for what he's put me through, what he puts Mom through," he vowed, and I finished wrapping him up.

"I'll help you. One day, we'll be the toughest assholes around and everybody will fear us, and you'll be the scariest of them all. You already have an excellent scowl, at least Olivia thinks so." I winked at him and he pushed me playfully. "Come on, you can stay over, my parents are at some party with Fish's parents tonight, and the girls are at a sleepover. We can stay up late and sleep 'til noon tomorrow."

"Kai... thank you. I don't know what I'd do without you. I love you," Sloane declared, and when I turned back to face him, he wrapped his arms around me and hugged me fiercely. Sloane Sullivan didn't hug, or do feelings, so he must have been really off his game tonight.

"Love you too, Sloaney Baloney." I chuckled and he shook his head in fake annoyance. He claimed to hate that nickname, but I knew that was bullshit. He fucking loved it.

I stumbled on my way to my bed, pain flaring up my spine, making me cry out.

"K? What's wrong? Did you stub your toe or something?" Sloane's

concerned voice came from behind me, and his fingers rubbed nervously over the rough denim of his jeans, his heartbeat increasing with each passing second. "Are you okay?"

The scratchy feeling intensified to an unbearable feeling, and I fell to my knees and rolled onto my back.

Sloane's face came into view. "Holy fuck, K. Your eyes. They're... yellow."

That was the first time I shifted. I still think it was the emotional reaction to seeing the full extent of damage that had been done to my best friend's body, him telling me how much I meant to him, the two of us swearing to one day kill his deadbeat dad... the perfect storm. The first shift was excruciating, and Sloane held me, soothed me.

Even after it happened and Bagheera was standing in my bedroom, Sloane took care of him, too. He didn't back down, or leave me. He was my brother, through good and bad, and I loved him with all my heart.

"Ya know, we still have to kill him one day," I murmured and Sloane's eyes flashed with fire.

"Trust me, I think about it often. If the bastard wasn't locked up in Seventh Circle, we would've done it a long time ago."

He wasn't wrong, but I still was convinced that he wouldn't ever be whole until that asshole was nothing but a pile of ash in the wind.

His gaze went to his book again, but I couldn't let it go. He was self-sabotaging and what kind of protector would I be if I didn't try to protect him from his own miserable ass?

"Don't push her away. She's good, and you deserve something good. Don't self-sabotage this, I can see the way you hold yourself back. She could be perfect for you, Sloaney Baloney."

Before he could respond, I hopped up and left him in the living room. His dad had been locked up for a long time, the only thing standing in the way of his happiness now was himself.

Saige

Chapter Twelve

Bryce hadn't spoken to me since last week at Dinner Thyme, and as much as I appreciated that, it also made me feel more on edge. I'd see him at random times, catch his face in the crowd, or walking down the street, and each time I had to push my panic deep down. He was probably plotting. And that was enough to make me want to puke. I was also feeling pretty guilty about not telling the guys about what had happened... but I was terrified of what Bryce would do to them.

I also hadn't seen much of Sloane, or their new roomie, Johnny. I'd seen a bit more of the latter, but I couldn't read him at all and every time I felt like I was able to look at him a little closer, he suddenly had something he needed to go do for work, especially if one of the other guys was near me. The way he scowled in my direction led me to believe he wasn't a big fan of mine, but I had too much shit going on to deal with yet another man.

Being iced out by Sloane stung, though. He'd seemed to revert right back to his true self and I wasn't even sure why. I guessed I should just be thankful that he was showing his true colors now, before I got involved any deeper with him. I didn't ask Fischer about him either, I didn't want to put him in the middle. Fish assured me many times that he and Sloane weren't boyfriends, or in any kind of relationship, aside from their BDSM sessions they did together, but I wasn't so sure that feelings weren't involved.

My fingers traced the pentagram that hung around my neck

and my heart ached a little when I thought of Bram. The necklace did its job well, and I hadn't had any more projections since the last one that had put me in a comatose state. Surprisingly, I found myself missing Bram and his crazy ways. Hopefully, he wasn't too upset when he realized I'd given him completely fake information about myself.

"What are you thinking about, child?" Gran asked, sipping on her mimosa as we took a break from gardening and kicked back in the lounge chairs on the patio.

"Oh, just everything. The guys. My birthday."

She chuckled, "I'd be thinking about the guys too." She held up her index finger and thumb in a circle and jammed her other index finger through them and I snorted.

"You're ridiculous, you know that, right?" I asked, shaking my head.

"You love it. I can't believe you're going to be twenty-eight in a few days! What's the plan? Party? Low-key hang out? Strippers?"

"Okay, settle down. I need to call Miranda later to sort out the rest of the details, but we're going to Magic Stixxx, so strippers are happening."

Gran squealed and clapped. I swear, she was worse than a teen.

"Well, call her now, we can get this planned out!"

Pulling my phone out, I called her and put the call on speakerphone.

"Hey girl, what's up?" My bestie's voice had me smiling and excited for my birthday.

"I'm sitting here with Gran and she's impatient to get my party planned, and since we're taking a gardening break, we figured we'd give you a call and see if we can sort it out," I explained, sipping on my coffee.

Miranda laughed. "Hey, Gran! Long time no see, how have you been?"

"I'm spectacular, as usual." Gran flipped her hair even though Miranda couldn't see her and we all laughed.

"Your birthday is Saturday, so that's perfect!" Miranda exclaimed, and I heard the sound of papers ruffling so I knew she was about to start taking notes. The girl had a serious pen and stationery obsession.

"I'm ready to cut loose." I smiled thinking about how much fun it was going to be with the guys at the club.

"Let me check Magic Stixxx's calendar of events quick." Miranda went quiet for a few minutes and then her loud squeal had Gran and I chuckling. "Oh my gods, this is perfect. They're having a Neon Night across all three levels. One cover charge gets you entry into all three clubs. This is epic."

"You're going to start laughing like an evil genius any moment, I can feel it..." I teased, and then she did a perfect impression of Dr. Evil.

"I'll be in the strip club! Maybe I'll venture upstairs if I'm feeling extra," Gran commented.

Miranda fired back, "When aren't you feeling extra?"

"Okay, okay, so Saturday, we'll meet at the club at ten. Sound good?" I asked, and she agreed.

"This is going to be the best birthday, I can feel it." I squealed and we ended the call. Gran and I stood and danced around the patio to nothing but the music in our heads.

"I only have a few days to get my outfit picked out," Gran grinned wickedly and I was only like... sixty percent scared of what that might look like. "I'm going to go see what I have to work with, I'll see you later." She stood up and practically sprinted across the lawn to her house. Gran is a spry bitch.

My phone went off, and I smiled when I saw who it was.

Guppy: I miss you, sweetheart.

Me: I know, I miss you too, I feel like we haven't had much time together lately.

Guppy: It's been a crazy few weeks.

An idea formed in my head and it was perfect. So perfect. Closing out of the messaging screen, I pulled up the number I needed. After making sure that tonight would work for my idea, I texted Fischer back, my heart racing with excitement.

Me: Guppy, will you go out with me tonight?

I chewed on my bottom lip waiting for a reply. Instead, my phone lit up with an incoming call.

"Hi, Guppy."

"Are you asking me on a date, sweetheart?" His deep, smoky voice filtered through the line and my stomach flipped with butterflies.

"Are you saying yes?"

"Of course I'm saying yes, I can't wait to have all of your attention on me for the night. Is that greedy of me?" His tone dropped an octave deeper and I squirmed on my seat.

"Maybe, but if you're greedy, then so am I."

His chuckle was so sexy, and I could picture him running his hand through those thick curls of his and shaking his head.

"What are we doing?"

"Can't tell you that, it's a surprise. Wear something comfortable but nice."

"You're a little sneak, but fine. I think I can work with that dress code."

"Did you guys get a rental car yet? I don't think I'll be able to make my outfit work on the back of your bike... " I trailed off and smirked when he groaned.

"Well, my curiosity is officially piqued. Yeah, I picked the car up this morning, I'll let everyone know it's unavailable tonight. I'll swing by and pick you up, what time?"

"Six. I'm so excited!"

I heard his smile through the phone.

"Can't wait, sweetheart."

"Gotta go, see you soon."

Ending the call, I stared up at the blue sky and let the sun's rays heat my face and rejuvenate my body. Not using my magic had been a struggle, but to be honest, I was kind of terrified of it. Made it easier to push down the desire to give in.

Maven trotted around the corner of the house and nudged my hand with his head.

"Hey, buddy," I cooed and scratched him behind his big ears and he hopped up onto my lap, putting his paws on my chest and his nose an inch from mine. I laughed. "You're nuts. What do you want? Are you hungry?"

I'd never met another animal who could scowl quite like Maven. If it was an art form, he'd be a master.

"Are you giving me attitude?" I asked him and he huffed.

"Fine, let's go inside. I'll hook you up, maybe it'll improve your bad attitude." I scooped him into my arms and he grumbled while we walked into the house and I deposited him on the floor in the kitchen.

Remembering that I had some lunch meat in the fridge that was close to expiration, I figured I'd give Mave something he didn't normally get. He tap danced across the floor in excitement as I mixed the salami and turkey in with his regular food, slamming his little paw on the floor when he felt I was taking too long. Bossy as hell, I tell you.

Heading upstairs, I wanted a nice long bath. Fischer and I hadn't been intimate since the mind blowing erotica that happened out in the garden with Sloane, and his little touches and kisses were building me up so much that when we finally did have sex, I was probably going to come as soon as I got a look at his dick. Hopefully tonight, but first, a soak, and then, I needed to pick out some lingerie.

Settling down into the steamy bath, I leaned back and let my eyes close. The smell of my bath salts and the heat of the water felt so good, I must have drifted off.

"Goldie."

My eyes snapped open and my hand flew to my neck,

breathing a sigh of relief that my necklace was still in place. I must've imagined that I'd heard Bram's voice.

Settling back, I closed my eyes once more and ran my washcloth over my stomach and breasts.

"You lied to me."

Shrieking, I almost threw my washcloth in the air.

"Bram!" I yelled, "What the fuck... how are you here?"

"Ah, it's nice to see you too, Goldie," he replied, walking over to the vanity and hopping up to take a seat. Thank gods for bubbles, at least I was mostly covered.

All I could do was stare at the demon who was *in my house*, where no demon should be able to be.

"Imagine my surprise when I texted you for weeks and called and got no response. I thought something horrible had happened to you, because never in my wildest dreams would I have thought that my Goldie would give me a fake number, and maybe worst of all, a fake name." He narrowed his amber eyes as he glowered down at me.

"Bram, listen—"

"No. You listen. I told you that I'd find you, and now that I have, I'm not sure what I want to do with you. Something that was even more disturbing was that I was watching, waiting to see who your lover is, but you don't just have one, do you, Goldie?"

My mouth dropped open, he'd been fucking spying on me?

"Maybe I should go find myself a group of hot women to fuck? What do you think about that? It's been a long fucking time, but I do remember what to do with my cock." He raised an eyebrow in challenge and the thought of him putting his dick in anyone had the heat inside of me flaring to an immediate wildfire. I was fucking pissed. *How dare he?*

"Fuck you, Bram!" I slapped at the bathwater and bubbles flew out of the tub. I couldn't stop the laugh that escaped my mouth when a big clump of suds landed right on his stupid face.

"I've seen some pretty women down at the park. They eye

fuck me every chance they get, you know? Kind of like how you pretend you don't. Can you picture it, Goldie?" He sneered my name and I gripped the edge of the tub. "Imagine me thrusting in and out of them while I feast between another's legs. How does that make you feel? Think about how they'd squeeze me and be the first women in fifty years to take my cum."

"Shut up." I was starting to sweat, and not because I was turned on. Oh no, I was disgusted and livid. There was no rationalizing it either.

"Nah, I don't think I will. Do you have any single friends? What about the woman with the dark hair and the little girl? She's got a banging body and I wouldn't mind—"

Flying up out of the water, I launched my soap covered naked self at him and he grabbed my wrists before I could get a swing in.

"I'm going to kick your ass!" I screeched and he chuckled darkly.

"I'd like to see you try." He snorted, smiling at me in a mocking manner.

"How dare you come in here while I'm bathing and, and..." I stuttered, unsure of where I was going with that line of thought.

"And what? What? Tell you how I'm going to go lose my secondary virginity card to some random chicks? Why does that bother you? You didn't even give enough of a shit about me to tell me who you really are or give me any way to contact you! You're unbelievable. Here you are, fucking how many guys and you think you have a right to get pissy with me?"

"You are infuriating. I'm going to call them right now and they'll get rid of you. You shouldn't even be in my house!" I shouted in his face and he laughed.

"No, I don't think you will be calling them," he grabbed my throat and I swallowed a moan. "What are you going to say? A demon who shouldn't be in my house is and I'm insanely attracted to him but I keep lying to myself about it. How do you think the truth would go over, Goldie?" He leaned forward, his breath hitting my neck, releasing a chill down my spine.

"You're acting like a spoiled, entitled brat!" I growled, my mouth against his while his grip remained firm around my neck. "What person in their right mind would give a man they don't know all of their contact information? I had no idea I wouldn't be coming back to see you and I did what I felt was best. You can't just call someone your soul mate and not have them be wary! It's about a five thousand on the creep-o-meter, Bram!" I shrieked, exasperated.

"So, you won't give your mate your phone number, but you will hop into a car with a stranger? I think you're full of shit, princess."

"Yeah? Well, I think you're an asshole, so whatever. I'm done with this. I have a date to get ready for and you need to leave."

His eyes narrowed and flared with possession that had my core clenching and I internally cursed my inner witch for being such a cock lover. He released me and I stepped back, momentarily forgetting I was butt ass naked. He didn't forget though, his eyes took in my body that was covered in bubbles and soap suds, I quickly slapped an arm over my tits and used my other hand to cover my vagina.

"Gonna need a bigger arm to hide those mountains from me." He smirked and hopped off the counter. "But fine, I'll go. Next time I see this body naked though, you'll be begging for me, mark my fucking words, Goldie. You and me? We're fated and it will happen."

I blinked at him and in a flash, he was gone, and I was left standing in a puddle of quickly chilling water, questioning my own sanity. Maybe I'd imagined that whole thing, but the lingering scent of his cologne had me thinking that wasn't the case at all.

CRUNCHING gravel underneath car tires signaled that Fischer had arrived and I slipped on my Mary Janes that completed my pin-up girl look to perfection. Bright red lipstick, a black retro dress in the same style as my lemon dress that I'd worn the last time we'd been intimate... what a memory. This dress though, had black lacey cap sleeves and a matching black lace overlay on the flared skirt. I felt sexy as hell in this outfit and I hoped my guppy would appreciate it. *Bet he appreciates what's underneath it even more...*

Snagging my clutch, I double checked that I had some cash, my lipstick, phone, keys, the essentials and then I pulled open the door and dropped the damn thing.

"By the moon, you are stunning, sweetheart." Fischer openly ogled me, but I figured that was fair because I couldn't get a grip myself as I took in his appearance.

Black on black on black. *I think I might be dead right now. No, nope, I felt a flutter down below so I guess at least my vagina is still alive and well.*

Sharp black slacks with a button down long sleeved black dress shirt that he'd rolled to his elbows, *because of fucking course he would do that to weaken me*, and black shoes. His hair was parted on the side, his curls tamed, and his oak colored eyes sparkled with mischief that I didn't see in them often enough.

Oh, this is going to be a fun night.

Fischer bent over and grabbed my clutch, handing it to me and pulling me against his body. A sigh rushed out of my mouth at being pressed against him. His finger traced my jaw and tilted my chin up, giving him access to my lips, and he didn't hesitate. Any time with Fischer was soothing and loving and romantic. The way he touched me, looked at me, his gentleness set my skin on fire and scrambled my brain.

"I've missed kissing this mouth, sweetheart," he rasped and I cupped his cheek. He had some three day scruff going on and it was working in all the right ways.

"I'm so glad I get you all to myself tonight." I smiled at him and he chuckled.

"Feeling is mutual." He offered me his arm and I looped mine through, letting him guide me out of the door and I quickly locked it up with a spell and the key. Fischer opened the passenger door of the large SUV and I hopped inside. Pausing, his gaze traveled down my body and I blushed under his scrutiny. Shaking his head, his eyes were full of lust when they met mine and he just closed the door and moved around the front of the vehicle before sliding into his own seat.

"So, where we going, sweetheart?" he asked, turning the car on with the press of a button and smoothly clicking his seatbelt into position.

"Head into town, we're going to Magic Stixxx tonight, Guppy."

His head snapped in my direction so fast, some of his curls bounced and I giggled.

"Don't worry, I have it all planned." I grinned and he put the car in drive.

"Those sound like famous last words, sweetheart. If you wanted me to strip for you, I could've given you a hell of a show right inside the house."

I gasped and he winked at me. *He's full of surprises.*

Fischer

Chapter Thirteen

The drive to the club was short, but it didn't stop me from slipping my hand in hers and getting as much physical contact as possible. I'd been craving her fiercely and everything had gotten so fucked up after that shit went down in the garden with Sloane. She seemed to be doing fine, but seeing her laying in her bed lifeless, for hours, had nearly killed me. There were definitely times when I wished I was able to read her, but then I remembered how free I felt being with her, and those wishes faded to nothing.

We pulled into the parking lot of Magic Stixxx, the neon sign all lit up, and the logo was oddly phallic in shape with bursts of color shooting from the end. I'd assumed there'd be some kind of event here tonight, but the parking lot only had one other car, I mean, it was a Wednesday night, but weren't strip clubs open all hours and days of the week?

Breathing a sigh of relief that I wouldn't have to be surrounded by so many people, Saige's laughter had me casting her a look that said what's so funny?

"Sweet Fischer, did you think I'd really take you on a date to your worst nightmare? A packed club? The only person I want to be around tonight is you." She grinned, and I lifted our hands to my mouth and kissed her knuckles.

"Alright, sweetheart, I'm ready to be wined and dined... or whatever it is you have planned."

She squealed with excitement and flung open her door before

I could get my ass over there to open it for her. Saige met me at the front of the car and grabbed my hand, her mood was infectious and I found myself smiling at her enthusiasm.

The double doors were royal purple with studded leather accents and... *by the moon, is that velvet? The doors are fucking velvet. What have I gotten myself into here?*

"I'm freaking pumped, Fish, I think you're going to love this!" Her heels tapped across the see through plexiglass floor that was lit up underneath with neon dicks and boobs.

"Welcome to Magic Stixxx, where witches, mages, and humans alike can let go of their inhibitions, worries, and stress and let your wildest fantasies come to life!" A booming voice came from above and we looked up toward it. The upstairs was open, a banister running around the large space. The biggest man I'd ever seen in my life appeared at the top of the stairs, which were coincidentally, also purple velvet, and Saige clapped her hands with glee.

"I am Master Rupert, owner of this fine establishment, breaker of hearts, and dance guru." He held his arms out wide magnanimously, his draping purple velvet robe only adding to the effect. Yeah, he literally had a plush cape tied around his neck, the guy had a serious thing for purple velvet.

My eyes widened when I noticed the six inch heels he was sporting walking down the steps like a fucking runway model, fishnet stockings ran up his hairy legs and disappeared under a pair of leather shorts that did nothing to hide that monster cock he must've had to try and suck in to zip those fuckers.

"Rupe!" Saige shrieked and they met at the base of the stairs. He took her hand and spun her effortlessly before bringing her back and tugging her against his chest, her face lit up with amusement.

"Darling, it's been too long. Can't tell you how excited I was to get your call earlier. And who do we have here?" Rupert eyed me like I was a fire grilled hot dog that he wanted to squirt some condiments on and I flashed him a flirty smile that had him fanning his face theatrically.

"This is Fischer, he's my boyfriend," Saige blurted out and then looked worried at her label. We hadn't ever made this thing official, but she was gods damned right. *I am her boyfriend, though the label actually felt lesser than what we were, to be honest. But if she wants to claim me publicly, I'll take anything I can get.*

I made my way over to them and offered my hand in greeting, but the big dude let out the deepest belly laugh I've ever heard and tugged the both of us against his huge body. Saige met my eyes and we both busted up laughing.

"Your handshakes are no good here, and with what we're about to be doing, this hug will seem like child's play. Now," he released us and clapped three times in quick succession, "follow me to The Ballroom." He turned and began ascending the stairs, and I shot a look at my girl.

"And what exactly are we about to be doing?" I questioned as we climbed the steps.

She just laughed and shook her head. "That will ruin the surprise."

"I suddenly see why Cam likes to spank your ass, sweetheart," I whispered and her pouty lips dropped open in shock that I would say something like that. There were a lot of things she needed to learn about me, and I was going to damn well teach her. For some reason, she thought I was this gentle guy, when in reality there was a monster that lurked beneath my skin, though she did seem to calm him.

Rupert pushed through the doors to The Ballroom, which had one of their staple neon signs above the doors.

"Holy Neptune," I breathed and Rupert cackled like an evil genius.

"What were you expecting when I said The Ballroom?"

My eyes were looking around the room so quickly my brain was having trouble processing what I was seeing, but one thing I knew without a doubt, this had to be the gay club level of the establishment.

There were rainbow crystal chandeliers above each table and when I got closer I snorted a laugh when I realized the crystals were actually dick shaped. *Of course they are. Why would I expect anything different?*

There was a main stage with poles and a back wall that had leather cuffs attached. Jesus.

"We have theme nights, the last one was Sexy Subs night and I was quite pleased with the amount of people who took advantage of the cuff wall." Rupert grinned, watching me as I continued to look all around the room.

The barstools were high backed and, you guessed it, dick shaped. The floor tiles, intricate phallic shapes that looked almost hand painted. Wouldn't surprise me, honestly. There were purple velvet couches and the front of the bar was tufted with the shit. What really had me choking was the 'Cock Climbing Wall' that was made up of erect cocks of all shapes and sizes that jutted out in different directions. This wall was circular and surrounded a small stage that had a pole in the middle with a huge bell at the top that I'm guessing you could only get to ring once you made it to the top of mount mushroom-heads.

"Don't bother trying to figure out where all the dicks are in this room, Fischer. This is my penis paradise and people fucking love it!" He held his arms out wide and spun in a circle, his cape billowing out behind him.

"Over here, party people," Rupert directed, leading us to the dance floor.

Saige put her clutch down on the table and she was trembling with excitement.

"Tonight, I will be instructing the pair of you in the art of dancing." Rupert shimmied and I barked a laugh.

"Private dancing lessons?" I questioned Saige and she beamed at me.

"Do you like it? I thought it would be a great idea for a date since it's just one other person and hopefully it won't be too overwhelming for you?" I just stared at her. She chose this taking into consideration my inability to do a lot of public activities due to the emotional overload and I was just speechless. My mouth hung open and redness began snaking up her chest; she was nervous I wouldn't like this.

Stepping up against her, I leaned down and pressed my lips against hers. I felt her smile as she kissed me and then we were both grinning, which made it hard to kiss properly. So, I relented and buried my face against her throat and whispered, "I fucking love dancing, sweetheart. And I love that you did this for me. Now, let me show you my moves."

Saige pulled back and gave me a stern look, "Mr. Bahri, have you been holding back on me?" Her whole face lit up and she looked positively radiant with her shiny red hair in big fat curls that I wanted to sink my hands into. She reminded me of a firefly. Vibrant and every so often, she'd flash those glimpses of pure light that made my chest ache.

"There's a lot of me that you haven't seen yet, firefly." She blushed at the nickname, but it suited her well.

"Come on you two, the sexual tension is absolutely killing me, let that heat transfer to the dance floor," Rupert said dreamily, and when I chanced a look, he was sitting at a table with his hands folded under his chin with hearts in his damn eyes.

"So, what kind of dancing did you have in mind?" I questioned and both Saige and Rupert laughed with an evil edge, but that was fine, I was about to blow their fucking minds and then we'd see who was laughing.

"Oh, my stars, Fischer, where did you learn to move like that?" Saige was still bouncing with adrenaline beside me in the car from our dance lesson and I felt like hot shit.

"Well, I've always found music to be kind of an escape, quiets my mind. When I was younger, I watched videos and stuff and taught myself. Kind of hard without a partner, but I convinced Kai to learn with me, so we practiced a lot. He can dance almost as well as I can." I smirked at her and she shook her head in disbelief as she fanned herself.

"I'm just... wow. The way you can move your hips is criminal!"

"Oh, I can show you in more detail how I can move them, sweetheart." My voice sounded husky even to my own ears, but the past hour had been a sick kind of torture. Saige had rhythm and the way she'd sway her curvy hips and the perfection of her soft body pressed against mine had taken all my willpower to kill my boner before Rupert got more of a show.

She spun her hair around her finger and quirked an eyebrow, "I think I'd like to see that."

"Oh, you think? Well, if you're not sure about it I can just—" I was cut off by her lifting my fingers to her lips and sucking two of them into her mouth while her eyes pinned me in my place. Her tongue swirled and she bit down on my fingers, a challenge.

Quirking an eyebrow at her, I used my other hand to grip her wrist that held my fingers captive and I pulled them out of her mouth. As great as it felt to have them there, I had other ideas. And those ideas did not involve fucking this woman in a rental car.

"Take me home, Fischer."

The ten minute drive it took to get to town earlier took seven on the way home. My cock was uncomfortable and after weeks of torturing myself with small touches and fleeting kisses, I couldn't take it anymore. I was fucking wired and this needed to happen. Now. Sliding into the parking spot by the garage, I grabbed her hand and squeezed.

. . .

"Stay right there, sweetheart," I ordered, hopping out of the car and running around to her side to open her door.

"Such a gentleman," she said with a fake ass southern accent that made me snort.

"I'm about as much a southern gentleman as Rhett Butler, and you're about to see exactly what I mean," I growled, and she shrieked when I leaned in the car and hauled her out, tossing her over my shoulder and kicking the door closed.

"Unlock the door."

Her hand glowed and a burst of gold hit the lock, and then we were moving inside and headed right for the stairs.

"You can put me down now, I'm not exactly a lightweight." She squirmed, *and did she sound embarrassed? That's not like Saige. I've never once heard her make any negative comments about her body.*

"You're perfect, and I'm carrying you to the bed. Don't insult me, sweetheart. I know I'm technically the smallest out of the four of us, but I'm solid, and if I want to carry my witch around like a caveman, then I fucking will."

She sucked in a breath and I knew she'd be blushing. The words coming out of my mouth had slightly surprised me, I wasn't usually this assertive or aggressive. It had been a while since I'd had a session with Sloane, and those always kept the darkness at bay… Shaking away those thoughts, I focused again on the feel of my witch against my body, running a hand up the back of her thigh. *I need to feel her...*

Entering her room, I lowered her to her feet and spun her around, my mouth going to her neck as my fingers traced down the zipper along her back.

"Firefly," I rasped, "tell me to stop if you don't want this to happen right now, because once I slip that little zipper down and see what's underneath this dress, I don't think I'll be able to stop myself from ravishing you."

"Take it off of me, Fischer," she whispered. The slight wobble to her voice was a clear indication that she was also being driven wild with lust.

Sliding her hair off to the slide, I ran my nose up her neck and smiled against her warm skin when she shivered. My hands found the tiny zipper and I pulled it down slowly, the only sounds in the room, her short breaths.

"I feel like I'm unwrapping a present just for me, sweetheart," I growled against her ear and she sighed, leaning back against me, pushing her ass against my cock.

"All for you, Fish." She spun out of my hold when the zipper was all the way down and gave me a lusty smirk. I still couldn't read her emotions for shit, but I was getting better at doing so without my powers, and right now, she was feeling sexy as hell and turned on.

"I picked this out with you in mind..." she trailed off. Her hands came up to the sleeves of her dress and slid them down her arms before letting the whole thing drop in a poof around her feet.

Dark green lace. So much lace. The corset was stunning on her figure, it squeezed her breasts to perfection, cinching in at her waist and stopping just after, my eyes trailed down and I swallowed roughly at the matching panties. Saige stepped forward out of the pile of tulle and I circled my finger in the air, wanting her to spin and let me see what the back looked like.

Her cheeks were pink with her blushing and she smiled softly as she did a one-eighty and stopped, looking back at me over her shoulder so she could see my reaction.

Cheeky little lace boy shorts disappeared between her ass cheeks and I groaned loudly at the sight, her little giggle making me bring my eyes back up to hers.

"So I take it you like it?" she asked sassily and I stalked toward her, the predator moving in for the kill.

"I fucking love it. The color matches your eyes, firefly. Now, get your pretty ass on that bed and let me show you how much."

Saige

Chapter Fourteen

There was a beast inside of Fischer. He'd alluded to that fact a few times, as had the other guys, and I was curious. Probably foolish of me, but I wanted to see it. He was always so calm and collected, quiet and reserved, gentle. I needed to see that darkness inside of him and see if I could tame it, because in this moment, I wanted everything he had to offer.

Lying back on my bed, my heels hit the floor with a thud, and I watched as he tugged his shirt off and dropped it by my discarded dress. Heat pooled in my belly and I licked my lips as I let my eyes study the dragon wings tattoo he had artfully displayed across his chest. The colors popped beautifully with his bronze skin and I stifled the urge to run my tongue over it.

He kicked his shoes off and removed his socks, his eyes staying locked on mine. When his hands moved to his belt, I sucked in a breath and wiggled on the bed, the need to be touched was strong. The weight of his belt had his pants sliding easily off of his narrow hips and a clang rang out in the air when his belt buckle hit the floor.

Fischer's body was stunning; he wasn't stacked with muscles or anything, but the definition was there. He was wider than Kai, not as jacked as Cam, and not quite as lean as Sloane. Delicious. Fish was fucking delicious.

"Wanna take a picture?" Fischer jokes, hands on his hips and looking at me with heat in his eyes.

Keeping my face even, I sassed, "I mean... maybe? Would you let me?"

It was so hard not to giggle and give away the fact that I'm fucking with him when his eyebrows lifted in surprise as he studied my face searching for any indication of what I was actually thinking. But nope. He can't read me. His gaze went right through me and my lip twitched just a hair, making him growl.

"You fucking with me, firefly?" His voice was so deep, the hairs on my arms lifted in warning... *is the real Fischer going to come out and play?*

Shrugging my shoulders, I bit my lip, the tension in the room rising with every second. Just when I was about to open my mouth to say something, anything, he moved. Like there was a tether between us and we were on a collision course.

"Tell me what you want, tell me what you need me to do..." he begged, climbing up onto the bed between my legs, running his nose up the length of my torso to my neck.

He's begging me? No. That's not what I want.

Reaching for his face, I pulled his mouth over mine and pressed a kiss to his lips. "I need to see you, Guppy. Show me who you really are in there." Nipping his bottom lip, he groaned into my mouth.

"I need you to tell me what to do, sweetheart," he whispers, but I shake my head.

"No. There's nothing here I need to pull your mind away from, you're here with me. If being submissive is who you are, that's what I want. If you've never had the chance to find out what else you might enjoy, then I want you to figure it out with me. We can have our own little world, Fischer." I smiled before leaning up to lick his bottom lip.

He's staring at me so intensely, I half expect to feel his presence in my brain at any moment, but he just holds my eyes. The need to be touched is traveling through my body, my hips started to lift, seeking out his body.

"I want to see what you like, I want to watch your face while I do every last wicked thing in my head to your beautiful body. I'm going to make you mine," he promised, his dark curls falling into his eyes as they flashed black, and fuck if that didn't make me wetter.

Suddenly, his arms were under my back and he was pulling me upright, undoing all of the little eye hooks that ran down the length of my spine. My breasts tumbled out of the corset and he sat back on his heels, his thick cock jutting out from between his legs. Leaning back on my palms, my chest automatically pushed forward, his eyes tracking the movement like an animal on the hunt. His hands landed on either side of my hips, still not touching me, and the anticipation drove me crazy.

"Lay back."

I let myself fall back onto the pillows, my hair fanned out around my head, and a moment later, his hands were peeling my panties down my thighs and I felt lightheaded.

"Fish..." his name nothing but a whisper in the quiet room.

Fingertips moved from my throat down my breastbone, over the swell of my stomach, and softly over my pussy. He's going to kill me with his gentle brushes and smooth caresses. Lifting one of my legs up to his mouth, he pressed his lips to my ankle bone and watched my face as he kissed down my calf, so softly that I felt his breath more than the slide of his mouth.

Whimpering, I reached for him and he shook his head.

"Please, please touch me," I begged, reaching for his hand in an attempt to put it where I needed to feel him but he pulled back and slapped me right on my cunt. I practically leapt off the bed with a squeal.

"Be still. I'm cataloging every square inch of this body, sweetheart, because I will taste every last part of you tonight. Be patient."

Oh, okay, we're going to just ignore the fact that you slapped my pussy then?

As if he could tell what I was thinking, his eyes glinted with darkness, and a sinister smile that I'd never seen on him before flashed, taking my gods damn breath away. And then in the blink of an eye, his face was buried between my legs, a dark chuckle vibrating against my clit.

"Keep these legs open for me, I'm going to slide my tongue up so far inside of you, you're going to see stars."

His mouth and tongue tortured me, nibbling, sucking, fucking. His groans drove me on and soon, my hips were bucking against his mouth.

"Fischer!" My body wound tighter and tighter, and just when I was sure my head was about to explode, he pulled back and flipped me over, tugging my hips up and going right back to lapping at me from behind, his tongue licking a line of fire from my cunt to my ass, and I moaned because it felt so fucking amazing.

"Oh gods, oh gods!" I called out into the pillows, unable to lift my head and give this the volume it deserved but then his fingers were there, pressing into my tight hole. It was impossible for me to know how many, but it felt like more than one, and then a smart slap to my butt cheek before he commanded, "Relax."

Inhaling a shuddering breath, I willed my muscles to chill the fuck out and the moment that happened, he slipped his fingers right up inside of my ass again and an anguished mix between a cry and a moan exploded into the pillow.

"Good girl," he praised me, reaching around to rub my clit while the fingers buried in me stroked and stretched. "Have you ever taken someone here, firefly?" Fischer asked me, his teeth nibbling against my ass cheek.

"Once," I panted while he continued his ministrations and I tried not to think about that one time and who it had been with. How unenjoyable it had been.

His chest pressed into my back as he stretched up and whispered in my ear, "I'm going to fuck your pussy, and then I'm going to finish in your ass."

"By the moon, Fischer," I moaned, my body temperature rising with each passing second. He pulled his fingers out of me and I pushed up onto my knees, his large hand turning my face to his so he could devour my mouth. With my back pressed to his front, he toyed with my nipples and ran his hands over every inch of skin he could.

"Wanna taste you," I murmured against his lips.

"You want to suck on this dick, sweetheart?" he rasped, running his tongue over my jawline.

"Yes, please. I need to see how you fit in there."

My head was pulled back and the slight sting of his fist clenching my hair sent a rush through my body. Lifting my eyes, our gazes collided and I sucked in a breath at the utter darkness that had taken over. *There's the part of him that he doesn't like to let out.*

"Lay down, Guppy, let me lick you."

Groaning, he flopped back against the pillows and I eased my way between his thick thighs, letting my breasts run over the hard length of him. Dark hair started at his chest and ran down straight to his dick, and it was sexy as hell. Puckering my lips, I pressed them on the large head, sighing at how smooth it felt against my skin.

"Fuck," he cursed under his breath when I ran my tongue over his slit, tasting his unique flavor and needing more. I gripped the base of his dick and sucked the tip into my mouth, swirling my tongue all over and he groaned his approval.

"Yes, sweetheart, suck my cock. Take it in as far as you can, I want to see it disappear down your throat," he growled, and I squeezed my thighs together, seeking friction. My sweet Fischer had a filthy mouth.

Doing as he requested, I let him fill my mouth with his hardness; he was thick and delicious. When he hit the back of my throat, I coughed, and pulled back a little, but then his hand was there, gripping my hair and pushing my face right back down onto his cock. Shit.

Trying to breathe through my nose before I passed out, I got ahold of myself and swallowed, locking him in and then I hummed.

"Fucking hell, sweetheart. You suck dick like a goddess," he grunted, his hips began to thrust and he fucked my mouth with no hesitation. Tears started building from the onslaught, but holy moon maidens, I was fucking loving it. Glancing up at him, his eyes were black and his free hand moved leisurely over his nipple and I watched with total fascination as he squeezed it.

"Gotta feel you," Fischer rumbled, pulling me up by the shoulders and smashing his lips against mine as he fluidly flipped us so that he was between my thighs and I squeezed him tightly, urging him to connect us in a way that we hadn't yet.

"Please, fuck me. Get inside of me, I can't wait."

His hand landed on my throat, his large fingers squeezing gently as he looked into my eyes and shook his head, like he was trying to clear his mind. The blackness of his eyes began receding and his features softened a bit.

"Shit. Shit. Did I hurt you?" He sounded pained and when he realized he was gripping my neck, he pulled his hand back like I'd burnt him.

"Hell no, you didn't hurt me. That was hot as hell, I want you. Just you..." I ran my fingers over his lips, his breaths hard and hot over my skin.

"Sweetheart, I don't want to hurt you. I've never done this before."

My eyes widened. What did he mean he hadn't done this before? Sex with a woman?

Chuckling, he shook his head like he'd read my thoughts. "I've been with women, I mean I've never been with someone that I couldn't read. Someone that I couldn't tell immediately that what

I was doing was wanted. I can't tell what you're thinking, there's no bursts of ecstasy swirling in the air, there's no lust rolling off of your body, no excitement," he explained, looking sheepish, like maybe he was embarrassed.

"Fischer. You might not be getting visuals or however it is that works for you... the ecstasy you usually see? Those are my moans when your hands are on my skin. The lust? That's every time you make me shout out your name and beg for more. And the excitement?" I grabbed his hand and pressed it against my cunt. "The excitement is right here. Do you feel how wet I am? I'm loving everything you're doing to me and there's nothing you could do in this bed tonight that I wouldn't fucking love."

"Fucking hell," he smirked, dipping his fingers inside my wetness. "You really want me, don't you, sweetheart?"

Wrapping my arms around his neck, I tugged him down and pressed my forehead against his "More than you know."

His lips never left mine when he buried himself to the hilt and when I tried to tip my head back to scream, he bit my lips and whispered against my mouth not to fucking move.

"You feel perfect, silky and hot. Jesus. Made for me." Fischer's mouth never quit dropping the dirtiest encouragements and my hips moved to match his pace, our bodies doing a different dance than earlier, and despite this being the first time, we moved beautifully together.

He stretched me, filled me, his thrusts increasing in speed, and when his mouth sucked on one of my nipples, I came so hard, I couldn't help but call out his name.

When I opened my eyes, his monster inside was back and he had a smile on his face that I'm positive Lucifer himself couldn't recreate. He pulled out of me and leaned over to my nightstand, the sound of the drawer opening let me know he was looking for something, but I couldn't be fucked to pay attention. Post orgasmic bliss was running through my veins. The drawer slammed shut and there he was, rising over me like a dark god, or maybe a devil.

Fischer had a small bottle of lube in his hand, which he opened and squeezed onto his fingers, looking at me with so much intensity, I moved to close my legs and he smacked my thigh in warning.

"Don't even think about hiding what's mine," he growled, and my stomach clenched with desire at his claiming words.

"What are you doing?" I asked innocently.

"You know what I'm doing, firefly," he rasped out, his voice deeper than usual, his fingers rubbing together, getting nice and slick. "Put that pillow under your ass and then open those legs," he commanded, and fuck if I didn't slip the pillow under my hips in two seconds flat. I spread my legs but frowned when he shook his head.

"Like this," he directed, pushing my knees back toward my chest. "Hold your knees."

This was quite possibly the most exposing position I'd ever been in, it made me feel like I was serving myself up to him on a platter. I could still see him from between my thighs as he got closer and ran his fingers up and down my ass, getting me ready. When his finger pressed against my ass, I clenched involuntarily and he moved his other hand up to rub at my clit, the distraction enough to make me relax for him to push through the tight muscles there.

"Oh stars, Fish..." I moaned, the feeling of him causing a slight sting before it dissipated into pure pleasure.

"I need to stretch you out before you'll be able to take my cock, firefly. And you will take it. All of it, nice and snug in your tight ass."

Words weren't possible from me at that point and I lifted my hips in encouragement. Another stretching sensation, another burn, and then *fuuuuuck*. I'd had no idea it could feel like this.

He'd barely been torturing me for five minutes and I was already climbing the mountain to pleasure peak.

"Look how you swallow up two of my fingers, so hot," he murmured, his thumb still swirling on my clit.

It was almost as though he had split personalities. The sweet, submissive mage who made me feel cherished and safe, and then this dominating, intense monster that he tried to keep chained up inside his mind. Why though? My thoughts were cut off when another finger pressed its way inside and I whimpered from the stretch.

"Keep still, firefly. Not much longer. Your ass looks so good stuffed like this. I knew it would. Can't wait to see how you squeeze my cock." Fischer teased me with pressure on my clit, swiping through my folds to gather more wetness that seemed to have no end in sight.

"You're ready for me," Fischer informed me, his voice soft and calm. The voice of a predator. The voice of a man who didn't get riled up, the kind of man who knew what he wanted and was going to fucking take it without any theatrics.

"Please," I begged. The need to feel him again was overpowering any anxieties about what was about to happen. I was too turned on, too addicted to him.

Fischer leaned over me, desire burning in his eyes, his face shiny with a slight layer of sweat, he looked beautiful and dangerous, and when his cock pressed against my ass, I took a deep breath, I'd never get what I wanted if I didn't let him in.

"Push when I push against you, firefly. Let me in," he encouraged as he pressed against me and I pushed like he'd told me and then he was there. Oh gods, he was there.

"Ahhh," I squirmed; it burned more than his fingers.

"Shhh, sweetheart. Look at me, it will feel better in a minute, I promise."

I wasn't so sure at that moment, but the look of pure bliss on his face and the trust I had in him, in all of them, had me nodding and tugging his mouth to mine. Our tongues lapped at one another, lazily, like we had all night. And I guessed we did, so when he moved further inside of me and I sucked in a sharp breath, his hand snaked between our bodies and found my clit again. The pleasure taking from the bite of pain, creating a heady fucking cocktail of endorphins and adrenaline that told me an earth shattering orgasm was in my future.

Fischer

Chapter Fifteen

My hands were gripping her hips so tightly, my fingers were leaving indentations in her skin. The beast inside perked up at that, loving every way that we were marking what was ours. I'd lived my entire life shoving this part of myself down into the deep recesses of my psyche because he made me feel out of control. Referring to a part of your own personality as another entity was highly fucked up, but *he* wasn't me... I'd done everything in my power to ensure that we never became one being.

He was sick and depraved. Dark, twisted, hungry for blood and darkness.

Sloane's domineering ways kept him away. In the past, when I'd been too far gone, when *he'd* taken the wheel, Sloane had been the only one who could dig deep and bring me back to reality. So why, in the name of Jupiter, was I sharing this sweet woman with *him*?

Because you know we're the same person and she wants me just as much as she needs you.

It wasn't often I heard his voice, I'd locked that shit down years ago, and yet, with my cock sunk to the hilt inside Saige's ass, his voice was loud in my head.

'She wants the monster. Give it to her. Show her what we can do,' he taunted.

'Shut the fuck UP, Faris!' I shouted at *him* in my mind.

Grunting, I started snapping my hips against her ass, each cry that slipped through her swollen red lips spurred me to go harder.

"Fischer, gods... yes. Fuck me harder!" Her hands squeezed my upper arms, the bite of her nails like kisses of fire on my skin.

'Fuck her ass. It's yours. Make. Her. Scream,' Faris growled and my balls actually shivered.

"You want me to make you scream, little girl?" I taunted her, an inch from her nose, her feet tickling the hair on my head.

"Yes," she moaned as she thrashed her head from side to side, my cock pumping in and out of her tight ass relentlessly.

'Show her what she needs. Show her what we want.'

'You're a sick fuck,' I snarled, disgusted.

Pulling my cock from her body, I flipped her over so fast, she barely had a moment to protest before I slammed back inside of her.

"Jesus, Fischer!" she screamed and I gathered her hair in my hand, pulling her head back so that her curvy body bowed beautifully. Creamy white skin that was glistening with a sheen of sweat and the red marks from my hands lit up like a work of art.

My free hand traced the curve of her spine, veering up over her shoulder and my fingers wrapped tightly around her throat. The devil inside me grinned wickedly and pushed himself to the front of our psyche when a squeak of surprise left her mouth.

My actions, my movements were no longer only mine as we shared our body for the first time. It's always been one or the other, either I'm in control, or he is. This was different and I wasn't sure how I felt about it yet. But if she wants all of me, she's got to experience him, too. This is me. This is us.

"Do you like the way our fat cock stretches your ass, firefly? You squeeze us so beautifully." We pulled her hair and straightened our bodies so we were both on our knees and our mouth pressed against her ear. "Now that we've had this ass, how are we not going to fuck it every day?" She moaned and we knew she was close to coming.

"You'd love that, wouldn't you, dirty girl? Touch yourself. We can't wait to feel your ass clenching our cock."

Our grip on her throat tightened and her fingers found her clit, and the sounds she was making were criminal. *Absolutely fucking criminal.*

"You're a filthy thing. Look how needy you are. We're going to fuck you all night long. Shit, maybe we'll video call the others and let them watch us defile your sweet ass."

At the first flutter, we squeezed her neck enough to cut off her air supply and her hand clawed at our forearm in an attempt to pull our arm away, but not yet. And from the way she was furiously rubbing herself, she didn't really want us to. Dropping her hair, we snaked our arm around her hips and fucked her senseless, her orgasm tore through her forcefully and we let go of her neck just in time for an earth shattering scream that had our cum thundering through our balls and firing deep inside her hot ass.

We continued swirling our hips slightly, ensuring she was thoroughly marked with our seed. Fuck, this witch was making us feel all kinds of crazy things.

Breed her. Breed her. Breed her.

What the fuck!?

Faris flashed images of my woman with a swollen belly and even rounder tits that startled me enough I pulled out from her body and pulled her down so she could rest her head on my chest.

'What the fuck are you playing at? I'm not knocking her up,' I promised.

'Yet,' Faris vowed.

'Get the fuck out of my head. You're deranged,' I argued with this other being that lived inside my head.

'You're deranged, Fischer. We're the same person. Accept it.'

'Never,' I swore.

'She loves when I call her firefly. Are you going to tell her that it's me calling her that? That I'm claiming that name for her? You can't

hide me forever,' Faris taunted and I really wished the bastard would just shut the fuck up.

"Fish? Are you okay?" Saige's small voice pulled me out of my internal war and I stroked her cheek.

"Yeah, sweetheart. I'm more than okay. That was amazing."

Saige popped up, her face directly over mine as she peered down at me, her hair falling over us.

"Your eyes are still black." Her finger ran over my cheekbone and her brow furrowed in thought.

"Kiss me."

Her soft lips pressed lightly against mine and her tongue teasingly licked the seam of my lips. Opening for her, she deepened the kiss and I felt myself returning to normal as I pushed Faris back and regained full control of my mind.

"Thank you, sweetheart. I didn't... hurt you, did I?" I'd never fucking forgive myself.

The corner of her mouth lifted in amusement.

"No. You didn't hurt me. You surprised the hell out of me, Fischer. I could tell there was some darkness in you, and I'm not sure what I expected, but that just surpassed anything I could've dreamed up." Saige smiled above me and she was so gorgeous it made me breathless.

"You weren't afraid?"

Part of me didn't want to know the answer to that question, but even then as my hand smoothed down her back, I wanted to know. Needed to know.

"Afraid isn't the right word. Excited, on edge, nervous to see how far you were going to take it. I'm not scared of you, Fischer. You've protected me, cared for me, and despite how hard you just fucked me, those things, the way you are so sweet with me lets me know that you would never hurt me. Even if you want to a little bit during sex. But I wanted to explore this with you. How do you feel now?"

"My girl. Always brave and selfless," I murmured, tucking

some hair behind her ear and pulling her down to lay her head on my chest once more. "There is something dark inside me, sweetheart. It's best if it stays there. That side of me doesn't deserve to see the light of day."

"But how can you say that?" she questioned softly, her fingertips moved across my naked chest, making nonsensical drawings, but the touching had my heart racing nonetheless.

"Just trust me, sweetheart. Nobody wants that side of me. Did you enjoy yourself dancing earlier?" I changed the subject because I couldn't talk about Faris anymore. Shit, I already let the bastard out to play earlier and he was still too fresh in my headspace to give him any more thought.

"I had so much fun. I hope Rupert didn't overwhelm you too much, I'd imagine he's pretty open with whatever emotion he's feeling," she chuckled.

I let my mind drift back to the club and then I jolted upright, Saige startling and looking at me with panicked eyes.

"Holy shit," I breathed.

"What? What's wrong?"

"I didn't feel any of his emotions, none of his thoughts, nothing," I confessed slowly, my brain trying to catch up with that. I'd been so wrapped up in my girl earlier, I hadn't even realized that my power had been muted.

"How is that possible, though? I thought it was rare for that to happen?"

"It is. I'm wondering now if you blocked my power."

"Me?" she squeaked and shook her head in denial. "I would never do that!"

"Not on purpose, sweetheart. We'll have to see what happens tomorrow when we're around other people to see if it happens again. There's been a lot of weird stuff going on, so it's not unreasonable to think," I said gently.

We laid there for a while, just softly touching each other. But I finally got out of bed and went to the bathroom to clean up.

When I came back, Saige was laying on her stomach, her legs crossed at the ankles, scrolling through her phone.

"Oh, I'm gonna clean up quick, then do you want to have a picnic with me in the kitchen?"

"A picnic. In the kitchen?" I grinned and she walked toward me without a stitch of clothing.

"Yeah, why not? Picnics are our thing, aren't they?" She winked and closed the bathroom door behind her, but not before I saw her bright red ass.

She was back in a couple of minutes, heading to her dresser to find something to wear. My feet were quiet as I stalked over to her, pressing myself against her back.

"A picnic with you sounds amazing, but I think I'm going to just have another snack first before..."

We made it to the kitchen an hour later.

Saige

Chapter Sixteen

Friday morning arrived and I knew I needed to get myself into The Pig today to get some administrative stuff done. Frank and Arlo were running everything else today, but I liked to be in charge of my paperwork and financials. The month was flying by and I couldn't believe tomorrow was my birthday.

After a quick shower and throwing on some comfortable clothes, I made my way to the kitchen and found Gran sitting at the table sipping her coffee with another mug of steaming goodness waiting for me.

"You're the best. Thanks, Gran." I slipped into my seat and moaned when the coffee hit my mouth. Sweet, sweet creation.

"What's your plan for the day, child? I need to put the finishing touches on my costu- I mean, outfit for your birthday party tomorrow. Other than that, I'll probably just do some upkeep in the gardens," Gran informed me, but I'd heard her little slip up. A costume, I didn't know whether to be amused or terrified. Okay, let's be real, I was equally feeling both of those things when it came to anything that woman did.

"Just need to run into The Pig for a few hours, the guys are taking care of some business today, something with that property, I'm not even sure exactly what each of their job titles are. Probably should ask that, huh?" I chuckled, shaking my head at myself. How have we never discussed that?

"Ah, well there's been a lot of shit going on lately, dear. You got the gist of what they do, and clearly, they're all intelligent men who have a steady income. Much better than some deadbeat freeloader. Like that limp dick Bryce. Has he been giving you any trouble, by the way? I saw him a couple of weeks ago skulking around town like the cockroach he is," Gran informed me, her cornflower blue eyes shining with concern.

Yeah, Gran knew what I'd gone through with him. I'd nearly lost myself during that shit show of a relationship, and I still got embarrassed thinking about how long I'd put up with his shit. But I didn't want anyone to know the levels of fucked up he was reaching now. Just thinking about the way he'd groped me in the middle of the grocery store had my heart racing and my stomach clenching in disgust.

"No, I think he knows better now. He's already been roughed up by Fischer, and Kai confessed the other day that he throat punched him a few weeks back."

Gran's laughter lifted my spirits and snapped me out of that horrible headspace that I always seemed to dive right back into when it came to him. Abuse will do that to a person, though. There's good days and bad. Days where you give yourself the credit you deserve for being an absolute badass and taking control of your own destiny, and then there's days where the tiniest event can send you spiraling down the cliff of unhealthy thoughts where you can't see the light through the darkness.

Refusing to be sucked into that black pit of despair, I focused on my vibrant grandmother as she talked hardcore shit about Bryce and praised my guys for their desire to defend my honor.

"I need to head out, Gran. I'll be home later tonight," I told her, standing and pushing in my chair.

"Take that lazy fox with you. He's been giving me crazy side eye the past week and I think he's plotting on me," Gran whispered conspiratorially, her gaze darting around the room as though Maven was lying in wait, ready to pounce her ass.

"You know I always take him, and he's been side eyeing you

since he moved in here, but don't act like you don't do the same thing to him. He's a fox, Gran, not some nemesis. Just ignore him," I suggested, grabbing my backpack and making my way to the mudroom.

"Be safe!" Gran shouted and then muttered a string of words that I was too far away to understand.

"Mave! Let's go, boy!" I called out and listened for movement. A soft thump upstairs, and the slow progression of little creaks in the floorboards let me know that at least the grump was up and on his way downstairs. *Worse than a teenager, I swear.*

Once I had my bike ready, Maven showed up with a mouthful of food and the most severe stink eye I'd ever seen on man or beast. Throwing my hands up, I picked him up and deposited him into the basket.

"IT'S YOUR OWN FAULT, maybe you should wake up on time next time if you want to eat breakfast. There's food at The Pig anyway, so quit your growling," I scolded.

I set off for the town. Damn, it was already getting hot outside and it wasn't even eleven yet. Today, I'd opted for a racer-back tank top that said 'I'm kind of a big dill' with the shop's signature logo, a crescent moon with a cartoon pig, on the back. Since I wasn't officially on the clock today, I also opted for girl's best friends, yoga pants. Hell yes.

"Oh great," I mumbled to myself when I got close enough to the store to see Sloane leaning up against the red brick front of the building. Decked out in all black with glimpses of his tattoos peeking out, he looked every bit the surly bad boy that he was. Sloane had been avoiding me. At least, that was the best I could make of the situation. Why else had I only seen him a handful of times in the past several weeks?

I guess a smoking hot threesome in the open air doesn't cause Sloane Sullivan to make any promises or change anything about his demeanor. At least I knew he was an asshole from the start, right? My expectations of him weren't high to begin with.

Hopping off my bike and helping Maven out of his basket, I planned on ignoring Sloane. I really did. But then I walked past him without acknowledging that he was there and I guess that was just too much for him to handle.

"Good to see you too, Red. I'm fine, thanks for asking," he smarted off, and my head whipped in the direction he was standing so fast, I felt something crack in my neck. But it felt good so I knew I hadn't just inadvertently snapped my own neck. *That would be something I'd do.*

Sloane's eyes sparkled with excitement at the promise of a verbal sparring, and I narrowed my own at him in warning.

"That last time I saw you, I'm pretty sure I said hello to you and you ignored me. Forgive me if I can't keep up with your mood swings, dear. So, you're acting like you know me today?" I snapped at him and his jaw ticked in annoyance.

"The last time you saw me was after I'd come home to my own apartment and been forced to listen to some rather interesting sounds." My eyes widened when I thought back to Kai fucking me in his room. "And trust me, there was nowhere I could have gone in there to escape those noises, Red." Sloane laughed without humor and I watched his forearm flex as he clenched and released his fist multiple times. Guess the urge to use his magic was strong at the moment.

Before I could open my mouth to respond, my phone started ringing, the ringtone alerting me to exactly who it was. My stomach dropped and Sloane must've noticed the change in my expression because he straightened up and closed the distance between us.

"Everything okay, Red?" He questioned as I dug my phone out of my pocket. Thank the gods for yoga pants with pockets. Pure magic.

Giving him a quick nod and a smile that I'm sure didn't reach my eyes, I hit the green accept button.

"Hello?"

"Saige, darling. How are you?" Her voice filtered through the earpiece and she couldn't even disguise her lack of interest over the phone.

"I'm fine, Mom. How are you?" I glanced at Sloane and an indecipherable expression flashed across his face before I could examine it closer.

"Wonderful as always. I just wanted to call and wish you a happy birthday. Unfortunately, I won't be able to make it to celebrate in person. The big twenty-eight, huh? Hard to imagine that it's been that long since you were born. When I was twenty-eight, I had a seven year old." Laurie sighed and my blood boiled, because no, no she did not have a seven year old. I'd been living alone with Gran for years already at that point.

"Well, thanks for calling..." I trailed off, unsure of what else to say because I honestly had nothing to say to the woman.

"Are you spending your birthday with anyone special this year?" she pried, and I rolled my eyes. Of course she'd ask about men.

"Actually, I am. My three boyfriends," I stated matter of factly and smiled smug as hell when I heard her choke on whatever she was drinking.

"Three? You have three boyfriends?"

"Sure do," I replied, locking my eyes on Sloane's. "Three really sexy mages. They're amazing."

"Why three? Why not four, or five?" She laughed.

"Hmm, well, there's potential for more. But I'm not sold yet," I informed her, but it wasn't Laurie I was having this conversation with. It was the asshole in front of me with eyes cold as ice and anger that radiated off of him in waves of heat.

"I see. Well, I have to go. Things to do. Happy Birthday."

The line clicked when she ended the call, not even waiting to see if I had anything else to say. Typical.

"Your mom?" Sloane questioned as I stuffed my phone back in my pocket.

"Obviously," I rolled my eyes and went to spin away from him to head inside, but he gripped my arm and held me in place.

"Everything okay, Red?"

Glancing down at his fingers, which were tightly wrapped around my bicep, I lifted my gaze and narrowed my eyes.

"What the hell do you care, Sloane? You've made it perfectly clear that not only are you not actually interested in me romantically, but you can't seem to even be my friend. I tolerate you because of the others. I've been nothing but nice to you and yet you still act like a pompous asshole. Let go of my arm, now," I snarled, surprised by the nasty tone of my voice. Honestly, I didn't even know I was capable of such venom. It did the trick though when moments later, my arm was released.

Spinning on my heel, I didn't even bother to look back for his reaction. *You're a bad bitch, Saige Wildes. Keep walking and don't fucking turn around.* Before I could even register what I was doing, I fired a burst of magic at the door of the shop and it opened forcefully just in time for me to stride right through and with a flick of my wrist, it slammed shut behind me.

Fuck Sloane Sullivan.

AFTER AN HOUR of isolating myself in the back room, I felt calm enough to come back out and face customers, and Frank and Arlo, who I had practically ignored in my haze of agitation and fury. I'd actually felt pretty light headed once I'd gotten inside the building and my body temperature was doing a lot of weird shit again. At least I haven't been being pulled into another realm... *no, the demon prince just decided to hunt me down, break into my home, and taunt me.*

The guys were going to be furious when they found out. Why hadn't I told them yet? When I'd first woken up from my time in Besmet with Bram the last time, I'd told them about him briefly. Not that he was borderline psychotic and had serious delusions regarding our 'relationship'. At the time, I never thought I'd see him again, but then there he was in my freaking bathroom while I was naked as a jaybird. Groaning in my head, I knew I'd fucked up. Cam for sure was going to be really livid.

But Bram wasn't a threat to me, for some strange reason, he just wanted me. *Did I want him like that?* The whole thing sounded so messy, I shut it down in my brain. There was enough shit going on that I didn't need to add to it by considering adding another boyfriend. *Would they get along?*

"You doing okay today, sweet thing?" Frank's question snapped me out of my thoughts.

"Oh yeah, I'm sorry, just have a lot on my mind this afternoon. Everything going okay here? I popped in to do some admin stuff," I explained, moving behind the bar to mix up an elixir for myself.

"Yeah, doing great. Miranda and her girl stopped in a few hours ago. Annie dropped off a couple of drawings for you, I put them by the register. We're probably going to need to harvest some crystals soon, they've been selling like hotcakes. Oh, and quite a few people were asking about the next Witching Hour event, it's been close to a month now since the last one," Arlo rattled off all of the important information and I followed along as I poured some water into a glass, a drop of azure spirit, a pinch of pink salt, and a dash of fairy sprinkle, which as soon as it touched the liquid, the whole concoction changed to a beautiful teal blue with pink smoke rolling off the rim.

"What are you mixing up?" Frank asked, peering over my shoulder.

"Hmm? Oh, I have this hellish headache, so it's just something to relax me a little bit and hopefully help stabilize this pounding in my head," I explained, reaching for the glass and frowning when he batted my hand out of the way.

"Here, let me add a few things to this, I know just the trick." Frank snapped his fingers, as if a brilliant idea had just come to him and he started grabbing different ingredients as Arlo directed me to a barstool. I sank down onto it with a sigh of relief, because damn, my head really was starting to hurt.

The doorbell alerted me that someone had come in but I didn't have the desire to look and see who it was, luckily, or maybe not so luckily, they made themselves known quickly.

"Saige, we must speak with you at once. The stars have been loud in our heads the past several hours and we have things to share with you," Roberta announced as she sat down beside me in a flourish of color and old lady perfume.

"Yes, yes, it is of utmost urgency, dear girl. When the stars speak, we listen," Matilda added, nodding her head so fast, I almost thought she was tripping on some damn fine drugs.

"Back off ladies, Saige has a headache. Let her drink this first before you make it any worse with your ramblings!" Frank ordered. The two women had the good sense to look slightly apologetic, even though I could still feel their excitement from the way their bodies were trembling which was causing their gaudy, dangling earrings to clink together like some sort of miniature wind chimes.

Frank slid the glass tumbler to me, the color now a glowing purple with blue steam rising from the top. Shit, at this point, I'd drink a jar of pickle juice if I thought it would cure this hell. I downed the whole thing in three swallows, it was delicious. Surprisingly, it had a raspberry taste with a cut of citrus.

Arlo stood on the other side of the counter watching me closely to see if the concoction was going to provide me with any relief.

"Well? How do you feel?" Frank hedged, his hands clasped over his rounded belly.

"These things don't work immedi- oh. Ohhh, gods, that's some good shit, Frank." I sighed, a bright smile taking over my face. Whatever he'd whipped up had done the trick because not only was the headache gone, but I felt wide awake and more alert than I had all day. "What the hell did you put in there? I need that spell, that's almost better than coffee."

The men chuckled, but Frank pulled out a notepad and scribbled down the spell. "This isn't something you can use daily though. If your headaches continue to be a problem, you'll need to see the healer. Magic only goes so far."

"Got it. Thanks, big guy!"

"Okay, now it's our turn! To the back room for privacy. Move it, girl." Roberta poked me in the side to get me moving and I felt like a sheep being herded by a pack of shepherds.

"Fine, fine, okay!" I scolded so they'd quit jabbing me to move my ass.

We filed into the tarot room and took the exact same seats we had the last time they'd cornered me and spouted their craziness about the prophecy. Turned out that it wasn't as crazy as it seemed seeing as how everything went to shit afterward. They exchanged a look and then turned to me in synchronicity that was creepy as shit.

"You must be careful, dear girl. Trouble has come to Emerald Lakes and more is on the way," Matilda said ominously.

"Betrayal. There will be betrayal and everything you know will be called into question. A transformation will soon happen. Lies will be exposed," Roberta shuddered visibly.

"So many lies," Matilda spat.

"Who is going to betray me? What lies?" I questioned, despite not wanting to take them seriously, I had to admit that there were a lot of strange things happening and the guys were taking the prophecy to heart so I should do the same, but it was hard.

"We haven't seen that, just that it will happen and you must stay true to the path," Roberta explained, like I should know what that meant.

"What path? I'm sorry you guys, I don't know what that means and there's not much I can do when I am only given cryptic messages. If the stars were really so concerned, they'd be more forthcoming with information!" I snapped, but I couldn't help it, I was getting so frustrated with all of this nonsense.

Roberta looked sad, her mouth frowning as she told me softly, "They didn't mean for it to happen like this. Just know that."

"The stars? Who didn't?" I leaned forward, but there was nothing more to be said.

"Just be on alert, child. That's all you can do. What's going to happen is already written," Matilda sighed, and with that, they stood and stalked from the room, leaving me sitting there wondering what the hell was going on, and how much worse could things actually get?

Letting their words sink in, I stared at the dead cactus in the center of the table. The same one that had bloomed so beautifully for me the last time the three of us had sat in this room, was now a spiky black blob and the petals were strewn on the table, shriveled up little blackened wisps of what once was a work of natural art.

Hopefully, that wasn't going to be a metaphor.

AFTER SEEING the Seers out of the shop, I flipped the open sign to closed and told Frank and Arlo to take the rest of the day off. There were only a couple hours left until close anyway and I just didn't feel like dealing with anything else today.

I put on some music and made my way back to my office to hopefully get some work done. So much for a productive day. Frank's drink was still in my system, and I felt fantastic aside from my sour mood. Wonder if he could mix me up something to fix that?

Worst part of owning my own business was all the stupid math. I'd been meaning to get an accountant to handle all of this but I was still dragging my feet in pure Saige fashion. Once I was positive my eyes were going to stay crossed if I did one more calculation, I pushed away from the desk and stretched, my eyes catching the clock on the wall. Holy moons, two hours had just gone by like nothing.

My evil inner witch took that opening all too smoothly; *you should stop by the grocery store and get some ice cream, and not look at another number for the rest of time.*

Couldn't argue with that logic. *Hmm, do I want peanut butter chocolate swirl or mint chocolate chip?*

"If I could turn back time, if I could find a wayyyy."

I jumped when Cher's voice started blasting from my phone and my initial shock faded to amusement when 'Thunder Daddy' popped up as the caller.

"Why hello, Thunder Daddy," I cooed, stifling a giggle.

"Is this some kind of new kink you want to try, baby girl?" Cam sighed, like he was no longer shocked by my bullshit.

"Ask Kai, I'm positive he's the one who came up with the nickname."

"Fucking Kai..." Cam huffed, and I could picture him running his hand through his hair with exasperation.

"What'd you say, Thunder Daddy? You wanna fuck me?" I heard Kai shout in the background and I laughed so hard, tears were making an appearance.

"Ignore him. I'm not even going to acknowledge his ass," Cam told me.

"You want my ass, Thunder Daddy? Is that what you just said?"

"Just one moment, little witch," Cam said calmly, and then I heard Kai shrieking dramatically and sounds of a scuffle. Hopefully Thunder Daddy didn't hurt my little pussycat.

"Sorry about that, had to deal with something," Cam apologized.

"Mmhmm. Sure. So, what's up? You called me this time."

"Oh, right. Well, we finished our workout and we have a few other things to take care of, but I forgot my backpack in the apartment. If you're still at The Pig, do you think—"

I cut him off. "I can grab it. Are you coming to get it?"

"No, not me. Sloane is on his way through so he'll just get it from you out front so we can finish up some things today."

Great. "Sounds good. You guys should come over tonight, I miss your faces."

Cam's deep chuckle came through the line and I grinned like a goofy ass.

"I'll see you later, little witch. Thanks for your help."

"Bye, Thunder Daddy."

Click.

I was excited to get to see all of them tonight. Maybe we could just drink and watch movies together in the living room, I was craving something normal. That was something people in relationships did.

My feet quietly carried me up the stairs to their apartment, Maven charged ahead of me, his sniffing loud as he no doubt scoured the new to him area. The apartment was surprisingly clean for a bunch of men living in it. I scanned the room quickly, seeking the backpack in question and a very clear thump had me freezing in my tracks. What was that?

"Maven?" I called out, approaching the hallway. His soft chittering was coming from Cam's room. "Did you break something?"

Pushing the door open, I spotted Cam's backpack on the floor beside his bed and Mave's head was buried inside, the distinct crinkling of some kind of snack wrapper told me all I needed to know.

"Maven! Get out of there. You can't just steal people's snacks," I scolded, dropping to my knees to pull him out of the bag.

"Cheetos? Really?"

His face was dusted with orange Cheeto dust. He looked ridiculous. Mave just snorted at me and gave me the evil eye for taking away his precious treat, but I didn't know how Cheetos mixed with fox's bellies, and I'd rather not deal with a fox who had a case of the shits.

"Go wait in the living room, you've caused enough trouble."

He huffed and walked slow as all hell out of the room. I swear, he was a vindictive little creature.

Some of Cam's stuff had of course fallen out of his bag, so I started picking up all the notebooks, loose change, hair ties... *dear gods, he has a lot of them. Wonder when his birthday is, I should get him a little accessories bag to keep his hair stuff in.* Laughing at the thought of his face receiving such a gift, I snatched a folder that had fallen open and was halfway under the bed.

Glancing down at the papers tucked away inside, I was about to close it up and shove it in the bag when something caught my eye. I did a double take so hard I felt my brain bounce. *What the fuck?*

A grainy photo was printed on a standard sheet of paper and I almost didn't recognize the face staring back at me. *Why the hell does Cam have a picture of my mother?*

Falling back to sit on my ass, I pulled out the rest of the stuff in the folder and right behind this one was another. Laurie was much younger, standing beside an incredibly handsome man, both of them dressed to the nines. What is going on here? I flipped over the photo and scribbled on the back in Cam's writing, 'Laura Walker, Khol Larson, Christmas 1991, last known location: Emerald Lakes, bring in alive.'

A drop hit the paper and I realized I was crying. More fell, tracking down my face and blurring the ink from his pen. My heart felt like it was going to explode, my insides were twisted up so tightly, my throat felt too small to get a deep breath.

He... he was using me? "No, please no," I begged, a sob breaking free.

Was it just Cam? Or were they all in on this? Oh gods. My stomach rolled and I staggered to a stand, rushing for the toilet where I made it just in time to heave. *How could he? How could they? This can't be happening...*

Somehow, I stumbled back into the bedroom, gathered up the papers, the only damning evidence being the two photos. Nothing else that alluded to why they were really here. I had to get out of here. Now. I zipped the bag closed and carried it out to the living room. What the hell am I going to do?

I didn't get much time to think about that because the door opened and footsteps came up the stairs, Sloane stepping in and seeing me as soon as he entered the apartment. His face paled and he moved toward me, but I stepped back, nearly stumbling over the coffee table.

"Red, what's wrong? Why are you so upset?" He reached for me, but I didn't want him touching me. I'd wanted to scream and yell but when I opened my mouth all that came out was the sound of a heartbroken woman. Words wouldn't work, my voice was broken. Hurt. So much hurt.

Collapsing back onto the couch, I hid my face as the tears felt like they would drown me at any moment.

"You're scaring me, woman. I can't handle tears. What. Happened?" Sloane demanded and I dropped my hands so I could slip the backpack off and hurl it at his stupid fucking face.

"Was it just Cam, then? Or have all of you been lying to my face the entire time, Sloane!?" I screamed, standing up and charging him.

The bag fell from his arms to the floor just in time for him to catch my hands and wrap his arms tightly around my body.

"What the fuck are you talking about? Would you settle the fuck down?" he hissed as I squirmed and fought against his hold like a wildcat.

"Fuck. YOU! Look in that folder, Sloane! Tell me what the fuck that is!" My breaths were rapid and shallow, my body temp heating up with the anger that was taking over the sadness.

"I'm going to release you and you're going to sit your ass down so I can look. Now, sit!" He barked, pushing me down onto the couch. I scowled at him as I wiped away the tears that just wouldn't quit. *Not these guys, please, stars.*

Sloane's face remained emotionless as he opened the folder and flipped through the papers inside.

"What exactly am I looking for here?"

My mouth dropped open because either he was a damn fine liar, or he really didn't know anything about those pictures. Deciding I didn't have the time to work out which one it was at the moment, I stood and pushed past him.

"I'm out of here," I muttered, proud that my voice didn't crack that time. I just sounded sad as shit and tired.

"Red, I'm going for a ride on the bike. How about you come with me? I don't know what you saw in here that has you all fucked up, but a ride can be therapeutic," he offered, his voice soft and deep.

Halting my progression to the stairs, I considered it. Something reckless right now sounded like a horrible idea, but what else could really go wrong? And a healthy dose of giving zero shits was just what the doctor ordered.

"Fine. But you better drive like the devil's chasing you. Maven will stay here."

His voice was so soft, I wondered if I'd imagined it. "I am the devil."

Sloane

Chapter Seventeen

Fuck. Fuck. FUCK!

Saige was stomping down the stairs with enough anger radiating off her that I feared she was going to turn green and hulk out on me any second.

She'd seen the pictures of her mom. Gods, I could murder Cam right now. The fuck was he thinking leaving those in his bag like that? They should've been destroyed.

The door slammed downstairs and I whipped my phone out, my fingers flying across the keyboard in the group chat with the four of us.

Me: Saige knows we're lying. I covered, but she's on a warpath. Taking her out on the bike.

Messages started flying in immediately and I skimmed them as I bounded down the stairs after her.

Cam: She WHAT!
Kai: Oh shit. How?
Fischer: What did you tell her? How does she know?
Cam: Where are you going? We'll meet you.

Cringing, I silenced my phone and put it back in my pocket. They couldn't meet us, because I was taking her to Larson.

SAIGE'S ARMS were wrapped tightly against my waist as we flew through the back roads out of town in the direction of Kingstown. When I'd gotten outside, she hadn't said a single word. When I'd straddled my vintage motorcycle, she silently slid onto the back.

Her silence disturbed me. She was never quiet. Her sassy mouth never quit.

She'd get some answers soon, though. The cover was blown and we were out of time. Larson had texted me earlier after my argument or whatever the hell that was with Red. I'd gone with the guys to work out and I knew I needed some excuse to head back to the apartment so I could get her. Without them.

Larson informed me that he was going to be in Kingstown within a few hours and he wanted to meet Saige to ask her himself about her mother. After some hesitation on my end when he asked me to come alone with her, he'd assured me he didn't intend to harm her. I trusted him. He'd brought me into his training academy and turned me into something worthwhile. And I had never seen him harm anyone who wasn't scum. Red was sweet, almost sickeningly so. And I was a soldier. A hired gun. Larson gave the orders, and I followed them. We all did. That was our fucking job.

Why does it sound like I'm trying to convince myself I'm doing the right thing?

We drove around a little longer than necessary, I'd been hoping that some extra time on the bike would bring her anger down from a boil to a simmer at least.

The wind was picking up and thunder rolled in the distance. Saige and I both flinched at the sound, knowing what it meant and who was causing it. I could only imagine how many texts and missed calls I'd have by the time we arrived at the warehouse.

It looked exactly the same as it had when Fischer and I came here weeks ago. Nobody had bothered to pull the weeds or clean it up whatsoever. Pulling the bike up alongside the aluminum siding, I killed the engine and Red's arms fell away from my body, taking her heat with her. Sometimes she ran almost as hot as I did and that wasn't really natural for someone that didn't have some kind of fire magic.

"Where are we?" Her voice was absent of all emotion as she got off the bike.

"This is the building we've been scouting for our boss. Thought you might like to see it?" I questioned, putting the kickstand down and swinging my leg over the seat on the opposite side of her.

Wrong thing to say. Her eyes narrowed on me.

"Sure, Sloane. Show me this building that you came to Emerald Lakes to buy. The one that you haven't bought yet," she sneered, turning on her heel and speed walking to the entrance.

Choosing to ignore her, I followed and when I got to the door, I entered the code that the realtor had given Fischer the first time we were here. She didn't even comment on that. Holding the door open, I gestured for her to enter and she flipped me off as she brushed past me.

Well, at least there's that.

I wasn't sure where Larson would be, but it was safe to assume he'd make himself known at some point.

"So, this is the elusive real estate?" she mocked, her eyes flitting over the lobby area, arms crossed over her chest.

"Yep. This is it."

"And what a wonderful piece of real estate it is," Larson's deep voice came from a hallway just off the front desk and we both turned to look. He stepped into the space, commanding it. That was just the kind of man he was, when he was in the room, everyone noticed. Everyone shut the fuck up and listened.

"Who the hell is this?"

Well, almost everyone.

"This, Red, is Mr. Larson, our boss. Head of Radical Inc." I told her, the title a warning. Watch your smart mouth.

"You must be Saige. It's nice to meet you," Larson addressed her, approaching her with his hand out in invitation.

"I'm sure it is, Mr. Larson. Sloane, I want to go home. I'll call Miranda to come pick me up," Red told me, digging her phone out of her pocket.

"Saige, I was wondering if you'd answer some questions?" Larson asked, looking pretty calm given the situation. Too calm. Everyone knows a predator goes still before the kill.

"What kind of questions would the head of Radical Inc. possibly have for a green witch from a small country town?" Saige questioned, slowly making her way toward the door, ready to make her escape.

"I found a conference room just down the hall here, we can sit and get more comfortable." Larson told her, avoiding answering her question about what the hell was going on.

My eyes darted to Red's face and she was getting redder by the second. *Probably should step in and calm her down a little before she goes back there and everything goes to shit.* Because I had a feeling that's exactly where this was headed.

"Follow me," Larson commanded, turning his back to us and disappearing down the hallway.

"Red, come on. Just talk to him and then I'll take you home," I offered.

She spun around, her eyes glassy with more tears, but she didn't meet my gaze.

"I don't have the answers he wants," she stated softly, but her accusing eyes finally pinned me down. She knew me bringing her here wasn't a coincidence. When I opened my mouth to respond, she slashed her hand through the air, silencing me. "Don't talk to me if you're just going to lie some more. I can take a lot, but fuck, Sloane. This really, really..." her voice cracked as she looked to the ceiling, trying to wrangle her emotions. "It hurts," she whispered and pushed past me to follow the direction Larson had gone.

My throat tightened as I watched her get further and further away from me. Some part of me wanted to apologize, but she didn't know everything yet. She'd seen the pictures of her mother, and suspected that we'd been lying to her about why we were there, but I couldn't open my mouth and give away any other information. My fucking scary as sin boss was down the hall and whatever information came to light today would be at his discretion, not mine. I'd worked too damn hard the past ten years to have it go to shit in a matter of minutes over guilt of doing my job.

I followed her, her vanilla scent surrounding me. Vanilla and salty sadness.

"In here, if you please," Larson called out and Saige didn't look back before stepping into a room to the right.

By the time I entered, she was sitting facing the door, eyes locked on her hands clasped in front of her. Larson caught my eye from the head of the table, Saige was seated beside him. He gave me a nod of approval and for the first time in my career, it didn't make me feel like hot shit. No, it made me feel like a piece of shit.

"Sit, Sullivan, let's talk."

I took my seat across from Saige, but footsteps behind me had fire bursting from my palms, ready to defend, but they dissipated almost as quickly when my magic processed that it was just Johnny. He was dressed in tactical attire, black pants with more pockets than I could count, and a skin tight black t-shirt that did nothing to hide the fact that he was a strong motherfucker. Johnny walked around the table and dropped into the chair beside Saige and I raised my eyebrow. Why are they boxing her in? She's not a threat, and there was no need to intimidate her.

"Saige, thank you for meeting with me today. I haven't been to this part of the country before, have you lived in the area your whole life?" Larson asked like it wasn't weird at all.

"Yep. Nearly twenty-eight years," Saige replied, still not looking up from her hands.

"I see, and w—"

A loud crash and shattering glass stopped Larson mid-sentence, Johnny and I hopped to our feet.

"WHERE IS SHE, SLOANE!?" Cam roared, followed by an absolutely savage growl from Bagheera. Oh fuck, this is a shitshow.

A familiar tingle started in my head and my mouth dropped as I felt Fischer, fucking Fischer, dipping into my psyche. What the fuck? He had never used his affinity on any of us except during training, but he was using it now, and I was pissed. *How dare he?*

Heavy footsteps approached the conference room and a blast of lightning blew the double doors clear off their fucking hinges. Bagheera soared through the air and landed on the table, all of his razor sharp teeth on full display, hackles raised, and muscles ready to kill.

"Are you all finished?" Larson inquired in a bored voice before gesturing to the empty seats, "You're all here, you might as well take a seat."

Saige was frozen in her seat as she watched Fischer and Cam drop into seats at the table. Bagheera was still snarling though, despite Cam telling him to shift.

"Kaito. Fucking shift and sit your ass down or you'll be removed from this room. You're pissing me off," Larson snapped, some of his calm resolve slipping.

In the blink of an eye, a very naked Kai was towering above us and Fish tossed him a pair of basketball shorts as he hopped off the table. He nearly fell trying to get them on so that he could get to Saige.

"Sprout, listen, let me explain. It's not as bad as it seems, I promise," he pleaded, reaching for her but she leaned away from his seeking touch.

"Don't," she whispered and I heard Cam's knuckles crack from three seats away.

"Please, Cub, just—"

"Enough!" Larson boomed, slamming a fist on the table. "I've been patient. Now, everyone sit down and shut the fuck up, it's my turn to talk."

Kai looked exasperated when Saige turned away from him and focused her attention on Larson, but he knew our boss meant business, so he sulked over to the seat beside Johnny and crumpled into it. I could feel Cam and Fischer's gazes burning holes through my head, but I couldn't bring myself to glare at them in return.

"Now, Saige. I understand you own the magic shop in town, the one below the apartment the guys are staying at?" he asked and I wondered what the hell that had to do with anything.

"Yeah. The Mystical Piglet. It's my store," she replied, her voice numb.

"And do you have any family in the area?"

"Yes," she snapped, her jaw clenching.

"Who?" Larson pressed, not taking his eyes off her face.

"My grandmother."

"Is that it?"

"That's all that's in the area, and she's the only one who matters to me," she fired back, lifting her chin slightly.

"Larson, what is the meaning of this?" Cam asked, clearly unable to take not being the one in control any longer.

"Cameron, I'm just asking Miss Wildes some questions. Do you have a problem with that?" he challenged and I held my breath.

209

Cam leaned forward on his arms. "No, I don't have a problem with it, but as you can see, she's clearly upset and if we could perhaps speak with her before you ask any further questions, it might help."

"I don't need to speak with him. Continue." Saige snapped, her eyes narrowed on Cam.

"Little witch, we really need to talk. You don't understand..."

"What exactly am I not understanding, Cam? You guys obviously aren't businessmen. You didn't come here to buy this building. You came here looking for somebody, and you used me to try to find her."

"Sweetheart, that may be how it started, but we care for you," Fischer said, his fingers furiously tapping on the table.

"No more talking from you three. Since you can't seem to follow orders, I will make it easy on you," Larson barked and he twisted his hand through the air, over his throat and when Cam slapped his palm on the table and I saw his mouth moving but no words coming out I leaned back in shock. All three of them were yelling now, but silently. Not a peep.

"Sit. The Fuck. Down," Larson warned and Johnny backed up the command.

When they were back in their chairs, Saige was staring at me from across the table.

"I'm happy to answer your questions, Mr. Larson, but I want to ask Sloane something first. He does still have his voice?" Red questioned without looking away from my face and my stomach sank.

"He does."

"Did you know? It's obvious all three of them did, by the way they're acting, but I need to know if it was all of you who are responsible for ripping my heart out and tossing it on the floor like garbage." She leaned forward and I glanced to my brothers, Kai looked like he was two seconds away from murder, lightning was sparking off in random places on Cam's body, and when I got to Fischer, I sucked in a sharp breath. His eyes were pitch black.

"Answer me. Now."

Sighing, I turned to her and ran a hand through my hair.

"Yes, it was all of us. I didn't discover Laura was actually your mother until after your first date with Fischer, I saw a picture of you, Bette, and Laurie," I confessed, ignoring the pounding on the table from the guys. "They didn't know she was your mom, not until this moment."

Nodding, she turned her attention back to Khol.

"I'm looking for your mother. Do you know where she is?"

"I have no idea. She called me earlier today, first time in months. We don't have a relationship. Never have and never will. Are we done here?" Saige pushed back from the table and Johnny's hand snapped out and grabbed the arm of her chair, halting her from moving.

"Not quite, Goldie." He smirked and she startled, lifting her eyes to his face as all the color drained from her face.

I watched in horror and fascination as Johnny's body began to shimmer and ripple, almost like water. A moment later, a new man was standing in his place. Red hair, short red beard, a million freckles.

Saige sucked in a breath and almost toppled the chair backward,

"B- Bram?"

"Hi, Goldie." He smiled and reached for her hand, which was the wrong thing to do. All of us were on our feet, moving toward this fucker. *Who the hell is he?*

"Who the fuck are you?" I shouted, "Don't fucking touch her!"

Suddenly, the four of us were frozen in our tracks, unable to move. My heart was racing, something was not right.

Larson stood and brushed his hands down the front of his suit. "Gentlemen. I appreciate your services on this assignment, but your mission is complete as far as you're concerned. I have what I need now and you can thank Sullivan here for your extended paid time off. He generously negotiated that when he agreed to keep some information discreet."

Thunder shook the building.

Johnny- Bram, whoever the fuck, pulled Saige up from her chair, and when she attempted to push him away, he pulled her snugly against his body and dropped his face to the crook of her neck taking a deep inhale of her scent.

"What is happening right now?" Saige whimpered, tears falling freely from her beautiful eyes.

"Since we're all here, there's some things you should know, gentlemen. My name is Kholvin L'argonne, Second Commander under Asrael Carlisle serving his royal highness, King Thane Carlisle. I was born and raised in Besmet before coming to this realm on a mission on behalf of King Thane." He looked at each of us and I opened my mouth to call him a son of a bitch, but no sound came out. I'd been put on mute just like everyone else.

Khol walked over to where Saige was being held and he pushed her wild hair back out of her face gently.

"Twenty eight years ago, Laura and I had been engaged to be married. I thought I was in love, I thought she was in love with me. I was wrong. So very wrong," he spat the words like he was purging his soul of poison that was tainting his veins.

"No." Saige gasped at the same time the pieces all connected in my head.

"You're my daughter, wild one. And tonight, we're going home."

NO! I was screaming in my head, agony burning through my chest. If they took her to Besmet, I had no idea how we'd ever get her back.

"No, I want to go back to my house. Gran, I need Gran, and Maven. Please don't do this," she choked.

"It's for the best, Goldie," Bram cooed, kissing the top of her head and making me see fucking red.

Tears fell like raindrops as Saige's sobs burst from her throat, her breaths coming so quick that she was near hyperventilation, but there wasn't anything we could do.

"Bram, don't do this," she begged, hiccoughing. "Please."

"You have a higher purpose, my girl. I'll let them speak, but they won't be able to move until you and Bram leave; he'll take over the holding spell from here. I'll see you soon."

Larson waved his hand and opened a portal right in the middle of the fucking conference room. Blues and purples swirled together, the inside of the circular shape moving rapidly, and when Khol walked into it, his body faded from our world, and a second after he was through, the portal vanished. Like it had never been there at all.

Saige was crying softly, and I found I was able to move my head and nothing else.

"Baby, look at me, please," Cam asked, his voice deeper and raspier than usual.

I watched as she lifted her eyes to Cam's face, heartbroken, betrayed, hurt.

"I know you're upset right now, and you have every right to be, but I don't want you to get hurt," Cam said.

"You don't want me to get hurt? It's a little too fucking late for that now, isn't it, Cam? Is that even your name? How much bullshit have you guys fed me over the past month? For someone who doesn't want me to get hurt, you didn't have an issue when it was you doing it!" She squirmed in Bram's arms. "Fucking hell, Bram! Let me GO!"

He dropped his hold on her and she stepped away from him a few feet, further from all of us.

"Firefly." Fischer. My insides felt like they were rolling.

"I thought I meant something to you, Fischer. How could you lie to me? And all because you wanted to find my mom?" Saige's voice increased in volume at the tail end of that sentence and her face flushed a deep red. "I trusted you guys, I let you into my home, my heart, my fucking bed! Fuck you!"

Kai whined, high pitched and agonized, and her eyes snapped to him.

"And you. Mates, huh? Is this what mates do to each other? Lie? Use each other? I would never do that to you. Any of you."

"We didn't know she was your mom, I swear. Apparently, that was a secret Sloane kept to himself," Kai growled, his upper lip curling in disgust.

"I was following orders, I had no idea this would happen," I replied in a level tone.

"Shut the fuck up, Sloane. You've done more than enough damage here!" Cam bellowed and I flinched.

"Enough chit chat. We're leaving now. Goldie, come here," Bram ordered and Saige looked to the hole in the wall where the doors used to be before the guys had shown up, like maybe she could get away.

"You could try. You won't make it out of this room, but I do enjoy the thrill of the chase," Bram smiled devilishly.

"You won't fucking touch her, you son of a bitch! Who the hell are you?" Kai yelled.

"He's Bram. He's the demon who kept me safe the other times I went to Besmet," Saige answered Kai's question, and then before we had a second to process that information, she was sprinting around the desk.

Bram threw his head back and laughed loudly with glee. *Is this guy fucking deranged?*

"Run, baby!" Cam encouraged, but then Bram disappeared out of thin air and Saige screamed when he popped up right in front of her, the momentum carrying her right into his arms.

All of us were yelling, begging, anything to make him get his hands off her, but he just hugged her tighter.

"I'm sorry, but this is what you need, and they can't help you.

Things are going to change, and you need to learn." And in the same motion Larson had done, another portal opened in the air.

"No, no, let me GO!" Saige screeched, her nails drawing blood up and down Bram's arms, but he wasn't even flinching. He had a smile on his face and hearts in his eyes.

"Let her go!" Kai.

"I'll fucking kill you." Cam.

"I'm going to melt your brain from the inside and watch it pour out of your ears and nose." Fischer.

Wait. What? My head snapped to look at him and holy shit, this was bad. His voice was cold, detached, dead.

"Sorry guys." Bram waved and stepped back into the portal.

"Let me go, Bram, please! Don't do this to me!" Saige screamed, her body flickering away before our eyes.

She'd just vanished from view when something came flying back out of the portal, landing on the ground by my feet. Then the portal was gone and our bodies all hit the floor, released from whatever hold Larson and then Bram had put on us.

Groaning, I pushed myself up onto my knees and looked to see what had been cast out of the demon realm and I could've thrown up when I saw it. The tether. The pentagram necklace, broken into two pieces and completely black. My hand shook slightly as I picked it up and straightened, turning to the guys. "Her neckla—"

Crunch. Pain exploded through my face and I dropped the necklace so I could grab my nose which was no doubt broken. My eyes watered from the pain and blood soaked the front of my shirt and hands.

"Shit," I grunted, and flicked my hands to fling the blood off.

I deserved that.

Looking up, I expected to see Cam standing there, but my black heart stopped beating when my blurry vision registered that it was Fischer towering over me with a mixture of fury and disgust. His breathing was ragged and his midnight black eyes penetrating, then I felt that tickle in my head.

"Don't." The last thing I needed was him in my fucking head right now.

He pushed further and I winced as I tried to fortify my mental shields against him, but he was insanely powerful in this state and he smashed them with hardly any effort. My memories were flying through my head so quickly, everything starting from the time we got the assignment from Larson.

Khol offering me the assignment, me accepting. Operation oldies. My jealousy of Saige. My insecurities and vulnerability. My anger. The warehouse. My... feelings for Fischer. Me texting Khol, talking to him on the phone, me finding the picture in her house. The suspicion. The lies. Larson ordering me to get involved with her. Me negotiating a personal mission for Cam. The garden. The attraction that was real, that I'd tried to deny. Me pulling away from her. Everything. Fischer saw all of it. Then he recoiled from my psyche as though he'd been burned.

"Fischer, I didn't mean to—"

"Yes. Everything you've done since we got here was because you meant to," he sneered. "We" —he motioned between us— "are done."

I opened my mouth to say something, anything, but all that came out was a choking sound that I didn't even think I was capable of. *What does he mean we're done? Our friendship? Our fucking? Both?*

"Just listen... you don't understand, Fish, just sit down and we can talk." I shook my head, trying to process everything, but he just laughed. A deep, dark, malevolent laugh that sent a chill down my spine.

"Now he wants to talk," he muttered, continuing to put distance between us. My chest was tight, I felt like I couldn't get a full breath, but I reached out to him regardless.

"Do not touch me. You're a selfish bastard. You took that side job with hopes of being promoted. Larson fed you compliments, called you son, and you fucked all of us over with stars in your eyes. But what, Sloane? You didn't feel dirty enough about being a liar until he ordered you to 'work your way into a relationship with her, just like the others'? And what did you do next, Sloane? You fucked with both of us less than an hour later, you had your hands all over her body! You make me sick!" Fischer roared, his breathing labored and I felt like I was going to puke.

"What the fuck did you just say?" Cam growled, stalking over to me, electricity crackling between his fingers.

"You touched her because you were ordered to?" Kai began prowling behind him toward me.

"It wasn't like that! Fuck!" I shouted, running my hands through my hair, not caring that I'd just covered my head in my own blood.

"I have a secret to tell you, Sloane," Fischer whispered, his eyes burning me from the inside out. "Those feelings, the ones you felt for me, the ones you struggled with in your memories? The ones you couldn't make sense of?" He sneered at me. "It's love, you motherfucker."

"Love?" I choked, shaking my head.

"That's right. You love me, Sloane. You're in love with me. But want to know something else? You're also in love with *her*. So how does it feel, now knowing that you just betrayed two people who you love and two others who you almost love just as much? Must be a record, two loves lost on the same day you realize you're in love with them."

My back hit the wall and I sank to the floor, my legs spread out in front of me. *Love? I'm in love? With Fischer* and *Red?* My throat tightened and my heart was pounding in my ears, blood running down my face. I raised a hand and wiped at my cheek, looking at my fingers for several moments before realizing that there wasn't any blood on them. But there were tears.

Cam

Chapter Eighteen

My body was shaking.

Towering above Sloane, one of my oldest friends, my brother, my ride or die... I watched as he fucking broke. Shattered.

And I felt the kind of rage a man gets when he'd been fucked over so royally his hands itch with the urge to feel bones snap and blood spray. Oh my gods, I was fucking pissed. How dare he go behind my back like this?

We all watched as he stared at his hand like it was some kind of alien appendage, his thumb smeared the tears into his skin and his eyes were wide, like he just couldn't fucking believe he was human enough to cry.

I couldn't speak to him right now, I could barely stand the sight of his fucking face. My woman was gone and it was his fault.

"Cam, I'm so sorry, I didn't know this would happen. How was I supposed to know our gods damned boss was a fucking demon?" Sloane said, but the last bit was like he was talking to himself.

My jaw hurt from how hard I was clenching it, but I could not open my mouth toward him right now. So I turned to the side and addressed Fischer and Kai.

"We're going to go back to the cottage. We will tell Gran everything. We'll take her wrath or whatever the fuck else she deems appropriate for our lies. Then we will do everything in our power to get our witch back because I will kill any motherfucker who stands in my way," I vowed. And I meant every word.

"I can't be without her." Kai's voice was pained and panicked. He had a mate bond, he would be in physical pain in addition to the heartache.

"I'm sorry, K. I'm so fucking sorry," Sloane rasped.

Kai ignored him.

"What about him?" Fischer inclined his head to where Sloane was slumped.

I let out a deep sigh, my hands forming fists at my sides.

"Do it, Cam. Beat the shit out of me, I deserve it."

Nope. You don't get off that easy.

"He can stay at the apartment, or he can fuck off back to wherever he wants. We will hopefully be staying at the cottage with Gran to work on this day and night. We'll get our clothes and belongings moved into her house as soon as possible," I voiced the plan as Kai and Fischer nodded in agreement.

"Brothers, don't. Please, let me help you. I can fix this. I'm sorry, I just wanted to get time off for all of us, for you, Cam."

Thunder boomed in the conference room, lightning bursting from my hand and obliterating the solid wood table into a million splinters.

"How fucking dare you use my childhood trauma to make yourself feel better about what you've done! Do you even hear yourself? I'm done with this," I turned and moved to the hole in the wall where the doors had once stood. "Let's go guys, we need to get our woman back."

Fischer was right on my ass, clearly done as well. When I glanced at him, his eyes were still black. He still wasn't in control of his magic and I could fucking relate. Electricity was licking up and down my spine.

"You said you'd always be there for me, Sloane." Kai's strained tone had us pausing for a moment to see what Kai had to say to Sloane. "You said that we'd take care of each other when others hurt us, when my own body hurt me when I shifted for the first time. Do you remember that night? How you held me and took care of me? Do you remember how much pain I was in? You soothed me, made me feel safe." Kai's voice cracked as he stared down at his broken, bloody brother. "This hurts worse than that, Sloane. And this time, instead of being the one to make me feel better, you're the one who gutted me."

Sloane dropped his face into his hands and I watched his shoulders shake for half a second and then I flew down the hallway and to my bike. Sloane Sullivan didn't deserve another moment of my time, not tonight. Probably not ever. And if Saige was harmed in any way, shape, or form, I just may kill him myself.

Straddling my Harley, I didn't hesitate for another fucking second before firing it up and tearing down the road, the rolling thunder above drowning out the roar of my own bike. I knew Fischer and Kai would be right behind me. We had work to do, and I could only put my faith in the stars that our woman would be okay and that Gran wouldn't murder our asses when we told her what had happened. *Ugh, I am not looking forward to telling her.*

My heart was racing and I had to push down the urge to tear the fucking sky open with a hurricane or a tornado. Something to get this fear and anger out of my system. Sloane... where did I go wrong? I'd always given him praise, just like the others. What did it say about me as the team lead that one of my fucking own would go behind my back like that? *Larson ordered him, and Larson is above you.* The voice in my head was already working hard to try and absolve me of the blame that I was surely going to be torturing myself with for the foreseeable future. Where and how did this get so fucked?

Fischer came up behind me and pushed his bike to the max, sending up a huge dust cloud in his wake as he gave his bike everything. Adrenaline junkie, always. My heart ached for him, too. Sloane and Fischer had this connection, a different one than anyone else on the team. When we were nearly out of high school, I realized what they'd been doing with each other, but I didn't say anything. It didn't bother me, and truthfully, I was glad they had each other. Fischer was drowning in emotional overload and he was miserable. Sloane was getting his ass kicked on the daily and needed some semblance of control in his life, and they figured out something that worked for both of them.

Their arrangement benefitted both of them, and it never interfered with our job or our friendships with each other. They fucked other people, too. It was never anything official. No commitment. I know Kai had done some things with them before too, and there was never any jealousy that I picked up on.

And now here we were, everything had gone to hell in a handbasket in the blink of an eye.

Khol had sent us here looking for Saige's mother. Had he suspected he'd fathered a child with the woman? Why had Saige's mother kept everyone in the dark? I'd bet it was also Laurie who'd warded the town to keep him out of Emerald Lakes. But why? I couldn't fucking believe we'd gone ten years not knowing he was a demon, doing all of his dirty work, who the hell knows what kind of missions we've been on thinking we were fighting for the right side. Fuck! I rubbed my temples in a piss poor attempt at soothing my brain.

We needed to find her soon, her knowledge of demons and Larson would be crucial to us getting Saige back. Saige, fuck. The look on her face, the pain and the hurt. When she cried, it felt like my heart was being stabbed, and when she screamed and thrashed in that bastard's hold, begging... that was when my heart broke and I hated myself so fiercely in that moment for having even an ounce of responsibility for putting her in that situation.

My little witch. Who I'd promised to protect. Gods, I'd fucked this one up epically.

I followed Fischer as he made the smooth turn into the driveway of the cottage, my stomach full of dread and regret.

Golden light spilled onto the grass from the large kitchen window and I figured that meant someone was home, and since it wasn't my baby, it could only be Bette. She was probably making dinner for everyone. She gave us our privacy but she often ate with us most nights.

We all parked and dismounted our bikes, Kai and Fischer standing on either side of me as they stared at the cottage.

"I grabbed the necklace on my way out... This is going to be brutal, man," Kai said softly.

"Yep. But we're doing this. No more secrets," I replied, gearing myself up to go in there and break an old woman's heart.

"Let's do this," Fischer's detached voice had me looking over at him, and when his eyes met mine, I swallowed the lump in my throat at the darkened unhinged look in them. We can't have a repeat performance from the last time he went off the rails.

"Are you good, brother?" I questioned, studying his expression. The corner of his mouth kicked up in a disturbing kind of way, a way that was inappropriate for the situation we were in, and without Sloane here to do whatever it was he did to bring Fischer back from the darkness, I wasn't sure what the fuck we were going to do.

"I'm great."

He pushed away from us, opening the screen door and disappearing into the house. I knew that I should probably be more concerned that he wouldn't have a way to work through the darkness quickly with Sloane out of the picture. However, the distant thunder and lightning strikes across the landscape around us were a harrowing reminder that I, too, had issues that were going to have to be my focus. Plus figuring out a solution of how we were going to get Saige back.

. . .

WE WERE A FUCKING MESS. Kai had a mate bond that was about to rip him apart, so Fischer was going to have to fight his own demons.

"Cam..." Kai warned, worry in his voice.

"I know. He'll be okay. He just needs some time to come back to normal, just... keep an eye on him, okay?" I clapped Kai on the back and we headed into the house. Something smelled delicious and my stomach growled in appreciation, but it made me feel like a fuck to be thinking about eating at a time like this. Would they feed Saige? Was she a prisoner?

Bette was in the kitchen, as I'd suspected. Fuck, the way we moved into the room made me feel like some kind of harbinger of destruction, which I supposed was fitting, but I didn't want to destroy this woman. She'd stopped her movements and watched us closely.

"I made eggplant parmesan tonight," she explained, pointing to the casserole dish that was on the stove.

"Bette," I began, but she waved me off, spinning to remove plates from the cupboard. She wouldn't look at me when usually she had trouble keeping her eyes off me. *She knows. She knows something terrible has happened.*

"If you boys could just set the table? Is Saige still outside? I caught up on all of the gardening earlier today so she doesn't need to mess with anything out there right now. Can you get her, Kai?" She stepped around the island with the plates and beelined for the table.

"Bette," I said more firmly this time and she froze in place, "we need to talk, okay? Can you sit down, please?"

"Where is she?" she breathed, setting the plates on the table and dropping into a chair.

"Taken. She was taken tonight," I confirmed and we all watched as her face paled.

Creaking above us had our heads tilting up and I strained my ears, listening to see if it was just the old house settling. Then the unmistakable sounds of someone walking around upstairs had our training kicking in. Kai immediately moved toward the stairs, no doubt using his senses to see what he could figure out.

"Who is upstairs, Bette?" I asked softly.

"A guest. The three of you better sit down and get to talking before I have a WF."

"What's a WF?" Fischer asked, confused, but also intrigued as he dropped into a seat at the table.

"Witch fit. And trust me, you don't want to see that," she cautioned, but I felt a little more at ease knowing that she knew whoever it was upstairs and some of the tension in my chest abated.

I called out to Kai, telling him to join us at the table. Once we were all sitting, Bette didn't waste a second.

"Someone better start talking or I'm going to start busting some asses," she threatened and I had no doubt she meant business.

Kai caught my eye, his pain evident. Fischer was suddenly incredibly interested in his fingernails, so I took the lead and began telling her everything. It was brutal. Watching as she processed how deeply we'd hurt her granddaughter. How badly we'd fucked up. *How I failed at keeping her safe. Another one I let down.*

We were just getting to the part where Khol had revealed he was Saige's father when whoever was upstairs began coming down the steps, the creaks and groans from the old wooden steps so loud that they'd give away a spider moving on them. The three of us looked to see who this guest was and I nearly toppled my chair with how fast I pushed out of my seat.

"What in the name of Neptune's nipples are you doing?" Gran barked as the three of us created a wall of muscle and magic between her and the woman who had caused this entire fucking situation.

"You," I growled and the windows shook violently with the thunderous boom I unleashed from the heavens.

Her auburn hair was down, hanging in soft curls to her collarbone, she and Saige shared the same face shape and arch of their eyebrows. Both were redheads, though Saige's color was a bit lighter than her mother's. I could see a hint of familiarity now that I was looking for it, but it was faint. She was petite, probably the same height as my little witch, but it was clear Saige didn't get her curvy body from her mother.

"Mom? Who are these men and why are they looking at me like they want to murder me?" Laurie squeaked, but I wasn't fucking buying it. Neither was Kai from the way he growled low in his throat.

"Boys, sit your asses down before I kick you out of this house. There will be no violence within these walls."

We inched backward to our seats, never taking our eyes from Laurie.

"Where's the birthday girl?" Laurie questioned innocently, and either she was the best actor I'd ever seen or she wasn't the evil creature that Larson had painted her out to be. Deciding that it was smarter to stick to the assumption that she was dangerous, I slammed a wall up around my mind that was built of suspicion and distrust. I'd trusted Larson, respected the fuck out of the man, and look where that had landed me.

Gran shifted in her seat, taking a sip of her coffee.

"Laurie, these are Saige's boyfriends," she pointed to each of us, "Cam, Kai, and Fischer."

Laurie's eyes ping ponged, following Gran's finger.

"Ah, she did mention that on the phone yesterday. Well, it's nice to meet you? But can someone explain to me why you're all looking at me like I'm Lucifer's daughter, and tell me where the hell my daughter is?"

"We were just explaining to Bette... perhaps we could continue our conversation in private?" I looked at Bette and she scowled so severely, I swear I felt my face heat.

"This situation is out of control. You four tried handling things privately and look what happened. No. We need back up, and if anyone knows how to get her back, it's this witch right here. As much as I loathe her demon obsession, we need her now. So get to fucking talking before I start punching dicks." Gran cracked her little knuckles and Kai's face blanched at the thought of those tiny granny fists using his nut sack as a punching bag.

"Fine. Laurie, I will give you the quick cliff notes version, because we've already wasted enough time. We work for Radical Inc. Khol Larson is our boss and he sent us here on an assignment to find a woman he'd been looking for for close to thirty years. Turns out, that woman is you."

Laurie's face paled and she scooted away from the table a few steps, but I held up my hand signaling for her to stop her retreat.

"We're not looking to harm you or whatever you might be thinking. We used a cover when we arrived, saying we were businessmen sent here to procure a new building for our company. The apartment above The Pig was for rent, and that's where we ended up, and that's how we met Saige. We all felt drawn to her, we'd do anything for her. We hadn't worked out yet what we were going to do about our jobs, obviously, we are not businessmen. We're operatives, spies, assassins— whatever Larson needed us to do, we did.

"He told us that you were dangerous, untrustworthy, and that he'd stop at nothing to get to you. He'd tried himself to infiltrate the town, but someone, who I am now assuming was you, had warded the town to keep him out."

At that tidbit of information, Bette raised her eyebrows and narrowed her eyes at Laurie.

"And why would you do such a thing, dear daughter?" Bette questioned, her knee bouncing.

"Mom, listen..." Laurie sighed and Fischer leaned forward,

resting his forearms on the dining table, eager to hear what she had to say and determine if she was full of shit or not.

"I'd hoped it never would come to this. That he'd never find me, or Saige. Everything I've done was to keep her safe, to keep her hidden from him. When I left Emerald Lakes, when I was younger, I ended up meeting Khol at a club and I quickly fell in love with him. He was older, insanely rich, and he made me feel cherished. After some time, he became more controlling and possessive. I overheard him on the phone one evening with someone named Thijs, talking about Besmet and how they'd never be able to return until they succeeded in impregnating a witch with a demon child." Gran gasped and I felt my mood darken another ten shades of shitty.

"So, you can understand that when I discovered I was pregnant a few days later, I knew I needed to escape him before he found out. I hadn't known he was a demon, thanks to his highly powerful demonic energy, he shielded so many of the signs. And I hadn't wanted to be pregnant at such a young age, but he was able to do something to combat my monthly contraceptive spells without my knowledge. Imagine my surprise seeing a positive pregnancy test, and knowing that it was a demon who had gotten me pregnant. That's unheard of. Trust me, I know my shit about demons," she trailed off, turning and walking into the kitchen and opening up the cupboard that held all the liquor.

"I'm going to need a stiff drink to continue this conversation." She shook her head as she pulled out several bottles and carried them over to the table. Gran snatched the Bailey's and dumped a healthy measure into her coffee. Fischer moved to the kitchen and snagged the coffee pot, which was thankfully, nearly full. *Guess it's a good thing the Wildes witches were addicted to coffee at all times of day, we were going to need the caffeine.*

"So, you're telling me that my sweet Saige, the innocent and goodhearted green witch, is actually sired from a beast? I won't accept that. It's not possible. There is nothing demonic about her," Bette swore, shaking her head.

"Well, actually, it makes sense. Her powers have been fucking up for weeks now, her temper, her body temperature... now that we know Larson is her father, all of those signs back it up," Fischer chimed in with a degree of nonchalance that really wasn't appropriate in this situation and I shot him a severe look when he simply sat back in his seat, sipping his spiked coffee.

"What do you mean her power has been fucking up?" Laurie asked, worry marring her features and I again had to wonder if she was genuine. Fischer wasn't calling her out, so I decided to wait to ask him afterward.

"Anything she used her magic on was dying. It started out fine, and then turned to ash. Then a couple weeks ago, she sent out a burst of magic so powerful into the ground that she raised a damn jungle in the yard. Not to mention, she astral projected twice to Besmet... or maybe that was dream walking? We'd thought astral projecting before, but dream walking is a strictly demonic power, and she was asleep those times, so maybe that's what happened? Then she definitely projected when she was awake and was in a damn coma for hours. Gran made a tether to keep her here, but as you can see," Kai pulled the broken necklace from his pocket and dropped it on the table, "it didn't stop them from taking her."

Laurie and Gran both sucked in a sharp breath and my body was itching for a fucking fight. I needed to split my knuckles and push myself until my muscles screamed for mercy. I didn't know that I would be able to calm the fuck down until that happened.

"Who is *them*? Who exactly took her?" Bette asked.

"Larson and Johnny. Or, is that even his name? I'm a little confused on those details..." Kai wondered as he removed the top from a bottle of vodka, brought it to his lips, and took a healthy pull. He slammed it down on the table, wiped his mouth with the back of his hand, and stood up to start pacing.

I ran a hand down my face. "Johnny is, or was, our handler. We've known him since we started at Radical ten years ago. He's always been a good dude, maybe a little on the quiet side, but we often hung out together when we were at the training facility between jobs. Turns out, he's also a demon, and has a shapeshifting ability, because he transformed right in front of our faces into a tall motherfucker with red hair and more freckles than a cabbage patch kid. Saige said he's the one who she'd spent time with during her time in Besmet, that he'd kept her safe," I explained to the two witches who were looking more and more uneasy by the damn second. Well, welcome to the party, girls.

"What did she say his name was?" Kai tapped Fischer on the arm, getting his attention.

"Bram. She said his name was Bram," Fischer responded, a glint in his eye that promised blood.

"Oh shit," Laurie gasped and we all turned to her. "Oh no, no. That's not good. You're positive? Fuck!"

Gran snarled, slamming her hand on the table. "Spit it out, girl! Who the fuck is he?"

Laurie shook her head, the look of defeat in her eyes had my heart clenching in pain.

"Bram is the Prince of Besmet. He's the heir to the throne, and he's insanely powerful, and rumored to also be, well... insane."

"My granddaughter is with her demon father and a psychotic prince?" Bette shrieked.

"I just can't see Johnny being some evil demon prince, can you?" Kai asked, but there was a thread of worry there that even I felt.

"Nothing makes sense. Why do they want her? Khol said she has a higher purpose to serve or something..." I recalled, trying to replay everything that had happened in that conference room, but it was difficult because when I'd been in there, helpless to do a damn thing to help her, I'd lost my fucking head. Fuck, the way she'd looked at me... like I'd shattered her with my bare hands, I'd never get that look out of my memory.

"The prophecy," Bette breathed. "It spoke of saving a race, having to find her five before turning twenty eight, which is tomorrow. What if this... Bram," she spat his name from her mouth as though it was poison, "is the fifth? And where in Jupiter's cock is Sloane?"

Kai growled at Sloane's name and I swallowed down my own.

"Sloane decided he was going to be Larson's bitch and feed him information that we knew nothing about. Like the fact that Laura, who we were looking for, was actually Laurie, aka Saige's mother," I explained and the anger inside of me rose up like a fucking beast.

"He also lifted her hair from a brush in her bathroom and mailed it to Larson. That's how he was able to conduct a paternity test to be sure," Fischer supplied like it was no big fucking deal and I pinned him with a stare so harsh a weaker man would've hid under the table, but not Fischer. Not when he was like this, anyway. And this time there was no Sloane to pull him back from the dark. It was worrisome.

"That motherfucker," Kai snapped, completely disgusted with our supposed brother.

"He's at the apartment, as far as I know," I looked to Bette, hoping that she would be okay with what I was about to ask. "We were actually hoping that we might be able to stay here, that way we can work on this around the clock and figure out how we're going to get Saige back here safely, where she fucking belongs."

She looked at the three of us for an uncomfortably long amount of time before giving a stiff nod, but I knew it wasn't going to end there. Oh no, Bette Wildes was livid, and Saige had to have gotten her fire from somewhere.

"You can stay here until we get her back. But I want to be very clear, so listen closely. You hurt the most precious thing in my life, I'm not happy with any of you right now. That girl has gone through enough, especially after her relationship with Bryce, she doesn't need any more boys pretending to be big men. So either step the fuck up or get the fuck out. I'll let her make her decision when she returns, but the least you three owe her is getting her back here safely. It's late. There's nothing we'll be able to do for her tonight, we'll sleep and reconvene in the morning. Her shifts at The Pig will be covered by one of you, work it out. I'll not see her livelihood suffer because of this. She will be back, and when she is, she won't be drowning in work. I'm going to call Miranda and cancel her birthday party festivities. Laurie, you're staying in my cottage now, so get your shit and get over there." Bette stood, walked over to the kitchen, and picked up the entire casserole of eggplant parmesan she'd prepared for dinner.

"I'm taking this with me, you three can fend for yourselves."

And with that, she stormed through the house and out the backdoor.

"I'm going to go grab my things then I'll be out of your hair, I think I still have some of my old demon texts hidden at Mom's, so I'll look through those tonight. But this isn't going to be easy. From what I know, you can't get into Besmet without a demon escort. They have to be the one to open the portal, there's no other way in," Laurie explained, taking her coffee mug to the sink.

Fischer was eyeing her, his face carefully blank, and I wondered what he was reading from her.

Laurie disappeared up the stairs, and Kai and I both looked at Fischer, waiting for his report.

"She's blocking me. There were a few hints of anxiety, some shock, anger. She's strong, but not like Saige and Larson, so I don't think she's a demon. Either she knew what I was capable of, or she trained herself to keep her shields up at all times, just in case. Regardless, it's interesting. Only trained witches are able to accomplish what she just did," Fischer pointed out, crossing his arms as he chilled in his chair.

"Well then, we'll be watching her even closer and we'll find out who Laurie Wildes actually is. Let's try to get some rest so we can hit the ground running in the morning."

Kai and Fish both drifted away, and I remained in my seat in my little witch's kitchen. Her scent was everywhere, her presence surrounded me and my throat constricted when I thought about how she'd screamed and fought like a bobcat as she was dragged into that portal. Fucking hell.

Stay strong, baby girl. I'm coming for you, and I'll cut down the demon king himself and set the whole realm on fucking fire if I have to.

Saige

Chapter Nineteen

The pain was indescribable.

Betrayed. Lied to repeatedly by the men I'd been falling in love with, and then there was Bram. Another liar. One who currently had his arm wrapped around my waist as he guided me to his living quarters in the castle. Larson hadn't been waiting when we arrived through the portal, and after I fought Bram, which was really just me pounding my fists against his chest as he grunted and took it, all of the energy left me. Like it had evaporated into thin air. My brain was shutting down, probably some kind of coping mechanism to keep myself from detonating. That was fine, I'd rather feel numb than feel all of that.

"Let me take you home, Goldie. You can rest, I'll get you whatever you want, food, coffee, anything," Bram promised, but I didn't really care. All I could see in my head was Cam's pained expression, Kai's panic, Fischer's darkness, and Sloane— *No, I can't go there*. So, I let Bram lead me through the castle halls, my feet shuffling because the energy it would've required to pick them up off the floor was too great. I was spent.

Bram obviously noticed because next thing I knew, my feet were swept up and I was cradled against his chest. The desire to fight him over his macho bullshit was nonexistent. If I wanted to be completely honest, being held right now felt nice, I just needed to ignore the fact that it was a big red-headed lying fucker who had his arms wrapped around me tightly.

We reached the door to his place and he somehow got it open

without putting me down and carried me straight to the bathroom that I hadn't been in the first time I was here. It was a massive space, easily bigger than my bedroom at the cottage. My eyes took in the huge shower with two benches that looked like they were made out of smooth multi-colored river rock on either side of the see through glass enclosure, jets built into the wall, and a rainforest showerhead in the middle of the ceiling. That wasn't the best part, though. There was a pool, a legit fucking pool against the far wall with steps leading up to a platform with the same smooth rocks as the shower.

Steam was rising out of the water and my skin actually tingled in anticipation of getting in and washing away the pain of the day.

He put me down, still standing close. "It's a natural spring, I just had the rest of the bathroom built around it. I thought you might like it?" Bram questioned, sounding vulnerable. But I wasn't able to speak yet. My throat hurt, my face was raw from crying, my eyes were still stinging. So instead of answering, I just began kicking my shoes off and pulling my shirt over my head.

"Goldie, can I take care of you? Please?"

I didn't answer, I just shimmied my pants down my thighs and stepped out of them, leaving me in my bra and panties. *Was any of it real?*

My lungs wouldn't inflate, and I felt like I was trying to breathe through a straw, a keening sound came out of my throat. I felt like I was underwater, everything was muted and then Bram's face was in front of mine, his lips moving, but I couldn't make out his words for a moment. *Need to breathe.*

"Breathe, princess," Bram encouraged, his hands rubbed my back and I buried my face into his chest and sobbed. *They used me, they gave me to Larson, why would they do that? Why?* Tears just continued falling as Bram stripped down to his boxers, lifted me into his arms once more, and carried me into the water.

He walked us out to the center, his height easily kept us both well above the water. Heat enveloped my body, the water was hot, and I imagined if I could feel things right now, it might feel great. As it was, exhaustion just set in further, making me feel like a boneless jellyfish.

"I know it hurts, Goldie. It will all be okay," Bram cooed, standing me on my feet and encouraging me to lean my head back to get my hair wet. I did as he wanted without a fight. He procured shampoo from somewhere and began massaging my scalp gently. I watched on as my tears hit the water, creating small ripples. With how I felt on the inside, the small physical disturbance that my heartbreak caused just didn't seem anywhere near enough. A tsunami wouldn't be enough.

"Want to hear something ridiculous? I had no idea who you really were. It wasn't until I saw you walk out of that grocery store and caught sight of you." He continued rubbing my head gently, moving down to my neck and massaging me there. "I followed you to your shop. You know, I called and called that number you put in my phone. I was worried, Goldie. When I realized that you were the woman that my team was claiming, I was angry. So, so fucking angry..." Bram trailed off, pushing me back to rinse the soap from my hair. I just floated there, letting him wash me. "That's why I said what I did in your bathroom. I wanted you to feel like I did. My heart fuckin' hurt," he admitted, shaking his head.

Steam rose up from the water, swirling in mesmerizing patterns. Bram cleared his throat, but I didn't move or give any signs of life. My lip trembled and I wanted to slip under the water and wait for this to pass.

"When Khol told me that he had a daughter, I couldn't believe it. I told you how our people have been having difficulty in the past years with fertility. Then he sent me to this tiny town, which was the absolute last thing I'd wanted to be doing because I couldn't get you out of my head. Don't you think this was written somewhere in the stars, Goldie? You and me?" he murmured softly, his touch soft and caressing.

He righted my body and went to work with the conditioner, it smelled exactly like the kind I used at home. *Home.* My heart stuttered in my chest, clenching tightly as I thought of Gran. *Oh gods, Gran.* She would be devastated when she found out about this. She'd already lost her daughter to demons, and now she'd find out I actually was one. Would I lose my green witch magic? I didn't think I could cope with that life.

"Shh, princess. Seeing you cry makes me feel seven shades of homicidal and there's nobody around for me to kill. Let me rinse your hair, hmm?" He poured water over my head and I kept my eyes closed. He continued talking but I wasn't paying attention, all I could focus on was the shaking of my body. *I think I'm in shock.* "You're the first hope our people have had in a century, and things you don't understand yet are about to change for you. We won't be here forever, but you do need to be here to learn. I promise, this isn't as bad as it seems."

Bram continued his pampering and he didn't push me to talk or make any demands. I allowed his lying ass to take care of me because I was exhausted. The energy for conversation eluded me, and I had no desire to dig deep and search for it. After we were done in the large pool, he carried me out and wrapped me in a huge towel before ushering me back through to his massive bedroom. I found myself parked firmly on the bed, my hair hanging limply around my shoulders, little drops of water making their trek downward before landing on the towel.

I must have been lost in my head when his bare feet suddenly moved into my line of sight. *Where had he gone?* "Do you need help getting your wet clothes off, Goldie? I won't touch you, or look, I just want to take care of you," Bram asked quietly.

Lifting my gaze to his for the first time since the shit show in that conference room, I mindlessly mapped his face, trying to gauge his sincerity. He'd already seen me naked, so what did it matter? What did anything matter? *I'm a fucking* demon.

I stood and let the towel fall, turning to let him unhook my bra. He made quick work of it and I pulled it off, dropping it at my feet. Bram brought the towel up around me once again, drying my back and I dried my breasts, quickly, using my other hand to slip my soaked panties down.

"Here, princess. I know you love nightgowns," he told me, dropping one over my head and letting me slip my arms through before tugging it down as he pulled the towel away so I was fully covered.

Glancing down, I noted that this was a t-shirt style nightgown, my favorite. It was cream with a variety of cacti printed on it, along with the words, "Don't be a prick". Normally, I would have loved this. Yesterday, I would have laughed at the pun and been excited to have a new nightie. Now? I climbed into Bram's big ass bed and slipped under the covers, not even bothering to brush my hair.

The lights dimmed and I stared at the wall for minutes, or maybe it was hours? Time was irrelevant. I was no longer feeling time or anything at a normal rate. Everything was muted. So when the bed dipped and I felt Bram climb into bed behind me, I didn't move. When he started brushing my hair out, I blinked. And when he started humming softly, I cried silently. Then, when he slipped down beside me and pulled me against him, I slept.

MY EYES FLEW OPEN. Something wasn't right. I mean, this entire situation wasn't right, but something with me. Feeling numb clearly wasn't an option for my body anymore, it felt like my very cells were zinging and rioting. My skin felt tight and hot, my nails were already digging their way into my neck and chest, trying to alleviate a persistent itch. Bram startled awake beside me, my restlessness wasn't just a disturbance to my own sleep, unfortunately. My other hand snaked down and clawed at my thighs, I was so fucking itchy.

"What the hell is going on?" Bram questioned, leaning over to put on the bedside lamp. The room lit up enough to where we could easily see each other and my hands were under the covers furiously scratching. Adrenaline was pumping through my veins now and I writhed beneath the blankets seeking friction.

His eyes widened as he dragged his gaze from my face down to where the covers were jerking with my frantic movement.

"Oh my, my, my. You are a dirty little birdy, aren't ya?" He brought his fist up to his mouth and bit down on it. *The hell is he talking about?*

"Shut up and help me," I whined.

"Oh stars, fuck yes!" Bram shouted and dove underneath the covers, his lips hit my hip half a second later and I jerked my hand and smacked him in the face.

"Hey, what was that for?" he shouted, but it was muffled through all the blankets.

"Get. Out. Of. There." I growled, and suddenly his face popped out from under the blankets.

"I thought milady was in need of assistance? I mean, that was a pretty quick one eighty from the tear typhoon that went down just hours ago, but what Goldie wants, she gets," he smirked devilishly and licked his bottom lip, and my mouth fell open.

"Bram. I'm itchy. I'm just scratching an itch, okay?" I narrowed my eyes on him, not in the mood for his shit.

"Yeah, you sure were, *scratching* an *itch*," he winked and I fumed.

"You honestly think I'm laying in bed beside you," I paused to scratch harder and rub my arm over my forehead, "and whacking off when my entire world just went to shit?" I rubbed my eyes and groaned. "My body feels weird and I'm getting another headache."

"Oh yeah, what time is it?" Bram scrambled to check his phone and I heard him mumble something under his breath that sounded like sexy demon.

"What's the time have to do with anything?"

"It's just past midnight, which means it's officially your twenty-eighth birthday," Bram smirked, "which of course means, you'll soon begin the manifestation."

Bram snapped his fingers and a giant cupcake appeared in his hand with a single candle and he peered down at me with a smug smile.

Stupid demon doesn't even realize I don't care about my birthd—

"Excuse me, *the what?*"

"The manifestation. The prophecy refers to you needing to find your five before your twenty-eighth, which you did, and now your demon powers will manifest. That's why it's called the manifestation," he nodded, like all the bullshit he just spewed made any sense to me at all.

"How do you even know about the prophecy?" I asked, still squirming around between his sheets.

"The team told me, of course. It's pertinent information. Granted, they told me before they knew who I was, but whatever," he shrugged. *No biggie.* Of course they would have told him, it was a job after all. *Ugh.*

Sinking back down onto my pillow, I felt a bit better at the change of position, but the dull ache in my forehead wasn't going anywhere.

"What are you feeling, Goldie?"

"Pressure in my forehead, my skin feels tight and itchy, I'm exhausted," I admitted, letting my eyes drift shut once more.

"You might shift, just a warning," Bram said softly, and my eyes flew open, but there was no mistaking the hint of excitement in his voice.

"Shift into a demon? I'm not a full demon, so I fucking hope not," I cursed, clenching my jaw.

"Oh, but you'll be the sexiest demon, those curves with a tail and wings?" Bram groaned and physically shivered, the bed even shaking, as if the thought of me in full demon form was enough to give him a stiffy. Then again, this was Bram, so he probably was hard as a rock already.

Ignoring his ridiculousness, I had some questions that I wanted answered now that I'd recovered the use of my voice.

"Does your dad know I'm here and what I am?"

"I'm sure he does. That's likely where Khol went running off to the moment he stepped through the portal. It's been a very long time since he was allowed to come back here."

"Allowed?"

He ran a hand over his hair. "Yeah. The Four were sent away to complete their mission of procreating and they weren't allowed to return until they succeeded."

"Who are The Four?"

Bram sighed. "The Four were my father's highest ranking demons a century ago. Asrael, Eronne, Thijs, and Khol. Known for their ruthlessness, loyalty, and desire for blood, they were tasked with the mission of furthering our race," he explained.

Wow. The king was crazier than I thought. Sending your highest ranking minions out into the world to fuck and make babies. Nice.

"What does he want with me?" I wondered, absently scratching my arm.

"You're hope. You're a promise of something that our people have long given up on. A future. Possibilities."

"So, he isn't going to want to like, I don't know, study me or something?" The thought of being used as a lab rat was enough to send fear rocketing through my body.

"He can fucking try, but I told you before, Goldie." He hovered his face over mine, his expression fierce. "You're mine and I will kill anyone who harms a hair on your head."

His eyes were such a strange color, like they were made from an actual piece of amber, slightly darker honeyed flecks sprinkled throughout. Bram was intense, he didn't say things without meaning every single word and I had no doubt he would do exactly as he promised.

"But I'm not yours, Bram. I'm not anyone's. Not anymore," I croaked, the faces of the men who I'd been falling in love with flashed in my head and tears stung my eyes again. How my body was able to keep producing the damn things was a modern miracle because I was certain I had to be dehydrated by now.

"As much as I want to rip their heads off for touching you, and for hurting you so badly, you have to understand a few things, okay?" Bram cupped my cheek, keeping my focus on him as though he knew how badly I wanted to roll over and bury my face in my pillow.

Shaking my head no, I didn't want him to say another word because I didn't want to hear anything yet. It was too fresh, too fucking raw.

"Yes, princess. You will listen. Seeing you ripped up like this is tearing me up, and the last time I felt a shred of empathy toward anything was when I was sixteen and my friends and I had a dick measuring contest. Obviously I won, and I felt very empathetic toward them and their less superior swords. Nothing I could do about that though, right?" I opened my mouth to tell him I didn't really think that was empathy, but he continued. "This time, I can do something to make you feel better. I have known those guys for a long time, since they signed up for the academy. They are fucking fantastic at their jobs, and for the past ten years, that is all that has mattered to them. Constantly in different countries, with different people, the thrill of life and the hunt driving their purpose. They are lethal," Bram explained, and my eyes widened at that word. *Lethal.*

"Yes, Goldie girl, it's true. They may have been sweet and laid back with you, that's how they are with one another, but believe me when I say that each and every one of them has a beast living in the depths of their souls and they can release it within the blink of an eye. Now, I don't believe that Cam, Fischer, and Kai were playing you. Maybe at first, just gathering intel about the town. Can you blame them? They moved into a perfect location with a friendly, beautiful witch who had lived there her whole life, the perfect informant."

Was that all I was to them? Kai told me that we were fated mates, and I'd felt something strong between us, binding us together, so how could he have continued lying to my face? Was he planning to leave me there at the end of this... mission?

"They respected Larson. Completely trusted him because he's never given them a reason not to, he gave them every opportunity to further their careers and rise to the top. I saw the way they were with you. That night I took you back to your cottage, I wanted to snap all of their necks so that they wouldn't be able to touch you ever again. I knew you were going out with Fischer that night I popped in and interrupted your bath." He smirked, obviously recalling the naked argument that had exploded, but before I could smack him, he continued, "I was so jealous. So I watched. Everywhere you went, I watched you. The smiles, the touches, the laughs, I saw them, Goldie."

A tear slipped out without permission and Bram swiped it away gently with his thumb. *Why does my heart feel like it's hemorrhaging?*

"I'm not sure when it happened, but I became—" he paused, searching for the right word, "grateful. Grateful to them for protecting you, for making you smile so hard and bright that your face lit up. When I showed up in your bathroom that day, all of my jealousy, insecurity, weakness... it all came to a boiling point and I behaved like an ass. Then I saw and felt their pain when I took you from them. Your pain and heartbreak nearly choked me, Goldie. How could I kill them when they clearly made you so happy? All I could hope is that one day you might look at me the same way," he breathed, his voice raspy and deep.

"But, they lied. How can I move past that? How am I supposed to trust them again? I've never felt pain so crippling, Bram," I replied softly.

"If you've never felt a pain so devastating, then you've never felt such tremendous love before, either." He leaned down and pressed his lips to my forehead before lying back and pulling me against his warm body.

"Try to get some more sleep, princess. Tomorrow is a new day and you're going to need to be sharp."

Love.

I'd been falling so hard in love with those men, and now, I wasn't sure if I felt the same way, or if hate was slipping into my heart, covering that love in darkness.

I WASN'T sure exactly how long I'd been laying in Bram's massive bed, but I couldn't seem to get out of it, aside from using the bathroom, which wasn't often thanks to barely eating or drinking. On top of being emotionally drained, I felt physically weakened, too. Bram told me it was probably because of this transition I was going through. It wasn't a transition I even wanted and I wished there was some way I could put a stop to it.

There was no light coming in from the window, so I assumed I'd been asleep all day. Fine by me. I wouldn't have to think. I wouldn't have to see their faces in my head, wouldn't have to think about the lies, or how Sloane...

No, I'm not doing that. I can't.

Hopefully, Maven was back at Gran's. She may not like him, but she wouldn't let him starve. I wondered if Gran was okay, was she helping Frank and Arlo with the store? What would she tell everyone about where I was? This can't be forever. *I won't be here forever.* And yet, I still hadn't asked Bram any more questions because what if he did intend to keep me here? Surprisingly, he'd backed up the guys, softened my anger toward them slightly. Which was good for them because now I would only kick them in their big stupid dicks at seventy five percent power versus one hundred.

A twenty five percent power decrease when it comes to dick kicking is very generous, everybody knows that. Kai would know that.

My heart fluttered in my chest as I thought of him. His flawless skin, his lean frame that showed all of his muscle. His black hair that often tickled me when he'd kiss his way down my body. Gasping, I curled into a ball when something sharp pricked in my chest. My hand ran up and down my sternum as I tried to apply some pressure to help dissipate the pain. When I screwed my eyes up in pain, that's when I saw him.

Yellow eyes, rippling black fur, a massive body with a flicking tail.

'Baggie?' I whispered, very much aware that I was probably losing my mind.

A low pitched sound left his throat, and it sounded very much like a whimper. *If panthers can whimper?*

'Are you okay?' I asked softly as he laid down in my mind, his arms stretched out in front of him, his head dropping to rest between them.

'Baggie, I miss you so much. And Kai. Is that what this pain is? The mate bond?'

I'm not sure how exactly, but I knew he answered me.

'Yes.'

'Does... does he miss me, too?' I whispered, tears welling.

'Duh.'

My mouth dropped open. *Did I just get sassed by a fucking jungle cat?*

Rumbling laughter filled my head. *Great. Now he's laughing at me.*

We stared at one another, but having him in my head right then was such a huge comfort, I wished I could snuggle against him, though.

'It hurts, Baggie. So much,' I choked out, gasping as the weight of everything crushed me once again.

And then something really fucking bizarre happened. I saw myself in my vision or whatever the hell this was, walking toward him and collapsing on his big body. I buried my face into his neck and squeezed him as sobs overtook my body. His purring vibrated my body with how loud it was and it was calming. Perfect. Soothing.

'Rest.'

My body slipped down beside him on the floor and he curled up against my back, flopping a big black paw over my waist, his nose nuzzled my neck and those deep purrs lulled me into a deep sleep.

THREE DAYS.

I'd been here for three days and every time I closed my eyes, Baggie was right there. He was my anchor to my life, the life I'd known up until it all went to total shit. My headaches had been excruciating whenever I opened my eyes, so I tried to do it as little as possible. Plus, it was easier to keep tears from falling if I kept them physically locked down.

Bram however, must have had enough of my moping. If the way he was glaring down at me with his hands on his hips, skin glistening with sweat after his morning workout, was any indication.

"Goldie, you're getting up today. Now, in fact. It's time for a bath. You stink." He clapped his hands like some kind of drill sergeant and I wanted to stab him.

I rolled over and gave him my back. These fuckers brought me here, they could kiss my ass.

A gust of air had my lungs sharply inhaling as he snatched the covers off my body. *Okay, now, I'm pissed. Who the fuck does that? It's barbaric!*

My eyes narrowed on him and I quickly launched a vine from my palm, snatching the blanket before he could get it in his hands again. *Holy shit, my magic was fast. Guess that's a perk of becoming a demon?* The second the blanket hit my body, I barrel rolled like a fucking crocodile and made myself into a nice little burrito and I encouraged the vine to wrap around me, nice and tight, so that demon dickheads couldn't steal my damn blanket again.

Bram was laughing so hard and it just pissed me off even more. *Why won't he just shut the fuck up and leave me alone?*

"That's cute, princess. But like I said, you're getting up and taking a bath."

My eyes were barely peeking out of the top of my cocoon, glaring at his dumb face. *Well, he could fuck off, I'm not going anywhere, and he can't make me.*

Then his arms were underneath me, lifting myself, the blanket, and the vine into his arms. Fuck, I hadn't planned on him doing that. I squirmed like I was trying to get a spider and it's web off me, but his arms were banded around me and there wasn't anything I could do.

When we were in the bathroom, he put me down on my feet, but the blanket had slipped up so my eyes were covered and the only parts of me that were exposed were my bare feet, and my hair. And I'm sure that looked like a bird's nest after three days in bed.

"You look like a walking joint right now," Bram cackled and if my hands were free, I would've given him double birds. Fucker.

"Are you going to strip or am I going to have to improvise?"

THE MAGIC OF BETRAYAL

his deep voice asked, and I could just picture him walking around me, surveying how he was going to solve this problem.

I didn't move. He could fuck off.

"Improvising it is!"

A moment later, I was once again being lifted and when I realized what he was doing, I found my voice.

"Put me down, you son of a bitch!"

"Ahh, she speaks! Praise the stars above and Saturn's silky—"

"I'm not joking, Bram. Put me down!" I shrieked, letting the vine around myself and the blanket fade away so I could attempt to fight him.

"No. I'm not going to put you down. You've done enough laying around. It's time to get the fuck up and sort your shit out."

And with that, Bram's crazy ass pushed off the ground and we hit the water with a splash.

Anger ignited in my veins like nothing I'd ever felt before and I twisted in the water, trying to find my footing because I was going to lay into him. When I broke free and pushed my soaked hair out of my eyes, taking ragged breaths, Bram was standing there, smirking at me. Fucking smirking.

Bellowing a battle cry, I launched myself at him, his eyes widening with shock a moment before impact.

"Why can't you just leave me alone?" I yelled, pushing him backward and he took it. "You, you fucking kidnapped me! And not some basic witch kind of kidnapping, you took me to another dimension! Who do you think you are? You and my, my... *him*," I snarled, pulling my fist back and slamming it into his nipple.

My breaths were coming in pants, my blood was sizzling.

"Did you just punch my nipple? Like, deliberately?" Bram cocked his head at me.

"Shut up! I'll punch you in the other one next!" I moved toward him.

Bram shrieked, covering his nipples with his hands as he shouted, "Please, not my beautiful chest raisins!"

"That's the stupidest thing I've ever heard, you're crazy! Do not touch me, I don't want to be here, don't you get that? Just leave me alone!" I screamed, really picking up volume at the tail end of that demand.

Bram crossed his arms over his chest, clearly unharmed by my attack on his body.

"You're turning pretty red there, Goldie. Can I wash your hair now or are you still having an episode?" he asked, sounding bored of my bullshit. But I was just getting started.

"If you try to touch me, I'm going to squirt shampoo in your eyes, I swear to the stars! You wanted me out of bed? This is what you get. I'm pissed the hell off!" I shouted at him, tears pricking the back of my eyes because I was cursed with being a pissy crier.

"Saige, stop yelling. Get your ass over here, now. We have things to do today and you need to accept that for right now, this is your reality. I've watched you do nothing but cry and sleep for days. Days! It fucking hurts me, too, damn it!" he boomed and I slapped my hands down, splashing water while we faced off, both breathing heavily.

"Don't you try to flip this around on me," I gritted out. He wasn't the victim here.

"Quit. Sulking," he bit out, moving toward me with each word, like a Scottish Highlander coming to claim what was his after a battle, and my thighs clenched. "And stop fucking pretending like you don't feel it. Like you don't feel this," he motioned his finger at the space separating us, "because if you want to keep pretending, well, then that makes you a fucking liar too, princess." He towered over me, looking down his nose into my eyes and I couldn't breathe.

His hand came to the back of my head, fisting my hair and pulling my head back, my neck straining. The only sounds in the large room were our harsh breathing and the gentle lapping of water against the stone sides of the pool.

"Fuc—" my curse was cut off when Bram smashed his lips against mine with brutality and determination. Fireworks detonated in my blood, and before I really processed what was happening, his tongue darted between my lips and I moaned as he stroked my tongue with his. Bram groaned into my mouth, his hard cock pressing against my stomach, letting me know just what he felt for me. My body was on fire, I was furious and sad and turned the hell on.

My nails sank into his shoulders, no doubt leaving marks. Good. All these men thought they could leave their mark on me, and while I may not have any physical representation of those right now, my heart was carved up with their names.

I felt my body shaking, trembling, a pain along my spine that made me wonder if he was digging his fingers into my back, but one was cupping my ass and the other was still tangled up in my hair. *What the hell is that pain?* Something that sounded like an umbrella snapping open, echoed in the room and my eyes popped open just as Bram's wings exploded from behind him.

Gasping, I pulled back and looked at his face, two black horns rose from his forehead and when I felt something long trailing up the side of my thigh, I knew it was his tail. Holy fuck.

"Oh my gods," I breathed, but before another word could slip through my lips, a quick, sharp pain had my back arching and that snapping sound came again, loud in my ears. A scream left my throat as I glanced back and saw a pair of light green wings. *My wings.*

"Fucking hell," Bram marveled, staring at me like he was seeing me for the first time.

"Bram?" I whispered, because my voice wasn't strong enough right now for anything louder.

"Yeah, princess?" he answered, still locked in a daze as he stared at me.

"Do I... do I have horns?"

I wanted to check myself, my hands were itching to fly up to my forehead and find out the truth, but I couldn't bring myself to do it.

"Yes, princess. You have the most precious, cutest little baby horns I've ever seen in my entire fucking life. Your wings are magnificent. I have never seen any that shade of green before, they're almost like... leaves. Like fairy wings." He stood there, breathless and staring.

Inhaling, I reached back under the water, past my hip and closed my eyes when I felt it. A tail.

Holy moon maidens, I'm a legitimate demon. Full on, all the shit.

"Breathe, Goldie. You're still you, this is who you've always been. It's just manifesting now. Nothing has changed, not really. You shift when you feel strong emotions, it's something I will teach you, okay? That's why I wanted you here, so you can learn. You need to learn."

Bram had a point. A very good point, but he still shouldn't have gone about it the way he had. We could have had a discussion, like normal people. You don't just grab someone and disappear with them to another realm.

My breathing slowed, returning to normal, and I was surprised when I realized that my wings were weightless. If I hadn't seen them with my own eyes, I wouldn't have noticed they were there at all. The back of my nightgown was shredded, the front of it wasn't much better from the force of my shift. I may have horns, but at least my tits were covered.

Finding the courage inside, I lifted my hands and felt the sharp little points on my head, just peeking out from my hairline. They were only about an inch long, and Bram's were more like four.

"I think I want to see what I look like," I murmured, thinking that maybe seeing my new form would help me wrap my head around everything.

"Let's get you cleaned up first and then I'll tell you everything you need to know and answer all of your questions. I know you have them," Bram joked, smiling shyly at me now, his cheeks red.

The fuck is he blushing about?

"Okay. But can you wash my hair like last time?"

Bram belly laughed and got to work.

Afterward, he left me in the bathroom and I'd been standing in front of a full length mirror for the past twenty minutes. Every time I thought I'd stared long enough, I stared some more. I was never going to get used to this. My wings moved with ease— if I thought it, they responded. The same was mostly true for my tail, though it seemed to have more of it's own mind. It was the same color as my wings, a sea foam green color with silver markings that almost looked like outlines of scales. My eyes fluttered shut and I searched for my anchor.

His purring calmed my racing heart. Baggie's yellow eyes flashed as he moved closer to me in my mind.

'I'm different, Baggie. So different.'

The big cat shook his head, like he was disagreeing.

'Can't you see my horns? The wings and tail?' I asked, spinning in my mind so he could see.

'Still ours, Cub,' he assured me, and I was still not processing how I was able to communicate with a panther in my head.

Just accept it, Saige. Stranger things have happened. That's what I told myself. It's what I had to tell myself to avoid some kind of psychotic break.

'You shouldn't abandon Kai, Baggie. Go back to him. I'm fine.'

Baggie sat his huge ass down and his tail flicked behind him.

'Don't be stubborn. Please, I'm sure he's struggling. I know he is. I can feel him sometimes. Take care of him, Bagheera. Go.'

He padded over to me and bumped his huge face against my stomach, my hands sank into his soft dark fur. The volume of his purring raised goosebumps on my skin.

'Thank you, my dark knight. Take care of him.'

Blinking, I felt Baggie's presence fade from my mind and while it hurt, I felt better knowing Kai would have him. Sure, I was still hurt and pissed, but I wasn't heartless.

Staring back at myself in the mirror, my waist actually looked a bit thinner, probably from hardly eating the past several days, but my hips were still large and in charge. Leaning closer to the mirror, I eyed my little horns and tentatively felt them. After almost cutting a finger, I realized real quick that they were quite sharp. I really needed to go get dressed, Bram was going to teach me a whole bunch of demon stuff this afternoon and for the first time since I arrived here, I actually felt excited about something. There was no changing this, it was who I was. Now I just needed to know what all I was capable of.

"First rule of Demon Fight Club?" Bram smirked, flexing his muscles and I rolled my eyes.

He'd jumped us out to the pine forest, we were in a clearing that gave plenty of room for whatever he had planned. He was still staring at me and I realized he actually wanted an answer. Of course he did.

"Uh, we don't talk about Demon Fight Club?" I guessed, distracted by my tail that kept winding around my leg.

Bram chuckled. "Good guess, but that is not correct. First rule is, always wear comfortable clothing." He snapped his fingers and I gasped as I took in his new look. Knee high purple socks, a pair of Nikes, really fucking short neon orange shorts, and no shirt. Oh, and of course, he had a fucking orange sweatband over his forehead.

"What in the name of moon beams are you wearing?" I laughed, and he grinned, striking a pose.

"Not to fear, dear warrior woman. We can be matching, all you had to do was ask!" He snapped his fingers before I could shout at him and then I too was wearing the same shoes, socks, and shorts. At least he'd given me a sports bra.

"Bram Winston Carlisle," I scolded. "Shirt. Now."

"Who the fuck is Winston?" he growled, stalking over to me, that wild look in his eye that was both exhilarating and terrifying. My wings wrapped around the front of my body, shielding my bare skin.

"Oh quit, I made the name up because I don't know your middle name. Now, give me a shirt," I warned, glaring.

"You can do what we need to do in that outfit, Goldie." He waved me off.

"Bram," I said a little more softly. "I'm not comfortable wearing this."

He spun around in a flash, his expression absolutely puzzled as to why that would be.

"Why not? You look scrumptious, princess."

My face heated and I let my wings pull back to reveal my midriff, Bram was still eyeing me like I was a scantily wrapped gift he wanted to open.

"If you haven't noticed, I don't exactly have the body figure to go waltzing around like this," I pointed out.

He stared at me like I'd grown nipples for eyes.

Then, he moved. His hands gripped my waist and I let out a soft squeak as he tugged me close, leaving only an inch between us. The smell of an aged book being cracked open slammed into me and I groaned, leaning closer to get more of it.

"If. I. Haven't. Noticed?" he growled and my insides flipped. "All I've done is notice, Goldie. The curve of your waist," he trailed his hands over my skin, "how your hips flare out." He bent to run his hands over those, too. My brain was melting.

"These thick thighs that I'm dying to have wrapped around my head, squeezing the fuckin' life out of me... and this," he moved his hands back to grip my ass, "this fucking ass, princess. I wanna see how it bounces when you're riding me," he rumbled, dropping a kiss to my neck and I moaned. This man, this demon, he was insane, dangerous, and oh so fucking sexy. Sinful.

"Bram," I whispered.

He straightened, leaving one hand on my ass and bringing the other up to cup my cheek.

"You're the most beautiful creature I've seen in my entire life, Goldie. If I have to spend the rest of my lifetime assuring you of that, then it would be my honor," he vowed, his words fierce and true.

"I... thank you," I replied, as a rogue tear fell and trailed toward his fingertips.

"Who made you think otherwise?" he inquired, studying my face.

I chuckled without humor, shrugging my shoulders.

"Society? Mean girls in school? My ex," I confessed.

Bram's eyes flashed with all the stabby feels, an expression of his I had quickly learned.

"Ah. The ex from the night I drank with you in your store?" He shook his head, piecing that evening together. "That's why you were blasting Lizzo? Body positivity?"

My cheeks heated and I tried to look away, but he held me steady, refusing to let me hide.

"Yeah. He uh," I cleared my throat, "he cornered me in the grocery store that day. Threatened me, tried to drown me, he's a water mage. Promised me that he was going to get me back, and that if I told the guys, he'd drown them in their beds," I told him, my heart racing as I recounted the event.

"What else did he say, Goldie?" Bram practically snarled, he knew I wasn't telling him everything.

"He told me that I should cut back on snacking because most mages don't like fucking fat witches," I said quietly, looking down, ashamed. Disgusted by his words and that they were still affecting me.

Bram blinked several times while he stood still as a statue. It was oddly owl like.

"Is that it?" he bit out between his clenched teeth.

Tears swam in my vision now, but I was going to tell him, because I needed to tell someone. Maybe getting it out there would help me move past it.

"He... he touched me," I confessed and Bram snapped, pulling me tightly against him as a sob wracked my body and I buried my face against his bare chest. He held me while I cried and cried. I cried because I was sick and tired of men thinking they could say what they want, touch when they weren't fucking allowed, taking my confidence, my safety, my fucking dignity.

"Oh, princess. I'm so fucking sorry. I'm so sorry," he soothed, rubbing his palms up and down my back.

I hiccoughed and pulled back a little to wipe my face that was now puffy and raw. Sniffling, I tried to get myself together, but I felt exposed. All of the things Bryce had done to me in the past, everything was at the forefront of my mind and those were memories I wanted locked down forever.

"I'm going to teach you, Goldie. I'm gonna teach you so many things that if you are ever in a situation like that again, you'll be able to get out of it. But, make no mistake, beautiful princess," he held my face and it was like time stood still, "when I see that piece of shit, I will not hesitate to end him. There won't be one second for him to open his vile lips and whisper poison into the air. He will never get near you again. This, I promise you. I will hunt him down the moment we return and his death will set you free," he vowed and I found myself nodding in agreement.

The old Saige would argue that nobody deserves death. That nobody is purely evil. The old Saige was no longer in the building. I was done and wanted vengeance with a longing I'd never felt before. My arms snaked around Bram's neck and I rose to my tiptoes, pressing my lips against his. He tasted like safety and danger at the same time and I moaned into his mouth. Most importantly, he tasted like mine.

Groaning, he used his wings to lower us to the ground gently. My legs wrapped around his hips and he ground against my core, his short shorts doing absolutely nothing to hide what he was packing in there.

"Bram," I panted when he broke our kiss to move down my throat.

"So soft, so gorgeous, so delicious," he murmured against my neck and I urged his hips to move against me.

"Where did you come from?" I questioned as I wiggled beneath his weight.

"Your best dreams and your worst nightmares, Goldie. You know I'm both. I straddle the line between light and dark and I'll never, ever let you go," he growled, taking my lips again in a brutal, punishing kiss that flooded my veins with heat.

"Need you, Bram," I moaned, tipping my hips to feel his cock against my clit.

"Bloody hell, princess," he stilled, then sat up to run a hand through his hair.

"What's wrong?" I asked, studying his face.

He bit his bottom lip, trailing his eyes all over my body.

"As badly as I want to fuck you, we don't have the time right now." He pushed back and stood, offering me his hand.

Not gonna lie, I pouted. Like a fuckin' whiny baby.

"Nuh uh. Don't give me that face. You don't understand, Goldie. The first time we come together, it's going to be epic. Monumental. A quickie in a pine needle bed isn't possible," he explained, shaking his head with a smirk kicking up the right side of his mouth.

"But you haven't had sex in decades." I followed behind him as he walked over to our water bottles. "Don't you think it might go a little quick?"

Bram threw his head back and laughed so loud, birds in the trees took flight.

"You're cute, Goldie. What do you know about demon mating?"

"Uhh... nothing. Is it different than regular sex?" I asked, feeling like an idiot for not knowing more about his species.

"Yes. It's very different. For starters, no, it will not be quick. We're fated, princess. That's why we have these special scents to one another, it's like pheromones. The first time we come together, we'll be locked together for hours," he explained, studying my face.

"Locked together? Like, in a room?"

"No. Like, our bodies will be connected. Have you ever heard of knotting, princess?"

My eyes widened. I may or may not have read a few romance novels that had knotting...

"You have a knot?" I choked.

"I do. And I cannot wait to fill you up with it and have you clenching around me for hours," Bram groaned and reached down to rearrange himself.

"Won't it hurt?"

"It won't hurt; it's going to feel like the best thing in your life. So typically, a male demon wouldn't be able to knot a female unless she were in heat. It works differently for fated mates. I'll be able to do it every time, but it will only last for extended periods of time if you lock on me, which means your body is fertile and wants to conceive. The first joining is always hours long, no matter the probability of reproduction," he explained, taking a swig of his water.

"But I don't want to be pregnant. Not now, anyway. I do monthly contraceptive spells."

"Then you won't get pregnant. It's just our bodies doing what they're programmed to do. You're going to love it, I promise. But when that time comes, it won't be in the middle of a forest." He tossed me my water and I greedily drank it down. Water dribbled down my chin, but before I could wipe it away, Bram was invading my personal space and licking the droplets from my chin before kissing me deeply. My knees went weak with the pure fucking passion behind his kisses and we were both panting when he pulled away.

"Had to do that one more time. Your lips were all shiny and glistening and shit," he groaned, lifting his hands to readjust his ridiculous sweatband. "Okay, enough sex talk. Let's get started on the basics. Oh, one sec." He snapped his fingers and a tank top appeared on my body. Glancing down, I saw that it said 'Demons do it better'. "The last thing I want is for you to ever feel uncomfortable when you're with me, Goldie girl. Though, I stand by my earlier statements about you looking sexy as sin."

I smiled at him, once again speechless at his thoughtfulness. "Thank you."

He cleared his throat and got right back into teacher mode. "One, in order to hide your demon appearance, just calm yourself and focus on hiding your demon form. Shifting is tied to emotion, so if you get too worked up on any emotion, you're more likely to shift. Especially at first, because you're still learning. The more skilled you become, the easier it'll be for you to quickly shift and also repress your demon form if you so choose.

"So, let's try. Take a deep breath, focus on hiding your demon form. Close your eyes if it will help you concentrate," he encouraged and I let my eyelids flutter shut.

I noticed the steady pumping of my heart, the rustling of the pine needles all around us as a breeze swirled through the forest, Bram's scent. Picturing my horns, wings, and tail, I imagined them disappearing. Hiding. *Hide!* I ordered and opened my eyes to Bram clapping.

"Great job, tiny warrior. Look at you, in control of your own shit." He grinned and I beamed back. I was on a fast track of no return with his crazy ass.

"What's next?" I bounced on the balls of my feet, excitement flooding my senses.

"I know we discussed this a while ago, but demons don't have a specific affinity like you. Although, we do have basic powers that every demon has. Then there are specialties, and you can have more than one, or you could have none. It just depends on the demon in question. There is shapeshifting, which means you can alter your appearance to anyone else. Now, before you ask, everyone in Besmet usually takes preventative measures to ensure nobody can steal their appearance, but it happens. There are charms, usually worn on the person, that blocks a shapeshifting demon from being able to copy their identity. Obviously, this is a power I possess since I was able to parade around as Johnny," he explained and I nodded, desperately trying to remember everything he was telling me. I was gonna need a serious notebook.

"Next, there's dream walking. Another specialty I possess. I'm able to move from my dreams into someone else's. I suspect this is an ability you have as well since the first couple of times you astral projected, it was while you were asleep. I believe it was just your powers not knowing what the fuck was going on and that's how it manifested. Just like with shapeshifting, others can protect their dreams from walkers by symbols, charms, spells, and a whole slew of other things," Bram explained and then chuckled at my wide eyed look.

"You following, princess?'

"Yes, it's just fascinating and I want to remember everything though I already feel like my brain is about to explode," I admitted. "But please, continue. Tell me everything."

Bram sat down and tugged me down so that we were sitting across from one another. Guess there was quite a bit more to know.

"So, these next powers are incredibly dangerous. Biokinesis, which is the ability to psychically manipulate someone's anatomy, physiology, or internal body regulation. It's somewhat similar to Fischer's affinity, though he can alter, erase, and plant memories. I once saw my father make someone's heart burst within their chest just by narrowing his eyes," Bram cautioned, another warning to never underestimate King Thane.

"Telekinesis is the ability to manipulate inanimate objects. Like that creepy kid in the Matrix who bends and twists that spoon with his mind? Telekinetics can levitate objects, move them, warp them, whatever they want. Demons also have our own version of seers, they harness the specialty of clairvoyance and we call them that exactly. Clairvoyants. Aside from being able to do basic demon powers, if a demon is given the power of clairvoyance, that is their only specialty. It's rare, and incredibly dangerous in the wrong hands.

"Perhaps the most risky of all though? Deal making. Desperate times call for desperate measures, and there are demons who thrive off of others' willingness to do whatever it takes to get what they want or need. Poor demons who cut a deal to make sure their children are fed, demons who get too deep into gambling and cut deals to try and work their way out of their debts... a lot of deal making demons run in gambling circles. The stakes are always high and the deal maker almost always wins. But just like any other kind of gambling, it sometimes becomes an addiction," Bram explained and I felt a shiver run through my body. *No deals. Never make a deal with a demon, Saige. No. Matter. What.*

"Wow," I muttered, feeling one hundred percent overwhelmed.

"Feel free to ask me anything as you think of it, okay? I want to tell you anything and everything you can think of," Bram grabbed my hands and squeezed them reassuringly.

"And you don't think I'm going to lose my green magic?" I swallowed roughly, not prepared to hear any answer other than no.

"Not a chance. Your magic is linked to your soul, Goldie. It's who you are as a being. If anything, it will be stronger now. The reason you were killing plants before was because of all the changes going on with you behind the scenes. We can practice a little soon, but first, I want to teach you something else that's very important," Bram smiled widely and my heart raced a little at how beautiful he was.

"Okay, what did you have in mind?"

He smirked, standing and extending his hand to tug me to my feet.

"Flying," he told me conspiratorially.

My mouth opened and he wrapped his arms around my waist and jumped up, his powerful wings beating against the air as we rose toward the sky.

"Oh my moons, oh my stars, oh my gods," I chanted as we went higher, well above the trees now and the whole of Naryan spread out below us. There were rivers and streams that intersected all across the terrain and it was beautiful.

Bram was chuckling at my theatrics, his hold still tight on my waist. Was he going to release me up here?

"I'm not gonna let you go, don't look at me like I'm a monster, Goldie. I'm going to hold onto your waist, I want you to extend your wings out, like mine. They will take over, it's like when you stand to walk, you don't think about telling your legs to do it, they just do," he encouraged and I did as he asked.

Looking back over my shoulder, I admired my wings in the sunlight. They were a gorgeous light green color and Bram was right, they did kind of resemble leaves with how the darker emerald color worked its way through them, like veins in a leaf. They were so thin, sunlight came through them with ease, but they were damn near indestructible. I knew, because I'd tested out trying to tear them in private. I needed to be sure I wasn't going to get in the air and have them blow out like a failed parachute.

"They're gorgeous, just like you." Bram kissed my throat and I swallowed my fear, working up the nerve to try and fly. The wind caught my wings and pulled us higher, making me squeal and Bram barked a laugh.

"Good, now flutter them. Like this," he demonstrated and I copied. We were doing it.

"I'm doing it!" I screamed and he smiled, pulling his hands off my waist.

"Wait, wait!" I started dropping down to the ground like a rock. *Fuck!*

"Flutter, Goldie! Open your wings and let them do what feels natural. They won't betray you," he directed and I let them span out to the fullest extent, squealing when I hit a pocket of wind that sent me upward at high speed.

"Bram! Look! Oh my gods, I'm fucking flying!" I cackled hysterically, swooping through the air and Bram chased me, taking part in my excitement and happiness.

He flew up beside me and we looked out over the rolling countryside, a huge mountain range in the background, the sun was hitting the water below and making it sparkle like millions of tiny diamonds.

"It's beautiful," I commented, awestruck.

Bram's hand slipped into mine.

"I know," he breathed, but I knew his eyes weren't on the landscape.

HOURS LATER, after we returned from the forest where Bram had taught me demon basics 101, I was exhausted. Despite my wings being light as a feather, it still required a good bit of strength to use them and they were muscles that I hadn't used in my entire life. And I don't work out. Like, ever. So I knew I'd be sore as shit tomorrow.

THE MAGIC OF BETRAYAL

Bram was sitting across from me on the bed, flicking through the TV, looking for something to watch. But I had more questions and now, I was starved for information. It was like my brain had needed that total shut down to put myself back together, kind of like a fail safe.

"Well?" Bram cocked a brow at me as he side eyed me.

"Well what?" I asked.

He sighed deeply. "Just ask me. You can't sit still. I know you have more questions."

"Okay, but can I ask them in rapid succession because I feel like that will be best for both of us and we can get this over with quickly? I'm getting hungry," I warned. Because my hanger needed a warning.

"Go for it."

Taking a gulp of air, I asked the first thing that popped into my head because of our earlier conversation on knotting.

"Does your dick shift into a demon dick?"

Bram threw his head back and laughed so loudly, I couldn't help but join.

"I'm not answering that. Next question."

I scowled, but whatever. *I bet it fuckin' does. But, I probably should ask something not dick related...*

"Do demons prefer cold or warm milk?"

"Are you high? Did you eat some of those mushrooms in the woods I told you not to touch?"

Shrugging my shoulders, I motioned for him to answer the damn question.

"We don't drink milk."

"I don't either. Guess that makes sense."

"Can I go make dinner now? I want lasagna," he questioned, looking at me full on now. I'd tucked my wings and tail away, but my horns were still adorning my head.

"One more question, then you can go cook me dinner. Can

you, ya know, use that tail as a spare peen or whatever?" I wondered, dead ass serious.

He choked, coughing into his elbow as he hopped off the bed.

"I'm done with you. You're awfully interested in sexual questions, princess. If you want a physical demonstration of exactly what I'm capable of doing with my 'demon dick' and 'spare peen'" —he actually used air quotes— "then I'd be happy to show you. But you might want to clear your schedule for a few days because I'm totally making a fuck nest to keep you in for days." Winking, he sauntered out of the room and I flopped back onto my pillow.

A fuck nest? So. Many. Questions. *Wonder if there's demon porn around here somewhere...*

"And don't bother looking for porn!" Bram shouted from the kitchen and I huffed.

Spoilsport.

Kai

Chapter Twenty

"Get up, man. We have work to do."

Growling, I rolled over and buried my face into Sprout's pillow, her scent surrounding me and making my throat constrict.

"Kai. You've been in bed all morning, it's one in the afternoon. You need to get up." Cam's voice was understanding, but firm. I just didn't have it in me to move today.

"Can't. Nothing is working."

"It's only been four days, K. We knew this was going to be an uphill battle, right? We're all battling our issues, man." Thunder rumbled from the sky and he pointed overhead, making his point. "There's a mile wide storm cloud hanging over everywhere I go, everything sets me off. We're lucky the area isn't under a fucking flood warning." He reached out and clapped my shoulder. "I get it, K. I fucking get it. We've all seen Fischer, who knows what the fuck planet he's living on right now!" Cam ran his big hands through his golden hair, looking like he might just rip it out. "Something is going on, Kaito. We all know that, but I can barely help myself right now. Our girl needs us to figure this out. Laurie has some spell she wants to try later tonight. She went to The Pig to get supplies, and if it works, we could have eyes on our witch as soon as tonight."

He was still hopeful.

I felt dead.

For three, well, I guess four days now, we'd done nothing but scour every old and falling apart text Laurie could find, we'd run through every possible scenario, considered finding a rogue demon that we could force to open the portal, but that was quickly dismissed because most rogues had been stripped of the ability to open the gateway, and what if she came back and we weren't here?

Three days without a single word from Sloane. That was cutting me up, too. I tried to stay angry, and it wasn't difficult at first, but the longer it went without hearing from him, the further I sank into the eager open arms of deep depression. *Was he okay?* Despite being appalled at his behavior, the thought that he might be hurt, possibly by his own hand, made me sick.

I hadn't talked about him with the others though. Cam and Fischer were on another level right now. Fish was downright scary, the evil glint in his eye hadn't broken once, the darkness gripping him days longer than I had ever seen. He was cold, detached, methodical. Often sitting alone, silently studying those books or looking at information on his phone, barely saying a word to us.

Bette was in full fledged denial. There was no way Saige wouldn't be coming home. She wouldn't, or couldn't, even entertain the idea that we may not ever get her back. Fuck.

Surprisingly, Laurie had stepped up. Big time. She'd told us all how she gave Saige up to keep her safe, figuring that if she wasn't near her, it would be harder for Khol to find her. Laurie had directed us on different articles and texts to look up online, plus she'd been giving us a crash course in Demonology that far surpassed anything we'd learned at Radical. Even Bette listened attentively to everything Laurie had to say, and I saw the pride shining in her eyes as her daughter used her knowledge for something Bette deemed worthy. There was no doubt that Laurie had a brilliant mind; she retained information like a sponge and I wondered if she had a photographic memory. It was impressive, but nothing had paid off yet. And I was sick of waiting.

THE MAGIC OF BETRAYAL

We'd returned to the apartment early the morning after Sprout was taken and packed our bags. Maven was missing along with Sloane. It looked like he had been at the place to grab some things, but most of his shit was still there. *That's just what we need, for Saige to get back and her beloved fox be gone. We couldn't even do that right.*

I could feel Cam's presence, he wasn't going anywhere.

"Fine," I snapped, "I'm going into town though. I want to get some things from the store." I rolled off the bed and pushed past him heading to the bathroom. I was being a little bitch, but I was fresh out of fucks to give.

The hot water pelted my skin and my arms hung loose against my body as I leaned my head against the cool tile in the shower. Why was everything so exhausting? I was always bursting with energy, and today, it was taking so much effort to just wash my hair. Crushing sadness. An unwanted blanket that weighed me down and stole any desire to shove it away, so instead, I pulled that bitch up around my neck and let it squash the pain.

Some time later, I got out of the shower and threw on some basketball shorts and a tank, grabbing my bike key and heading downstairs. Chatter from the kitchen and the sounds of dishes told me they were probably eating lunch, but I didn't want to socialize. At all. So I hung a sharp right and headed out of the house, eyes focused on my bike.

Nobody came chasing after me.

Rolling into town a few minutes later, I saw Frank and Arlo through the big window at the front of The Pig. Thankfully, they were able to pick up a lot of slack, and yesterday, I'd worked for a few hours to give them a break. It was weird as hell being in the shop without Sprout around. It was weird as hell *being* without Sprout around.

Even Bagheera had abandoned me. Whether it was the depression that pushed him out of my mind, or if it was his doing, I wasn't sure. All I knew was that it was radio silence and it made me feel even more empty.

I needed to refill the beer supply at the house, so I rounded the corner and parked on the street in front of Dinner Thyme. Hooking my helmet on the handlebars, a gust of wind whipped through the building lined street and I caught a scent that I hadn't in a while. The water mage. I inhaled deeply and frowned when another scent mixed with his. Laurie?

My nose led me past Dinner Thyme, past the bakery, Earth, Wind, and Flour and I peered around the corner into a narrow alleyway between the two stores.

Laurie and Douchemage were having a heated, yet hushed, discussion. What was she doing talking to him? I suppose she would know who he was, Sprout had dated the bastard for two years after all, but didn't Laurie know what he'd done to her?

Suddenly, her palm shot out and the clap of it catching his cheek echoed against the brick walls on either side of them. She said something else, the distance too far for me to hear, and took a step in my direction so I spun backward quickly and made my way to Dinner Thyme. *Guess she does know how he treated her and gave him a taste of his own medicine. Good.*

I loaded my cart up with a couple six packs and a bag of Flamin' Hot Cheetos, because what the hell? Perhaps the biggest testament to my mental state was that I walked past the fresh cut meat counter and didn't get a semi over the massive tomahawk steaks that were chilling in there. Grilling would require effort. The only effort I had in me today was stuffing my face with these spicy devils and getting my buzz on.

The cashier, Joanne, smiled brightly when I put my items on the counter for her to ring up. Ever since I'd throat punched douchemage in front of her, we often bantered whenever I came in here. Which was often enough with my penchant for cooking and trying new recipes.

She was speaking to me, but I wasn't hearing it. I nodded, not caring what I was agreeing to and handed her forty bucks, mumbled "keep the change" and stalked back outside.

On the way out of town, I did a double take when I spotted Sloane and Maven walking side by side down the sidewalk, Sloane's arms full of books. *What the hell?* I probably should have kept driving, but I just couldn't. Sloane's eyes widened as I pulled my bike over and stopped right in front of him.

"Kai," Sloane started, moving toward me as I got off and stepped up onto the sidewalk. His ice blue eyes were full of pain and the dark bags beneath them told me that he likely hadn't been sleeping.

"You found him," I commented, pointing at Maven.

Sloane looked down at Maven who was sitting beside his feet obediently. "Yeah. He was in the apartment, that's where Red left him when we..." he trailed off, not needing to continue that sentence.

Shifting my weight to my other foot, I nodded, "Good. I was worried he was gone."

"Is she... has anything happened?" he asked, looking at the ground.

"No. Everything is a dead end."

Sloane nodded gravely. "I've been searching for information, anything that might work."

"And why haven't you contacted us? I thought you were gone," I scowled.

"I didn't want to until I had something useful. I'm going to do everything I can to make this right, K. I'm so fucking sorry. How did Larson hide his true nature from us for so many years? I swear, I never would have taken her there if I had known he was a threat."

He was being sincere. I could count on one hand the number of times I'd ever heard him apologize.

"Why'd you have to fuck up so spectacularly, Sloane?" I asked softly, shaking my head at him.

"I don't do anything unless I do it well, brother. You know this," he replied, a small smirk tugging at the corner of his mouth and my own lips twitched in response.

We just took each other in for a beat, unspoken words passing between us. We'd been together forever, we didn't need to verbalize right now. His eyes said, I'm so sorry. Mine said, I know, brother.

His hand ran through his hair, which was getting longer than he usually wore it and he exhaled a deep breath.

"Is um, I mean, I know I probably shouldn't ask but... is he okay?"

"No, Sloane. He's not okay. None of us are okay, but Fischer? He's battling with his demon, or maybe he's not really fighting it anymore, I don't know. He's not talking," I admitted and watched pain bloom on his face again before he stiffened and shoved it down.

"He will be okay. We all will. Red, too. You'll see, K. I'm close to coming up with something to try, okay? Just don't give up on me, brother."

"Laurie has something she wants to try tonight."

"Laurie? Red's mom? She's back? What the fuck, man?" Sloane snapped, looking at me as though I'd lost my damn mind, and maybe I had. Shit, maybe we all had.

"Chill. She's gone above and beyond the past three days working around the clock with us. She hid Saige here and left to keep her safe from Larson. He played us, man. He played us all," I bit out, teeth clenched tightly as my hands fisted with violence. *I can't wait to get my hands on that son of a bitch.*

"You trust her? Do they?"

"We really don't have much of a choice right now, we're doing what we have to. So far, she's been useful and hopefully whatever she's planned for tonight will work." I wasn't holding my breath.

Sloane nodded, "Okay then. Call me if you need help. Tell them... I'm sorry."

"You can tell them yourself when you pull your nuts out of your ass and show up." I grabbed his neck and pulled his forehead against mine, letting my eyes shut, his smokey scent invading my senses.

"It really hurts here." He pounded his closed fist over his heart, his voice cracking as he echoed the words that he'd told me so many times in my childhood bedroom.

"I know, brother. I fucking know."

He pulled back and turned away, continuing down the sidewalk. Maven stared up at me, his brows furrowed in that grumpy foxy way he'd perfected.

"Are you coming back to the cottage? You'll have to run, I can't take you on the bike."

Cocking his head to the side, he paused for a second and then took off after Sloane. Guess they really were kindred spirits.

My arms were full of my beer and Cheetos when I walked into the kitchen ten minutes later.

"Where did you go?" Fischer's raspy voice startled me, I hadn't even noticed him sitting in the corner like some kind of malevolent spirit, his honey oak eyes being blacker than the devil's soul only added to the eerie effect.

"Fuck, dude. Can you quit being so creepy for like two seconds? Damn," I huffed, dropping my haul onto the counter before swinging the fridge door open.

"You're guilty of something. What?" he questioned, and I sensed movement.

Ignoring him, I put my beer in the fridge. It would be nice and chilled in a couple of hours.

Cam strode into the space next, his long golden hair hanging around his shoulders, spilling onto his hunter green t-shirt. He was going full casual today, rocking some dark grey joggers.

"Laurie got back just before you, she's out with Gran prepping some things for later," he told us, that hope still shining through his words and I didn't have the energy to attempt to give him a dose of reality. Guess I should've noticed the slight drizzle from the sky had finally stopped when I'd gotten back to the cottage. If he wanted to get himself all worked up over something that probably would fail, that was on him. I was protecting myself. I'd get excited when I had eyes on my cub again.

"Kai is hiding something from us. He was just about to tell me what when you walked in," Fischer so graciously provided.

Cam's gaze snapped to me and I rolled my eyes. But I knew they weren't going to let it go and it was probably best to just rip off the proverbial band-aid.

"I went into town to get beer and I ran into Sloane," I confessed, suddenly feeling exhausted and wanting to go take a nap. If I went and took a nap, time would pass quicker than this snail paced hell, and I won't have to talk to anyone. I was just so damn tired.

Fischer's face remained perfectly expressionless and Cam's eyes narrowed.

"And what did Sloane have to say, K?" Cam's voice deepened to a scary growl, and the room darkened from the clouds blocking out the remaining hints of sunlight, but I knew it wasn't directed at me.

"He told me he'd been working around the clock, searching for spells, anything that could fix this. He told me he was so sorry, and that he hadn't wanted to contact us until he had something concrete that we could try and use," I relayed the information, it was up to them if they wanted to do anything with it. "He told me to call him if we need his help."

Cam scoffed, but before he could reply, a woman's voice drifted from the back hallway, "Actually, that would probably be the best plan. If all four of you could be present for this, I think it will boost our chances of being successful. You're all incredibly powerful, and this is going to take a lot of fucking magic," Laurie suggested, snagging my bag of Cheetos and ripping them open, stuffing one in her mouth.

Is this witch serious right now?

"Excuse you, but those aren't for sharing," I grabbed for the bag and she backed out of my reach.

"You brought them into the kitchen, they're fair game. House rules. Sorry, kitty cat. So, can someone let Sloane know we need him here at eight? I just came in to tell you to find a fourth for tonight, and it sounds like you have that covered, so I'm heading back out to prep the location." Snatching a handful of my Cheetos from the bag, she tossed it back to me and left the room.

"Well, I can see where Saige's sassiness comes from. The nerve of some people," I growled, hugging my snack to my chest.

"Fischer, what do you think about having Sloane here tonight?" Cam asked our friend, who was staring out of the large window in the kitchen.

"I'll do whatever I need to in order to get her back here and keep her safe. She would have been better off if we had never shown our faces in this town," he stated matter of factly before striding away from the two of us, going who knows where. Probably to fantasize about murder or something.

"Call him. Eight tonight," Cam grumbled, leaving me standing in the kitchen. Pulling out my phone, I dialed Sloane's number and he picked up right away.

"Be here at eight. Don't be late. Bring Mave, and for the love of Jupiter's cock, don't do anything fucking stupid."

Bram

Chapter Twenty-one

There was a baby goat sniffing my neck, it's whiskers tickling my skin and making me giggle. Yep. Giggle, like a schoolgirl. Who brought this baby goat into my room and how did I get so lucky? I fucking love babies, all kinds of babies. Animal babies, bug babies, although sometimes those can look nasty as fuck, I don't really like those kind. Demon babies, although it had been years since I'd laid eyes on one, I still loved holding them. So small and cute and special.

"Be still, baby goat, you're tickling me," I scolded, but secretly loved it.

Sniff. Sniff.

"I'm sorry," the goat whispered against my throat.

Goats don't talk.

My eyes flew open, the dream evaporating from my mind in a flash. Goldie was wrapped around me with her face hidden beneath her hair and pressed against my neck. Her chest was shaking with her crying and nope—I was going to put a smile on this girl's face come hell or high waistcoats.

"I don't want to lose my green magic," she cried into my neck, her little baby horns stabbing me a little bit. *Oh, I like that.*

"Goldie, it's okay. You used your green magic the other day when you made yourself into a witch sized blanket burrito. I promise, it will all be okay. Now that your birthday has passed, you should have access to things you hadn't before. You need to learn, you told me about your magic being off, you don't want to keep decimating all of your plants, do you?" I questioned gently, hoping that she might see some reason.

Her head shook back and forth as she sniffled, trying to get a hold of herself.

"Good girl," I soothed, stroking her hair.

"I TRIED to get my horns to disappear and they won't go away, Bram. I did what you taught me and it's not working! I can't let my gran see me like this, it'll break her heart! You can shift so easily, I'm frustrated," she growled, the sound was demonic, dark, and oh so delicious.

"YOU HAVE to understand that at first, it can be a little tricky to master while you're still learning. Your shift is tied to your emotions, so if you feel any kind of strong emotion, you're at risk of sprouting horns and keeping them visible until you learn self-control. This is why it's good that you're here. I can teach you all of these things and you don't have to worry about harming anyone."

"Why would I harm someone? I'd never hurt anyone." She sounded offended and slightly concerned. It was precious the way her brow furrowed and her lips pursed. I wanted to kiss those lips off her face.

"Not intentionally. Like I said, it takes a lot of self-control. Accidents happen. Everyone fucks up when they're learning, and everyone here is used to that, it's to be expected. We can't have you walking around Emerald Lakes shapeshifting or making all the old people in town float through the air with your mind," I explained, smiling down at her softly and her face twisted in horror.

"Oh shit. Do you think I'll get those powers? I might not, you know? But yes, you have to teach me everything because I would never forgive myself if I harmed someone, accidental or not," she breathed, the horror in her voice of causing someone pain just showed her innocence and her loving heart.

"Don't worry, princess. We'll work through this together. But I would be expecting powers, and several of them. Khol is extremely powerful, so I think we should pay close attention. If you feel anything new or off, tell me right away, okay?" My hand cupped her cheek and her eyes flitted to my lips, and I watched as she licked her own.

Settle it down, you dirty demon dick, it was different on her birthday because we clearly thought she was already using her fingers to get a one way trip to pleasure town! Now is not the time because we don't have enough time, again. We're going to wait 'til she's begging for it, and then we're going to claim her for days. Sometimes, a man just needed to have a heart to heart with his cock. This was one of those times. The cheeky bastard.

But quiver me timbers, the way she's staring at me.

Nope.

Rolling away from her and out of bed, I walked over and threw open the curtains, letting the light spill into the room and hopefully, killing the mood. No way in Naryan was I gonna fuck her when she was so emotional over the others.

"Can you get some coffee for me?" she asked from behind me and I didn't turn to look at her as I power walked across the room, heading for the kitchen.

"Sure thing! Clothes for you are in the closet!" I called out, her laughter was like a siren song in the air, she knew exactly what she did to me.

Marching over to the expensive coffee machine I recently purchased, I began making her a big ass cappuccino, with frothy milk. The whole nine yards for my princess. I'd had to watch about fifty Youtube videos to figure out how to operate the fucker, but now I was practically a pro at this, and I used my artistic skills to make her a beautiful picture on the top of the milk.

I smelled her before I saw her. She smelled of my favorite things, burning fire, damp soil after the rain, and that underlying vanilla, coconut, and sunshine scent that was all Goldie. *Delicious*.

"I thought you could just snap your fingers and get anything you wanted," she teased and I turned to her, holding the mug between both hands.

"If that worked, I would've snapped my fingers after the first time I met you in your dream, princess. But yes, usually I can, but I wanted to make this for you. Personally." I smiled, handing her the mug and when a laugh burst from her mouth, I grinned so hard my cheeks hurt.

She was staring down at the snail I'd designed, it was just a normal one this time, nothing phallic about it. But it did have little horns, just like hers.

"You're insane," she chuckled, moving to take a seat at the island.

"Never claimed to be anything else, Goldie. You like it, though," I flirted and started making my own coffee.

"Ahh, so good."

She moaned. *Moaned*.

My cock was hard enough to chop a tree down right now. *Fuck you, Paul Bunyan*.

"Glad you like it, Goldie," I rasped, adjusting myself against the cabinets.

"What are we doing today?"

"Well, after breakfast, I need to go have a meeting with my father. I've stalled for the past three days, told him that you were out of it with your powers manifesting, so I bought some time. But he wants to talk this morning. Khol will likely be there, too. He's also asked how you're doing," I confess, looking back at her to gauge her reaction to that.

"Seems a bit like bullshit, don't you think?" she asked, lifting her mug to her mouth and making an obscene noise yet again.

"It's up to you if you want to get to know him. He's obviously never been a father to anyone, and he fucked up in the way he went about getting you here. We all did, princess. But talking to him a little might be good. For both of you?" I moved over to the island and sat down beside her, sipping on my own coffee. *Damn, this is some good shit.*

She didn't respond, just stuck her finger into the foam of her coffee and swirled it around, lost in thought.

"Do you think, is there some way I could contact my gran?" she questioned, her voice pained.

She was doing better than she had been, much better. She was actually speaking and out of bed, but her heart was still shattered and it was painfully obvious that I couldn't mend it. Not on my own, anyway.

"Let me get through this meeting first, and then I'll see what I can do, okay?" I reached out and pressed my hand against her round cheek, loving the way she leaned into the touch. I loved touching her, any part of her, that electric jolt that filtered through my skin and sizzled my veins every. Fucking. Time. Saige Wildes was an addiction. She was a blessed sin that was wrapped up in stupid pun t-shirts and yoga pants that held *the* fattest ass. My heart skipped a devilish beat thinking about peeling those fuckers over her juicy butt, I bet my fingers would sink into it so deep, I could leave the prettiest marks.

"I'm going to use your bathroom pool," she told me and I barked a laugh.

"That's a first hearing it called that, but I like it. And it's all yours."

With a snap of my fingers, a plate with an assortment of bagels appeared in front of her and she groaned.

"Carbs, thank the stars."

"Not the stars, but you can thank me if you want to."

She glanced at me and I winked. Her cheeks reddened instantly. *I love that.*

Standing up, I snagged a bagel for myself and trailed my hand over her back as I moved around her. "Eat up, princess. I'll be back in a couple hours."

"Quit standing around out there, get your asses in here!" My father's voice bellowed from within his private quarters and Khol and I glanced at one another before pushing the double doors open and walking inside.

"Fuck, Dad." I shook my head, disgusted.

He was sitting at his desk, a woman bouncing up and down on his lap, his fingers buried in another.

"Yes, son. That's what's happening here, but I can understand how you might have forgotten what it's like seeing as how you refuse to let the snake out of the cage," he grunted, throwing his head back and clearly finishing.

Khol raised a dark eyebrow at the sight and cleared his throat. I'd tried telling him what my father had been like in the time he'd been gone. He's gotten crazier with each passing day.

"Someone has to try and save this race," he snarled, pushing the woman off of him and shooing them both away. "Close the door on your way out."

Khol and I moved to the chairs that were in front of his massive wooden desk that had intricate carvings etched into nearly every available surface. I'd always loved this desk, knowing one day I would be sitting behind it.

"The people that have heard the news are thrilled. Hope has been restored to the community and we need to celebrate. A party will go a long way to restore the fighting spirit our people have been stripped of in the past years." He leaned forward, clasping his hands in front of himself on the desk.

"When?" Khol asked.

"Tonight," my father replied, his voice hard. There would be no arguing this.

Khol turned to me. "And is my daughter... is she well enough to attend a party this evening?"

Concern flashed in his eyes before he covered it. He was good at that. So fucking good at hiding his feelings.

I opened my mouth to respond but was cut off when Dad's massive hand slammed down on his desk. "I have been patient. Three days this girl has been in my home and I have let her recover. I'm done waiting. She will be there tonight. End of discussion."

Rage burned behind my eyes and I pushed my demon down. If he thought he could have a say in anything about my Goldie, he had another thing coming. I already fucking hated him. She had seemed better this morning though, and perhaps a party would be good for her, get her out of my house and introduced to some new demons. Maybe she could make a friend who had horns. A friend who didn't have a cock, one who had tits and a vagina. A girl. She could have a friend who was a girl.

"She'll be there. What time?" I bit out, trying to keep the anger from my tone, but gods damn was that hard to do.

"Dinner will be served at six followed by dancing and entertainment at seven," the king stated, sitting back in his chair.

"Sire, have you spoken with Asrael, Thijs, and Errone? Are they going to be returning soon?" Khol questioned, and I wondered if he really gave a shit. He despised Asrael. Like, with a fucking passion. Maybe that's why he wanted to know if he'd be here, so he could kill him. I'd watch.

"I have not. They haven't completed their missions, so they are not welcome back in my kingdom. Simple as that."

Wow, what a prick face.

From the corner of my eye, I saw Khol's jaw tick and I wondered what the hell he was thinking.

"Where is the girl's mother, Khol?"

"I don't know. I suspect she'll show at Saige's home soon, once she realizes she's missing. Why?"

"You know why," my father's eyes narrowed, challenging.

My eyes widened. "You want to bring her here? To what? Fuck her? See if you can knock her up yourself?"

"Don't sound so scandalized, son. I'd do anything for my people. She's carried demon spawn once before, I have no doubt she can do it again. Whether it's mine or not, I don't really give a fuck."

"I'll keep an eye on the area to see when she returns. I don't give a fuck what you do with her," Khol snarled, his horns erupting from his head.

A knock on the door broke the conversation.

"What?" My dad barked and the door cracked, one of his little bitch boys coming in to whisper something in his ear and I watched a wicked smile grow on his face as he listened to the words.

"Thank you, Nigel. Gentlemen, you'll have to excuse me. There are things I need to do that are more important than sitting here with you both. Do not be late to dinner," he growled as we stood and moved to the exit, slamming the door behind us as we stepped out into the hallway.

KHOL WALKED beside me through the castle and I observed several of the staff's eyes bugging out when they saw him. Everyone knew who Khol was and knew that if he was back, it could only mean that he'd been successful in his mission.

"The king has... changed."

I snort. "Yeah."

"Do you think he's stable? To lead?" Khol asked quietly. He may be a badass, but even asking such a question was treason.

"He hasn't been stable in a long fucking time, Khol. I've tried telling you, but it's really not something that hits properly until you've seen it for yourself. And now you have. All he does is drink, fuck, and sleep. Oh, and kill people. Ones that have supposedly wronged him in some way." I shrugged my shoulder, our steps clapping against the stone beneath our feet as we approached my home.

"Does she... does she want to see me?"

He didn't need to say her name, we both knew who he was referring to.

"I'm not sure. She shifted the other evening. Completely, a full shift." I smiled when his face lit up.

Khol twisted his hands together in front of him and it was strange to see him uneasy. Vulnerable.

"She's okay then?" he asked softly.

"She's far from okay, man. You went about this whole thing in the worst possible way. She misses all of them. Her home, her store. Bette."

"Fuck, I know. I'm horrible at this. All I could think about was getting back here, coming home. It was selfish. I'll tell her as much. I never thought I'd get a chance to be a father and now that she's grown up and doesn't really need one, I'm not sure how to do this," he admitted and I felt for him. But I felt for her, too.

"Let me go in and see if she wants to talk? No promises, though."

He nodded and I slipped through the door.

"Goldie? Where are you? I need to talk to you about something," I called out, my eyes darting over the room but not finding her anywhere.

My heartbeat picked up and I was about to bellow her name when a giggle had me slowly turning around, but she wasn't there.

"I swear, princess, you better come out from wherever you're hiding. As much as I'd love to hunt you down, there's— oomph!" All the air whooshed from my lungs as I hit the ground.

"Gotcha!" Goldie laughed, rolling over onto her back. Pushing myself up on my hands, I glared at her. Wings out, hair splayed across the dark hardwood. "I was floating up there in the corner," she breathed, trying to catch her breath from all the laughter.

"Hmm. Well, it seems I'll have to be more on guard if these are the kind of games you want to play. But you have no idea what you've started, pretty princess. I love games, and I always win in the end," I growled and smugness settled into my bones when her cheeks flushed and she squeezed those thick thighs together.

"What did you want to talk about?" She changed the subject, but that was probably for the best right now.

Jumping up, I extended a hand to her and pulled her to a stand.

"Khol is outside. He wanted to know if he could come in and hang out with us for a bit. We have a dinner party tonight at six, so it won't be for too long," I added, hoping to ease some of her anxiety by letting her know that this wouldn't go on for hours. Her eyes widened and she nodded slowly, wringing her hands together.

"Oh, well, okay. Do I need to change?" she asked, looking down at her outfit. She was wearing a pair of ripped up jeans and a loose navy blue tank top.

"You're perfect," I promised, leading us to the door. Before I could open it, she slipped her small hand into mine, squeezing tight. Looking down at Goldie, I gave a supportive smile and opened the door to let Khol in.

His arms were clasped behind his back, his face serious and intense. That's how he was all the time though, so I was used to it. But if he wanted to win her over, he might need to not look like he had a cactus lodged in his ass.

"Hi," he said with a hint of shyness, eyes on my girl.

"Hi," she responded with a degree of wariness, eyes on her toes.

"Come inside," I offered, gesturing for him to get in here.

We moved over to the sitting area, Goldie taking up the corner of the sectional with the chaise so she could have her legs out in front of her. While they got situated, the minibar was calling my name.

"Drink, anyone?" I offered.

Khol and Goldie both said, "Yes, please," at the same time, and I chuckled.

I poured two glasses of whiskey for myself and Khol and made a vodka cranberry for my girl. I'd seen her drink one before and I didn't want to get her fucked up on dragon fire before the party. When I turned around, Khol was sitting in a chair across from the couch, nervously twisting his hands together. I'd never seen this man nervous in my fucking life. Goldie was staring at me, though. *That's right, princess.*

After passing out the drinks, I didn't hesitate to sit down right beside her, our thighs pressed together. Khol cleared his throat, shifting uncomfortably and Goldie blushed. Didn't bother me in the slightest.

"So-"

"I-"

Goldie and Khol spoke at the same time. They both froze and I squeezed her hand and gave Khol an encouraging look.

"Saige. I want to apologize for the way I brought you here. For the way I went about looking for your mother. I didn't know you were my daughter, I didn't even know you existed. I'd given up any hope at being a father a long, long time ago. It's been a century since I've been in Besmet, in my home. I was desperate to get back here and see old friends, family." He grimaced at the word when Goldie shifted in her spot.

"Family? Do I have more family?" she questioned, biting her bottom lip, nervous for his response.

Khol smiled and visibly relaxed knowing that she was interested in hearing what he had to say. "You do. A fairly large one, in fact. There have been a few additions in the years I was gone, so if you'd like, maybe we could meet them together?" he offered, looking hopeful.

She nodded, taking a sip of her drink.

"You're right, though. You did fuck up," she told him and he choked a little on his whiskey. *Bet that burns.* "When exactly did you find out that I was your daughter?"

Khol's face pinched a little and I kind of enjoyed seeing the big bastard in the hot seat. His daughter was a gods damned ball buster and he was going to get a grade A verbal smackdown.

"I suspected when Sullivan revealed that you were actually Laura's daughter. Though honestly, I didn't want to believe it. That would mean that the woman who I'd loved had left me and hidden my child, probably the only one I'd ever have, from me. That I'd missed her entire childhood and a big chunk of her young adult years. Not only that, but none of the other three had been successful in reproducing, so I didn't want to get my hopes up," he admitted, leaning back in his chair and running his hand over his face.

"Keep talking. I want to hear everything. You and Laurie. The guys. The orders you gave them. Did you know that we were involved romantically? Was that part of their—" her voice cracked, "mission?"

"I met your mother in a bar. We had a fast and intense love story. Or I should say I did. She never loved me." He shook his head and diverted his eyes to the carpet for a moment before continuing, "She was intelligent, beautiful, witty. She told me she was a research student and was in the city working on a project for an employer who'd snagged her out of college after reading some of her reports. When I convinced her to stay, she assured me her boss was fine with her working remotely and building up business in Portage Falls. I proposed four months later. She'd told me how much she wanted a family of her own, despite being so young. She was only nineteen at the time, you know? But I couldn't deny her a thing. I wanted to give her the whole world, and knowing that I likely wouldn't be able to give her a baby fucked me up. But I was selfish and I figured what the hell, not thinking that she would actually get pregnant. I really loved her and I'd long given up hope on returning to Besmet, so why not be selfish for once? We could adopt kids and have our own family if that's what we wanted," Khol explained as I twirled Goldie's hair around my fingers.

"But she did," Goldie responded.

Khol nodded, taking another drink of his whiskey.

"She did. She must have found out very early on, because of how everything lines up with your birthday," he added, his voice low.

"Did she know you were a demon?"

"No. After I fell so hard for her, the thought of telling her the truth scared the shit out of me. I was afraid she would leave, that she'd be scared of me, or worse, disgusted. Demons don't exactly have the best reputation, if you hadn't noticed. I let her believe I was a mage since I could do all of the same kind of magic." Khol leaned forward and placed his empty glass on the coffee table.

"Why would she have run away then? You were engaged and in love." Goldie sounded skeptical, and I didn't interrupt. This was between her and her father.

"That part, I don't know. That is why I've been searching for her for the past twenty-eight years. She destroyed me. Then to find out she also stole my chance at being a father?" Khol's knuckles turned white as he gripped the arms of the chair.

"I'm sorry she did that to you," Goldie said quietly and I quickly glanced down at her. Her eyes were wet. *Ah, fucking shit, if he makes her cry again, I'm going to have to kill him.*

"You're apologizing to me, wild one?" Khol asked, his tone full of disbelief. Or maybe it was wonder.

"She wasn't a good mother, she didn't want me either. So, I kind of know how it feels to be rejected by her," she murmured.

Khol's mouth was hanging open at this point and my heart was aching for my princess.

"Saige, I am the one who is sorry. I became obsessed with finding her, getting answers, making her pay for what she'd put me through. Did I know that the team was involved with you? Yes, I did. I sent them there with direct orders to get any information they could, by any means necessary."

Goldie sucked in a sharp breath, but Khol didn't stop.

"When Sullivan found that picture of Laura, you, and your grandmother, he sent it to me. I had him get some of your hair and mail it to me so I could test it. I didn't get the results until you had the unresponsive episode after projecting here. But, Saige, there's something I need to tell you. I want there to be total transparency here, and while I could have defended my actions before, claiming a broken heart and just being in the line of work that I am... but please, believe me when I tell you that I am so very sorry. If I could take it back, I would. I wish I could."

The ice in Goldie's drink clinked as her hand trembled. Watching him though, whatever he was about to say, it wasn't going to be good. His face was pale and I could feel Goldie's heart pounding from her back as I draped my arm around her and pulled her closer.

"Just tell me." Her voice shook and a tear slipped down her cheek.

"Cam, Fischer, and Kai... as far as I know their feelings toward you are genuine. When I learned of your relationship with them and I felt like I was getting closer and closer to my target, I made an order and I regret it." He shifted in his seat and the beast inside of me was two seconds away from attacking him for her sake. "I ordered Sloane to get involved with you," he finally admitted quietly.

Goldie dropped her head, her hair spilling forward to shield her face.

"He argued with me. He didn't want to, didn't want to betray his brothers. I think he knew that they would be devastated when it was time to leave and he also didn't know what to think about that photo he'd found. I wouldn't take no for an answer... he negotiated with me. He wanted a personal mission for Cam, so they could find some answers on what happened to his family, and I agreed. Knowing now that you're my... my daughter, having met you, I can't stand to look at myself in the mirror."

"Khol," I snarled his name as Goldie cried silently beside me.

"I'm so fucking sorry, Saige. I understand if you never want to speak to me again, but I couldn't live with myself without telling you the truth. I'll give you some space." He stood up and moved across the room to the door.

"Wait," she choked out as she pushed herself up off the couch and darted after him to where he was standing.

He stood so still it was as though he'd been frozen and when she collided with him, her arms wrapped around his waist, he looked at me like what the hell do I do now? Then he exhaled and pulled her tightly against his large body, tears glistening in his green eyes.

"I don't forgive you yet, and I don't know where this will go, going forward," Goldie told him, her cheek pressed against his chest. "But, I always wondered what it would have felt like to get a hug from my dad."

"Oh, sweet girl," Khol's voice cracked as he held her tighter. "I've wanted to hug my own child for over one hundred years. I will make this right, I promise. I'll see you two at dinner."

A moment later, Goldie stepped back, wiping her eyes and Khol nodded once before he disappeared from the room.

"Princess, are you okay?" I asked as I stepped up behind her and pulled her against me.

"I will be."

Warrior woman.

"Yes, you will," I promised.

She turned to face me. "It's kind of strange, but I feel more calm than I have since I got here. For some reason, getting the answers from him, knowing that my other relationships weren't just part of the job... it helps. I'm still upset, but I miss them, Bram," she frowned.

"Even Sloane?" I cocked an eyebrow and she breathed a laugh.

"Surprisingly, yeah. I'm still level thirty-eight pissed at him, though. That number needs to come down to more like a fifteen before I'll be able to speak to him without ripping his tits off."

"Jesus, woman. Don't arouse me right now. We have a dinner to get to," I joked, attempting to lighten the mood, and she smiled.

I love when she smiles at me.

Saige

Chapter Twenty-two

After Khol left, I started getting ready for the party. I was in the large bathroom again, utilizing the massive walk in shower and Bram was using the smaller bathroom to get ready.

My mind felt like it was so full with everything I'd learned in such a short time. I had a father, one that I could get to know, if I wanted. He seemed to genuinely want to get to know me, and that made me happy. When I'd first met him, I was horrified. He was so... demanding, scary, and intimidating. I wanted to trust him, and knowing what I did of my mother, his story didn't surprise me much. But why did she leave him, and why did she hide me like that?

The words he'd spoken about the guys had given me some peace. I'd wanted to believe with all of my heart that our relationships hadn't been a lie. They were so intense with me, and I just couldn't see how someone could fake that. Even Sloane, I wanted to forgive him. After hearing about what Cam went through as a teenager, I couldn't act upset that Sloane wanted to get time off for them to look into everything. Not having closure on something so horrible had to take its toll.

I knew I needed to get back home sooner, rather than later. Who was running the shop? Were the guys even speaking at this point? What had happened after I was pulled out of that room? Cam must be losing his fucking mind... and while I was still pissed that they'd lied to me, I was trying really hard to put myself in their shoes. Plus, I had lied as well. Bryce's face flashed in my head, the way he'd threatened to kill them, and how I hadn't told any of them because I didn't want them to be harmed.

Of course, I probably would have said something if I'd known they were fucking killing machines. My gut twisted uncomfortably at that. Who exactly did they kill? Bad guys? Has to be bad guys or people who deserve it, because they did have a moral code.

A knock on the door cut off any further thoughts.

"Princess, I have a dress for you on the bed. I'll be in the kitchen, come find me when you're ready," Bram told me through the door.

"Okay, I'm almost done!" I called out in return and started putting on my make-up. Bram had everything I needed. Liquid black liner, red lipstick, foundation that matched my skin perfectly. Fucker had probably gone through my bathroom and looked at all my stuff, but I couldn't even bring myself to get upset about that because it was comforting to have some things from home.

I went with a smokey look on my eyes that made my green eyes look brighter than usual. Nerves fluttered in my belly when I thought about what might happen tonight at this party. I hadn't met the king yet in any official capacity, and from what little I'd seen of him, plus what Bram had told me, I wasn't really sure I wanted to meet him, but I had no choice.

After applying my lipstick, I made sure my robe was tied securely and I walked out of the bathroom, eyeing the garment bag that was draped over the mattress. I sucked in a breath as I pulled the zipper down and caught a glimpse of the black beading that shimmered in the light. As I removed the bag, I saw that the dress had a nude mesh bodice with long sleeves and the intricate black beading swirled in floral patterns that would make it look painted on. The black tulle skirt flared out at the waist and trailed down to the floor. This dress was gorgeous. By far, the nicest thing I'd ever worn in my life.

I breathed a sigh of relief when I realized it had a built in bra, because there was no way I was going to let the girls go unrestrained anywhere that I might have to dance. Weapons of mass destruction needed to be contained.

Bram had given me my own dresser, and I needed some panties, so I laid the dress down and went to grab a pair. I shook my head when I saw a pair sitting on top of the dresser with a note that said 'wear me'. The pair he'd chosen were sexy as hell, and red. The front was lace and the sides had three straps that wrapped around to the back which dipped into a thin piece of lace that would be lost between my cheeks. Blushing, I pulled them on and peered at myself in the mirror. Holy moon balls. *I'm so taking these back home with me. My ass looks amazing.*

I then worked on getting into the dress. It was lighter than I expected despite all of the beading and material. Hopefully, that means I won't sweat to death and end up looking like a roasted chicken. Looking in the mirror, I hardly recognized the woman staring back at me. My horns were still on display and I found I kind of liked them, but my wings and tail were hidden, though the back of my dress dipped low, nearly to my tailbone, so if I wanted my wings out, they could be. Easily.

Smiling at myself, I just wished that my guys could see me dressed up like this. I wondered what their reactions would be and my heart ached at the thought. *Just get through tonight and then I will work it out when I can get back home.*

"By the moon, Goldie girl. You're stunning," Bram breathed and my eyes met his in the mirror as he approached. His hair was styled, the long red strands combed to the side, giving him a classy look that somewhat didn't fit with what I knew of him, and he was wearing a tux. My mouth dried up as I turned and blatantly checked him out. *Damn.*

He smirked because he knew exactly what I was doing and he knew he looked like a ginger god.

"Do you need help zipping that dress up, princess?" he asked, his voice a low rumble.

I didn't. I could've used my magic to zip it, but I turned and gave my back to him. There wasn't much to zip since the back was so low, but when he sucked in a sharp breath I knew he'd seen the panties he'd picked out, his eyes flicking to mine in the mirror.

"I knew those would be perfect," he whispered, his breath spread over the side of my throat and goosebumps erupted over my skin. Once the zipper was up, he trailed his fingers up my spine, our eyes locked together.

Leaning closer, his lips pressed against my neck and I sighed. We hadn't kissed since that one time in the pool, but I'd be lying if I said I hadn't thought about it. A lot.

One of his hands pressed against my stomach, moving up over my chest and wrapping around my throat. He looked massive behind me, like he could protect me from any enemy, and I found that I really liked that.

Turning my face toward his, he didn't hesitate to press his lips to mine. He swallowed a soft moan that escaped me and kissed me so thoroughly, I knew I'd need to reapply my lipstick over my now swollen lips. I liked the idea of walking in there and everyone knowing that he'd already put his mark on me.

"It's time to go, princess." He smiled against my mouth.

I nodded and reluctantly looked to the mirror once more to check my make-up. The red of my lipstick was smeared and a good portion of it was on Bram's mouth. Chuckling, I walked to the bathroom and cleaned up my face and reapplied. Bram followed me into the bathroom, waiting patiently for me to hand him a make-up removing wipe.

"Part of me wants to leave this on so every fucker in attendance knows that I'm the one you've been kissing," he admitted and I shook my head.

"I don't think your father would appreciate it, and I don't want to piss him off tonight. Let's go before we're late."

Bram wiped his face quickly and tugged me back out to the sitting area, urging me to sit down on the chair. "Be right back," he told me and disappeared for about five seconds before popping up again, kneeling at my feet.

"Shoes, princess," he smirked, reaching under the skirt for my foot.

"Those are beautiful, Bram."

And they were. Nude heels that had the same beading and stitching as the bodice of my gown. Thankfully, they weren't too high so I wouldn't make a fool of myself.

"Not as beautiful as you." He took my hand and pulled me against his body, pressing a kiss to my forehead that triggered a soft sigh from my lips. "Okay, I'm going to jump us there," he warned and I nodded.

We hadn't practiced jumping on my own yet. To be honest, it still freaked me out and I was scared I'd end up somewhere I shouldn't. Bram's hands gripped mine and a blink later, we were standing in the massive throne room that I'd been in a few times before. A string quartet was playing somewhere and the scent of delicious food swirled through the air. There were people everywhere, laughing, drinking, talking. Everyone was dressed to the nines, some had their wings and tails out proudly, and others looked human. I looked around the room in awe, there were so many different horns, too. Some curled, some had two sets, all different colors.

"You okay, princess?" Bram asked and I smiled up at him.

"Yeah, just taking it all in."

"Let's get you a drink, I'm sure people are going to be talking your ear off as soon as they realize you're here," he warned, wrap-

THE MAGIC OF BETRAYAL

ping an arm around my lower back and ushering me through the crowd.

He wasn't wrong, as soon as the people realized Bram was here, with me on his arm, most discussions cut off and whispers went up in the air. That's the thing about whispering, if it's just a couple of people doing it, it's not noticeable. When it's hundreds of people, well, it kind of loses its purpose of being discreet.

Trumpets sounded and everyone turned to look at the front of the room where the king appeared, moving toward his throne. Clapping and cheering started just as I felt someone move to stand on my other side. Looking over, Khol was staring at the throne, also dressed in a tux. I wasn't sure how old my father was, but he didn't look a day over forty five. His black hair was streaked with silver that made him look more distinguished in a way, and fine lines wrinkled at the corners of his eyes that I imagined were more prominent if he smiled, or scowled.

He was tall, too. Probably six-three. Looking around the room, it appeared that nearly all male demons were tall as hell. Even the women.

"Great people of Besmet, thank you for joining me today for this momentous occasion!" the king boomed and the crowd cheered. "Some of you may have heard rumors that we have a new demon with us tonight, a hybrid." The crowd quieted, hanging onto his words. "It is true, my people. Khol the Merciless has returned home and with him, he brings his daughter!"

It was dead silent for about five seconds and then everyone went crazy. The noise was deafening and I felt a little overwhelmed. What was it about me that was so important? I was one person, was it just the fact that now they knew it was possible to have babies with witches?

"Let us eat and drink, afterward there will be music and dancing. I will introduce you all to the lovely Saige after dinner!"

My face was burning. They wanted me to go up there and get

introduced to the hundreds of demons in this room? I was going to need several drinks before that happened.

All at once, people started making their way to a large dining hall that was just off the throne room. There were tables that must've been thirty feet long. Serving staff immediately started to bring out plates of salad.

"Come on, Goldie. We have to sit with my father at his table," he sounded apologetic.

"It's fine, I kind of figured that would be the case," I smiled at him and hooked my arm through his.

"May I also escort you?" Khol asked, offering his arm as well. I smiled and Khol took my arm, wrapping it around his. Together, the three of us moved to the dining hall.

Khol surprised me. Going from the villain to the father figure in the blink of an eye, I'd hardly had time to process what I wanted from our new found relationship. He'd been so nervous when he walked into Bram's home, I could tell by the shine on his forehead that he was sweating a little. Khol did not seem like the kind of man to get nervous, and that softened me toward him immediately. The nervousness he'd shown before was nowhere in sight now, though. He moved us through the crowd with purpose and from the nods he received from others, to the wide berth we were given, I knew he was respected here. Revered, probably. He'd done the impossible, after all.

After years of being rejected by my mother, I was a little taken aback at how quickly I'd warmed up to him. Daddy issues? Probably. But if Khol wanted to genuinely get to know me, I'd take everything he was offering because deep down, I really wanted to know who he was.

I felt so many eyes on me as we walked through the crowd and my body was starting to heat up from the unwanted attention.

"You're doing great, wild one. You look beautiful tonight,

THE MAGIC OF BETRAYAL

that's the main reason they're looking." Khol patted the top of my hand in a reassuring gesture that made my heart squeeze.

"Thank you. You look... well, almost exactly the same as the other times I've seen you," I chuckled and Bram laughed out loud.

"He's kind of obsessed with suits and looking put together all the time. Once, I invited him to the gym and he showed up in dress slacks and a crisp white button down shirt with suspenders. Suspenders, Goldie!" Bram laughed and so did I at the image, because I could totally see it.

"Laugh all you want, children. I still beat your ass, Bram. Didn't get a drop of blood or a wrinkle on my shirt either," Khol reminded him, puffing his chest out.

"Yeah, yeah, old man. You need someone to loosen you up a bit."

Khol stiffened slightly at that comment, but recovered quickly. "Having my daughter around will be sufficient. Anyone beyond her is unnecessary."

Well, that is just plain sad, but I couldn't deny the warmth that spread in my chest at his declaration. He really wanted to be a part of my life. Before we could say another word, we'd reached the table and it looked like we were getting lucky tonight by sitting right at the head of the table next to King Thane. He was dressed in a tux as well, a crown on his head that was a gold band with words scripted on it. *I wonder if I yank it off, will he Gollum out on me?* Bram resembled his father only slightly. Thane's hair was black and his eyes were nearly matching. It was the shape of his face that was the same, the arch of the eyebrows, the shape of the eyes. Where as Bram always had this look about him that was a mixture of fun and crazy, Thane just looked... off.

As a woman, I'd lived through a lot. My asshole alarm was going off full blast as I eyed this man. The way he stared too long, like he was trying to make me uncomfortable, the way he didn't initiate any conversation, waiting for one of us to do so first, I knew this man was not a good one. I held his gaze, though. Fuck being intimidated by men who thought they were powerful and could just treat everyone else around them like shit. I recalled all of the little comments Bram had made about his father, and it bothered me that his father didn't treat him better. It bothered me a whole lot.

"Father, may I introduce Miss Saige Wildes, my date this evening," Bram bragged as he added that last part onto my introduction.

King Thane's eyes never left mine and in the awkward moments after Bram had spoken, they narrowed slightly before Bram leaned down and whispered, "You are supposed to greet him now, Goldie."

Fine.

"Your Majesty, thank you for having me tonight. Dinner smells delicious and the castle is decorated beautifully."

Thane held out his hand, but not in a way that I would be able to shake. It was palm up, like I was supposed to put my own in his. *Weirdo.*

"Go on, princess. I'm right here." Bram nudged me and I placed my hand in Thane's.

"I'm very glad you're here tonight, Saige. We've been waiting a long time for you. Come, you'll sit beside me tonight, you are, after all, the guest of honor." His hand squeezed mine a bit too tightly and I winced, but he directed me to the chair to the right of his at the head of the table. Khol was right behind me, pulling it out and waiting for me to sit before he pushed it back in.

"Thank you," I told him, but my throat was dry as sandpaper. I needed water.

Thane dropped my hand and sat in his own chair, Khol dropped into the seat beside me and Bram sat across from me. That kind of surprised me, I'd assumed he would've been the one beside me, but what did I know about how royalty sat at dinner parties? Nothing, I knew absolutely nothing, which was why I snagged my glass of water and chugged half of it before realizing the other twenty people seated at our table were all staring at me with open mouths.

Oops.

I put my glass back down and shifted in my seat.

Thane started laughing and the tension at the table broke, some of the others joining in nervously. *Are they scared of him?*

"I'm sorry, I don't know your customs here. That was likely the first of many faux pas I'll make tonight, Your Majesty," I admitted, holding his eyes.

"Sweet girl, I couldn't expect you to know our traditions when you've only been in the realm for three days. Enjoy yourself tonight, that's what we're all here for anyway."

Glancing across the table, Bram was burning a hole in the side of his father's head with those striking amber eyes. Luckily, the rest of the food began coming out and that gave me something else to focus on.

"They will serve four courses. A salad, a small appetizer, an entrée, and dessert," Khol whispered and I nodded, grateful that someone was giving me a heads up on what to expect here, even if it was only about the food.

"The king will take the first bite and then everyone else may begin," he added, his voice playful, like he was teasing me. I turned to the left to look at him and caught his fading smirk just in time.

The food was amazing. It was probably the best food I'd ever eaten, actually. The main dish was homemade pasta with a delicious spicy garlic sauce and shrimp. *Fuck, I'm stuffed.*

Chatter was loud in the large room, but our end of the table remained mostly quiet. That surprised me a little, I was expecting a bit of an interrogation from King Thane about who I was, but that never came.

"Everything okay, Goldie girl?" Bram asked me from across the table, the candlelight flickered on his face giving his beautiful features a more sinister appearance.

"Yes, the food is fantastic here. You've been holding out on me," I joked.

"You trying to tell me you don't like my cooking, princess?"

"Just telling you this is better," I bantered back at him and he chuckled. He was a great cook though, and he knew it.

"You're cooking for her, son?" Thane questioned, sounding disgusted at the thought.

Bram turned slightly in his seat. "I am."

"He's been very hospitable, I'm thankful," I added, unsure why his father sounded like that.

Thane's eyes darkened and he narrowed them on his son just as several servers placed our dessert down in front of us, seeming to distract him from his temper.

Khol tapped on my arm and I gave him my attention, letting those two demons sort their shit.

"Dancing will be next. You'll be expected to start the festivities by dancing with Bram," he explained and I nearly choked.

"What?" I hissed. While I loved to dance, I did not love the idea of being the center of attention in a room full of demons.

Khol sighed. "He didn't tell you?"

Glaring at Bram now, I waited for him to take notice as I answered Khol, "No, he didn't tell me I'd have to dance this evening."

"You would've just freaked about it, kind of like now," he flicked his eyes to Khol, like it was his fault for worrying me. I would have found out about it in a few minutes, anyway.

Ignoring him, I took a bite of the cheesecake in front of me and a moan left my mouth. Chocolate and caramel deliciousness. Reaching for my wine, I realized once again that nobody was speaking at our end of the table, so I looked around to see what the hell was going on now. Bram was staring at me like he wanted to drag me back to his bed, and when I braved a look at Thane, I was more than a little sickened to see the same look on his face. My

THE MAGIC OF BETRAYAL

stomach dropped and I pushed the dessert away from myself, what a travesty. It was no secret that I was a vocal eater, or whatever you call it. A moaner. I just enjoyed my food, gods dammit. *Men.*

"Right, let us begin the fun part of the evening," the king announced to us, standing up and clapping his hands three times. The chatter ceased, all attention on Thane.

"I hope dinner was enjoyed, our chefs really outdid themselves tonight. Our guest of honor was impressed!"

Clapping and cheering erupted and my cheeks flamed. I really did not like this attention.

"We'll take a fifteen minute break between dinner and the opening dances, you're all excused."

Bram stood, walking around his father to my seat, pulling it back and taking my hand as I stood.

"Be ready in ten minutes, Bram," Thane ordered, turning his back and walking away. I took a deep breath, feeling like I was able to breathe for the first time since I'd sat down beside that man.

Khol took up my other side once again and the two of them guided me back toward the throne room where the center of the room had been cleared while we ate, leaving ample space for dancing.

"So, what kind of dancing are we doing?" I asked, nervousness fluttering in my chest.

"It's a waltz. Just follow my lead, princess. You'll do great," Bram assured me, but my nerves only slightly dissipated.

"The dance is not a hard one, you have nothing to worry about," Khol whispered in his calming tone. It was bizarre because I didn't know this man, but for some reason, I trusted him not to bullshit me. If there was ever going to be some hard truths, he'd be the one to give them to me straight, even if it hurt me or painted him in a bad light. His confession about what he'd ordered Sloane to do... while that had hurt, a lot, the fact that he'd told me when he didn't need to yet... well, it went a long way toward how I viewed him.

A small group of women were in our direct path and the way their eyes lit up when they landed on Bram and Khol, I had to bite my tongue. The four of them curtsied when we got close enough, they looked young, maybe a couple of years younger than me. Then again, they were demons so they could've easily been hundreds of years old and I wouldn't know.

"Ladies, thank you for coming this evening," Bram addressed them, nodding his head.

A few giggled and I tried really hard not to roll my eyes, but maybe if I did, then I wouldn't have to look at the fuck me stares they were giving him.

"It's our pleasure to be here to celebrate with you tonight," one of the demon girls said, innuendo clear.

"And we're so happy you're back too, Khol," another one gushed.

Okay, so they're just going to act like I don't exist?

"Maybe you two can come find us after?"

My eyes widened at the brazen balls on this bitch. And when she reached forward and touched Bram's arm, I didn't think. I reacted.

A snarl that I didn't even know I was capable of burst from my mouth and I felt my wings snap out, fast and angry as I stepped in front of Bram and narrowed my eyes.

"Do not fucking touch him," I growled, the hair on the back of my neck lifting, almost like a wild animal's would when they felt threatened.

The four of them gasped and clutched their non-existent pearls, but it was a little late for the innocent act. They had just been propositioning my man and my father for some kind of orgy.

Bram and Khol both chuckled behind me and I felt Bram's large hand wrap around my waist, tugging me back against him.

THE MAGIC OF BETRAYAL

My heart was thrashing in my chest but the longer he held me, the more I felt like I was able to calm down.

"I'm otherwise engaged. If you'll excuse us, we have a dance to start," Bram announced, pushing us past those women and I glanced back to make sure they kept their distance, but I did see Khol wink at them. *Ew.*

Bram ushered us to the middle of the large room, staring down at me with amusement.

"What?" I snapped.

"You were jealous," he said all smug like.

"You're mine, Bram Carlisle," I told him firmly. Surprised by how much I meant it, but it was the truth. He cocked his head, studying my face. "I wanted to rip her arm off even after she backed away just to make sure she could never touch you again," I admitted, and I didn't feel guilty about it either. There was just this part of me that felt pleased with my actions because I had defended what was mine.

Bram smiled. "That's our bond, Goldie girl. I've been waiting for you to accept it, feel it, let me in. I told you long ago that you were made for me, princess."

My arms wrapped around his neck as I tugged his face down to mine, capturing his lips in a claiming that everyone in attendance would see. They needed to know their prince was spoken for, and the thirsty bitches needed to back off. He groaned against my lips and people started cheering and applauding our performance, just before the music started playing softly.

Bram pulled back, smiling widely. "Let's move, Goldie. Follow my lead," he ordered and then we were floating across the stone floor. He held me tightly as I let him direct my body, spinning me at the right times, pulling me close, and then letting me twirl out of his embrace. He was clearly an experienced ballroom dancer, he moved with confidence and sex appeal that was just all *him.*

As he tugged my arm, spinning me against him so that my back was to his front, I turned my face to look up at him and we paused for a moment, staring at one another. His mouth landed on mine and the cheers from the room were deafening. Warmth was spooling in my core and I thought about what it might be like to claim him fully.

Bram looked sharply away from me, and I realized his father was standing next to him, hand stretched out, waiting for me. Was this part of their tradition? Did I have to dance with him? The thought of his hands on me made my skin crawl.

"Miss Wildes, may I have this dance?" Thane bowed and I flicked my eyes to Bram. He looked murderous, but he gave me a slight nod. *Okay.* This was something I had to do. Hopefully, it would be over soon.

He placed his hand on my waist, squeezing slightly too hard and I winced against the pain as he gripped my other hand and began moving us around the room.

"My son is quite taken with you, Miss Wildes," Thane stated, his eyes flashing with something I couldn't put a name to.

"It's mutual," I told him as he tugged me closer against his body.

"Yes, well, he's not king yet, is he?" he asked, sliding his hand down from my waist to the exposed skin at the base of my back.

"What does that mean?" I bit out, trying to remain somewhat calm and polite, but I didn't like his hands on my skin. It made me think of Bryce.

"It means that I have been without a wife for quite some time and I have been looking for a suitable replacement. The fact that you will be able to bear more of my children makes you perfect for me. You'd be queen, my dear," he whispered in my ear and I felt the blood run from my face.

"That- that is quite an offer, Your Majesty, but I'm afraid I cannot accept."

The music in the room was speeding up, the notes hitting a crescendo as I looked into Thane's eyes, and for the first time since I'd stepped through that portal I felt true fear.

"I think I'd better just—" I tried to squirm from his grip, but he dropped my hand and held my waist with his two large hands, keeping me from going anywhere.

"It wasn't an offer, my dear. I was simply telling you what would be happening. You will be my wife, and you will give me more children. Now, follow me," he ordered and I stared at him with my mouth open. *Where is Bram? Where is Khol?*

Thane guided me up the steps to the raised platform that held his throne and all eyes were on us. My stomach was churning, I needed to get the fuck out of here. Something bad was about to happen, I could feel it.

"Great citizens of Besmet!" Thane boomed and the room quieted. My eyes were darting across the room wildly, searching for the only two men here who I thought might give a shit about what was coming. Then I spotted them, against the back wall of the room. Those women from earlier were running their hands over their bodies, but my eyes were locked with Bram's. The way his were moving, I knew something was wrong. It was the only part of him that was moving. They were frozen like that. They wouldn't be able to save me now.

"Allow me to properly introduce Saige Wildes, daughter of Khol the Merciless, and future queen of Besmet!"

Applause rang out and trumpets started blaring loudly. *This isn't happening. This can't be happening.*

"I'd like to say that I would be able to wait to claim this woman until after our wedding, but with times as dire as these, I don't think any of you would mind if I put a royal Carlisle baby in her belly?" Thane bellowed, holding his hand out as his other one held me tight against his body and once again, the crowd cheered. Maybe they thought I wanted this, that being a queen is all any woman here would hope for in their life, but if Thane tried to put his dick in me, I would chop it off.

"How about a public demonstration?" Thane asked, his hand

sliding up on my waist, brushing the side of my breast that was only covered by thin mesh.

Looking at Bram and Khol again, their faces were red and murder was in their eyes. They had no idea this was going to happen. That much was apparent.

I needed to get to them. Quickly, before this went any further. If I harmed the king though, would they kill me? They needed me, right? Maybe I can just subdue him long enough to escape.

When Thane moved behind me and lowered his mouth to my shoulder, I felt like I was going to faint. Or throw up. Or probably both. Breathing in deeply, I called on my green magic and felt it flicker in response. I felt his mouth open, trailing wet kisses up my neck and I swallowed bile as I waited patiently for his hands to leave my waist.

They did, finally. Just as I figured he would, he slid his hands down to cup my ass and that's when I made my move. Small vines exploded from my hands, seeking out his wrists and securing them tightly, I didn't even hesitate for a second before I jumped and let my wings carry me halfway across the room, my feet hitting the stone floor just as the king roared, "Get her!"

But that wasn't going to happen. I wasn't going to let him rape me. I was strong, and I only belonged to men I chose to give myself to. There was screaming and the off note chord of a violin as the music came to an abrupt halt. Bram's eyes widened and I held my hands out, more vines coming to my aid and a symphony of gasps rang out around me as the vines pushed all of those handsy bitches away from him and Khol. People were diving out of my path, yelling for more guards, but I didn't stop. I wouldn't. There was movement at my back and I knew I only had moments before I'd be captured and then who knew what they'd do to me.

Both men in front of me were frozen, just like Khol had done to the guys in that warehouse before. *How am I getting us out of here?* I needed to jump. Fuck, fuck.

I slipped my hands into theirs and remembered what Bram had told me about jumping. You just picture in your mind where you want to go and use your mind to push it into motion. *Jump. Why can't I just open a fucking portal? Of course nobody wants to teach me that.* I thought about Bram's living room, if we could get there, we could regroup. Plus, we'd be far enough away that whatever Thane had done to them would wear off. Guards were running straight for us, hands reaching, wings extended, faces angry. I kept my thoughts on Bram's house. Jump. Jump. JUMP!

The three of us hit the rug in the living room.

"Holy shit, holy shit, oh my moons," I swore, my breathing ragged as I searched the room to make sure they were with me and we were alone.

"Khol, you okay? We need to get out of here. Now. He'll come looking here first." Bram scrambled to his feet and Khol was hot on his heels.

"Where are we going?" I breathed, my heart pounding so hard I thought it might burst.

Bram looked at me over his shoulder as he threw his hand out toward the empty space to his right, the portal shimmered and grew instantly.

"Emerald Lakes," he reached for my hand and Khol grabbed my other, "now."

The two of them pulled me through the portal just as I looked back and saw armed guards bursting through Bram's door.

Home, I'm going home. My heart skipped when I thought about seeing my guys.

Fuck, I've missed them so much.

Fischer

Chapter Twenty-three

This was becoming a shit show.

Kai was off the rails, his depression was in the driver's seat and until we got Saige back, I didn't see how that would change. The mate bond was probably making it worse. I would say it sucks to be him, but his shields had slipped and I could feel everything he was broadcasting, and on my own level, I understood. Having him around was uncomfortable though, and the beer run he took earlier was actually a relief.

Cam was refusing to face reality. Silly viking. He still kept a good hold on his shields, but try telling that to the gods damn storm cloud that followed his gigantic ass around. He did nothing except research and strategize with Laurie and Bette. I listened in, of course. But I really hadn't seen anything that would suggest any of these plans would end in success. Much to my dismay, I also hadn't been able to catch Laurie in a moment of vulnerability, either.

I was in control these days. After Saige convinced Fischer to let me out of my internal prison the night we'd fucked, he hadn't really locked me back up. Then, at the warehouse, it was like he dropped all shields and begged me to take over. Too much pain for *him* to take. That was fine. I lived off pain and blood. This is why he *needed* me.

The interesting part of all of this was that I really did miss firefly. I liked her spirit, her sassiness, her unabashed ability to just be herself. Fischer could really take some pointers from her in that department. It was high time he stopped denying that I was a part of him. He'd been a wreck ever since the warehouse. Realizing his beloved Sloane had been in love with him and yet betrayed him so blatantly... tough pill to swallow. Pfft, I was sure Saint Fischer would be back soon, ready to send me back to the mental prison he saved just for my bad boy ass.

The sun had set an hour ago, Sloane would be here soon.

Sloane. The motherfucker who always tried to keep me locked up. Well, I'm out now, and I'm not going fucking anywhere. And if he thought he could try that alpha shit on me, he had another thing coming. Fischer put me in charge because it was too much for him to feel. I suppose feeling heartbreak from other people was easier to swallow than your own. Either way, I was going to keep the both of us safe, and I needed my firefly. Also, I was desperate for some bloodshed, but I swallowed that down.

"Fischer?" Bette asked, and when I blinked in her direction, I realized it was likely not the first time she'd addressed me, but also, that wasn't my name.

"Yes?" I answered.

"Are you okay? You've been really quiet." She stood beside me and we both stared off into the darkness. Laurie was out there in the woods, setting up who knows what. She was also still blocking me from her emotions, but I didn't want to rock the boat if she was willing to help us. Some people were just more private, though I did wonder where she'd been trained to learn such a skill.

Not looking at her, I answered, "Yes. I'm fine. I'm ready to see if this works tonight."

She hummed in agreement. I knew she was anxious, because unlike her daughter, she did nothing to hide her feelings. Bette's feelings fluctuated between angry, sad, anxious, and worried. *'Probably should ask her how she is, asshole,'* Fischer reprimanded me and I rolled my eyes at the polite prick.

"And you?"

"I just want her back," she gritted out. *There's the anger again.*

The roar of an engine in the distance had me clenching my fists. I knew exactly who that engine belonged to.

"I'm going to go grab some things from my place. I'll meet you guys down there." Bette walked away toward her cottage and I heard the crunch of gravel as Sloane got closer to the house.

Letting myself back inside, Kai and Cam were in the kitchen, having a beer.

"Sounds like Sloane is here," Kai stated. *Captain Obvious, this guy.*

Cam grunted and I said nothing as I dropped into the seat beside Kai. The shifter seemed to be a little brighter in the eyes tonight. The despair wasn't rolling off of him like it had been, so maybe he did have a bit of light left in him. The door to the mudroom squeaked and I stared down the dimly lit hall waiting for him to come around the corner. Sloane appeared a second later, his eyes catching mine instantly and I smirked, which didn't match Fischer's heartache at seeing the asshole. Sloane's heavy boots thudded on the hardwood. Dark jeans wrapped around his thighs and a black Breaking Benjamin t-shirt was tight against his chest.

Sloane's eyes widened a little when he realized it was me, *Faris,* smirking at him, no doubt wondering what the hell was going on. *Good, let him wonder.* I'd pushed Fischer down into our psyche and the others hadn't been bothered by having me around all this time, so he could suck it. *Literally.* Granted, they didn't technically know Fischer had left the building, but they knew something was *off.* We all watched as Sloane removed his backpack and gently sat it on the ground, but before he could get it unzipped, Maven exploded from the thing, growling.

"Didn't have anywhere else to put him while I rode over," Sloane explained as Maven scowled at him.

"You literally piss off every living creature you're around, huh?" I asked, slouching back in my chair, watching his face.

"Fischer, I'm sor—" he started, but I cut him off.

"Good for you. Can we get on with this?" I stood up looking at Cam, but he was staring at Sloane.

"Yeah, let's do that," Cam agreed with me, but I waited for the explosion that was brewing.

Sloane sighed, his pain clear. In fact, that was the majority of his emotions right now. He was hurting, big time. He was ashamed, embarrassed, scared.

Boo hoo.

"I am so fucking sorry. I fucked up and I have been doing everything since to find a way to fix this, to get her back."

Cam stared at Sloane for an uncomfortable amount of time before running a hand through his long hair and rising to his feet.

"I don't trust you anymore, and I certainly do not forgive you. I'm not sure I will ever be able to forgive you. But let's get our asses out there and try to get Saige back. That's what's important tonight, not our bullshit," he added, staring at each of us. A warning. Stay focused.

Not bothering to wait, I turned and walked out to the backyard. There were flames dancing in the distance and I guessed that was where we were doing this spell. As I led the way, I felt a twisting in my head, *he* wanted to come out.

'It's my turn,' I thought to him, shoving his presence down deeper.

Nobody spoke as we marched through the woods to a small clearing where Laurie was finishing setting up. Bette wasn't here yet. Maybe she wouldn't come.

There were four chairs arranged in a square, facing inward. Laurie had a basket at her feet that she pulled different things from and sprinkled over the ground, mostly in the middle of the chairs.

"These seats for us?" I asked, tilting my head toward them when she looked up from what she was doing.

"Yeah, this spell is going to take a lot of power, so you guys might as well sit while we do it."

I stalked over to the chair closest to her little basket and sat my ass down. Hopefully, this wouldn't take long and then I could get back to my own plan of how to fix this shit. Which consisted of heading to the nearest city and finding a demon and forcing them to open the fucking portal. I wasn't even gonna ask. We were beyond pleasantries. I'd slip right in and plant the thought right in their head. Problem. Solved. We should've done this days ago.

"Evening, gentlemen. You must be Sloane," Laurie said to him over her shoulder as she knelt down and added a few more things to the grass before pressing her palms down flat and pushing her own magic into the ground.

"I am, and you must be Laurie." Sloane shifted on his feet and I picked up immediately on his nerves and... regret. Regret is a bitch. That's why you should always be damn certain that what you're doing is what you want because we almost never get a second chance to fix it. I sure as shit don't. That's why everything I do and say is intentional. When you don't get the luxury of correcting mistakes, you learn real fast to act with purpose and with confidence because there'd be no time for apologies. He was learning that lesson right now.

"What's the plan, Laurie?" Kai asked, taking the seat to my left.

She stood, brushed her knees, and returned to her basket of stuff. "This spell is ancient, I had to translate several old texts, but in theory, this should work," she told us.

Cam sat down to my right and Sloane was across from me.

"Where's Bette?" Cam asked, running his palms down his thighs.

"She was too upset to come out. Didn't want to get her hopes up if this doesn't go the way we want," she explained. "Shall we begin?"

"Let's do this, I want to see my girl as soon as possible," Cam nodded, his voice gruff and deep.

"I will give you directions as we go and I'll chant the spell, just focus on what I tell you to do and this nightmare will be over in less than fifteen minutes." She clapped her hands and I caught a flicker of excitement coming off her body. *She must really think this is going to be successful.*

A breeze ruffled through the forest, the leaves above us rustling in the wind and Cam quickly pulled his hair up to keep it out of his face.

"Sloane, if you could please cast some of your fire at the ground, then I will ask Cam to do the same in a few moments, okay?" Laurie directed and I watched Sloane's face illuminate briefly as he pushed fire from his hand and dropped little flames against the grass. A whoosh and then a burning pentagram was ignited, surrounding us.

"Perfect, now, Cam, add your magic to Sloane's."

Purple sparks flew from Cam's fingers and the flames around us surged to ten feet high as his electricity crackled and the flames changed from orange to blue before they shrunk down to only a few inches high.

"By using your power in the flames, it will keep them going when the storm comes," Laurie explained, holding a book that was practically falling apart from age. "At this point, I am assuming the prophecy is real and that you four are a part of my daughter's 'five', so I am running off the hope that by combining your physical powers, along with Fischer's cognitive abilities, and Kaito's mate bond, I will be able to use an advanced locator spell which will give us access to the portal. Does that make sense?"

It did, actually. This might actually work. Then I felt *him* again, pushing against my restraints I'd put in place to keep him away.

'Just chill out,' I told him.

"Yes," everyone agreed.

"Great, when I tell you, cast your magic as forcefully as you can to the center of the pentagram. It will feel draining, that's normal. It is going to take a tremendous effort to get this spell to work, so push yourselves. We'll get her back."

I could feel the excitement from the others, the hope. *He* certainly was hopeful.

'Let me out of here, you psychopath!' he screamed in my head.

'Not yet.'

"Kai, add your magic," Laurie directed.

A burst of yellow magic fired from Kai's hands to join the red fire and a sparking line of electricity from Cam. The earth actually shook beneath my feet and I grinned.

After a few moments, Laurie looked to me and nodded. Holding my own hands out, I let my own black and silver magic fly toward the center of the pentagram to join the others last, just as the first raindrop hit my cheek. The wind increased, blowing my hair around my head as our magic swirled in the center of us, cycling around and around until it resembled a tornado. A tornado of fire that flashed with lightning and produced the sounds of Kai's animal and the screams my power induced.

It was scary as fuck. And I didn't scare easily, fuck, I didn't scare at all.

Sweat was running down my face and I could hear the groans of the others as they continued to funnel their magic into the cyclone.

But this felt... unnatural. Not right. Something wasn't right.

"Keep going, not much more now," Laurie shouted and then continued her low chanting as she moved around the outer circle, careful to stay back from the flames as her hair whipped around her face. The book was no longer in her hands and I saw a slow smile on her face as she looked out into the woods where a figure moved in the darkness.

Is it Saige? Did it work?

Suddenly, there was pressure around my ankles and my torso, which caused me to break my concentration for a moment as I glanced down and saw a vine twisting around and around, securing me tightly to the chair I was in. Before I could call out, my wrists snapped down to the armrests and more vines made sure those were equally secure.

"What the fuck is happening?" Cam boomed. "LAURIE?!"

Our magic died as we all realized something was wrong. Very, very wrong.

Tinkling laughter danced in the air and a chill ran up my spine. No.

"You boys are fools," Laurie chuckled just as the figure in the woods stepped forward.

Bryce.

The flames of the pentagram burned out, leaving smoke in its wake, wafting up to the dark sky.

Kai let out a savage roar and I knew that Bagheera must've returned. That wasn't a sound a human could make.

'Faris! Let me out, you fucker!' Fischer screamed, my brain aching.

My eyes looked around at the guys, we were all tightly secured to our chairs. Kai was about to lose his fucking head, rocking his chair and snarling. Cam had closed his eyes, like he was trying to get a hold of himself, and when I looked at Sloane, he was still as a statue, his eyes locked on my face.

Laurie moved to the center of the pentagram, Bryce beside her, a smirk on his face.

"I honestly expected Khol to have trained you all better than this, it's slightly disappointing," Laurie taunted, her blue eyes, the same shade as Bette's, were cold and full of fury.

"What the fuck are you doing, Laurie?" Cam barked, his eyes narrowing.

She laughed and tutted, like he was a six year old asking a stupid question.

"Cameron Jacobs, thirty-one years old, storm mage, brother to Hunter Jacobs. Such a sad story," Laurie sighed, holding a hand to her heart in mock sympathy.

Fischer snarled in my head. "Gods dammit."

"Fuck you, you crazy bitch," Sloane growled.

Laurie threw her head back and cackled. Unhinged.

"Oh, poor Sloane Sullivan, aren't you tired of never being *good enough*? You just keep trying, bless your pathetic little heart. Daddy didn't love you, did he?" she teased, getting closer to him before she leaned over in front of his face. "Don't hit me, Dad! Please, I'll be a good boy."

Holy fucking shit. This bitch is insane. Maybe crazier than I am.

Sloane's body was trembling with rage. It called to me like a beacon in the darkness. Unfortunately, it also called to *him*. I felt *Fischer* shatter the cage I'd locked him in and my awareness faded as he pushed forward, but I refused to give up total control. Never. Again.

"Sloane," I rasped. Shaking my head free of that fucking psychopath who had possessed me for the past several days.

His gaze snapped to mine from across the grass, I could make out the icy coldness in his eyes, the pain that flickered there.

"Don't listen to her. Nobody listen to her," I told them, "we have to keep our heads."

"Shut. The fuck. UP!" Laurie screeched and I shifted in my chair. *How the fuck are we going to get out of this?* Our powers were depleted, as I reached for mine I felt a tendril of magic, but I needed to save it until the perfect moment. Until she revealed herself, what her end goal was.

"Was this your plan all along?" Cam asked, his voice not wavering a fucking octave.

"Of course it was. I made it twenty-eight years without Khol finding me or learning anything about this shitty fucking town. Then one day he magically finds me on an ATM camera in Emerald Lakes? Please. He played directly into my plan, just like you all have. This has been a long, long time coming."

"Why is douchemage here?" Kai spat venomously and Laurie snorted.

"What an interesting nickname, Bryce. Maybe I should start calling you that? It's fitting for you." She raised a brow in amusement as Bryce glowered at Kai.

"How long has he been working with you?" Sloane asked, getting back to the important shit. Keeping her talking to get as much information as possible, like we learned in training.

"Working with me? No, he works for me. And we both work for Montague Industries. It's amazing, state of the art training, you know? Fun fact, Asrael runs that company. He used to be best friends with Khol. He's the king's brother, and when he takes his throne, I'll be the one beside him," she grinned maniacally, spilling all her secrets like an unhinged psychopath.

Bryce stood dutifully beside her, his emotions rotated between anticipation and desire, but my powers were so weak that the colors of his feelings were dimmed. But the desire wasn't directed at Laurie, nor anyone in this circle. My jaw ticked when I thought it was probably for Saige. *I'm going to kill that motherfucker. Slowly.*

'Yes, yes we fucking are,' He growled darkly from the depths of my psyche.

"I've had enough chit chat, boys. Let me tell you how this is going to go. You've no doubt figured out that your powers are depleted. You're not getting out of those chairs until I let you. I was seventeen when I first learned about the prophecy. It's about me, did you know? I found four of my five, but without being able to get to Besmet, I wasn't able to bond with King Thane before my twenty-eighth, such a shame," she singsonged, shaking her head.

"If the prophecy is real, Saige has already completed it. She has her five, you dumbass," Kai snarled.

"Hmm, does she though?" she cocked her head to the side as she glared at Kai.

"One of you isn't completely tapped out. Any guesses on who?"

My blood turned to ice. *She knows. She planned all of this. Everything. Right down to the order in which we were instructed to use our magic, having me go last so that I'd use my power the least amount of time. I'd be amazed if I wasn't so disgusted.*

Sloane's face paled and Cam lunged against the vines that were keeping him captive.

"I wonder, how would the prophecy come to fruition if four of my lovely daughter's five don't remember who she is? Do you think it would still be her? It's never fucking been her. I created her, hid her for this purpose. I sent Bryce here to keep her occupied, to keep her uninterested in other men. It was going great until he fucked up." Bryce scowled at her, but didn't comment. "Luckily for Bryce, I'm a quick thinker."

"How could you do this to your daughter?" Cam growled, his face red, sweat glistening on his brow from his useless efforts to free himself.

Horror slid down my spine as a thought hit me. No. She wouldn't.

"Laurie," I spoke, my voice sounded like someone else's, "where is Bette?"

The guy's heads all snapped to me with matching looks of shock and fear.

"My darling mother is none of your concern, Fischer Bahri. But I'll tell you what is!" She clapped her hands. "You're going to use that little remaining bit of magic that's coursing through your

THE MAGIC OF BETRAYAL

veins and you're going to dip inside your friend's heads and erase every last memory of Saige."

Shouting and cursing echoed throughout the woods from my brothers.

"Get fucked," Sloane snarled.

"He would never, ever do that," Kai yelled.

"Oh, but I think he will. Otherwise, I'll just kill you all." She shrugged. Fucking shrugged, like this was just a discussion about what television show we would watch later.

"Don't do this, Laurie," Cam growled, his face pained.

"Oh! But Cameron, I almost forgot! Must have slipped my mind earlier when we were discussing your dead family. Did you know that Montague Industries studies rare affinities?"

The hairs lifted on the back of my neck.

"This is actually good news, so don't look so pissed off." She walked over to him and knelt between his thighs. "Where did you hide that day we came and burned your little cabin to the ground?"

Cam's mouth fell open and nobody breathed.

"Don't get too hopeful, your mothers are still deader than doornails, but your brother? Hunter?" She tilted her head to the side, and my heart pounded in my chest. *No fucking way.* Cam was frozen in his chair, I wasn't sure he was even breathing at this point. "You'll all return to the compound with myself and Bryce once Fischer does as I asked. It'll be a lovely little family reunion." She reached forward and smacked him patronizingly on the cheek.

"You're lying," he spat, venom dripping from his words.

She crossed her arms. "And why would I lie about that? Fischer can tell I'm being honest, can't you?"

Cam glanced at me, his face pale. I observed Laurie, not wanting to use my power to sort through her crazy, but this was important and I gasped as she literally pushed an image into my head of a young man, likely in his early twenties and my eyes flew to Cam's.

"He's alive. By the fucking stars, Hunter is alive, brother," I choked, emotion taking over.

Cam tilted his head back and roared like a beast. A feral, terrifying, murderous beast.

"Moving on, Fischer, let's focus. Erase everything from the moment before you were given this mission. I want them to have no memory of Emerald Lakes, Saige, my mother, nothing. Then you will plant in their minds that they work for Montague Industries and they'll leave willingly with me."

Bryce cleared his throat and Laurie snapped her head around to glare at him. "But he will remember. He will know even if he removes their memories," he unhelpfully pointed out, but my gut was already twisting with the words I knew she'd say next.

"That's why I'm going to kill him afterward."

All hell broke loose. Well, as much hell that could break loose when four incredibly powerful mages are powerless and strapped to chairs.

"Like fuck you are! I'm going to rip your gods damn head off!" Sloane screamed, the veins in his neck protruding.

"I'm going to rip your throat out!" Kai promised, his teeth flashing in the night.

"And if I refuse?" I questioned, trying to remain calm.

"That's why Bryce is here. I'll give you a moment to say your goodbyes because afterward, you'll have one minute to do what I said, or he will drown them where they sit, you included," she sneered.

"Fischer, don't you fucking dare," Cam's eyes met mine, they were shining. *Fuck.*

"You don't want to do this, she'll never forgive you." I tried to reason with Laurie. *What the hell else can I do?*

"You think I care about that, Fischer? We've already established that this plan has been in the works for years. Let's give them a moment, Bryce." She grabbed his arm and pulled him with her.

"This isn't happening," Kai breathed.

"Fischer, don't even think about it. We'll figure something out. Don't do it," Cam begged, his voice hoarse. Our gazes connected and he was pleading with his eyes, his expression pained. He must've seen the acceptance in mine and I watched a tear as it trekked down his red cheek. It broke my heart.

My eyes closed and I went over my options quickly, I had none. The amount of magic I had left wasn't enough to try and break through Laurie and Bryce's mental shields. Cam's brother was alive, he was going to get him back. Asking me not to save my brothers was futile, there's nothing I wouldn't do for them, and I know if the situation was reversed, they wouldn't hesitate either. I inhaled a deep breath and opened my eyes again.

"I love you guys—"

"NO!" Cam bellowed.

"And the past month has been one of the best of my life. Our bond, our brotherhood. Saige," I breathed.

"Fischer." Sloane's voice cracked, but I couldn't look at him. I wouldn't be able to do this if I did.

"She healed me in a way I didn't think was possible, or that I deserved. Not after what I've done. The blood, the screams... the fucking pain."

"Look at me, Fischer."

I can't.

"You three will fix this, okay? It will be okay. The stars will shine down and fate will guide you, but you have to be alive to do it." My heart was pounding in my chest, my throat was so tight it was hard to breathe.

"Brother," Kai whispered, tears on his cheeks, "don't."

"I think we both know that I have to, brother."

"Fischer, gods damn you. Fucking look at me!" Sloane yelled, and my heart cracked when my resolve broke and he caught me in his gaze. We just stared at each other for a beat before I smiled softly.

"I love you, Sloane," I murmured, needing him to hear the words, needing him to understand.

"Don't say goodbye to me, Fischer, I need you. I've always needed you. I barely survived the past three days, I won't survive a lifetime. Do you hear me? If you die, I'm going to chase you into the afterlife. *Do you hear me?*" He was desperate. Wildly so. It was devastating.

Sloane was straining to get free from his binds. The cords in his neck on full display in his fight against his restraints. Tears trekked down my cheeks as I studied him. He was so beautiful. He'd always thought he was the dark one of the two of us, but he was my light. My savior. All I'd ever hoped for him was that he would one day allow himself to feel. He screamed in frustration before stilling, his chest heaving. Those icy blues slammed into my honey oaks and the emotional exchange that happened between us in those seconds was more than we'd ever had. It was brutal honesty. Sloane accepted that he was not only capable of love, but that he was deserving of it. *Gods, I am going to miss him so much.*

"You saved me, Sloane. I never would've made it past twenty if I hadn't had you. And now, I'm going to save you." I looked away, trying to block out the screaming, the pleading, the begging.

"I love you, Fischer. I fucking love you, don't leave me. Fuck! FUCK!"

He loves me.

Laurie stepped back into the center of the pentagram. "You have one minute, Fischer."

Bryce lifted his hands and the yells and screams from my brothers were replaced with gasps and gurgles. They should be able to hold their breath for a minute, but just in case, I didn't hesitate.

"I love you guys. Forgive me," I begged, closing my eyes and letting my power manifest, letting it slink from my body toward the three men I loved like family. I would do this for them. I'd always known I wouldn't live a long life, not in this line of work, and not with my demons.

'Fucking melt her brain!' Faris screamed.

'I'm too weak to penetrate her shields,' I sighed.

The fear of drowning had lowered theirs, though. My essence slipped right into their psyches with zero resistance.

The meeting with Larson. Driving to Emerald Lakes. Meeting Saige for the first time. Her beautiful face and wild green eyes. The barbeque at the park. My magic flipped through all of those memories at a rapid pace, I didn't want to risk taking too long. When I reached this moment, I let them believe we were all doing a spell together. One that had gone wrong, very wrong. A spell that killed me.

Did it make me a coward that I didn't want them to hate me when I was gone?

You work for Montague Industries. You're going to stand up and leave with her and Bryce when she says. Those words burst from my head and slipped right into their brains, they wouldn't even be able to fight it. My shoulders slumped forward, my power was absolutely gone now. My heart already felt slower, exhausted. My eyes fluttered shut and my head bobbed.

Sharp intakes of breath and coughing rang out around me and I grinned, happy that they'd be okay.

"Let's go," Laurie commanded, her vines falling away from their bodies instantly and the three of them stood, like puppets. My heart ached, but one way or another, this would work out. Saige was safe with Bram, I don't know how I knew that, I just did.

"Goodbye, Fischer," Laurie whispered in my ear as the rest of them moved behind me through the woods and tears fell down my face. A small gust of wind brushed against my skin as she moved away from me and I stared up at the stars, wondering if it was going to hurt, but even if it did... *it's fucking worth it.*

Their footsteps faded to the point that I had to strain to hear them, the vines surrounding me were still holding me tight to the chair, until they weren't. Confused, I watched as they fell away and I stood quickly, looking around. Nobody was there, and I heard nothing in the forest.

I took a step outside of the pentagram and that's when it happened.

A vine snaked up my leg so fast I didn't have time to react before I was flipped in the air and slammed down onto my back, other vines converging on my body, wrapping, twisting, tighter and tighter. My pulse hammered when I felt them wrap around my neck, and my eyes watered when I was no longer able to take a breath. I would've clawed at my throat, but my hands were bound.

I'm so sorry, sweetheart. I wish we'd had more time. I wish I'd told you how much you brightened my life and that you made me feel worthy of being loved. I was drowning when we met and you grabbed me by the hair and held my face above the water. Being good was never in the cards for me, but you made me great.

Black dots exploded in my field of vision and it was getting harder and harder to cling to consciousness, but I just kept thinking of her big green eyes, and I didn't stop thinking it until oblivion claimed me.

I love you, sweetheart, I love you.

Saige

Chapter Twenty-four

The three of us crashed into my kitchen like bats out of hell, and I guess we kind of were in a sense.

"Will they follow?" I panted, my hands flat on the floor before I was hoisted up by Bram and righted on my feet. We all tucked our wings, horns, and tails away. *The last thing I need to do is give Gran a heart attack.*

"They would've had to have been touching us to follow," Khol explained, looking around my kitchen.

"Wait. How are you here? In Emerald Lakes?" I asked, remembering that he'd been unable to pass the town lines before.

"Maybe the ward ended on your birthday?" Bram guessed.

As my eyes took in the kitchen, I noticed there were a few empty beer bottles on the table and a nearly empty bag of Flamin' Hot Cheetos. Kai must be here somewhere. My heart raced at the thought.

"Hello?" I called out, smoothing down my dress and kicking my heels off. *Sweet mercy.*

Barking from the little bathroom started and my brow furrowed. *Why the hell is Maven in the bathroom?* His tiny paws were scratching violently against the door as I darted down the hallway and pushed open the door. He was a blaze of white as he flew out of the room, running straight to the back door and staring at me.

"Maven, what's wrong? Where is everyone?"

He began whining, spinning in circles, scratching at the door. Khol and Bram exchanged a look and when I tried to pass them in the kitchen, Bram stuck his arm out to stop me.

"Animals sometimes know more than we do, Goldie girl. Let us check it out first, yeah?"

Unease settled in my stomach as I watched Khol and Bram move to the back door, pulling it open so Maven could dart out into the night. I trailed behind them, stepping onto the patio, the smell of smoke hitting me, making my nose wrinkle.

"Something's burning," Khol murmured, mostly to himself as we all glanced around the property. A light was on in Gran's cottage. Gran. A smile spread over my face as Maven ran full out to her cottage.

"That's weird. He usually can't stand Gran..." I told them and I led the way through the yard to her little home. Bram stepped in front of me before I could reach for the door and he pushed it open slightly, enough for Mave to slip through before opening it wider.

"Gran?" I shouted, "Gran, I'm back."

I stepped through the door after Bram and when Gran didn't answer, my heart picked up its pace. *Where is she?* Pushing past Bram, I came to an abrupt halt when I saw Gran lying on the floor of her kitchen, a large bruise forming on her head and a small puddle of blood beneath her.

"Gran!" I screamed, running to her and slipping on some of the blood that was on the linoleum as I threw myself on her. She was so still. Khol and Bram were on their knees beside me, and I watched as Khol felt for a pulse.

"She's breathing, wild one."

Relief flooded my body and tears sprang to my eyes. If I lost Gran, I don't know what I'd do. Growing up without many people loving you, the loss of that... I couldn't imagine. She was okay. She was alive.

"Who would do such a thing?" Bram questioned.

I brushed her hair gently out of her face, her curls wild, just like she was. Her eyes fluttered and opened a tiny sliver, before she startled and tried to sit up, batting her hands at us, like she was scared.

"Gran, Gran, calm down, it's us. It's me, Saige. You're okay," I soothed, and her wild eyes landed on my face.

"My sweet girl," she breathed, almost like she couldn't believe what she was seeing.

"Bette, who did this to you? Who hurt you?" Bram asked gently and Gran tried to scoot backwards to put space between them.

"Gran, it's okay. They're safe. Tell us," I encouraged.

"Laurie," she bit out.

"Laurie is here?" Khol growled, eyes flashing.

"Why the hell would she do this, Gran?" I asked, horrified.

"They were going to do a spell," she explained, shaking her head and wincing when the motion likely caused pain.

"Who? Who was going to do a spell?" I urged as ice ran down my spine. *Something is wrong.*

"Laurie and your men. To get you back, did you see them?"

"Where?" Khol asked as he and Bram stood to their full height.

"About a hundred yards into the woods, there's torches," she breathed, her voice weak.

"We'll go check it out, stay here with your grandma, okay, princess?"

My brain was at war. Laurie had fucking attacked Gran, she was obviously not in her right mind and I knew without a doubt the guys never would've allowed Gran to be harmed, so they didn't know what she was up to. They were probably in danger, too. The urge to go with Khol and Bram was nearly suffocating, but Gran needed me right now. I'd help her first then get my ass out there.

. . .

"Okay, I'll be out there as soon as I get Gran situated." I nodded and they left the room. Slipping my hands under Gran's arms, I lifted her upright and got her on her feet before I threw one of her arms over my shoulder, guiding her to her bed. She needed to rest.

"Let me just get you into bed, then I'm going to go see if the guys are out there," I told her, spreading an extra blanket down over her bedding so it wouldn't get blood on it. "I don't have time to get you cleaned up yet, are you okay?"

I was anything but calm, but I didn't want to upset Gran. She'd been through enough tonight. Her own daughter had harmed her, the least I could do was swallow my agitation and not add to her stress.

She took my face with both hands and something in her face twisted my stomach.

"I'm fine. Your mother... she's not right, child. Be safe out there, go. I'm fine. Go find your men," she encouraged.

"Gran," I shook my head, ready to tell her I'd go soon, but wanted to make sure she was okay.

"Go Saige. Hurry," she ordered, her tone firm.

With a lingering look, I turned and ran through her house, bursting through the open doorway, finding Maven waiting for me, pacing. When he saw me, he yelped and ran ahead, leading the way.

I didn't hear any voices, *why aren't there any voices?* It was almost too silent. Even the forest was quiet.

Maven led me through the forest to where the smoke was getting thicker and I almost screamed when Bram materialized in front of me through the fog.

"Did you find them? Where is everyone?" I asked, trying to continue walking but his hands landed on my shoulders.

"Is my mother still here? I'm going to fuck her up for hurting

Gran like that. Who would do something like that to their own mom?" When Bram didn't respond to my questions, I tilted my head up and looked at his face at the same time I heard a howl from Maven that sent thunder through my veins. He sounded... mournful.

"Bram?" I whispered as I took in his pinched expression, the way his eyes were shining.

"S- Saige," his voice cracked.

Why is he calling me Saige? He's never once called me Saige.

"Don't call me that," I snapped. "Let me past, Bram."

"I can't, you don't want to go over there right now, okay? Just– just stay right here with me," he pleaded, his pained eyes locking on mine. As if he were begging me. *What's over there?*

"What's over there, Bram?" I choked out as I held my stomach.

He shook his head, running both hands through his hair.

"You're scaring me," I rasped as my chin trembled and the ache in the back of my throat threatened to suffocate me.

"Let's go see your Gran, okay?" He took my arm and started to pull me with him, away from whatever it was he didn't want me to see.

"No," I said, but he didn't stop, he picked up his pace. "NO!" I screamed, making a sudden break from him that he didn't expect and as soon as his hand left my arm, I was sprinting toward the smoke, and then I was in it. Bram was calling my name behind me.

"Grab her, Khol!" he roared.

My feet skidded to a halt when I nearly tripped over a chair. What the fuck was a chair doing out here? Adjusting my vision, I could make out three other chairs and then I saw a figure hunched over.

"Khol?" I asked, walking toward him slowly as Bram nearly ran me over as he burst through the lingering smoke.

"Saige, please. Don't," Bram begged and I felt sweat run down my back.

My feet carried me the remaining ten feet to Khol and he turned his head to look back at me, tears on his cheeks.

"Khol, what is wrong? What's happening? Someone had better start fucking—" my voice shriveled up in my throat when he fell back on his ass and I saw what they hadn't wanted me to see.

"F- Fischer?" I croaked. He wasn't moving. "FISCHER!" I screamed and threw myself down to the ground beside him, looking at where he was hurt so I could fix it. There were bruises all over his skin, the kind ropes would cause. His beautiful eyes were shut, a soft smile on his mouth. *He's not dead then. Dead people don't smile. Dead men don't fucking smile.*

"Saige."

There was no blood. There was no wound. *How can I fix him if there's no wound!?*

My hands were shaking so badly when I brought them to his face, I was scared I was going to slap him accidentally. *Cold. His cheeks are cold. Why are his cheeks cold?*

"Saige, baby, please."

Someone was talking to me.

"Fischer, wake up. Where does it hurt, Guppy? Tell me where it hurts so I can fix it," I ran my hands down his chest, but he didn't move.

Arms wrapped around my waist and I tried to peel them off immediately.

"Put me down, help him! Can't you see he's hurt? Why aren't you fucking helping him!?" I screamed. *Why aren't they helping him?*

Khol's face appeared in front of mine, his features blurry.

"Saige. I'm so, so sorry," his voice cracked.

"No," I said. "No. No. NO! *NO!* Help him, Bram!" I squirmed in his grip like a wild animal that was trying to be tamed. I wouldn't be tamed.

"Let her go, Bram," Khol commanded and once his arms fell away, I ran right back to Fischer.

"Fischer, Guppy, no. Please, I can't, let me help you, baby. This isn't real, this isn't happening." I shook my head violently back and forth, my face felt numb. My entire body felt fucking numb and I collapsed over top of my sweet Fischer, wrapping my body against his still form. A horrible keening sound was in the air and it made me want to cover my ears, but I couldn't because then I'd have to stop holding him. *I'll never stop holding him.*

My hands slipped underneath his body and I felt the dirt as it got wedged under my fingernails, but I had to get closer. *Maybe if I hold him hard enough, if I love him hard enough, he won't leave me. He can't leave me.*

"Honey, he's gone. I'm so fucking sorry. He was a great man, he's a legend," Khol said solemnly.

"He's not gone. He's right here, he's with me. We belong together. I love him! How fucking DARE she? I'm going to kill her. I'm going to hunt her down and fucking destroy her," I vowed, not removing my cheek from Fischer's chest.

Heat was prickling at my body and I felt my tail elongate and my wings snapped out at the same time as my horns. My wings wrapped around both of us, like a cocoon. Safety. We were safe in here.

Fischer's dead.

The thought slammed against my skull.

Fischer's dead. He's dead. She killed him.

Magic exploded from my body, through Fischer, and into the ground. Golden light exploded around us, and it was all I could see. A cracking sound that was deafening filled my ears as the crashing of trees hit the forest floor. The ground shook and I gritted my teeth as my magic took over.

They were calling my name, screaming at me to stop. I'd sooner be able to stop a speeding fucking bullet. This had to come out. *Now.*

My chest was cracked, my heart shattered, my soul darkened.

And all I knew in that moment as I pressed my face against my love's quiet chest, was that she would pay.

I would get my revenge.

Careful, Mother, you may have given birth to a daughter, but tonight, I was reborn a monster.

And I will find you.

THE MAGIC OF REVENGE: *Emerald Lakes Book Three, Coming Soon!*

WANT MORE?

WHEW WEEEEEEE HOHOHO

Are you punching me in the face right now? Did you break your reading device like I broke everyone's hearts?

Damn, I'm a freakin' assshole.

HOWEVER! THE PATH TO GREAT CHARACTER DEVELOPMENT IS LITTERED WITH MANY LANDMINES AND THAT IS JUST THE WAY IT IS!

When I started writing this book, I knew kind of sort of where I wanted it to end. It wasn't until I was about halfway through that I decided for sure what was going to happen. And side note: I fucking BATTLED with Fischer during his date with Saige. It took me days to figure him out. Something wasn't right. It wasn't clicking. Then I sat down and just wrote what he was telling me. Yeah, I sound crazier than a pile of bat turds, but that's the damn truth.

And thus, Faris was born. I legit messaged my content editor 'I DID NOT PLAN FOR THIS! WHAT IS HAPPENING RIGHT NOW!?" Then she read it. And my other alphas read it, and they loved it. I mean, holy shit. He mind fucked me just like every other enemy in his life.

Fact of the matter is this: I couldn't continue writing their stories if it weren't for you. Not the general audience, not you all. *You*, right here, right now. *You* picked up the second book in my debut series and gave me another chance to let you escape reality and that means so much to me.

The past eight months have been nothing short of a dream come true for me and every single time you recommend my book in reader groups, on your bookstagrams, your blogs, I see that. Each time you interact in the reader group and discuss these characters? I SEE THAT. And it is literally everything to me.

I hope you'll stick with me for the next book. Who knows what will happen.

THANK YOU!

Now for the sappy shit.

Cassie Hurst, my development/content editor. My Jiminy Cricket who leaves things like, "TOO CRAZY LADY. TONE IT DOWN." and then in the next paragraph leaves me the filthiest suggestions. I see you, ma'am. I couldn't have done this without you. Book three is gonna be off the charts.

Stacy, my book boo. My alpha bitch. Thank you! You were my first cheerleader and your support and friendship means so much to me. Also, the amount of TikToks and NSFW images you throw my way has really solidified you as a bestie for life.

Polly and Dani, your editing and proofreading is next level. Polly, your thirst comments and reactions to my stories is literally something I CRAVE and I'm going to need that with every book I write. Thank you, ladies. Check out Proofs by Polly and Black Lotus Editing if you're in the market for author services.

Nicole Babinsack, my friend and PA. I'd be lost without you managing my things. Your enthusiasm for every single word I write is a bright light in my day that keeps me going. Thank you so, so much.

To my ARC team, you guys are the freaking best. Also, the thirstiest crowd I've ever had the pleasure of knowing.

Bloggers and bookstagrammers, you guys are the real MVP's. I see you everyday tearing it UP on Instagram, TikTok, Facebook... and you do it for free. Incredible. The edits and reviews are nothing short of amazing and I can't thank you enough for giving me a little more visibility as a newbie author.

Last but not least, my husband. I love how when I read you scenes I've written you pretty much react the same way every time. Whether it's steamy or funny, you mostly turn red in the face and shake your head. You know all about me and you love my weird self. Your love and support means so much, I can't even express it with words. And no, I won't be trying with a blow j. HA! Love you.

STALK ME! It'll be fun.

Come join the reader group to talk about The Magic of Discovery and for all kinds of other filthy shenanigans! Gran makes regular appearances:

Britt Andrews' Magical Misfits:
https://www.facebook.com/groups/187380059350040

Join my newsletter:
https://mailchi.mp/c95f361e79a2/britt-andrews-newsletter

facebook.com/authorbrittandrews
instagram.com/authorbrittandrews
bookbub.com/profile/britt-andrews